MOURNING
IN
MALMÖ

Torquil MacLeod

M^CNIDDER | & GRACE CRIME

Published by McNidder & Grace
21 Bridge Street
Carmarthen SA31 3JS
Wales, United Kingdom
www.mcnidderandgrace.co.uk

Original paperback first published 2020

© Torquil MacLeod and Torquil MacLeod Books Ltd
www.torquilmacleodbooks.com

All rights reserved. No part of this work may be reproduced or transmitted
in any form or by any means, electronic or mechanical, including
photocopy, recording, or any information storage and retrieval system,
without permission in writing from the publisher. Torquil MacLeod has
asserted his right to be identified as the author of this work in accordance
with the Copyright, Designs and Patents Act 1988.

This book is a work of fiction. Names, characters and incidents are either the
product of the author's imagination or are used fictitiously. Any resemblance
to actual persons, living or dead, is purely coincidental.

A catalogue record for this work is available from the British Library.

ISBN: 9780857162076

Designed by JS Typesetting Ltd, Porthcawl
Printed and bound in the United Kingdom by Short Run Press, Exeter

To my grandson and all those with type 1 diabetes.

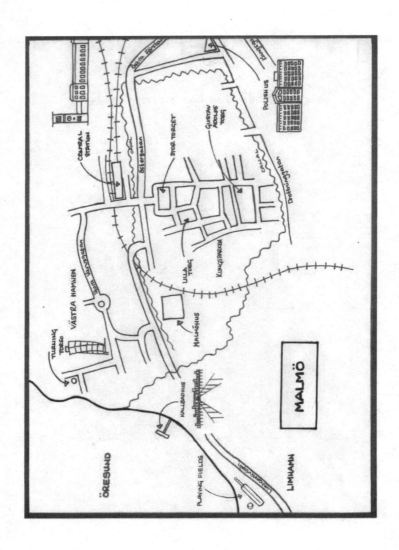

SITE OF THE SINKING
OF THE
MS ESTONIA
28th SEPTEMBER 1994

FINLAND

Helsinki

Stockholm

Tallinn

ESTONIA

SWEDEN

LATVIA

LITHUANIA

BALTIC
SEA

Malmö

RUSSIA

BELARUS

POLAND

PROLOGUE

The ship lurched. The crossing had been getting progressively rougher. Jens Ullman knew that he should have gone to his cabin when his two friends, David and Sven, had retired for the night, but he was enjoying the company of the young Estonian man Romet in the Admiral bar. Romet turned out to be a fledgling electrical engineer who was studying in Stockholm and was keen to hear about Jens's experiences at Electrolux. As Jens wobbled over with another drink from the bar – this would definitely be the last – he noticed that it was nearly one o'clock in the morning. He wasn't bothered – the drink and convivial conversation were warding off the seasickness he'd felt a couple of hours after their slightly late 19:15 departure from Tallinn.

Romet thanked Jens for the beer. The waves were crashing against the windows. There weren't many other drinkers left, though a bunch of Swedes were still noisily making the most of the end of their holiday. Jens hoped that they'd have time to recover before going back to work. He himself had the rest of the week off.

'Have you got a family?' Romet asked. Like all the questions he posed, it sounded as though he was genuinely interested in the answer.

'Yes. One daughter and one grandson,' Jens said with pride. 'They live in Lund. My son-in-law, Björn, lectures at the university. English. I think he's what you call an academic high-flyer. He'll do well.'

'Is your daughter at home?'

'No. Anita was off work for a while after she had Lasse but she's back now. She's in the police.'

'The police?' Romet said with surprise. His experience of the Estonian police in the recent pre-independence days had not been good.

'Yes. I've no idea why she went in for it. Enjoys it, though.'

Jens fished a photograph from his wallet. He held it out for Romet to inspect. It was a close-up of a family group: a young blond boy sitting between his parents.

'I didn't think policewomen could be so attractive,' Romet found himself saying, the drink having loosened his tongue. She had shoulder-length, blonde hair, parted in the middle. Her high cheekbones were accentuated by the spectacles she wore, framing bright, laughing eyes. The mouth was shapely, the lips not too thin. It was a mouth that was used to creasing into a smile. She looked truly happy. 'Sorry,' Romet quickly apologized.

Jens gave him an indulgent grin. 'That's OK. I think she's the most beautiful girl in the world, though she can be strong-willed,' he added as an afterthought. 'Once she gets an idea into her head...' He took the photo back and looked at it. 'Lasse has brought new meaning to my life. He'll be four in November.' He shook his head in disbelief. 'They grow so fast. You know, I was dreading being a grandfather. That melted away the moment I saw him.'

'They look a contented couple,' Romet remarked, hoping to atone for his earlier slip.

'They are. Long may it last. I'm afraid Anita's mother and I haven't set them a very good example.'

'Separated?'

'Divorced.'

'I'm sorry.' Romet found himself apologizing again.

The ferry gave another lurch, sending their drinks sliding across the table. Romet caught them both before they vanished, though the beer splashed onto the plastic surface.

'Quick reflexes,' said Jens with admiration.

Romet smiled as he took out a handkerchief and wiped his fingers. 'I play handball.'

The ferry suddenly rose and fell in quick succession. This time, Jens had his glass clasped in his hand. It was clear that Romet was nervous about the excessive movement.

'Don't worry. These ships are well built. Wave collisions like this are just like turbulence on an aircraft.'

'I've never flown.'

'Ah.'

Jens drained his glass. 'I think it's time I made for my cabin. He got up and nearly stumbled as the ship rolled again. ''Night, Romet. Maybe see you before we dock in Stockholm tomorrow.'

As Jens got to the bar door, he heard a loud bang. It was like an explosion, and it penetrated through the general hum of the ship. He steadied himself and made for the stairwell. He wasn't too worried; it would be something or nothing. But as the ship reared again, he was unbalanced and found himself tumbling down the narrow staircase. He was momentarily dazed. Recovering, he realized the ship had listed dramatically. It took him a moment to work out that the configuration of the corridor was all awry – everything was tilted. He staggered to his feet. Something was seriously wrong. He must get to his cabin and warn his friends. The ship should have righted itself by now. As he wobbled along, cabin doors were swinging open at unnatural angles. Passengers began to emerge; most of them half asleep, many of them alarmed. He heard children crying. A woman screamed. The ferry groaned.

He reached the next stairwell. People were desperately pushing their way upwards. He forced his way down the steps but could hardly move when he reached the bottom. He tried to negotiate the constricted corridor full of yelling, terrified passengers. Another massive creaking and a further tilt lifted him off his feet. He landed awkwardly and felt a sharp pain in his ankle. He was pushed aside and he crashed through one of the cabin doors, which had now, owing to the list of the ship, become part of the floor. Winded, with his ankle and ribs hurting, he found himself in a darkened room, his back against the porthole. In increasing pain, he managed to winch himself up to the door opening by using the handles. Lights were still on in the corridor when he got out. There was now no point trying to find David and Sven – they would have to fend for themselves. Then he felt water seeping into his shoes. The decks below must already be flooded, including the one where his friends were *sleeping. Cradling his ribs with his left arm, he gingerly stepped round the frames of the cabin doors, avoiding the gaping holes where the doors had swung open, and reached the stairwell, now askew. It was little more than a metre wide, and the angle was so acute that he was forced onto his knees. Clutching the handrail, he eased himself along as though he was wriggling through a shaft. In front of him was a frightened child being steered by a frantic mother. A man in underwear elbowed his way past them all, and the child slid backwards into Jens. He pushed him onwards, instinctively aware that every second counted. His engineer's brain was asking why the ship was going over so quickly. It should be righting itself by now.*

At the end of the stairwell, he staggered on, ignoring the screams and pleas around him. The ship's loudspeaker burst through the panic and a woman's strained voice repeated the word 'Haire'. He didn't understand the Estonian. Then he found himself in an enormous space: it was the nightclub. He'd been in here on the trip over from Stockholm. Except now, the large dance floor had morphed into a mountain, its slope sheer and slippery. At the bottom, he was surrounded by debris – loose chairs, broken bottles and glasses, coffee cups and ash trays, items of cast-off clothing – and people; unconscious, dazed or dead. Anything that wasn't nailed down had slid into this gruesome abyss.

Jens's strength was ebbing away. He was aware that his ribs were broken and his shoulder and ankle were throbbing. He was an out-of-condition, fifty-four- year-old man, and the effort of getting this far had sapped his energy. Only adrenaline was keeping him going – and the thought that if he didn't make it up that slope, he'd never see Anita and Lasse again. He knew that the nightclub was on an upper deck – and there was an exit to the outside. Make the climb out of here and he would be on the port side and well above the water. Then there would be a chance.

Jens recognized his only hope was to use the floor-mounted tables as arm bars and foot jams, as though he was on a rock face. He couldn't do it slowly and methodically as he didn't have the physical reserves left – or the time. The ship was creaking heavily. He must make a dash for it. With a yell to encourage himself, he launched his aching limbs at the nearest table, then onto the next. He could hardly breathe and his body was doing its best to impede him, but he kept on going. He could now see the open door ahead of him in what was effectively the ceiling. Someone was hovering there. A hand waved encouragingly and a voice called out. Jens didn't catch the words above the din. His feet were now on the legs of the penultimate table and he reached up to the last one... The ship abruptly pitched back to port, and as he was thrown forward, he smashed his head against the corner of the final table. Within seconds, the vessel had resettled onto its starboard side. Dizzy from the impact, Jens lost his grip and tumbled back down the dance floor, ricocheting from table to table like a steel marble in a pinball machine. He crashed into the wreckage at the bottom.

Then the lights flickered and went out.

CHAPTER 1

The sea rippled gently against the sand. It was a calm day with a few fluffy clouds in a blue sky. Lilla Vik was at its most peaceful at that time of the morning; it was a working week and too early for the holidaymakers. The path running parallel to the beach still funnelled the occasional jogger and dog walker, but Anita and Lasse had the sand to themselves. Lasse carried the plastic container in which lay the remains of his grandmother. Anita wasn't quite sure why her mother had wanted her ashes to be sprinkled in the sea at Lilla Vik. She hadn't been aware that it was a particularly special place for her; certainly not the haven that Anita had cherished from her teenage years onwards. When she'd been told of the request by her aunt, who had lived with her mother in Kristianstad for the last ten years, she'd wondered if it had anything to do with the fate of her father, who was lying somewhere at the bottom of the Baltic. Jens Ullman had been the love of her mother's life, and she'd never wanted anyone else after their marriage fell apart. Though there was no third party involved in the break-up, her mother had always remained bitter. And she took that bitterness out on Anita, who had adored her father and had remained close to him, especially when he was based in Stockholm and she was at the Police Academy there. His death in the *MS Estonia* ferry disaster had shattered Anita's world, and she had only been able to get through that terrible time because of her husband Björn's support – he'd been amazing. At that point, she hadn't been aware of his roving eye. And, of course, there was young Lasse to keep her focused; though part of her sadness was that Lasse had never properly got to know his grandfather. He would never be taken fishing or delight in Jens's off-beat sense of humour, marvel at his inventiveness and love of all things technical, be exposed to his passion for politics or revel in his ability to spin a good yarn. That's how she remembered her father. Of course, she'd edited out all his negative character traits – the ones that had probably contributed to the family break-up. After his death, she'd compensated for the huge hole in her life by throwing herself into her work. Not for a moment had she stopped to think what losing Jens had meant to her mother – sad and lonely, unable to emotionally connect with her daughter and grandson. Anita had hoped that when Lasse's daughter, Leyla, was born, her mother might involve herself more with her family, but it was only when Leyla was diagnosed with type 1 diabetes at the age of two that she had shown some compassion. That news had shocked them all, and caring for the little girl was a huge strain on Lasse and Jazmin. The grinding routine of sleepless nights and difficult days constantly monitoring blood sugar levels, regulating diet and calculating insulin intake enveloped them like a blanket through which no light could penetrate. But then, slowly, as they became accustomed to the routine, the darkness melted into shades of grey and sometimes even pastel hues. And Leyla's own strong character, tolerance and resilience was such an inspiration; her eyes sparkled through it all even though her little body was letting her down and her moods often fluctuated. But despite her mother's concern for her great-granddaughter, Anita could never forgive her attitude towards Jazmin. Though Swedish born, Lasse's partner was always an immigrant in her eyes and she had never accepted her.

Nevertheless, when her mother had been diagnosed with oesophageal cancer, Anita had done the right thing. It took her six months to die, and during that time, Anita had travelled to Kristianstad as often as work allowed. Whatever resentments she harboured – and there were many – it was awful seeing her mother decline so swiftly. She'd organized the funeral and she and Lasse had both given eulogies, though none of their words had rung particularly true. In the end, it was the recognition that their fifty-year relationship had been such a waste that had upset Anita the most. Mother and daughter should have had a special bond – she envied her friends who had that closeness. The emotional connection had never really taken flight after the family's two-year spell in England: that was the last time she remembered any real harmony. Maybe the fault was her own, Anita reflected. Not having enough empathy... whatever. Now for the last rights.

Anita hitched up her dress and tucked it into her belt. It wasn't very elegant with her knickers showing. She knew she should have hired a boat so that they could be more distant from the shore. Too late now. She took the plastic container from Lasse and waded out into the shallows until the water came up over her knees. It was bloody cold even on a sunny early-July morning.

She looked back at Lasse. 'Should I say a few words about your *mormor*?'

He shook his head. 'You said it all at the funeral. Are you OK?'

She felt faintly ridiculous. 'Fine.'

Slowly, she unscrewed the lid and began to tip the ashes into the sea. She couldn't believe how much volume there was. Instead of a dainty sprinkle disappearing sedately into the water as she'd imagined, it all came out in a great graceless whoosh. A lot of the ash was floating in what was fast becoming a gooey mess around her legs. She quickly tried to disperse it with her free hand. In mid-manoeuvre, her phone went off and shattered the fast-evaporating solemnity of the occasion.

'Christ!' she muttered furiously. Not the time for a call.

'Are you going to answer that, Mamma?' Lasse called from the beach.

Anita threw the plastic container towards him to free up her hands. She hadn't realized that it still held a residue of her mother, which spilt out as it came to rest at the water's edge. She retrieved her phone. It was Hakim. He *knew* what she was doing today. Honestly!

'Sorry, Anita,' Hakim put in immediately. 'Hope this isn't a bad moment.'

It was. Her knees were surrounded by unsunken ash. Even in death, it was as though her mother was being critical – Anita couldn't even disperse her remains without getting it wrong.

'What is it?' she snapped.

'It's an attempted murder.'

'*And*?'

'You're needed.'

'No, I'm not. Surely to God you and Brodd can sort it out!'

There was a nervous cough at the other end of the line. 'Zetterberg insists you have to take charge.'

'But she knows...' Of course, Alice Zetterberg knew why she was taking the day off. The bitch! This was yet another chance for her to make Anita's life as difficult as possible. There was no point taking it out on Hakim. 'Right. SMS me the address and I'll see you in an hour.'

Anita glanced up at the sky and let out a loud expletive.

'Mamma!' called a horrified Lasse. 'You shouldn't say that in front of *Mormor*!'

CHAPTER 2

An hour later, she reached the sheltered housing complex in Riseberga, having dropped Lasse off and cancelled the lunch she'd planned with her old Simrishamn friend, Sandra. All the way back into town, she'd been mentally cursing Alice Zetterberg. Zetterberg had been their temporary boss now for nearly two years. This was frustrating for everyone. Erik Moberg had been scheduled to return to his post after his heart attack. Complications had set in and his return had been delayed. Another couple of minor attacks hadn't helped. The Skåne County Police was still keeping his job open. This may have seemed altruistic, though, in reality, it was more to do with economics. Zetterberg was still head of the Cold Case Group as well as doubling up as acting head of their Criminal Investigation Squad for the same salary; Moberg was on half pay. It might be saving the force money but was unsatisfactory for all concerned. The team desperately wanted Moberg back, while Zetterberg had expected her role to become full time. She'd envisaged a move up the career ladder, which she felt she deserved after assisting the security services five years before. This state of limbo didn't improve her temper or her attitude, and she took her frustration out on Anita whenever she could. The team's only respite from Zetterberg was when an important cold case emerged and her attention was diverted. Fortunately, some of the year had seen Zetterberg working away from the polishus. And with Chief Inspector Moberg's return only a few weeks away, the team were looking to a brighter future. Zetterberg would soon be gone for good. Until then, she could still pull a few nasty strokes – like the summons this morning. Anita knew that was deliberate.

Hakim was waiting for her at the door of the retirement apartment. Sympathy was written all over his face.

'Don't say anything!' Anita said, holding up a hand.

Hakim followed her in. 'The kitchen,' he said.

She went through a tidy living room. It smelt like her aunt's house in Kristianstad – an old person's dwelling. Old furniture, old décor, old things – expensive old things; everything was of good quality. The kitchen wasn't so tidy. The cooker and the wall above were spattered in blood, as though flicked from a paintbrush. There were great daubs of red on the linoleum floor. The instrument of all this carnage was obvious – a bloodied kitchen knife lay on the table.

'It's an old couple. Markus and Nina Jolis,' explained Hakim, who was still wearing latex gloves. 'Markus attacked his wife with that.' He nodded at the knife. 'Amazingly, she's still alive. An ambulance took her off to hospital about fifteen minutes ago. It'll be touch and go. And forensics are on their way.'

'Where's the husband?'

'In the bedroom with Bea.' So Zetterberg had sent both Hakim and Erlandsson to the scene of the crime and yet had summoned Anita, too. She was trying not to fume.

She glanced around at the devastation. The crockery in the sink was all smashed; some pieces littered the floor.

'Who reported this?'

'He did.'

'*He* did?'

'Yeah. Markus Jolis. After he'd attacked his wife, he calmly rang the polishus.'

What bizarre behaviour!

'I've already spoken to the warden. Naturally, she's horrified. When she'd got over her hysterics, she told me that the Jolises had been in here a couple of years. Devoted, apparently. He's eighty and she's five years younger. Nina is more of a carer these days. Markus has Alzheimer's. He's been getting steadily worse. He often lost his temper. Nina usually managed to settle him down. This time, obviously, she didn't succeed. Anything might have set him off.'

'The washing up?' Anita speculated as she surveyed the sink.

Hakim shrugged. 'He doesn't remember much, apparently, though he has the odd lucid moment. Might explain the phone call.'

There was a ring at the door.

'Probably forensics.' Hakim disappeared, leaving Anita to take in the scene. Thank goodness her mother hadn't succumbed to dementia. Small mercies.

It wasn't Eva Thulin who appeared at the door. Young Lars Unosson bounced into the room. He hadn't Eva's worldly-wise cynicism and caustic humour that Anita so enjoyed – he was like a puppy which had just been let off its leash. His enthusiasm was as infectious as it was tiring. Each crime scene was an exciting new playroom, and he had the technical toys to keep him happy.

'No Eva?'

'On holiday. Somewhere quiet and sunny. Said she'd found a place where there were no distractions for her husband, except her. Reckoned she hadn't been getting enough sex lately.'

'That sounds like Eva. Well, I'll leave you in peace.'

Unosson scoped the room with his forensic eye. 'No body?' He was almost disappointed.

'She's still alive. But treat it as a murder scene. It may become one.'

'Okey dokey!'

Anita entered the bedroom. Again, it was neat. Nina Jolis liked to keep a pristine home. Not that Anita really took in the surroundings. It was Markus Jolis who was the centre of her attention. He was sitting on the double bed, head bowed. He dwarfed the petite Bea Erlandsson, who was seated next to him. She stood up when Anita entered. By the window stood a uniformed officer. Erlandsson wasn't taking any chances. Jolis might turn violent again.

'He's not really saying anything,' said Erlandsson. 'Except he keeps asking for his wife.'

Anita took the place on the bed that Bea had just vacated. Markus Jolis was wearing a blue dressing gown that was covered in dried blood. His cupped hands were also streaked in red from the attack. His grey hair was thinning. He was unshaven with a couple of days' growth. His most prominent feature was his large ears. They would be cartoonish if the circumstances weren't so tragic.

'Markus,' Anita spoke softly. 'Can you tell me what happened here this morning? With Nina?' He continued to stare silently at his hands. 'Nina's gone to hospital.'

He slowly turned to Anita. For a moment, his brown eyes flickered with fear.

'Why has Nina gone to hospital?'

'She was hurt.'

'Hurt?'

'Do you remember anything? Do you remember calling the police?'

He shook his head in bewilderment.

Anita glanced up at Erlandsson. She gave a shrug in return.

'Better let Lars have a quick look at him then get him cleaned up. He'll have to be assessed before anything else can be done.'

With the help of the uniformed officer, Erlandsson gently eased up the bulky Markus Jolis and took him out of the bedroom.

Anita went to the window. The gardens consisted of a pleasant lawn and bright, flower-covered borders. A grey-haired lady sat on a bench, gazing at nothing in particular. Old age was something Anita dreaded. Not being old itself but the infirmities that might come with it. Losing her memory was her biggest fear. Already she was absent-minded; Lasse teased her about it. Maybe she'd become more conscious of it since turning fifty last year. To distract herself from her morbid thoughts, she started to examine the room. Or to be more precise, the photographs on the walls. Children, grandchildren: smiling faces all around. How would they take the news of the attack? There was Markus presiding over a barbecue, Nina at a park with young kids, an excited family group opening presents at Christmas.

The only picture that seemed unrelated was one of a much younger Markus in a *tullverket* uniform; he had obviously been in the Swedish Customs. Years of service and respectability had come to this.

CHAPTER 3

He tapped his desktop impatiently. He had so much to do today that this call was an inconvenience, albeit a rather important one.

'Yes, I saw it in the newspapers. It's nothing to be concerned about.'

It had given him a jolt if he were honest. After thinking about it, he realized that it shouldn't be a problem – but it had been flagged up: hence the call.

'Are you sure?'

'I can't see any difficulties.'

There was silence at the other end of the line. The caller wasn't convinced.

'All we have to do is keep an eye on things,' he said, trying to sound reassuring. Why the hell was be being bothered by this? Maybe he should take the initiative; he didn't really want them getting involved. 'Look, do you want to monitor the situation, or do you want my people to handle it?'

After a pause: 'I think it's best if I leave it to you.'

He smiled. He knew that would be the answer. 'Fine. It'll be strictly softly, softly.'

'Good.' Another pause. This was annoying. The man was a puppy. His predecessors had not been so mealy mouthed – they'd been stronger, more resolute: tougher by far. 'You'll keep me updated?'

'Of course.'

He put the phone down before there were any further quibbles. He tapped his desk again. Not impatiently, but thoughtfully. Then, after a couple more minutes of contemplation, he knew exactly whom he was going to call. At least they would know what they were doing.

*

'It's awful, really. Sad. I haven't had a chance to talk to him again over the last couple of days. His wife is still in intensive care, and they're not sure she's going to pull through.'

Anita was sitting on her bed, FaceTiming Kevin Ash, her long-distance British boyfriend and fellow detective based in the north of England. They communicated most Sundays when their respective shifts allowed. Anita had expected Kevin's enthusiasm eventually to wane, especially after she'd turned down his hasty marriage proposal two years earlier which, at the time, almost ended their relationship. But the opposite had happened and he seemed to love her all the more. Maybe it was a case of absence making the heart grow fonder. It made her all the more anxious whenever they hooked up that she might not match up to the idealized image of her that Kevin kept in his head when they were apart. So far, she'd passed each test, despite the fact that she was increasingly aware that she no longer had her youthful looks. She looked down at her tummy, which was looser than she liked, and felt grateful that her glasses were a distraction from the lines on her face, which was why she was wearing them now even though she was still in bed with her third cup of coffee of the morning. And she'd combed her blonde hair, which was getting to the stage when it might need some help to keep its colour.

'Does he know he did it?' Kevin asked with a mouthful of toast. He was already dressed despite the UK being an hour behind.

'No, I don't think so. Unless he's a very good actor. The girl who took the call at headquarters said he was very calm. He just said "I think I've killed my wife.". By the time we got there, he couldn't remember a thing. Anyway, I hope to speak to him this week. But I need to find out a bit about his background. I think he worked in customs.'

Kevin slurped his tea. There was the cultural difference. Britain got going on tea, Sweden on coffee.

'How did spreading your mum's ashes go?'

She harrumphed. 'I was just sprinkling them in the water when Zetterberg got in touch via Hakim. She knew I'd taken the day off but she insisted I go to the crime scene. What a cow!'

'Deliberate?'

'What do you think? She's never off my case. Whenever she can, she finds fault.'

'She did save your life.' As usual, Kevin was trying to be the voice of reason. He was remembering Anita's near fatal ordeal at the hands of Kristina Ekman.

'That was an accident. It's something she regrets daily. However, there is light at the end of the Zetterberg tunnel. There's a rumour that she's getting a job in Stockholm. Pulled a few favours, no doubt. But she's hanging on until Erik Moberg comes back.'

'Blimey, that'll have been nearly two years, won't it?'

'I know. Of course, he's had two relapses since the big heart attack. But he's lost a lot of weight and claims he's given up smoking.'

'I'm surprised he's not taken early retirement.'

'Can't afford it with three ex-wives. Besides, he's been going round the twist without something to do. That's the trouble when the only thing in life is your job.'

'Lucky you've got me then.'

'I've got a son and granddaughter to distract *me* from work. You're just an occasional hobby.'

'That's the first time I've been compared to origami or stamp collecting. Mind you, it's still the nicest thing a woman has ever said to me.'

Monday morning was dull and overcast. It reflected the general mood in the office, when Anita sidled into the polishus. She didn't enjoy coming into work these days. The atmosphere that Alice Zetterberg created was one of disharmony. She liked to inject uncertainty into the mix, with the result that many of the individual members of the team often started to question their own judgement. This, in turn, resulted in a general lack of confidence. And they were often on edge. Though it was unsettling for the rest, the smarmily compliant Pontus Brodd didn't seem affected by it, as he was in thrall to his boss.

Klara Wallen, Anita's friend and contemporary, reckoned he was too thick to pick up the signals. Wallen herself was constantly nervous. She worried every time she thought she might get into trouble; in consequence, she was reluctant to make decisions. With regard to Bea Erlandsson, Zetterberg just instilled pure hatred. Bea was a constant target of Zetterberg's unsubtle jibes about her sexuality. Anita was always happy to weigh in in Erlandsson's defence, which only heightened the tension between her and their temporary boss. Hakim was more sanguine. He was just grateful that Zetterberg had grudgingly accepted his fiancée, Liv Fogelström, into the team. It had been at Anita's urging that she do so, despite the fact that Liv was wheelchair-bound. Anita had seen at first hand how good she was with computers and that she'd be perfect for following up complicated technological research that was beyond the others. Anita argued that Liv would be a real asset, but what swung it was when she mentioned to a reluctant Zetterberg that it would look good for the department having a serving officer who had suffered a disability in the line of duty usefully reemployed by the police. Zetterberg realized that this would gain her brownie points with the powers that be, and when it did, she was quick to take credit for the appointment. Liv was the one bright spot in the dispirited group. She always had a ready smile and, unlike the rest, didn't moan about her lot, even though it was tangibly far worse than anyone else's. But there was another reason for Anita's despondency, which was more personal – she felt she should be helping Lasse and Jazmin more with Leyla.

Hakim came into her office shortly after her arrival. He had a coffee in his hand, which he handed to Anita.

'Thanks a million.' She smiled at the young detective, who was now maturing into a responsible and effective police officer. The small moustache had long gone – Liv hadn't liked it – but he was still a string bean. However much he ate, he never seemed to gain any weight. Life was so unfair, Anita reflected as she consciously pulled in her stomach and mentally cancelled her planned buffet-style lunch at the Spanish restaurant on Östra Förstadsgatan.

'Liv wanted you to have this.' Hakim handed over a couple of sheets of paper.

'Ah, good girl. I asked her to dig up some background info on Markus Jolis.'

'It won't make much difference. I can't see him going to prison for attempted murder in his condition. It'll all depend on how dangerous they think he is.'

Anita didn't answer as she scanned the notes Liv had made. 'Born in Eskilstuna in 1939. Usual education... joined the Swedish Customs in 1963... married Nina two years later. Three kids, five grandchildren. A pretty ordinary life.' She turned to the second sheet, which had his service record. 'Most of his working life was in Stockholm. Worked his way up through the ranks. Transferred to Malmö October 5th 1994. Started work for Zander Security in Malmö six months later – April, 1995. Stayed there until his retirement in 2000 aged sixty-one.'

'That's early.'

'Maybe he quit for health reasons.'

'Or he didn't need the money. Probably got a good pension from thirty-odd years in customs. The apartment was nice. Expensive stuff in there.'

'Those sheltered retirement places don't come cheap.'

'Police record? Any hints of violence?'

Anita shook her head. She was staring fixedly at the paper in her hand. Hakim saw she was frowning.

'Seen something?'

'It's just the date of his transfer.'

'Is it significant?'

'Probably not.' Her mouth twisted. 'It's just that it's a week after the *Estonia* went down.'

CHAPTER 4

The *MS Estonia* was a ferry that ran thrice weekly across the Baltic Sea between Stockholm, and Tallinn in the newly independent Estonia. Fact. It left Tallinn at 19:15 Estonian time on the evening of September 27th 1994. Fact. The weather worsened as the ship progressed to the midpoint in its journey. Fact. The ferry listed badly to starboard in heavy seas in the early hours of the morning of September 28th. Fact. The *Estonia* only took thirty-five minutes to sink. Fact. There were 989 people from seventeen countries on board that night. Fact. 852 died in the tragedy, 501 of them Swedes. Fact. Among the Swedes that perished was Jens Ullman. Fact. He was Anita Sundström's father. Fact. The cause of the sinking? That's where fact strays into fiction.

The official version, according to the Joint Accident Investigation Commission (JAIC), made up of members from Sweden, Estonia and Finland, stated that the cause of the tragedy was the bow visor being ripped off, which allowed water to pour into the car deck, resulting in the vessel capsizing. A number of parties were not satisfied with the conclusions, among them many relatives of the dead. They continued to campaign for the truth. Anita was not one of them. She was numbed by the tragedy: she had lost the father she idolized. But she was also a servant of the government; a government that, as a young policewoman, she believed in. Like most Swedes, she accepted the official findings. Not to do so would have been to question the state that she so diligently worked for – and constantly revisiting the event, as some of the families of the victims had done, would have rekindled the grief she had taken years to come to terms with. Being drawn into all the conspiracy theories, which were still abounding, had been unthinkable. She couldn't contemplate a scenario other than that her father had died in a tragic accident that had been wrought by nature and not by man.

So why had the date of Markus Jolis's transfer piqued her curiosity?

Her faith in her country's judicial system had eroded over the years: it no longer seemed just. The criminals the police spent so much time and effort apprehending either didn't get punished at all or didn't remain in prison for long. She'd also seen and been disenchanted by the converse side of the state machine in the aftermath of the deaths of retired diplomat Albin Rylander, and her friend, the local Simrishamn historian, Klas Lennartsson. It was during her unauthorized investigations that she had become reacquainted with fellow Police Academy graduate Alice Zetterberg, who had played a corrupt (in Anita's view) part in the secret service cover-up. Disillusioned, Anita's belief in the values she had upheld since the day she joined the Police Academy had been severely dented. Throw in a polarized world of Brexit, President Trump and fake news – her own Sweden had just as many divisive issues – and she was forever finding herself questioning motives and seeking elusive answers. Might the sinking of the *Estonia* not have been as straightforward as she had always forced herself to believe?

She hadn't been among the four hundred questioning friends and relatives who had gathered at the Estline's Frihamnen ferry terminal in the days following the sinking. She had felt that going up to Stockholm would make it all too real. At that stage, she was still clinging to the faint hope that her father might have survived. No, she hadn't been there. But someone else had. Markus Jolis had been among the customs officials that had regularly checked the *Estonia* every time she docked.

Did this explain why she found herself walking across a sun-drenched Pildammsparken a week later? She was going directly from her apartment to the psychiatric section of the vast Skåne University Hospital complex. She'd fixed up a ten o'clock appointment to talk to Markus Jolis. Zetterberg thought this was a complete waste of time. Hakim had agreed. Jolis had severe Alzheimer's and was unlikely to stand trial. Even if he was up to it, there was only a remote possibility that he'd be given a custodial sentence. His wife Nina was still fighting for her life in another part of the hospital, and she was visited constantly by her horrified children, who couldn't understand why their father had attacked their mother. To them, the culprit was the disease. End of story.

Anita wasn't entirely sure why she was doing this. Maybe it was an excuse to put off going into work. She'd had a good weekend. She'd babysat Leyla on the Saturday. Now that she was getting used to administering the numerous injections Leyla needed, this had been relatively uneventful. Getting her to eat the correct amount of food was the biggest obstacle. Every carbohydrate served up had to be accounted for in order to calculate the right amount of insulin to ensure the stability of Leyla's sugar levels. Any huge swing one way or the other still produced moments of panic, and Anita was full of admiration at how calm Lasse and Jazmin had become when the readings were too low or too high. She'd got it now – in its simplest form: more insulin if too high, dextrose tablets when too low; but she knew there was far more to it than just that. She'd had the usual FaceTime with Kevin. He still couldn't commit to a week's holiday, as he was heavily involved in an ongoing investigation, so she was putting off her summer vacation until he became free. They hadn't decided where to meet up – home, away or on neutral territory.

She entered the building on Jan Waldenströms gata. She was shown into a very basic room with a table set against a wall, and four chairs. It could have been in any part of the hospital. What she was going to ask Jolis she wasn't entirely sure. On her walk over there, she'd started to question the point of the interview. From what they had gathered from the submitted psychiatric report, there was little likelihood of getting much sense out of him.

Markus Jolis came in, accompanied by a strapping male nurse. She hoped he wouldn't be needed but felt safer that he was present. They had been warned about Jolis's temper. What surprised Anita was the third person who entered the room. He was a smartly dressed man of about forty. He had the regulation white shirt opened at the collar and a tailored, tight-fitting, light-blue suit – a common sight on any main thoroughfare in Malmö, Gothenburg or Stockholm. His brown hair was centre parted with a slight wave each side. He was clean shaven, unlike many of his hipster brethren. The expressive brown eyes were piercing through expensive spectacles. In Anita's experience, the less material used to manufacture a pair of glasses, the more expensive they were. This man's glasses didn't have much beyond the lenses. He had lawyer written all over him.

'Inspector Sundström,' he said, proffering a well-manicured hand. 'I'm Filip Assarsson from Ekvall & Ekvall.'

'It's not a company I've heard of.'

Like a magician pulling off a trick, a business card miraculously appeared at his fingertips. Anita took it.

'Stockholm? It's a long way to come.'

'Herr Jolis is a client of long-standing. He used our services when he was based up there.'

'And why are you here?'

'My client is entitled to have a lawyer present when being interviewed by the police. We wouldn't want you putting words in his mouth now, would we? Anyway, it was the family who requested that I attend the interview.'

'Given your client's state of mind, I'd hardly call it an interview.'

'What would you call it then?'

Anita couldn't answer. She wasn't sure what she'd call it.

'OK.'

Assarsson helped Jolis into a seat. Jolis clearly had no idea where he was, though he disconcerted Anita by switching on a broad smile. It was almost as if he recognized her. Then, in a twinkling, it was gone.

'Hello, Markus. I'm Anita. We met at your apartment.'

Jolis smiled again. Then a frown crossed his face, accentuating his hooded eyes and saggy skin. This was a man who was disintegrating physically as well as mentally.

'She didn't give me any *fil* this morning with my muesli.' He was referring to *filmjölk*, a sour milk that health-conscious Swedes added to their breakfast bowls – Kevin had found it tasteless.

'Who, Markus?'

'Nina, of course!' The anger was instant.

'Nina can't, Markus. She's in another part of the hospital.'

His expression became blank again. He wasn't going to enquire further.

'Markus, do you remember anything about what happened at your apartment last week? When you took a knife... a kitchen knife. Do you remember what you did with it?'

Jolis turned to the window and stared out of it. He didn't speak.

'I think this is a waste of time, Inspector,' sighed Assarsson theatrically.

He might be right, but she wasn't giving up yet.

'I wouldn't want you to have come all the way from Stockholm for just five minutes. I presume you're charging for a full day.'

'On your head be it,' he said, crossing his legs and folding his arms.

'Markus, I see that you worked for *tullverket*. You were in Stockholm during the nineties.'

'What has this to do with the price of fish?'

'I know that people with Alzheimer's have little short-term memory but remember things from the past. Maybe that's a way of getting back to the present.'

It wasn't the real reason she was taking this tack. Assarsson shrugged.

'Do you remember working for the customs? In Stockholm?'

Jolis slowly turned to face Anita. The eyes were no longer blank. Was that the stirring of a memory?

'You were working at the EstLine terminal, weren't you? In fact, you were probably there at the time the *Estonia* sank.'

Jolis's head didn't exactly jerk up, but it was plain that she had struck a chord, however remote.

'You see, my father was on the ferry that night.'

'The *Estonia*.' He looked troubled. He leant across and patted Anita's knee gently. Then he sat back. The hand that had touched her knee was trembling.

'Do you remember working that night, or around that time?'

'I think you should stop now,' broke in Assarsson. 'You can see you're upsetting him.'

Jolis's whole frame began to shake.

'It shouldn't have happened!' Both Anita and Assarsson were startled by the sudden shout. 'He was wrong.' This was whispered.

'Who? What shouldn't have happened? Something to do with the ferry?'

By now, Jolis was trembling and his cheeks were streaked with tears.

'This has to stop now!' commanded Assarsson.

'You're right. I'm sorry, Markus.'

Assarsson glanced at the nurse and nodded his head. The nurse led the distressed Jolis away.

'Well, I hope you're proud of yourself. That man is in no fit state to answer questions, let alone be reminded of an event that not only scarred him but also most of the country, including you by the look of it. I may well have to report your unprofessional behaviour.'

Zetterberg will have a field day with this one, Anita reflected ruefully.

'Have a nice trip back to Stockholm.'

CHAPTER 5

The Pickwick was quiet at that time of the evening. Despite it being warm enough to sit outside, Anita and Klara Wallen plumped for an inside seat. Anita was halfway through her pint of *Bombardier*. Wallen was on the red wine. Anita was happy to have her friend's company. Since Klara had moved back to Malmö permanently, they'd got closer. It had been a brave decision to walk out on the controlling Rolf, who hadn't taken Wallen's bid for independence well. There had been a couple of nasty incidents since. Now things seemed to have settled down, and Rolf was rotting in Ystad. Wallen even lived near Anita on Kronborgsvägen.

Anita was glad to escape the polishus and come to familiar surroundings. All day, she'd been awaiting a call from Zetterberg, following up Assarsson's complaint. Yet nothing had come through yet. Or Zetterberg was sitting on it, waiting to pounce. It had been two days since the meeting at the psychiatric centre. Anita had regretted asking Markus Jolis about his past, but the whole *Estonia* episode had been simmering in the back of her mind, and she'd been unable to pass up the opportunity to ask someone who might have more inside knowledge. The fact that the man was mentally unfit hadn't stopped her. Yet he obviously remembered it, judging by his reaction. 'It shouldn't have happened!' was a natural response. Everyone in the country felt like that. The bow visor shouldn't have been torn off even in bad weather. But what Anita kept harking back to was Jolis's follow-up remark: 'He was wrong.'. Was he still talking about the disaster? Who was wrong? What was *he* wrong about? Maybe it was the ramblings of an old man whose mental faculties had been destroyed by a merciless disease. Was she trying to read something into nothing? She put it out of her mind. There were more interesting things to talk about.

'Liv told me about the wedding,' Wallen said, putting down her wine glass before shovelling out some more peanuts from the packet on the table. 'Sounds a bit hush-hush.'

'Ah, I wondered when that was going to become public.'

'You knew?'

'Jazmin blabbed. She can't keep a secret.'

'Liv said it was going to be a civic one. No religion at all. Got the impression that she would have liked something fancier.'

Anita sighted. 'Poor Liv. It's all very tricky. Uday and Amira are adamant that Hakim should have a traditional Muslim wedding. As Liv has no intention of converting to Islam, he has no choice. I think he feels awkward about it. Naturally, Jazmin is vocal on the subject. Stuff their parents! If they want to get married, then just do it. Of course, Jazmin has conveniently sidestepped the issue herself by not marrying Lasse. And he's quite happy about that. Björn and I weren't exactly a good advertisement for wedded bliss.'

'So, are Hakim's parents going to turn up?'

'Doesn't sound like it at the moment. I don't think they've even been told the date. It's going to be a very small affair. Liv's brother and family, our lot... not much more.'

'Well, good luck to them. Liv's great. She won't let Hakim control her.' Wallen couldn't keep the resentment out of her voice.

'I take it you've not heard from Rolf recently?'

Wallen drained her glass. 'No.'

'Then I suggest another drink.'

Wallen suddenly grinned. 'Yeah. Actually, we've got a reason to celebrate. That rumour that the hideous Alice is leaving... it's true. I've heard she's being lined up for some high-profile job in Stockholm – something to do with a government advisory committee on crime. The word is that she's going sooner than expected.'

'I hope that's not fake news.'

'The not-so-good news is that Erik Moberg is coming back sooner.'

'That's good. Moberg's fine.'

Wallen pulled a sulky face. She had never been able to cope with Moberg, who could be an intimidating figure, especially when investigations weren't running smoothly. Wallen had always been rather scared of the chief inspector. Anita had learned to deal with him and in the last year or so had started to regard him with grudging affection. Just the mention of his name made her feel guilty – she hadn't visited him much recently. Her mother's illness and Leyla's condition had rather preoccupied her non-working hours.

'Well, I'll certainly drink to Alice Zetterberg's quick departure.' Anita's spirits were immediately lifted. 'Maybe we should have a whip-round to pay for her train ticket.' Wallen smirked. 'Same again?'

Leyla was chasing after a butterfly in Pildammsparken. She was giggling because she couldn't quite catch it. The exercise was doing her good – keeping her blood sugar levels down. She was as bright as a button and kept Anita amused when she was like this. When her levels went awry, the moods took over. Throw in inheriting her mother's determination and, at times, she could be a handful. What all the family were looking forward to was the Omnipod. This insulin dispenser, attached to Leyla's body, would do away with the eight injections a day, and the doses would be calculated from information fed into a hand-held gadget called a Personal Diabetes Manager. They would still have to test her sugar levels by taking blood from her fingers, but even for that there was more gadgetry available in the shape of a Continuous Glucose Monitor. Research was developing fast, and Anita hoped that such strides would help her granddaughter to live a relatively normal life in the future.

Her musings were interrupted by her mobile phone. It was a Saturday afternoon and she wondered why Hakim was ringing her up. Cold feet about the wedding?

He began with an apology. 'Sorry to disturb you, Anita.'

'No, that's fine. I've got Leyla for the day.'

'How is she?'

'She's having a good day today.'

'Great. Look, just thought you might want to know. Markus Jolis.'

'What about him?'

'He's dead.'

'What do you mean *he's dead*?'

'Cardiac arrest, apparently.'

Anita was taken aback.

'Did he have a heart condition?'

'Angina. He was taking pills for it. But perhaps the business with Nina just triggered an attack.'

'Right.' She could see the reasoning. 'I suppose that puts that one to bed. Zetterberg will be pleased that no more needs to be done. Save the tax-payers, too.'

After the call ended, Leyla came up to Anita and pointed towards the lake in the centre of the park.

'Go to birds. Give bread.'

'OK, let's go and find the geese.'

Anita lifted her granddaughter into the baby buggy, and they headed off to the water's edge; Leyla cradling the plastic bag of unused pieces of bread that they'd collected up in the kitchen before setting off.

After the usual Sunday FaceTime with Kevin, who had appeared rather fragile after a colleague's leaving party the night before, Anita was making her way to the main part of the hospital. She wanted to see how Nina Jolis was and convey her sympathies to the family. She still felt mortified that she'd upset Markus Jolis earlier in the week, especially in light of the fact that he'd died a few days later. Had she stirred up dreadful memories? She was relieved, however, that the lawyer Assarsson hadn't gone through with his threat to make an official complaint. Maybe she had to be grateful to the family for that. Assarsson struck her as the sort of lawyer who'd have enjoyed getting official with officials.

The smells of a hospital are familiar to a cop. That mix of disinfectant, food and people; relief, despair and hope. Anita had spent many hours in this particular one, seeing colleagues or criminals or witnesses – and there'd been that awful week when Leyla was whipped in and diagnosed. And she'd been in as an outpatient on a few occasions.

She found Nina Jolis's room with little difficulty. Through the glass, she could see a battery of machines surrounding her. At the side of the bed sat a middle-aged couple. The man must be a son, as he had his father's build and his father's ears. He noticed Anita and came out.

'I'm Inspector Anita Sundström. I was called out to the incident at your parents' home.'

He held out a hand and gave hers a firm shake.

'Tord Jolis.'

'I was wondering how your mother was.'

His head swivelled back towards the room. 'She's still fighting.'

'Sorry to hear about your father.'

His eyes moistened. 'Possibly for the best. I don't think the family could have coped with what he'd have to go through. Public humiliation. He'd not know what was happening. I'm sure he never meant to attack Mamma. He was devoted to her. It's that...' He shook his head.

'The investigation will be wound up. Nothing to concern yourselves about. You and the family need to concentrate on your mother now.'

There was nothing else to do but go. She nodded to Tord Jolis, who turned to open the door to the room.

'I'm sorry if I upset your father.' Jolis appeared nonplussed. 'I just wanted to apologize.'

'What for?'

'I tried to interview Markus last Monday. And I strayed into an area that distressed him. I assumed your lawyer told you.'

'What lawyer?'

Anita fished out Assarsson's card and handed it to Jolis.

He read it out: '*Filip Assarsson, Ekvall & Ekvall, Stockholm.* What has he to do with Dad?'

'He said he was at the interview at the request of the family. Apparently, your father had used his firm for years when he was based up there.'

Jolis was still frowning. 'I don't understand. I know my father's lawyers because we've just been dealing with them when all this blew up. And it's certainly not this lot. And we definitely didn't send anyone to any interview. This Filip Assarsson has nothing to do with us.'

CHAPTER 6

Alice Zetterberg viewed her team with her usual attitude of superiority. In fact, she thought of them individually as 'a bunch of losers', in the immortal words of Donald Trump, though she had to admit that collectively, under her guidance and expertise, they got results. Of course, she knew they didn't like her but, so what?, they meant nothing to her. The only one who consumed her thoughts to the point of obsession was Anita Sundström, the bitch who'd slept with her husband, Arne – she knew she had, despite Anita's fervent denials. Nothing could adequately describe her feelings of antipathy towards Sundström. But she'd be moving on in a few weeks' time, and then the whole lot of them would just be an unpalatable memory. At the end of August, she would be out of this hellhole and into a cushy number in Stockholm.

She'd already got her eye on a nice apartment in Södermalm. She was looking forward to the social scene as much as the increased prestige. A career that had stalled for many years had only been resurrected by a stroke of luck – the secret service had needed her to keep the lid on information that could have caused serious damage to national security. And doubly gratifying had been the fact that in the process, Anita Sundström's efforts had been thwarted. Zetterberg had been promised that her contribution would not go unrewarded. Initially, that had seen her move from a Scanian coastal backwater to running the Cold Case Group in Malmö. Then, after Chief Inspector Moberg's heart attack, she'd been put in temporary charge of the Criminal Investigation Squad, as well. After fleetingly enjoying the triumph of being Sundström's boss, she'd become increasingly frustrated that Moberg hadn't been pensioned off and she given the position on a full-time basis. When it became clear that Moberg would eventually return, she decided to call in her favour with Stockholm. They hadn't let her down. Her new job would be one in the eye for Linnea, too. Zetterberg had always thought that her sister, a policy advisor for the Ministry of Foreign Affairs, looked down upon her, a mere cop. Now Alice would also be working for the government. And, of course, the other advantage of being so close to her sister was that she'd have ample opportunity to work on Linnea's husband, Christer, whom she'd convinced herself fancied her. So far, the odd drunken fumble hadn't led to anything, but now she'd have time to do the job properly.

Until all these prospects unfolded, she would keep her head down and leave with her reputation enhanced. She had a good clear-up record and didn't want it tarnished by any difficult, last-minute case suddenly rearing its head.

'Right, if that's all, let's get back to work,' she concluded. They had been through the ongoing cases – and this briefly included the attempted murder of Nina Jolis. Their only suspect for that was now dead. Case closed.

'I've just got one thing,' put in Anita.

Zetterberg sighed in exasperation. Why was it always bloody Sundström?

'Something odd happened when I tried to talk to Markus Jolis at the hospital.'

'I told you you were wasting your time.'

'From that point of view, you were right. He didn't remember attacking his wife. It's just that there was this slick Stockholm lawyer present. Called himself Filip Assarsson.' Anita produced his business card.

'Jolis was perfectly entitled to have a lawyer there.'

'Granted. But the family didn't know anything about him. They hadn't asked for him to be at the hospital.'

'Does it matter now?' Zetterberg said impatiently. Why was

Sundström dragging this out? She had a drink with her name on it in a Lilla Torg bar.

'It might. The fact that he was there was strange. But what's even stranger is that I called the firm, Ekvall & Ekvall, just before this meeting. They'd never heard of Filip Assarsson. He certainly doesn't work for them.'

'Maybe he handed you the wrong card.'

'Unlikely. All I'm wondering is why he was there. Don't you think we should look into it? Are we missing something?'

'For God's sake! There's no point. Man with dementia—'

'Alzheimer's,' interrupted Brodd.

'Same bloody thing. Mental man attempts to kill his wife. Can't remember doing it. Conveniently dies himself. Cardiac arrest, according to the quacks. Wife might snuff it and then it's murder, but we've got nobody to charge. If she survives, she'll have to be interviewed at some stage. But for the time being, that's us finished with it, bar paperwork. End of story. So don't go and waste any more of the department's time on this. Understand?'

Zetterberg didn't wait for Anita's answer as she gathered up her things and swept out of the meeting room.

'What's on your mind, Mamma?'

Lasse always knew when there was something worrying his mother. It was a sensitivity that he hadn't inherited from his father.

'Nothing really.'

Anita and Lasse were having a coffee in Möllevångstorget. Leyla was uncharacteristically asleep in her buggy. They'd been at the play area in Folkets Park when the rain had started. The café was a good place to take shelter. Anita gazed at her son. When she'd chucked the rapacious Björn out, it had been Lasse who had quickly become the man of the family. He'd made mistakes in his youth – the awful Rebecka being one – but he'd grown into fatherhood with maturity. Jazmin seemed perfect for him. She was tempestuous where he was calm, she took risks where he was reticent, she was voluble where he was quiet, she was a bundle of energy where he was laid back. They complemented each other. He would be more than happy to be a full-time househusband – one of the *lattepappas* – while Jazmin went out and earned. This lack of ambition infuriated Björn, who felt his son was frittering away his life. Now with Leyla's situation, it was more important than ever that someone was around for her. As it was, both he and Jazmin were in menial jobs. That was why Anita was encouraging Jazmin to go to college and get qualifications for a career.

'Come on, tell me.'

Anita pushed her coffee mug away.

'It's just something at work.'

'Alice Zetterberg?'

'Not exactly. There's something that doesn't quite make sense on the case I was called to when we were disposing of the ashes.'

Lasse smirked at the memory. If the occasion hadn't been so solemn, he would have caught his mother, floundering around in the sea surrounded by his grandmother's remains, on camera.

'Not my finest hour!' she grinned, too. 'It's just that the old man who tried to kill his wife had Alzheimer's. It reminded me of my *farfar*.'

'Your dad's father?'

'Yes.' Recollecting, an expression of sadness flitted across her face. 'I remember the moment when I realized that my grandfather's fading memory had mutated into dementia. He was a very practical man; good with his hands. Inventive. Must have been where my dad got it from. *Farfar* had a large collection of clocks: long-case down to travel clocks. Whenever I visited him in Västerås, I was always surrounded by constant ticking and chiming. He would offer to stop them if they kept me awake at night, but I found the sounds reassuring. Comforting. Magical, even. *Farfar*'s home was a place of calm, especially when my parents' marriage started to fall apart after we came back from England. Later on, when I was at the Police Academy, I spent a few weekends with him, as it wasn't far by train. When I arrived this one time, I couldn't find him. Then I heard crying from the back room. I went in and he was on his knees, tears rolling down his cheeks. He was surrounded by the workings of one of his favourite clocks. Each piece was meticulously laid out on the floor. All had been cleaned. He was weeping in frustration because he couldn't remember how to reassemble it.'

'How awful.'

'He went downhill pretty quickly after that. Spent his last months in a home.' Anita's face suddenly brightened. 'He caused all sorts of trouble because he kept trying to dismantle the clocks there.'

'Wish I'd met him.'

'He was lovely. And clever, like your own grandfather. I'm so sorry that *he* never got to know you properly. You brought real joy into his life.'

'I only have the vaguest memories of him. Sometimes, I think I don't remember him at all and that my memories are only there because I've seen photos of him since.'

'That's another thing this case has raised. This man, Markus Jolis, was working for the customs at Frihamnen at the time the *Estonia* sank. I asked him about it and it seemed to spark some kind of reaction. Made me start to think.'

'Do you really want to go there again? I know how close you and your dad were. It'll only stir up past feelings. Let sleeping dogs lie.'

Anita played with a crumb on her plate.

'You're right, of course.'

Lasse shook his head with a knowing grin.

'But you won't, will you?'

CHAPTER 7

Anita had been through a directory of Stockholm lawyers and had failed to find Filip Assarsson. She had to be sure that there wasn't a rational explanation for him being at her 'interview' with Markus Jolis. Then she grabbed her bag, headed out of the polishus and made her way along the canal towards the hospital.

The day was blustery and the wind whipped up the dirty water. Not the best day for a pedalo outing, though one couple were trying their best, their machine wobbling precariously. The scene reminded her of what she'd been reading on the internet over the past few days after her conversation with Lasse. Whether or not it was because her mother had now gone and she felt more able to think about her father, she'd found herself compelled to revisit the whole *Estonia* disaster. She'd found a summary of the official JAIC report into the incident. The weather that night had been bad, with the increasing wind velocity and the significant three-to-four-metre height of the waves causing the ferry to roll and pitch. Shortly before 01.00 hours, a seaman of the watch reported a metallic bang from the bow area as the ship crashed into yet another wave. At 01.00 hours the crew changed shift. The seaman returned from his round and caught up with the captain on the bridge. He was sent back down to the car deck to find the cause of the sounds. He never reached it.

At 01.15 hours, the visor separated from the bow and tilted over the stem. This resulted in the ramp being pulled fully open and allowing huge volumes of sea water to enter the car deck. The ship very rapidly listed to starboard. At around 01.20 hours, a weak female voice was heard calling in Estonian '*Haire, haire, laeval on haire*' over the public address system: 'Alarm, alarm, there is alarm on board'. The first Mayday from the ship was received at 01.20 hours. A second distress call was picked up two minutes later by fourteen ship-to-shore-based radio stations.

By this time, all four engines had stopped. The emergency generator kicked in, supplying power to essential equipment and limited lights in the public areas and on deck. The water was entering the accommodation decks with considerable speed, and the starboard side of the ship was submerged at around 01.30 hours. During the last minutes, the list was more than 90 degrees. The ship sank quickly, stern first, and disappeared from radar screens.

During the thirty-five minutes the *Estonia* took to sink, those passengers who had reached the boat deck were given lifejackets by crew members. They either jumped or were washed into the churning sea. It took an hour after the sinking for four ferries in the vicinity to arrive on the scene. The first rescue helicopter appeared at 03.05 hours. Thanks to the combination of helicopters and assisting ships, 138 people were rescued – one of these died later in hospital. During the following two days, a further 92 bodies were recovered. The rest had gone with the *Estonia* to the seabed, including fifty-four-year-old Jens Ullman.

According to the final findings, JAIC believed that the *Estonia* had been perfectly seaworthy and properly manned and that the cargo had been secured and displaced to normal standard before departure. The visor had been in place. They concluded that the accident was caused by a technical fault in the ship – the bow visor locks hadn't been strong enough to withstand the level of wave forces on that particular night.

With the deaths of 852 people, the *Estonia* was the largest peace-time loss of life in European waters in the 20th century. However, it was clear that a number of people – some families of the victims, various maritime experts and a whole bunch of conspiracy theorists – disagreed with the official findings. Many of the theories appeared ludicrous to Anita, though some obvious questions still needed answering.

The main one was how a ship that hadn't been torpedoed or been in a collision could sink in only thirty-five minutes.

It took Anita a little less than that to reach the hospital. She just needed the official version of Markus Jolis's death for the file. After asking around, she saw a doctor who had been involved in overseeing Jolis's medical care. He said that there was nothing untoward – he'd had a massive heart attack. He was already suffering from angina. It had been unexpected, but 'these things happen'. He handed over a file – '...that includes the psychiatric reports as well. Always bloody paperwork...' – and rushed off to see a patient. Anita didn't envy him his job. Medics were even more overworked than the police.

On the way out, she decided to pop along and see how Nina Jolis was faring. At the entrance, she passed the male nurse who'd been in attendance at her interview with Markus.

'Sorry, excuse me. I saw you the other day when I talked to herr Jolis.'

He nodded in recognition.

'That lawyer... Filip Assarsson. Do you know when he turned up?'

'He was brought up from reception.' The nurse's accent was thick – he sounded Slavic. 'I saw him when I brought herr Jolis along.'

'And afterwards?'

'I took the patient back to his room. I presume the lawyer left then. I didn't see him after that.'

'Have you ever seen him before?'

He shook his head.

'Were you around when herr Jolis died?'

'Yeah, I was on duty then. But I didn't find him. It was the uniformed police officer on the door. Noticed he was lying slumped over his bed. Unlocked the door; found he was unconscious. Alerted us. Tried to revive him, but ...'

'I'm sure you did your best.'

'At least the officer was thankful – not because the patient was dead, you understand, but he was bored hanging around here.'

'Shifts like that aren't much fun.'

'Said the only thing that kept him going was chatting up the nurses... the female ones! And the doctor. Actually, I think he was confused. There wasn't a lady doctor on duty that day.'

Nina Jolis's condition hadn't changed. She was still hanging in there. Tord Jolis wasn't among the family members gathered round her bed. Anita didn't want to intrude, so she left.

Back at the polishus, she leafed through the dossier that she'd been given at the hospital. There was little chance that they'd have been able to progress with an attempted murder charge. And the heart attack had conveniently solved that potential problem, anyway. Reluctantly, she knew that Alice Zetterberg was right. She closed the file. But there was one last thing to do before she completed her side of the investigation. She needed to have a word with the officer who was outside Markus Jolis's room. He was the person who found the body and alerted the medical staff. She just had to confirm the details, and then she would hand everything over to Hakim or Erlandsson.

She pushed her chair back, took off her glasses and rubbed the bridge of her nose. Suddenly, she felt very tired. She needed her annual summer holiday. The last six months dealing with her mother had taken its toll. She'd felt strangely flat after the funeral. Nothing since had raised her spirits. At times like this, a case might have piqued her interest; been a distraction. But the whole fleeting Jolis business was just sad for all concerned. She would chivvy Kevin along into making a decision about taking time off. If not, she might take a break away by herself.

It wasn't until the next morning that she managed to catch up with Simon Eriksson, the officer who'd been on duty at the hospital when Markus Jolis died. Eriksson was in his early forties, slightly podgy and with a ready grin. It was obvious that he was naturally flirty. That reputation was already well-established at the polishus. But he wasn't lascivious, as Westermark had been. He was harmless; he just couldn't help himself. She'd come across him before on a couple of occasions. He was pleased to see her.

'Hi, Simon. I'm just putting the Markus Jolis case to bed. I just need to get your side of things.'

'Nothing much happened other than he died. I was keeping an eye on things. Checking up on him from time to time. The last time, I saw that he was lying on the bed at a funny angle. More crossways: legs hanging over the edge of the bed. Like he'd just fallen back. I unlocked the door and was going to sort him out when I realized he wasn't breathing. I shouted for help. They called in an emergency response team, which arrived from the main hospital within minutes. Amazing, those people. I kept out of the way. Turns out it was too late. Nothing they could do.'

'That's straightforward enough. Can you just write it up and pop it along?'

'No problem, Inspector.'

'Thanks.'

She could sense that he didn't want her to go.

'Yes?'

'There's just something. Not sure it's worth mentioning.' He was embarrassed now. 'Erm... the doc.'

'What doc?'

'Well, she went in to see him... Jolis... about fifteen, twenty minutes before I found him.'

'You mean a doctor went in to see him shortly before he died?'

'Yeah. Coincidence, I suppose... that his heart attack kicked in so quickly afterwards. It's just that she wasn't with the other medics who turned up when I called for help.'

'And it was definitely a doctor?'

'Oh, yeah. Very nice looking. Gave me a big smile. Badge hanging round her neck. Docs did pop in from time to time. Sometimes the shrink ones, other times the medics. All perfectly normal.'

'Had you seen her before?'

'Not that one. But there were quite a lot. Just thought it was a new one. Or she might have visited when someone else was on duty outside the room.'

Then Anita remembered the male nurse saying that there weren't any female doctors on duty that day and that Eriksson must have been confused.

'Could you describe her?'

'Oh, yeah. Black hair in a ponytail. Dark complexion. Quite tall. Around one point eight metres. Good figure.' She could tell he was enjoying the memory. 'Well, she looked to have a good figure, but those things they wear are quite baggy.'

'Age?'

'Mid-thirties.'

'Did she say anything to you?'

'Asked me to unlock the door. Thanked me when she came out. Sympathized with me sitting there. Hoped my shift would end soon. That sort of thing.'

'You didn't look in through the window when she was with Jolis?'

'No. I took advantage and nipped off for a pee.'

Anita didn't like the sound of this.

'OK, Simon. Get your report written as quickly as possible. And mention the doctor.'

Eriksson didn't seem so sure of himself now.

'Is anything wrong?'

'I don't know.'

CHAPTER 8

It was too simplistic to say that it was gut instinct. Obviously, there were things that didn't make sense – Filip Assarsson's presence at the hospital (he didn't seem to exist), then Simon Eriksson's attractive doctor who just happened to appear shortly before Markus Jolis's heart attack. In theory, there could be rational explanations for both: Anita just hadn't found the lawyer, and Eriksson's female might simply be one of the many doctors assigned to a patient with both mental and physical problems. Yet Anita had never liked the unexplained. Not the result of a logical brain – one of her teachers at school had described her mind as a mess, and Anita herself was the first to admit that her thoughts were often as scrambled as a plate of spaghetti. But her years of police work had inculcated the feelings and hunches that people tend to attribute to gut instinct.

It was after another visit to the hospital that she definitely knew something wasn't right. After her talk with Simon Eriksson, she'd scurried down there again and checked who'd been on duty at the time of Markus Jolis's death. As the male nurse had said, there was no female doctor in that part of the hospital at that time. Could she have come from another department out of professional curiosity? She was told that that was possible, if unlikely. After an hour's wait, she'd managed to view some CCTV footage. There was the doctor, as described by Simon Eriksson, black ponytail and all, though the only available angle didn't give a clear picture of her face. A secretary had run off a copy of a still from the footage. No one in the psychiatric unit recognized her. Of course, this didn't mean that she wasn't a member of staff elsewhere. That would take a lot more time and effort to establish in such a big hospital. Anita was unwilling to do anything officially, as the case was being closed. The last thing she wanted was Zetterberg giving her a hard time until she was surer of her facts and had something more concrete to present her with.

Erik Moberg was most definitely looking thinner. Then again, it was all relative. He'd still be obese by most medical measures. His face wasn't as rubicund as it used to be in the days when he was a regular drinker. He appeared fresher. More vibrant. Again, a relative term when applied to the chief inspector.

He was pleased to see Anita, who felt that she had neglected him in recent months. One thing was sure: when he returned to the team, they would have a better working relationship than they'd had before the heart attack. They would appreciate each other more.

'Take a seat, Anita. Coffee?'

'Are you allowed?'

'No more than two a day. This will be my first.' He picked up a chunky electronic cigarette that he'd put down on a table next to his armchair. 'I've even given up proper smoking.'

'Doesn't that count?'

'You sound like my ruddy doctor. These aren't dangerous.'

Moberg blew out a cloud of vapour and moved towards the kitchen. Anita looked at him suspiciously. She could detect the faint whiff of tobacco – you can't kid an ex-smoker.

He returned with a thermos of coffee and two cups.

'No biscuits or goodies, I'm afraid.'

'Good for you,' she said encouragingly, though she *was* feeling peckish.

As he poured the coffees, she noticed a blue rubber pedometer on his wrist.

'Doing your steps?'

He shook his wrist. 'This fucking thing. It drove me mad at first because I thought I had to walk everywhere to reach my daily target.

Then I worked out I only have to swing my arms. Now I don't even have to leave the house.'

'I'm not sure that's really the point.'

'I'm giving up all the things I love. Why waste time on things I hate? And I do hate exercise! Anyhow, I'll get enough of that once I'm back at work.'

'That can't come soon enough.' Anita sipped her coffee. Even for her, it was strong. Two of these a day would be the equivalent of her six!

'*She* still on your case?' He didn't even have to mention Zetterberg by name.

'She's on everybody's case. Believe it or not, we're all looking forward to your return.'

'Never thought I'd hear that,' he beamed. 'Even Klara Wallen?'

'Even Klara.' It wasn't exactly true.

He took a long slurp of his coffee and then smacked his lips. 'Anything happening that I need to be up to speed on?'

'Not really. We haven't got any juicy murders lined up for you.'

'Pity. Naturally, I heard about the old guy who tried to murder his wife. And now he's dead.'

'She's still alive.'

'So, it's all straightforward?'

'Seems to be.'

'But...?' She managed to look puzzled. 'Oh come on, Anita. Jesus, I wasn't born yesterday. I've seen that expression on your face too many times before. And I always knew it meant trouble, and that you were going to do something that was bound to drive me mad. One thing I did learn, eventually, was that you were usually onto something the rest of us had missed.'

'Honestly, it's nothing really.'

'Spit it out. When we start to work together again, I want complete honesty between us.'

'You never liked that before,' she joked.

'I'm a different person now. Two years of inactivity gives you time to think. Time to regret the bad choices. I intend to be a benevolent dictator.'

'That would be a change from the malevolent one we've got now.' Anita knew she was prevaricating. Was she unsure about the whole Jolis business?

'Just bloody tell me!' Maybe Moberg hadn't yet reached the anger management stage in his recovery.

'OK.' Anita proceeded to tell him about her meeting with the elusive Filip Assarsson and the appearance of the unknown doctor shortly before Markus Jolis died. Throughout, Moberg puffed on his electronic cigarette, clouds of vapour escaping from his mouth.

'I must admit, the lawyer seems odd. Why would he be there if the family hadn't asked him to be present?'

'It wasn't even a formal interview.'

'As for the doctor, there's bound to be a simple explanation. They're always going in and out of rooms and wards. I should bloody know!' There was a pause while he vaped. 'Unless you're suggesting that something untoward went on while the doctor was in the room?'

'Sounds daft, doesn't it? There hasn't been a post mortem. I wouldn't expect one anyway given he was in hospital already and had angina. And the family didn't ask for one. I think I'm seeing a conspiracy theory where one doesn't exist. Who would go to great lengths to monitor and then get rid of Markus Jolis? He was only a customs official.'

Moberg put down his cigarette. 'Unless he was a corrupt customs official.'

CHAPTER 9

Hakim sat silently in the living room while his mother made him sweet tea in the kitchen. Uday, his father, sat opposite. He wasn't speaking either. He'd hardly said a word to Hakim since his son had announced he was marrying Liv and that it wouldn't be a traditional Muslim affair. Hakim was making one last attempt, at Liv's urging, to win his parents over to the idea that they were going to have a secular ceremony. Why was Amira taking so long? He'd contemplated bringing his sister, Jazmin, along for moral support but had decided against it. She was too volatile and would probably wreck any chance of reconciliation. Liv had volunteered to be there. But he'd declined her offer – he was too afraid of his father saying something irreparably hurtful.

After what seemed an age, his nervous mother appeared with the tea. She'd only made it for him. She retreated to the other side of the room and sat next to his father. Staring across at them, Hakim felt he was in an interrogation, but without a lawyer present.

Hakim had always had a good relationship with his parents. They were a typical immigrant family. He and Jazmin were both born in Sweden but had lived a double life: an immense disparity between the strict cultural restrictions at home and the openness of the society outside. His father, as a Baghdad-based art dealer who travelled extensively outside the Middle East, had been used to Western ways, but had become less liberal when he'd been unable to carry on his career after fleeing Iraq in the early days of Saddam Hussein's régime. Though Uday had always been grateful that he'd been accepted by a then more-welcoming Sweden, his inability to find anything other than manual work had been frustrating. Promises of help from those art dealers he'd done business with in Europe had failed to materialize. He was no longer any use to them. This lack of opportunity for an intelligent man had driven him back into the norms that he had been familiar with in his homeland. Religion was the most dominant. The mosque played an increasingly important part in his life. When his hot-headed daughter was driving him to distraction with her independent views, which he'd forgotten he'd shared to a lesser degree in his globe-trotting days, he could always rely on Hakim. He was a good, sensible boy. And though, initially, he'd found it difficult to come to terms with him joining the police – after his own experiences of being harassed by them in Iraq, that was understandable – he'd become proud of what his son was achieving in their adopted land. When Jazmin had started to date Lasse Sundström, the arguments had got worse. Even more so when she walked out of their small Seved apartment and moved in with her boyfriend. He felt that Anita should have stopped that from happening. Then they'd had a beautiful baby, Leyla. Rather hypocritically, he'd forced himself to accept the situation for the sake of the child – he couldn't abide the thought that he would never see his granddaughter. He found the easiest way to cope was not to talk about Jazmin to anybody else, especially at the mosque or when idly chatting to Iraqi acquaintances on the benches in Möllevångstorget. He was just coming to terms with this uncomfortable dilemma when it was Hakim's turn to let him and Allah down. He had nothing against Liv – she was a lovely young woman. But she was not for Hakim. There were plenty of eligible girls in the Iraqi community. Any one of them would help his standing at the mosque. It was important that the family kept their faith intact; so much around them was undermining it. Then came the day when Hakim had announced that he was going to marry this woman. His horror at that news was only tempered by the natural sympathy he felt when Liv was shot and confined to a wheelchair. His son, he knew, was going through hell, so when Hakim had moved back into the family apartment, Uday had striven to conceal his true feelings. It had been a difficult year for everyone, and it was a huge relief when Hakim was able to leave Seved and move with Liv into an adapted bungalow in Arlov, at the north end of the city. Yet Uday could never approve of the match. The only way out was for Liv to convert to the One True God. He had pressed his son to persuade her that this was the right thing to do.

Hakim's inquisitors sat motionless as he sipped his tea. Whatever he said, he knew it wasn't going to end well. He put down the cup.

'Liv loves you both.' There wasn't a flicker. 'She wants you to be at our wedding.'

Hakim wanted to go on but the words failed him. His father put him out of his linguistic misery.

'How can you do this to us? Your family? If she were to embrace Islam... that would be another matter.'

Hakim had already had that discussion, and it was a non-starter. Liv wasn't an agnostic; she'd been a churchgoer in her youth, though that had slipped after the early deaths of her parents. But she wasn't prepared to convert to a faith that she didn't believe in just to please others.

'That won't happen. But Liv is a believer.' He knew he was stretching the truth. 'She is a Christian. Doesn't the Koran say "the People of the Book", Jews or Christians, can marry Muslim men? She's an unbeliever because she doesn't accept the Prophet, but she is a believer because she doesn't deny Allah.'

'*Ahl al-Kitāb.*' His father waved this away with an airy flutter of his hand. 'That's a mere interpretation. It's not one that your mother or I adhere to.' He glanced at a fidgety Amira, who nodded meekly.

'Liv is a good, honest woman. She would have liked to marry in a church. But to spare my feelings and yours, she has arranged a simple wedding in the garden of our new home.'

'We will not be there,' Uday said firmly.

Before he arrived, Hakim had decided that he would remain calm whatever his father said. It was to spare his mother, whom he knew to be more understanding, though she'd never admit it in front of her husband. Now he lost his temper.

'Are you so bitter with your lot that you have to take it out on the people who love you? You came to this country because you were persecuted in Iraq. You were given a home, protection. No knocks on the door at midnight. No secret police interrogations. No fear that when you walked into your home, your wife wouldn't be there – "disappeared", like so many of your friends. You were marked out because you embraced the world. You loved art and culture in all its shapes and forms. You loved Allah, but it didn't mean that you were petty minded. By living here, you've given your children a better life than we could have had in Baghdad. Now look at you. Where has that idealist gone? Your big worry is what they'll think of you at the mosque. Oh, look how sinful Jazmin and Hakim have become, corrupted by Western ways. You don't care about how we feel, about our happiness. You're turning into a narrow-minded fundamentalist. You may be disappointed in me, but it's nothing to the disappointment I feel in you.'

Hakim couldn't remember whether Uday had said something to him as he marched out. All he remembered was the loud clunking of the front door as he slammed it shut.

At the same time, Anita was again pushing her way through the entrance door of the hospital. She wanted a word with Tord Jolis if he was there. Ever since she'd spoken to Moberg, she'd been thinking about Markus Jolis. Moberg's last remark had set her off. In a quiet moment, she'd got Liv to check out all the hospital staff to try and find the missing doctor. And while she was about it, could she dig up anything on Zander Security, the outfit Jolis had worked for after leaving his customs job? Liv was under strict instructions not to mention it to anyone else in case Zetterberg got wind of the fact that she was still pursuing, albeit in a low-key way, an investigation that was now being shut down. As it turned out, Liv hadn't been able to find the ponytailed doctor, or indeed anybody who matched Simon Eriksson's description.

45

That had led Anita to speculate about what the doctor had been doing in the hospital room shortly before Jolis's death. Could she *really* have had criminal intentions? Like killing Jolis? There must be numerous ways to simulate a heart attack, especially when the man already had a cardiac condition. It all seemed so fanciful. But the most obvious question was *Why?*. *Had* he been a corrupt customs official as Moberg had suggested? Even if he had been, why would anybody want to shut him up? And if he *had* been a threat during his professional career, it was twenty years ago – if anyone had wanted to murder him, they'd had two decades in which to do it! What Anita needed to do was have the body examined before it was buried or cremated. With no post mortem, there'd been no way of determining if it had been tampered with before death. The problem was she couldn't go through official channels – Zetterberg wouldn't countenance it. Her only route was through the family. Ask them to request an examination. That wasn't going to be easy; they'd been through enough already. To spring on them the notion that their father could have been murdered might be too much for them to take. It was going to be a difficult conversation. And if there *was* an innocent explanation for his death and she'd put the family through extra anguish, Zetterberg would hang her out to dry.

Anita found Tord Jolis at the coffee machine. She bought herself one in the belief that a casual conversation, coffees in hand, would somehow make her request easier to broach.

'How's your mother?'

He gave her a weary smile. 'Not much change. She's no worse, which I suppose is a positive.'

'How are the rest of the family bearing up?'

'Not brilliantly. At least we were all here a couple of days ago.'

'That's good. To have her family around her.'

'It seemed right. We all came after the funeral.'

'The funeral?'

'Yeah. My father's.'

This was a real blow. There was no way she'd get permission to exhume a body.

'That was quick.'

'We were lucky a slot became available at the crematorium at short notice.' That closed that avenue. 'It was all arranged. It was a blessing. After all that's happened… it was good that it was done quickly and went under the radar. No press or anything. Quiet family ceremony.'

'You said it was arranged. You didn't organize it?'

He gulped his coffee down.

'Well, yes we did. But a well-wisher actually paid for the funeral. We organized a small wake afterwards. We covered the cost of that.'

'Who was the well-wisher?'

'We don't exactly know. Someone who knew my father, I suppose.'

'How did he or she get in touch?'

The coffee was getting cold in her hand. She hadn't taken a sip since the conversation had begun.

'Well, he didn't directly. I'd started the ball rolling the day after Dad died. I went to a funeral parlour here in Malmö. We discussed arrangements. They said they would organize everything. They came back to me with the date and the time. I couldn't believe the crem could fit us in at such short notice. But, as you can imagine, we were grateful. It was when I was going to settle up, the funeral people said the bill had already been paid. Well, I wasn't going to argue.'

'Didn't you wonder who it was?'

'Of course. All the funeral director could say was that an old friend of my father's understood the sensitivity surrounding the family's situation and the potential embarrassment. So, he'd pulled a few strings.'

'As well as picking up the tab.'

'Yes.'

A thoughtful Anita left her coffee undrunk.

CHAPTER 10

The Wennås Funeral Agency was on Östra Rönneholmsvägen, one of Malmö's more extravagant streets. Between a bar with pavement seating on one side and a cosmetic store on the other, it was housed through a stone-faced entrance below a late 19th-century apartment block. Black, semi-circular awnings indicated that it was a place of death, but with refinement. This wasn't one of the more trendy establishments that would make the occasion a thing of colourful frivolity: it oozed discretion. The atmosphere inside wasn't austere, but it was respectful. Soft classical music played in the background. Anita was met by a young woman dressed in a black skirt and jacket. Her pretty face was framed by appropriately raven hair. It was an expressive face, which seemed wasted in such reverential surroundings. Her smile of greeting was welcoming yet already compassionate.

'Hello. I'm Anna. How can the Wennås Funeral Agency help you at this difficult time?'

'It's not a difficult time for me,' said Anita, pulling out her warrant card.

'Oh dear,' Anna replied, gazing in dismay at Anita's police photograph.

'Don't worry, Anna. Nothing for you to worry about. I've just got a few routine questions to ask about the funeral of Markus Jolis. It was a couple of days ago, I believe.'

'Yes. At Limhamn crematorium.'

'Are you the right person to talk to about the arrangements made?'

'Herr Wennås actually oversaw the funeral itself. I did most of the admin. Please, take a seat.'

Anita sat down as Anna took her place on the other side of a mahogany desk. She pushed aside a thick book of coffin designs.

'As I say, it's just routine. As you are probably aware, Markus Jolis was suffering from Alzheimer's. He attacked his wife. She's still fighting for her life in hospital. That's why we opened the case. Now, of course, he's dead. But we have loose ends...'

'I understand.' This was an excuse to inject some sympathy into her voice. A default setting.

'Markus's son, Tord, came in to talk about organizing the funeral?'

'Yes. Apparently, he is the only member of the family living down here. In Copenhagen, actually. His siblings live in and around Stockholm, so it was natural that he should make the arrangements. Which he was pleased to do.'

'I'm sure he was. And you managed to get a slot at the crematorium very quickly. Is that normal?'

'No. We were just very fortunate. They were able to squeeze us in. And herr Jolis was pleased that it could all be dealt with swiftly.'

'That was lucky. It was also good fortune that an anonymous benefactor paid for the funeral.'

'Yes, indeed. It was a huge surprise to herr Jolis. It was obviously someone who held his father in high regard.'

'Do you mind if I ask you how the "well-wisher", as Tord called him, got in touch?'

'Not directly, if that's what you're thinking. It was carried out through an intermediary.' Anita's ears pricked up. 'Amazingly, he paid in cash. That's almost unheard of these days. Certainly not that amount.' Her face now registered the correct degree of astonishment.

'Why was that?'

'The lawyer said it was for discretion's sake. So that the anonymous benefactor couldn't be identified. Didn't want any fuss that might distract from the funeral. That was the important thing.'

'You said it was a lawyer you dealt with?'

'Yes. Very professional. All the way from Stockholm.'

'Has he got a name?'

'Erm... I can't remember offhand. But I'll have his card in my file.' Anna stood up and left the reception area. A couple of minutes later, she returned with a business card in hand. Anita already knew what it would say: *Filip Assarsson, Ekvall & Ekvall, Stockholm.*

Anita gave it twenty-four hours before she bit the bullet and went in to see Zetterberg. Though she had nothing concrete, she'd rechecked as much as she could. With Liv, she'd been through all the staff at the hospital again – still no sign of the mysterious female doctor. She'd asked Simon Eriksson to look through the files, and he'd confirmed that no one looked like the woman he'd seen. She'd rung round and searched the internet for a Filip Assarsson, lawyer. No sign of him, either. Over a couple of drinks with Klara Wallen, she'd raised her suspicions. Wallen's advice was to ignore it – she was just making extra work for herself. The case was closing. Markus Jolis was dead. All Anita would do is stir things up and piss Zetterberg off. Besides, though admitting that Assarsson's involvement appeared peculiar, she thought it was too far-fetched to surmise that Jolis had actually been murdered. In her more rational moments, Anita had to agree. Wallen also sensibly pointed out that the lawyer might have made up his identity just to protect the benefactor so nothing could be traced back. It might all be perfectly innocent. As Anita's head hit the pillow that night, her thoughts were confused. Maybe Wallen was right. But by the morning, she'd changed her mind. She'd give it one last shot.

Zetterberg proved negative from the moment Anita entered her office. Same old, same old, thought Anita. She explained that the non-existent Filip Assarsson had reappeared, this time paying out cash for the Jolis funeral on behalf of an anonymous benefactor. Zetterberg came back with the same argument as Wallen had in the bar the night before – Assarsson was working for a client who didn't want to be traced, so he made himself untraceable. Anita couldn't challenge it without further evidence.

When Anita suggested that there might actually be something suspicious about Markus Jolis's death – now totally unprovable thanks to the speedily-arranged cremation – Zetterberg was scathing.

'Are you seriously suggesting that some doctor just wandered in and killed Markus Jolis? It's a ludicrous notion! And why, pray, would this doctor kill an eighty-year-old man who was out of his fucking mind?'

'I don't know. I need to look into his past. The whole thing is just—'

'Just what? You're one of these people who see bloody conspiracy theories everywhere. You're losing the plot.'

'I saw a conspiracy when Albin Rylander and Klas Lennartsson were killed. And you helped put a lid on that!' Anita wasn't going down without a fight.

Zetterberg instantly rose from her chair, a shaking finger pointing directly at Anita.

'You're a crap cop who shouldn't be near this police station. If I had more time here, I'd make sure that you had no future in the force. But, thank fuck, I'll be away from this dump soon. Until then, you'd better keep out of my way. And if I have the slightest inkling that you're still wasting time on Markus Jolis, I'll swing for you, so help me God. Now get out and pretend to be a proper inspector until your fat friend comes back.'

Anita felt like screaming at the woman. With difficulty, she managed to control herself and quietly left the office.

Zetterberg sat down. She was seething. She mustn't let Sundström get under her skin. Her breathing started to settle. There was no way that she was going to allow that tramp to muck up her future plans. When she'd calmed down, she took out her mobile phone and rang a number in Stockholm.

CHAPTER 11

Andreas Pressner was in two minds. He'd just been to the café at the Kallbadhus, where he'd enjoyed a *fika* with the *lattepappas*. It had been fun, though the kids had played up, especially Silas, his five-year-old. To be honest, he'd been a pain in the neck recently. Little Lotta, in her buggy, was usually as good as gold. The conversation had rattled around the usual subjects – football, working partners, computer games, the cost of children's clothes, cars and what was on television last night. Not that any of them stayed up that late these days, as the kids were tiring them out. Even so, Andreas didn't resent the joint decision for his wife to be the bread winner. Her job was better paid, and he wasn't exactly distraught at giving up his. And the kids were good to be with – most of the time. What he missed was the workplace banter. Or popping out to the park for lunch by himself in the sunshine. Or a drink with colleagues after a hard day at the office. Or going for a relaxing sauna in the Kallbadhus itself. But they were small sacrifices in the great scheme of things. And he did enjoy flirting with some of the mothers in the play area of his local park.

Now they were heading home along the pathway that stretched the length of Ribersborgsstranden. To the right, the wide-open grassed area that bordered the city's beach and the Sound beyond. To the left, through the cover of trees and bushes, were the playing fields used, mostly at weekends, for a variety of sports. There were rugby posts on one section. To Andreas, that seemed to be a version of American football but without the padding. Very odd and masochistic. Many of those he'd seen taking part didn't look or sound particularly Swedish. It was typical of the modern Malmö – an ethnic mix of people perpetuating their own cultures. He didn't mind, though some of his friends did. That was one of the reasons why politics was a no-no at *fika* gatherings.

Where the hell had Silas gone? He was always disappearing. Andreas stopped pushing the buggy and called out for his son. He'd be hiding in the trees somewhere. Andreas was starting to get irritated. He had to get back and get them all lunch. And then he had to plan supper for when Hannah came home. He was already thinking about that bottle of wine he'd put in the fridge. It had been recommended by one of the *lattepappas*.

'Silas!' Andreas bellowed. 'You won't get any lunch if you keep wandering off.'

No sign. Andreas cursed under his breath.

'OK, I'm going without you!' Andreas started to push the buggy. His shouting had woken Lotta, and she began to cry. Bloody Silas!

Then Silas appeared behind him.

'Stop messing about! We've got to get home.'

'Daddy!' The cheeky grin that usually accompanied his naughtiness wasn't there. If anything, he appeared perplexed. 'There's a man asleep in there,' he said, pointing to the trees from which he'd just emerged.

'Don't be daft.'

'There's a man asleep in there,' Silas insisted stubbornly.

'If this is another of your games...' Despite himself, Andreas thought he'd better check. It was probably some vagrant, or an alkie sleeping off a drinking session.

Andreas rocked the buggy to stop Lotta crying. 'Come here, Silas, and I'll have a look.' Lotta reverted to a tired whimper. 'Keep an eye on your sister.'

Andreas stumbled down a small depression and went into the trees. Through them, he could glimpse the wide expanse of playing fields that stretched to the bank beyond, along which sped the traffic on the main coast road to Limhamn. Some way ahead of him was a hut, which he knew was used by one of the sporting clubs for their equipment. Then he saw the legs jutting out from behind a bush. He pushed a branch away, and there was the rest of the body. His first observation was that the man was dressed in a new, dark-green tracksuit. The second was that he was coloured. It was probably an immigrant who was living rough, though the tracksuit belied that. He appeared to be sleeping peacefully. Maybe he should leave him be. Except something wasn't quite right. The man was very still, and his body wasn't in a very restful pose. Andreas leant down to poke him. There was something on the back of his head and some dark spots on the ground. Andreas instinctively recoiled. Dried blood. Despite a sudden wave of nausea, he forced himself to look closer. Then he really did feel sick. The man's head had been bashed in.

CHAPTER 12

Anita found that police tape had already been wound round some of the trees. There hadn't been enough room to erect a tent round the body, so she could see the forensics technicians moving about in their white suits. Hakim, arms folded, was leaning against a tree, watching the examination. Other officers, under the orders of Brodd and Erlandsson, were scouring the undergrowth, the edges of the fields, and the seaside path.

'We're trying to find a murder weapon,' said Hakim as Anita approached. 'Our victim had his head split open.'

'Bludgeoned.' This was Eva Thulin. She'd heard Anita approach. She got up off her haunches and came over. 'Blunt force trauma. Hit from behind. Struck across the back of the head, a little to the right. On the face of it, it appears to be two well-aimed blows in quick succession. I expect the first probably stunned him, and he may have slumped down, as the second blow appears to be from a higher angle. That was the one that fractured his skull. There are no defence wounds, so he probably wasn't expecting the attack.'

Anita glanced around. 'Plenty of potential clubs round here.'

'Don't think so. Whatever it was has created some sort of groove. You can see the second blow has almost obliterated the first.' Anita was quite happy to take Thulin's word for it. 'Something smoother than a branch.'

'Time of death?'

'Last night. I'd say between ten and midnight.'

'So it would be dark.'

'Not till about eleven and then it was a moonlit night,' put in Hakim.

55

'Anything else about the victim?' Anita asked.

'Possibly Asian.'

'Do you mean Arab?' said Anita, noticing the brown skin of the man's hand.

'I don't think so. I'd expect a typical Arab to be lighter skinned. Like our handsome Hakim. Anyway, I'd say in his sixties. Wearing a tracksuit, so he may have been out jogging. It's new.'

'Late night jogger? Hmm. There seems to have been no effort to hide the body.'

'Robbery?' Hakim suggested without much conviction.

'He's still got his iPhone. It was next to his body. It had been switched off. I suspect that he was in the process of switching it back on when he got hit. That's why he dropped it. And this small torch was in his pocket.' She held up a couple of plastic evidence bags. 'And he's wearing an expensive watch. That wasn't taken, either.'

'Was someone waiting for him? Or was it on the off-chance?'

'Your call, guys.'

Hakim wandered off to see how the search was going.

'Nice to see you back, Eva. Good holiday?'

'Gone too quickly.'

'I hear you wanted to get your other half away from distractions.'

'Oh, yes! I made sure *I* was the main attraction. He's gone back to work for a rest!'

'You're incorrigible, Eva Thulin!'

'I've got to make the most of it. It was nice to grapple with living flesh for a change. And something that wasn't stiff because of rigor mortis.'

'Enough, woman!'

She flashed Anita a salacious grin. 'You'd better have a look at the body.'

A forensic photographer was snapping away at every conceivable angle. The dead man was lying on his right side, one arm beneath him, his left hand near his head. The trees weren't so tightly packed at this spot, so the attacker had room to raise the murder weapon and swing it hard.

'A man do this?'

'It seems most likely. Though could have been a woman. Someone with strong wrists. Right-handed.' Thulin moved to the left of the body and mimicked the action of the attack. 'The murderer was probably standing over his left shoulder as opposed to directly behind him.'

Thulin bent down again and resumed her scrutiny of the corpse.

'It definitely hasn't been shifted?' Anita asked.

'No, nothing indicates that.'

'OK, I'll let you get on.'

Thulin squinted up. 'Will this be your boss's last case before she heads off to lick arses in Stockholm?'

'Yes,' Anita sighed. 'She'll want this solved before she goes. That means she'll make life hell for the rest of us until it is.'

His name carried weight. That's why he was put straight through.

'You've nothing to worry about,' he said quickly.

'I'm pleased.' The man at the other end of the phone sounded relieved. 'You can never be sure of these things.'

'The subject has been silenced permanently.'

'I don't need to know the details.'

'Thought not.' One of these days, they'd have to do the dirty work. 'Well, that puts an end to that.'

He could hear the man's breathing. 'There aren't likely to be any more...' he seemed to be searching for the right word '...complications?' The worry was back in his voice.

'Why should there be?'

'I don't know.'

'Look, we'd know if anything cropped up. I assume it's the same at your end?'

'Erm... yes, of course. Anything that registers on our radar, I'd let you know immediately.'

'That's good then. I hope we won't have to speak about this again.' He couldn't help being curt. He had much to do and felt he was wasting

precious time placating this man whom he'd never actually met, or ever wished to meet.

'No... goodbye,' the voice faltered.

He didn't bother responding. He clicked his mobile phone off to end the conversation. He pushed his chair back from his desk. Thank goodness that was sorted! It could have been a problem.

CHAPTER 13

When they gathered later that day, it was clear that Alice Zetterberg wasn't happy that they'd brought in a murder case at the eleventh hour of her temporary tenure. She was at her most brisk.

'What have we got?'

'We don't know who the victim is at this stage,' Anita started. 'He was wearing a tracksuit. Eva Thulin thinks he's Asian.'

'An immigrant,' huffed Zetterberg.

'Not necessarily. Might be second generation.'

'Same thing.'

Anita ignored the remark. 'He's in his sixties. He could have been out jogging.'

'Isn't that obvious?'

'Not obvious, no. But whatever the reason for the attack, which took place between ten and twelve last night, it wasn't robbery, as he was wearing an expensive watch. A Cartier.'

'That model's worth well over 400,000 kronor,' chimed in Liv.

'It appears that he was a man of means,' added Anita.

'Unless he'd nicked it.' Brodd's remark didn't produce the expected smirks.

'There was also a mobile phone, switched off.'

'That's with forensics,' said Liv. 'There's a blood spatter on it that they're checking out. We'll get it back first thing in the morning, and we'll unlock the pass code. That'll tell us who he is.'

'And a small torch, though the night was bright enough,' continued Anita.

'Murder weapon?' asked Zetterberg.

'We don't know yet. It left a furrow in the victim's skull. Two, actually, as there appear to have been two blows. That was Eva's first analysis. Whatever was used, there's no sign of anything in the vicinity that's the right shape. We're still looking.'

'Couldn't have been a branch?' Zetterberg suggested snidely. 'He was found among trees.'

'Not according to Eva.'

'Footprints?'

'The area's covered with them. It's right next to one of the most used paths in the city.'

'So, you don't seem to have come up with much so far.' The accusation was mainly aimed at Anita, though it implicitly applied to the whole team.

'Early days. As we've ruled out robbery, we think the victim was either meeting up with someone and it ended in his death, or somebody knew his routine and was lying in wait. We'll put out feelers in the Asian community. Hakim will co-ordinate that with Bea. With any luck, he'll be reported missing. If he *was* out for a run or a walk, then he'd be expected back. And we're appealing for people who may have been in the vicinity at that time. Late-evening walkers, etcetera.'

Zetterberg had had enough.

'When we get forensics back, I'll give the media an update. I'll play down the immigrant angle. It'll just cause tension. Right, I want this wrapping up as soon as.'

After the meeting, Liv wheeled herself into Anita's office. As usual, she was beaming. It was as though she relished every day and every challenge she was set. Maybe being that close to death made you appreciate life, even if it confined you to a wheelchair. Anita had had her own close shaves in the past – some alarmingly close – yet they hadn't given her the added zest that Liv seemed to have. Appreciation of the importance of family? Definitely. A sunnier outlook? Not really. The world was made up of too many bad people.

'Zander Security; the lot that Markus Jolis worked for. I've done a little bit of unofficial digging. No one knows. Not even Hakim.'

Complete discretion. That was another quality that Anita knew she didn't possess.

'I just don't want Zetterberg to know.'

'Makes it more exciting,' Liv said with a mischievous grin. 'Anyway, Zander Security still exists. It was set up in 1986. Originally in Stockholm, though they worked all over Sweden, then abroad. Basically, they do everything from providing bodyguards to parking security, patrolling compounds to guarding private functions – ones that need to be kept discreet or with important people present. High-profile business conferences. That sort of thing. They'll also vet personnel for companies working on sensitive projects. That's over here. Abroad, they seem to do a lot of stuff in developing countries. Middle East. Pakistan and India, and a number of African countries. That appears to involve working for some of the more, shall we say, dubious political figures around. But also protecting large installations. For example, our own Surt Oil. Guarding oil fields, mines and such like.'

'Isn't Surt Oil one of Henning Kaufer's many companies?'

'Yeah. Surt, the Norse fire giant. They've got various locations in Africa that need protecting. But they're just one of Zander's clients. It's impossible to get a full list of them, as some won't want it known that they're using a private security firm, often for political reasons. As a result, Zander like to keep a low profile, so you won't hear them trumpeting their successes publicly. They've got an official website, though it doesn't give much away. I've had to dig a bit deeper to find out what I have so far. Not exactly hacking but... well, best not to ask.'

Anita raised a hand. 'Then don't tell me. And don't get yourself into trouble for my sake.'

'I'm happy to help.'

Anita pushed her seat back from the desk. 'It seems an odd company for Markus Jolis to join.'

'Not really. They have a security compound here in Malmö. Stuff coming in and out through the docks for clients. His customs experience might have been very useful.'

'I suppose.' Anita wasn't really getting anywhere. 'Do you know who runs the company?'

'Not really. All a bit shadowy. There's no contact name on the website – just a phone number. I do know it was started by a Rickard Zander. A German. Despite being a failed businessman over there, he succeeded over here. Died ten years ago.'

'I'm just speculating as to who might have been the Jolis family benefactor. Clearly not Zander himself. A colleague at the company?'

'There probably aren't many people left who were working for Zander around twenty-odd years ago when Jolis was there. And he only spent five years with them. Not exactly a long-serving employee.'

'Oh, you're right, Liv. I'm getting nowhere with this. I'll have to admit defeat.'

'I think we've got him,' announced Klara Wallen as she came into Anita's office just after two the next day. Anita was going through a plan of action with Hakim and Erlandsson. 'A call came in yesterday from the daughter of a Bismah Nawaz. Bismah's husband, Iqbal, went out on Monday night and hadn't returned. She was told to give it twenty-four hours and see if he turned up. She's rung again saying he's still missing, so it's only just been flagged up.'

'Where does she live?'

'Limhamnsvägen.'

'You mean near the playing fields?'

'Not sure yet, but must be somewhere down there.'

'So if it's him, he hadn't strayed too far from home. Look, you go down there with Hakim and see if he *is* our victim. But go easy on her if he is.'

'Actually, I think you'd better go, Anita.'

'Why?'

'The daughter said her mother hasn't any Swedish. That's why she phoned in. Her mother does speak English, though.'

'Ah. OK. I'll take Hakim, and you can let Zetterberg know what I'm doing. But wait until we've left the building. Don't want her interfering.'

'Given that he died close to home, maybe it's a domestic,' said Hakim, getting to his feet. 'We might be able to clear this one up quickly for her ladyship.'

Anita hoped he was right. Then she might have more time to dig into Markus Jolis. She knew in her heart of hearts that she wasn't really going to admit defeat.

CHAPTER 14

The large, crescent-shaped block of upmarket apartments on Limhamnsvägen overlooked the playing fields of Limhamnsfältet. In the distance, through the trees, Anita could see the fluttering police tape at the crime scene. The only building in the vicinity was a long, green wooden hut. If the dead man lived in these apartments, he was decidedly wealthy. This was a million miles away from the dismal blocks in areas like Rosengård and Fosie that many of his compatriots called home. They now knew that the victim was definitely Iqbal Nawaz, as Liv had cracked the phone's pass code just before they left the polishus. This wasn't going to be an easy conversation.

Anita and Hakim were let into the penthouse apartment by a woman in her twenties, who turned out to be the victim's daughter and the person who had rung headquarters this morning. She wasn't pretty, though her strong-boned features weren't unattractive: she had large, dark eyes and her jet-black hair twisted over her shoulder in a thick plait. Her *shalwar kameez* – loose, pleated trousers underneath a long tunic – in rich pink shot through with gold thread suited her colouring. Her expression was of natural concern. She said her name was Muneeba. Anita asked if she could speak to her mother and assured her that she would be happy to converse in English.

Muneeba showed them into one of the reception rooms. The furniture consisted of a long, sumptuous sofa; several chairs; a quartet of brass-inlaid rosewood tables; and a magnificent, symmetrically patterned, carved wooden cabinet, stunningly hand painted in bright contrasting colours. An antique Ralli quilt dominated the longest wall; and calligraphy, abstract geometry and floral motifs decorated the smaller spaces. A beautiful single-knot Kashmir carpet adorned the floor. This place was definitely more Lahore than Limhamn. Bismah Nawaz was sitting in one of the chairs. She also wore a *shalwar kameez*, the dour beige colour in sharp contrast to her daughter's. Unlike Muneeba, she wore a *dupatta* – a long shawl which completely covered her hair. It made it difficult to tell her age, though Anita reckoned she must be around fifty. Her cheeks were full and chubby, but they softened the prominent nose. The lips were tightly pursed and the eyes intense; eyes that, at that moment, registered anxiety. Anita was not about to alleviate that.

Muneeba spoke to her mother in what Anita assumed to be Punjabi or Urdu. Bismah sat impassively, though she couldn't stop her hands continuously clasping and unclasping in her lap.

'When exactly did your husband go missing, Bismah?' Anita began tentatively.

'We only realized the next morning,' put in Muneeba in English.

'When did he go out on Monday night?' Anita again addressed Bismah.

She spoke before Muneeba could jump in. 'He left at about ten. When I went to bed.'

Muneeba didn't contradict her. 'I was out.'

'Were you worried when he didn't come back?'

'No.' She was very matter-of-fact.

'They sleep in separate bedrooms.' Muneeba clearly felt she needed to explain.

'Did he often go out at that time?'

'Yes. He likes exercise. Jogs. He also goes out to do business.'

'Do business?'

'He runs a company.' Again this was Muneeba. 'Electrical stores. He often visits them after closing. You may have heard of Happy Electricals?'

Both Anita and Hakim instantly knew the stores she was refer-ring to: the logo was a smiling plug. They were part of a national chain offering cut-price goods. The company was successful and had made many of the traditional Swedish electrical shops, who couldn't compete on volume and price, unhappy.

'My father is often out at night, late. So it was nothing unusual when I came back and he wasn't in. That was about half past eleven. It was only yesterday morning we were aware he hadn't come back. His bed hadn't been slept in.'

'Is that unusual?'

'Yes. He usually tells my mother if he isn't coming back. That's why I rang the police, but they told us to wait twenty-four hours, as he would probably turn up.'

'Did you hear him go out on Monday night?'

'It was after we had eaten,' Bismah explained slowly. 'He got a call.'

'Call? A phone call?'

'Yes.' That would be the first thing she'd get Liv to check out.

'Did he go straight out afterwards?' Anita insisted.

'Yes, it was about that time; a short time after.'

'Does he wear a tracksuit when he goes out running?' Hakim asked.

Bismah's head jerked up in alarm.

'Yes,' confirmed Muneeba. 'A dark-green one. He also sometimes wears it when he goes to the stores at night. Finds it comfortable. Why?'

Hakim glanced at Anita.

Anita cleared her throat. 'You may have noticed activity over on the other side of the playing fields.' She pointed out of the window. 'I'm sorry to have to tell you that we found a body.'

Bismah suddenly shrieked. 'No! No, it can't be!'

Muneeba rushed to her mother's side and enveloped her in her arms.

'The victim was dressed in a dark-green tracksuit. From the mobile phone we found next to the body, we bel—'

Anita couldn't say any more, as the wailing of the two women drowned out any other noise.

*

It wasn't until the next afternoon that Eva Thulin was able to bring them up to date with her findings. Anita had hoped they would have made more progress in the forty-eight hours that had elapsed since the body of Iqbal Nawaz was discovered. So far, they hadn't gleaned very much. At least they now had a positive ID: his daughter had confirmed it, as her mother had been too upset. No one who might have heard or seen anything within the timeframe that the murder took place had come forward. Ongoing calls to all the houses and apartments within sight of the murder scene were well underway and had yet to produce anything concrete. A couple of residents had seen a man in a dark-green tracksuit going for a leisurely jog some evenings, but not on Monday night.

They had looked into Iqbal's background. He'd been born in Lahore in 1955. He'd come to Europe as a young man and settled in Sweden in 1981, becoming a citizen five years later. He'd started selling electrical equipment from a stall at various outdoor markets around Skåne. His first shop opened in Malmö in 1987. Then in the early nineties, his business had really taken off, and outlets had sprung up all over the country, including Stockholm. He still had a family home in Lahore and owned a couple of factories out in Pakistan, making many of the own-brand electrical goods he sold through his chain of shops. He didn't have any criminal record, though, the team speculated, he must have had business rivals who were jealous of his success. They'd talked to staff at the company's main Bulltofta warehouse as well as the store in the Mobilia shopping centre in town. Iqbal appeared to be liked and respected by his workers, many of whom were of Pakistani origin, and they confirmed that he was in the habit of suddenly turning up at an outlet in the evening and going through the stock by himself after closing. He was very hands-on. That could have had the effect of alienating employees, and a disaffected member of staff might have had a grudge against his boss. That would have to be looked into.

Liv had spent time working through Iqbal Nawaz's mobile. She reported that he must have spent half his life on the phone, as he made and received dozens of calls per day. He had received a call at 21.49 on the night he died, which fitted in with what Bismah had said. It was from a Mohammad Abbas – one of many to and from the same number. The majority of calls and SMSs in Swedish, English, and Urdu using Latin script (Liv had discovered that though the natives of Lahore speak Punjabi, they often write in Urdu) appeared to be business associated, though some seemed to involve a cricket club called Malmö Gymkhana, and an anti-drugs charity. It seemed that Iqbal's two main passions outside of the business were cricket, and the charity, which he had set up to work among the ethnic communities in Malmö, Helsingborg and Trelleborg. He'd begun it after two sons of employees had died from heroin overdoses. The charity was much lauded and had gone down well with those in authority in the various communes.

With so many Muslim names in his address book, it was difficult to know which contacts were professional and which were personal. There were also some emails on the phone. Liv had used a translation app to decipher the ones in Urdu as much as she could.

His domestic life was harmonious, as far as they could gather. Bismah was the result of an arranged marriage, sent over from Pakistan in 1988. She was thirteen years his junior. They had had two children. A son had died at the age of one from meningitis. Muneeba was the second born. Neither woman was involved in the company – Iqbal clearly kept his business and domestic lives separate. Bismah, whose lack of Swedish can't have helped her integration, appeared to be a stay-at-home wife. Conceivably, she wasn't interested in mixing outside the Pakistani community. Or maybe Iqbal hadn't encouraged it. Muneeba, on the other hand, was more outgoing and was studying economics at the city's university.

'OK,' Eva Thulin began. 'Time of death I now estimate between ten and eleven.'

'That fits in with the victim's known movements,' Anita observed.

'As I deduced at the crime scene, the deceased suffered two blows to the head, the second of which killed him. The first wasn't fatal but had the effect of making him slump to his knees. We found evidence of that from the knee areas of his tracksuit, and from the ground he sank into when we'd removed the body. This would explain why the second blow came from a more elevated angle and slightly more downwards – he'd have been an easier target for the assailant. The second blow caused an extensive, impacted fracture of the temporal bone extending backwards into the parietal bone and forwards through the sphenoid bone and the zygoma, disrupting the right orbit. There was damage to some major blood vessels, including the right external and internal carotid arteries, and extensive damage to the underlining brain tissue. Death would have happened quickly. As there were no defence wounds, it's likely that he wasn't expecting to be attacked—'

'Or didn't feel threatened,' said Wallen.

'Absolutely.'

'Are you any nearer to pinning down the murder weapon?' Anita asked. 'It would be helpful to find it.'

'Sorry,' apologized Thulin. 'Though I did find something rather puzzling in the wound – minute flecks of what I later identified as silicone wax, which makes me tentatively speculate that the weapon may have been made of wood. It was certainly smooth, but with a ridge, as you can see from these.' They all peered at the close-up shots of the victim's head.

'That rules out a baseball bat,' Hakim said, twisting his mouth. 'Wrong shape.'

'Garden implement?' suggested Erlandsson.

'Not one that I can think of,' said Thulin.

'Given that it's not a broken branch or something you'd find lying around,' Anita said thoughtfully, 'the killer must have taken the murder weapon with him to the scene of the crime. That suggests that it was a pre-meditated killing. Either someone was meeting Iqbal Nawaz or was waiting for him, knowing his routine.'

'An educated guess is that he was about to turn on his phone when he was attacked, as it wasn't in his pocket and was lying close to the body.'

'Why would he switch it off in the first place?'

'There might be a reason for that. He didn't want to be disturbed. I'm not sure he was doing the exercise you think he was.' Thulin's comment raised heads around the room.

'Come on then.'

'We found traces of semen in his underpants and the inside leg of his tracksuit.'

'So, he was out meeting someone.' Wallen voiced what they were all thinking.

'Well, he had either had sex with someone unknown shortly before he was killed, or he was hiding in the bushes having sex with himself.'

'Ugh,' shuddered Wallen.

'Don't knock it until you've tried it,' joked Brodd.

'This throws a totally different light on the case,' said Anita, holding up a photo of Iqbal Nawaz in a business suit, that they had borrowed from Bismah. 'He could have had an assignation. Maybe the woman he had sex with killed him.'

'Why a woman?' pointed out Erlandsson. 'If it was done surreptitiously in among the trees and bushes, it might have been with a man. A rent boy.'

'I can see that,' agreed Anita. 'Maybe these night-time trips were cover for regular meetings with whoever.'

'Or maybe he was just a perv,' Brodd suggested. 'He knew couples have it off down there, and he's a regular watcher. Gets his kicks that way. They caught him having a wank and beat him up.'

'I doubt that's a regular rendezvous for amorous couples. It's too near the main coastal path.' Anita put Iqbal's photo back on the table. 'But I suppose any one of those scenarios is possible.'

'According to his wife, he left his home at around ten,' said Wallen. 'In theory, couldn't he have had sex with her just before he went out?'

'Yeah... theoretically,' conceded Thulin. 'But if he had, don't you think he might have cleaned himself up before he left the apartment?'

'Still, we'll have to ask the question,' sighed Anita.

'That won't be easy,' said Hakim knowingly.

'If Iqbal had just had sex in the vicinity of the crime scene, it might explain why he wasn't expecting an attack, from his sexual partner or anyone else.'

'Good point, Bea,' agreed Anita. 'What we urgently need to do is work out the weapon used, and then maybe we can work out who our killer is.'

CHAPTER 15

'Do you think you'll clear it up before I get back?'

Despite the long day she'd had, Anita had gone out of her way to call on Erik Moberg. She thought that he should know about the new case, which he might well inherit. It also made her feel better that she wasn't neglecting him. And despite the fact that a glass of red wine would go down very nicely, she had turned down Moberg's offer of a beer. Interestingly, he wasn't drinking; he wasn't even vaping.

'Well, Zetterberg certainly hopes so. I'm going down tomorrow with Klara to ask the awkward questions of the widow. I can't imagine she'll be very forthcoming. I've asked for her daughter to be there. Bismah's English is good, but I still don't want any linguistic misunderstandings. I'm spending my life on thin ice as it is at the moment.'

Moberg guffawed. 'What makes you think you won't be when I come back?'

'I can handle you most of the time. Anyway, I thought you were turning into a teddy bear.'

'One that can still growl.'

Anita didn't doubt that he would still be able to put the fear of God into the team when needed.

'Anyway,' she said, getting out of her chair. 'I'd better get back home. I've got another awkward call to make.'

'Who to?'

'Kevin. As Zetterberg has put me on this case, there's no chance I'll get time off. We were going to meet up somewhere. He'll not be pleased.'

Moberg eased his slimmer frame off the sofa. He really had lost weight.

'Any developments on your customs officer?'

Anita slung her bag over her shoulder. 'Dead end. Haven't got time now, anyway. But there was another odd thing happened. Remember that lawyer I told you about – the one who turned up at the hospital?' Moberg nodded. 'He reappeared. Jolis was cremated last Thursday.'

'That was quick.'

'Very. Understandably, the family wanted it out of the way. The funny thing is that a...' Anita made an inverted commas sign with her fingers '..."well-wisher" paid the funeral parlour bill. The family has no idea who it is: he wants to remain anonymous. But who should be this well-wisher's go-between? None other than the untraceable Filip Assarsson.'

Moberg pulled a face. 'Doesn't smell right.'

'To me, neither. But at the end of the day, I can't prove anything. Basically, an old man with dementia died after trying to kill his wife. His death has put his family out of their misery, and some kind benefactor has helped them out.'

Moberg regarded her closely. 'I know you. It'll be like an itch.'

'Shut up. I've got enough on my plate, thank you.'

He grinned. 'Don't be a stranger.'

Anita opened the door and looked back. Was she even starting to regard Moberg with real affection?

'You'll be sick of the sight of me when you're back in harness.'

Anita knew she was procrastinating. Not only did she make herself a meal with a much-needed glass of wine, but she also found herself tidying up the kitchen cupboards, which hadn't been sorted out properly since Kevin's last visit. When she returned to the living room and found herself with a duster in her hand, she realized she couldn't put off ringing him any longer. She knew he'd be really disappointed, and then he'd offer to come over even while she was working. Then she'd have to refuse, as she knew he'd get under her feet while she was involved in the case. OK, food and drink waiting for her on her return from work would be nice, but it was all the other stuff that would drive her mad – the sort of things they avoided when they actually went on holiday together. Like the way he'd appropriate her favourite mug. She knew it was irrational, but it was bloody irritating. Or like changing the shower setting or rearranging her CD collection. He couldn't help himself. She felt more at home with a bit of domestic disorder, but it was anathema to Kevin. She was convinced he had OCD – something he vehemently denied, usually while tidying up something that she didn't want tidying.

'Not sure if I'll be able to take that holiday now.'

Kevin didn't exactly explode. He was still taken aback at getting a personal call at ten to eleven UK time: almost midnight in Sweden. In fact, he'd just switched off the news and was heading for bed. He wasn't a natural night owl. He was also surprised to hear Anita's voice. It usually meant bad news. She'd chickened out of using FaceTime – she didn't want to see his disappointment.

'We've got a new murder case.'

'Bloody typical! Who is it?'

'It's a man called Iqbal Nawaz.'

'Sounds Arabic or Pakistani.'

'The latter. He's a local businessman. He was the owner of a successful chain of cut-price electrical stores around Sweden. Do you know he had a 400,000 kronor watch on him? Why do people pay that much for a watch? I've got a Sekonda which cost me a few kronor. It tells the same time as a Cartier or a Rolex.'

'Have to agree. But that's nothing compared to some brands. Buy a Patek Philippe or a Breguet and you could be paying over two hundred thousand – that's pounds, by the way.'

'So now I know what you're buying me for my birthday.'

It sounded like a raspberry coming down the phone line. 'I might be able to buy you a new strap for your Sekonda.'

'That makes a girl feel good.'

'Anyhow, have you got any suspects?'

'No. We haven't even got a murder weapon. He was hit over the head. Can't work out what with. Wooden probably; couple of neat grooves in his skull where it made contact. All it seems to have left is some silicone wax.'

'Where was he killed?'

'Down near the city beach. In the trees off the path. We've been for walks along there.'

'I know, I know. The sports grounds on the other side.'

'Victim lived across the road from them in one of the fancy apartments. He was found in the trees in between the grounds and the path.'

'I watched a bit of a cricket match there last summer when you were busy.'

'Iqbal was involved in some cricket club. Malmö Gymkhana. Funny name.'

'It's an Indian word. We apply it to equestrian events over here; I think it has more to do with general sports over there. Actually, that rings a bell. I think that's the name on some hut down next to one of the fields.'

'We'd better check that out. We're down there tomorrow to speak to the widow again.'

The conversation petered out soon after. Both were tired. Anita promised she would FaceTime at the weekend.

Anita wasn't sure how long she'd been asleep when she was woken by her phone buzzing next to the bed. Bleary-eyed, she checked the digital clock – 2.06. Her hand fished for the mobile. Without her glasses, she couldn't see who was calling. She answered it with a grumpy 'Yes?'

'It's me.' What on earth was Kevin ringing about now?

'I've been thinking about your murder weapon. The cricket ground. Wooden weapon, grooves. I think it's a cricket bat.'

Anita sat up and turned on the bedside light. She groped for her glasses with her free hand. 'I've seen cricket bats. They've got a smooth surface.'

'Not on the back of the blade. They're almost triangular in cross-section, and a lot of the modern bats have a pronounced ridge running down the spine. And bats are usually treated with silicone wax to give them protection. I had to look that up to make sure. Get belted with one of those and it would leave a distinctive mark on someone's bonce.'

'Oh, you could be right!' She was suddenly excited despite her tiredness. 'You're not just a pretty face. Actually, not a pretty face at all, but you're a very clever little Englishman.'

'How come you can insult and compliment in the same sentence?'

'It's a talent. Look, that's really great. Thank you.'

She finished with a 'Love you.' and put down the phone. There was no way she was going to get back to sleep now. Her mind was whirring. If a cricket bat turned out to be the murder weapon, the case really was getting somewhere.

CHAPTER 16

The apartment was full of people – mainly women. There was a pile of shoes at the front entrance, which Anita and Wallen added to. The visitors had come to express their condolences to Bismah Nawaz as part of the usual three days of mourning. Bismah's own period of grieving would last far longer. Hakim had warned Anita and Wallen that hanging onto the body of the deceased – for obvious reasons in this case – would be upsetting to Bismah, as it was the Muslim custom to bury the dead as quickly as possible. She would be feeling bad enough because Iqbal hadn't died in his own home, as most Muslims would wish to do. The post mortem would also cause extra angst. Muslims believe in the sacredness of the human body. Basically, he advised them to go gently.

After Muneeba had managed to shepherd the visitors into the further recesses of the apartment, they settled down in the reception room. Bismah was dressed from top to toe in black with a headscarf drawn tightly over her head. She was unsurprisingly agitated.

'When will the body of my husband be handed back to us?'

'I appreciate that you want to bury him as soon as possible,' Anita started slowly. 'You have to understand that this is a case of murder, and, as part of the investigation, we have to examine Iqbal's body.' Bismah winced. 'I'm truly sorry. We will be as quick as possible.' None of this seemed reassuring. 'However, we are making progress.'

'What progress?' asked Muneeba.

'We believe we might know what the murder weapon was, though more tests need to be done before we're totally sure.' Anita had passed on Kevin's conjecture to an incredulous Eva Thulin – 'Do we play cricket in Sweden?' – who then returned Anita's call after a quick internet search. She confirmed that it could well have been a cricket bat and was now in the process of trying to procure one to test out the theory.

Bismah shook her head. 'What do you think it was?'

'We'll let you know as soon as it's confirmed. We've been looking at Iqbal's phone, and a number of the texts seemed to be about cricket, or a cricket club.'

'Oh, Father was obsessed with cricket.' Anita and Wallen both glanced at Muneeba. 'From his young days in Pakistan. That's why we live here.' She pointed to the window. 'They play cricket on one of those fields over there. He set up his own team. They play there.'

Muneeba explained that when her father had come to Malmö, there had been only one team. He'd got involved with that but had fallen out with other members of the club, so he set up his own. Nearly all the team are Pakistani expats, many of whom work for Happy Electricals. And that was why he wore a dark-green tracksuit – the colour worn by the Pakistani national team. This wasn't all news to Anita, who had come across members of the multi-cultural Malmöhus cricket team at The Pickwick.

'Where does the team keep its equipment?'

'It's in the hut next to the field. That's where the club keeps all its equipment for matches. Obviously, some of the players have their own pads and gloves and bats, which they keep at home. But there are extra ones kept in the hut for those who can't afford these things. They can be quite expensive. My father paid for everything in there. He always liked to keep a check on his investment.'

'Do you think that's why your father was down there on Monday night?' asked Wallen.

'Possibly. There was a cup match on Sunday, but my father was away on business. He didn't get back until Sunday night. He could well have gone down to check everything.'

'In the dark?' Anita queried.

'He did sometimes. There's no electricity, but there are a couple of battery lamps. Normally, they don't need them because they play in daylight.'

'Presumably, it's locked?'

Muneeba nodded.

'We didn't find a key,' Wallen said, looking at Anita for confirmation.

'Can you check if it's here?' Anita asked. 'And we'll need your father's computer.'

Muneeba left the room. This was the time to tackle the thorny question of what Iqbal Nawaz had been up to.

'I'm afraid something else has come up, Bismah.' Bismah was distressed enough as it was, but there was no way of avoiding it – and no way of putting it delicately. 'It's not easy to tell you. It appears that your husband had sex shortly before he died.'

At first, Anita thought she hadn't understood. She was about to repeat herself.

'You cannot say this! That is not true!'

'We have forensic evidence.' Bismah appeared puzzled. Anita paraphrased: 'Evidence was found on his clothes.'

It was clear that Bismah didn't believe her.

'My husband was a good man. A true believer. I will not hear such things said about him.'

Just then, Muneeba reappeared with a computer bag and a key in her hand. She saw how distressed her mother was.

'What's happened?'

Bismah came out with a stream of Punjabi. Muneeba's horror was obvious.

'She wants you to go now,' said Muneeba. 'You can't believe that my father would do such a thing.'

'I'm sorry to upset your mother. I'm afraid we have to ask these questions.'

'There must be a mistake.'

Anita was faced by two women who could see no wrong in Iqbal Nawaz. Had he another life that he'd kept from his wife and daughter? She could see at this juncture that she wasn't going to achieve anything more by trying to probe further.

'We'll go.'

Muneeba accompanied them out of the room.

'Can I take that key? We'll need to have a look at the hut.'

Muneeba handed it over.

'Was your father the only key holder?'

'I think there are others. Some of the players will have one.'

'Who is the best person to talk to about the cricket club?'

'The captain.' Her gaze dropped for a second. 'Mohammad Abbas.'

'Where will we find him?' The name had immediately put Anita on alert – he was the last person Iqbal had spoken to before leaving his apartment.

'He is the manager of the company warehouse at Bulltofta.'

'Thank you.' The young woman looked drawn: not surprisingly, coping with the strain of her father's death and a distraught mother. 'I apologize again for causing you and your mother distress.'

Muneeba gave a wan smile. 'You have a job to do. But you are wrong about my father.'

They walked across the road from the apartment and down a steep bank that led onto the expanse of playing fields in front of them. The scopious swathe of grass made it difficult to see where the demarcation lines were between the sports grounds. The only distinctive one was marked by the H-shaped rugby posts. The hut was in the area adjacent to the rugby field, so this must be the cricket pitch. It was another grey, windy day, and the trees and bushes on the boundary were being tugged back and forth. In the distance, the Turning Torso brooded over the city, as though listening in on its deepest secrets.

'I'm amazed cricket is played here,' Wallen remarked as they crossed the empty expanse. 'It's so English, isn't it?'

'Yes, Kevin's into it. When I was at school in England, the boys used to play it in the school yard. I never understood it then; I'm none the wiser now even though Kevin has tried to explain it to me.'

'Is it just Pakistanis that play it over here?'

'Don't think so. I've heard them talking about cricket in The Pickwick. Australians, South Africans, Brits... all sorts. Indians and Sri Lankans are heavily involved, apparently.'

'Expats. Can't believe Swedes play it, though.'

'I think a few do. The Malmöhus club was co-founded by a Swede.'

'Takes all sorts,' Wallen said, shaking her head. 'And as for that,' she said, pointing at the rugby posts. 'That's alien too. These people are taking over in every way. I can't believe how much Sweden is changing.'

Anita ignored the comment. She wasn't going to have that battle with Wallen again unless they were both armed with alcoholic drinks.

The dark-green hut had recently been painted and looked smart. Anita was surprised she'd never really noticed it before the investigation. A sign next to the door proclaimed: *Malmö Gymkhana Cricket Club*. The police tape was flapping about a hundred metres further back along the edge of the trees.

'I suppose it's quite possible he came down here to check it out,' Wallen said as Anita slipped the key into the lock. 'That would explain the torch.'

'He can't have. His key was in the apartment.'

'True. Unless he met someone down here who had a key themselves.'

The wooden door creaked open. It was light enough not to bother putting on the two battery lamps which were suspended from the ceiling. To Anita, it was surprisingly tidy. Cricket paraphernalia was neatly stacked on the floor, against the walls and on some floor-to-ceiling IKEA shelving: cricket pads in white and green; chunky, padded gloves; wooden stumps; white umpire jackets hanging from hooks; a metal scoreboard with a stack of numbers; and a strange, slatted-wood, cradle-type object that Kevin later told her was called a slip catcher and was, unsurprisingly, used for practising catching the ball. There were a couple of green cricket shirts bearing the Happy Electricals logo, and three large cricket bags with the capacity to hold bats, pads and an assortment of clothing and other forms of protection. There was also a smaller cricket bag. Along one wall was a neat line of half a dozen cricket bats, and leaning against the opposite wall was some fold-up furniture – a picnic table and a stack of camping chairs for spectators to sit on. Obscurely, amongst all this neatness, one of the chairs was still opened out.

'Do you think this was the place where Iqbal had sex?' Wallen asked as she looked around at all this weird stuff.

'Could be. You're not likely to be disturbed here, are you?'

'Maybe they used that chair,' Wallen suggested.

'Yes. Better have that checked.'

'So, the sexual partner, if they had a key, could have been waiting for him here. Let him in, then they had a quick rumble and, for some reason, argued, and that person whacked Iqbal on the head. Plenty of weapons to hand.'

Anita put on a pair of latex gloves before she picked up a bat. It felt heavier than she'd expected. She ran her finger down the spine.

'I can see that doing the damage,' remarked Wallen.

Anita swung the bat to and fro for a minute. 'This is tiring. Kevin says it's all in the wrists. He says the Indian subcontinent players are particularly adept. They don't need to belt the ball to hit it hard.' She replaced the bat. 'If you're right, Klara, then we need to find out who the keyholders are – it would mean that the murder is connected to the club.'

'I presume all the keyholders are men. That last call was from a Mohammad Abbas, the same name that Muneeba just mentioned. Maybe it was to arrange to meet down here. Was Iqbal gay?'

'Possibly. But they might have wives or girlfriends who could have access to a key.'

'But do girls play cricket? I mean wielding one of those things?' Wallen bent down and lifted up the bat that Anita had just put back. 'They're quite weighty.'

'Don't know. We can't rule anyone out at this stage. Iqbal might not have come to the hut at all that night; maybe he was just using the trees as somewhere to meet a lover. He wasn't dragged from somewhere else, so he can't have been killed in the hut. But first, we need to get forensics down here. And all these bats will have to be checked, along with that chair. I don't want this place disturbed until Eva Thulin, or whoever, gives it a thorough going over. If you can organize that, Klara, I'll get hold of this Mohammad Abbas. We're going to have to check the bats of every player in the club without them suspecting anything's up.'

Wallen giggled. 'It's going to be like a gun or knife amnesty. Except all these people will be handing in cricket bats.'

'I'm sure Zetterberg won't be laughing.'

This call came at a more awkward time. He was entertaining guests for lunch and had to be fetched. He took his mobile into the quiet of his office.

'Yes?' he said irritably. He had enough on his mind already.

'Sorry if this is a bad time.' The man didn't sound that apologetic.

'What is it?'

'Just to keep you up to speed. There has been a slight problem on our side of things. My technical people have picked something up.' He felt his stomach tighten. 'Nothing that we can't handle; I've got someone on top of it.'

'Is it something to worry about?'

'Don't think so. Maybe you weren't as thorough as you led me to believe.'

'My people are professionals,' he said with an edge in his voice. He didn't like the thought that someone might have messed up. There was too much at stake.

'I'm sure the problem will go away.'

'Is it a problem we can deal with at this end?'

'No, no; it would be difficult to ignore if we took that route.'

'Right. Well, let me know if things change.'

Thoughtfully, he put away his phone. That was an unexpected jolt. He hoped that they could keep whatever it was under control. Nothing specific was ever mentioned in the calls. That had always been the drill with the man's predecessors, too. Though he hadn't met this one, he didn't have the same confidence in him. Others before him had been ruthlessly efficient. He sensed this one was weaker – too soft for the tough business he was in, too easily swayed by political considerations: a pen-pusher who would let him down at some stage. He would have to watch his back.

As he made his way towards the door and back to his guests, the call wasn't the only thing making him anxious. He had failed to mention the other complication; something the man might not even know existed. That had really come out of the blue.

CHAPTER 17

Anita had to cross town to reach Bulltofta. The Happy Electricals warehouse was on an industrial estate just off the ring road. It was a low, capacious, nondescript, grey metal edifice surrounded by wire fencing. Anita drove through the gates and parked next to a line of other cars in front of a strip of grass that ran alongside the building's exterior. Near a loading bay at the far end were half a dozen sizeable vans sporting the Happy Electricals logo. The boss might be dead, but it was business as usual.

Mohammad Abbas turned out to be a handsome man in his thirties. She could understand why Muneeba had gone a little shy when she mentioned his name. Was there something there? He had deep, dark eyes; thick, slicked-back, black hair and a strong chin. His intelligent countenance and air of confidence suggested that he was more than capable of managing this side of Iqbal Nawaz's business enterprise as well as captaining his cricket team. A self-assured character who thrived on responsibility. And, Anita noted, he was strong and well-built; perfectly able to give his boss a deadly whack with a cricket bat.

Anita had been led into the bowels of the warehouse by the young man on reception. It was clear that most of the employees were of Asian origin, though she had spotted a couple of white faces. She met up with Abbas in one of the aisles between the high-stacked metal shelves on which there were hundreds of serried ranks of boxes containing toasters, kettles and the like. He had a tablet in his hand.

Anita introduced herself.

'I'm Anita Sundström from the police.'

He inspected her for a moment. 'We've already had the police round here. They were asking about ex-employees. People who might have taken against Iqbal.' His Swedish was excellent and even came with a Scanian accent. She surmised he was second generation.

'I know.'

'Iqbal's death has been an awful shock to everybody. He was a great man.' Anita would reserve judgement.

'It's not about that. As you are probably aware, the murder took place close to where you play cricket.'

'It's unbelievable. We were playing there the day before. Iqbal was away, checking the outlets in Kalmar and Karlskrona. He liked to pay sudden visits to stores, often when they least expected it. And they wouldn't have expected a Sunday visit,' he said with a wry smile, 'because they'd assume he was playing or watching the team.'

'He was still playing at his age?'

'Sometimes. Friendly games, yes. In league matches, he'd want the strongest team to play. He liked to win. I understand he was quite a player himself when he was in Pakistan before he came over to Europe. That's why the club is called Malmö Gymkhana, after the most prestigious sporting club in Lahore. He was never accepted as a member, so this was the next best thing.'

'Do you have a key to the hut down on Limhamnsfältet?'

'Why, yes.' He looked puzzled.

'Who else has a key?'

'There are three other key holders. Iqbal, of course. And Sarfraz and Usman.'

'Do they work here?'

'No. Sarfraz runs the company store in the Mobilia centre. Usman lives in Lund. He's the Happy Electricals main buyer; works out of the Lund head office. He's a nephew of Iqbal's wife.'

'Bismah?'

'Yes. I don't understand. Why are you asking about the keys?'

'Just checking at the moment. Where is yours?'

'Right here.' He jangled a large bunch of keys hanging from his belt. He touched a key that was the same as the one Anita had used earlier to unlock the hut. 'You don't think the murder had anything to do with the club?'

'We're just exploring every possibility.'

Mohammad Abbas thought it best to carry on the conversation in private. They retreated to his office. The walls were covered in maps and charts showing a constant update on the movement of goods to stores around the country. There was a line of computers on the desk. He supplied Anita with a rather horrid coffee from a nearby vending machine.

'How long has the team been going?' she asked as she ran her tongue round her mouth to lessen the taste.

Abbas had already provided her with a list of the club members and their phone numbers, including the other two keyholders, Sarfraz Khan and Usman Masood.

'Iqbal began it back in 2002. Fell out with the only other team in Malmö at the time. Didn't think they were ambitious enough. And that club was made up of players from all over, including some Swedes. He felt more comfortable with people from—'

'Pakistan.'

'The subcontinent. Though to be honest, we don't have any Indians in the club. Or Sri Lankans. We've got a token Bangladeshi and two lads from Afghanistan.'

'Can't believe they play cricket there!'

'You'd be surprised. The up-and-coming force in the world game despite all the fighting in their homeland. You know, the only thing that unites the Afghan government and the Taliban is the national cricket team. Sport can do a great deal of good bringing people together.'

'Except Pakistanis and Indians.'

'Except us and Indians, of course.' He had the grace to smile.

'Most of my colleagues didn't even know cricket was played in Sweden.'

'It's a growing sport even if not many Swedes take part. Besides us, there are now five other teams in Malmö alone. There are a lot more in Stockholm. About twenty-five up there. It's now recognized as a national sport in Sweden, and we even have a national team, though you won't find a white face among them at the moment.'

'That's really interesting. But going back to Iqbal Nawaz... Could there be anyone at the club who might have a grudge against him – a grudge big enough to want to kill him?'

He shook his head vehemently. 'He was greatly respected.'

'Respected doesn't mean liked.'

'I can't think of anybody.' Anita sensed he was being evasive.

'Was he particularly "friendly" with anybody?'

'I don't know about his friends. I worked for him. I played cricket for him.'

'What I'm saying is: was he over-familiar with any of the players?'

Abbas frowned. 'I don't understand.'

'Did he prey on any of them? Sexually?'

He was absolutely horrified. 'That is against our religion! It's an appalling thing to say about a man who has just died!'

'Women then?'

'He wasn't like that. He was a married man.'

This wasn't getting her anywhere, so Anita switched tack.

'Tell me about the business.'

She could see him relax: this was a less sensitive subject. 'What do you want to know?'

'Is it doing well?'

'Yes. Trading is pretty good, and we haven't been too affected by the internet. Of course, if Amazon opens up in Sweden, that might be another thing altogether.'

'How do you sell things so cheaply?'

'Well, our most successful lines are sold under our own brand. They're made in Pakistan. Iqbal owns... the company owns a couple of factories out there, so they're cheap to make. But good quality,' he added quickly. 'Lahore and near Faisalabad. Most of the rest we import from the Far East. China mainly.'

'And who will run the business now?'

'I'm not sure. I don't know if Bismah will step in. I assume that she'll now be the main shareholder, though she's never really been involved.'

'What about Muneeba?'

He suddenly took an interest in his biro. 'Possibly,' he muttered. 'Then again, Usman might take over in the short term. He's family. I'm sure he would if Bismah asked him.'

'Not you?'

'Oh, no. I wouldn't know anything about the buying or selling side of things. I'm happy here, being the middleman.'

Anita pushed her half-drunk coffee away and stood up.

'Have you got a match this weekend?'

'Yes. Against a team from Helsingborg tomorrow. Two o'clock start. We weren't sure whether to postpone it out of respect for Iqbal. But Muneeba said he'd want us to carry on.'

That was fortunate. Anita needed to get hold of all the cricket bats that didn't live in the hut without alerting anyone beforehand. She didn't want any mysteriously disappearing. Confiscating the bats might ruin their match, but she supposed they could always borrow ones from the opposition.

She slung her bag over her shoulder. 'By the way, when was the last time you were down at the hut?'

'Sunday. The match. Actually, I've been meaning to go back there all week. I left my cricket bag. Some of us took the other team off for a curry after the game. I was going to go back for it. Didn't have time in the end.'

'Oh, just one more thing. Where were you on Monday night between ten and eleven?'

'Erm... I was here. Until getting on for half past eleven.'

'That's late, isn't it?'

'We had a couple of big shipments going out first thing Tuesday morning. I had to make sure everything was in order.'

'Were you working with anyone?'

The implication of what she was saying dawned on him. 'No,' he said slowly. 'I was here on my own.'

'Why did you ring Iqbal Nawaz on Monday night?'

'How do you know about that?'

'We've got his phone.'

'It was nothing really,' he said airily. 'I was just reporting in that the shipments for the following day were ready. He liked to keep on top of things.'

'You realize you were probably the last person to talk to him?' She let that sink in. 'Apart from the killer.'

Abbas shifted uneasily in his seat.

'I'm sure your wife wouldn't be happy about you coming home so late.'

'I don't have a wife.'

'Girlfriend?'

He shook his head. That bashful look had returned. It immediately got Anita thinking. Mohammad Abbas was definitely a person of interest.

CHAPTER 18

'Right. The cricket match starts at two o'clock tomorrow. We all need to be there at about a quarter to. I want half a dozen uniform with us, too. The players will soon realize what's happening when we start taking their bats away. If there are club members missing, then we go straight round to their homes – we've got the list. However, Mohammad Abbas was expecting everyone to turn up out of respect for Iqbal Nawaz, so, hopefully, they'll all be there.'

'Sorry to butt in, Anita,' said Hakim. 'Just a word about the names. Pakistani names, Muslim names in general can be complicated. It'll be confusing if we use them in the Western way – first name, surname. Each person chooses one of his or her given names to be known by, so it might make our lives easier if we simply talk about Iqbal because that's what everyone calls him. Same with Abbas.'

'That's fine. Thanks, Hakim. Getting back to bats... we'll pass them straight over to Lund for examination. They won't look at them until next week, but at least they'll be in the system.'

'What if the murder weapon's already been neatly disposed of?' Hakim interjected.

'All the players will know who owns a bat or who doesn't. If one is missing, that person may have a lot of explaining to do.'

Anita was running the meeting. She was thankful that Zetterberg was out of Malmö on something they thought might be to do with a cold case she was supposedly wrapping up. Or that's what she'd told Brodd. It had already been a long day, and Anita wanted to get through the evidence so far as quickly and efficiently as possible.

'Klara, have forensics been down to the hut?'

'Yes. That enthusiastic young man Lars Unosson came down. He's taken all the spare bats away.'

'Did you find a bat in one of the cricket bags?'

'Yeah.'

'That'll be Abbas's. I'm particularly interested in him.'

'They took his whole bag with all his equipment in it. Lars also took away the folded chair we found open. As for prints, he said it was a nightmare. Lots of sweaty people in and out of there whenever a game was on. He was intrigued by those hard plastic scoop things.'

'They're called boxes.' Kevin had shown Anita his old one from when he played the odd game. 'They cover the male genitals.' Brodd pulled a face. 'Those cricket balls can be very hard.'

'Oh, my God, I was playing with one!' cringed Wallen. 'Anyway, we'll hear back next week. They won't be doing anything over the weekend.'

'Good. At the moment, all we can surmise is that Iqbal left his apartment, dressed in his tracksuit, around ten. He'd received a phone call from Abbas at eleven minutes to ten. Abbas says it was just about a next-day shipment. He might be lying. Did he arrange to meet Iqbal near the hut? He has a key. Whatever happened, Iqbal turned off his mobile phone. He was dead within an hour of leaving home. In that hour, he had sex, either with someone unknown or with himself, though that is unlikely. Did he have sex with Abbas? Abbas doesn't have a wife or girlfriend that he admits to. We know Iqbal sometimes went down to check the hut, even after dark. That may explain the torch. However, he didn't have a key on him when he was found – his key was back in his apartment. So, he may have had no intention of inspecting the hut and was in the vicinity to meet a sexual partner. Or he did go to the hut, and it was opened up by someone else with a key. We know there are three other key holders. The first is Abbas, who is manager of the Happy Electricals warehouse and team captain. Unfortunately for him, he has no proper alibi. Claims he was working late at the warehouse. No one can verify that.'

'Could someone else have used his key?' Erlandsson asked.

'He carries it on him in a bunch, so unlikely.'

'I got the impression Muneeba might be sweet on him,' opined Wallen.

'I noticed that, too. I think there might be a mutual attraction. He went all coy when her name was mentioned.'

'Would Iqbal approve of an employee marrying his daughter?' asked Hakim.

'Iqbal blocking Abbas's path to happiness? We need to find out more. One thing we need to consider is that no attempt was made to move the body. Does that indicate that it wasn't planned – a crime committed on the spur of the moment? A moment of passion? A lover spurned?'

'If it was passion or a loss of temper,' came in Erlandsson, 'wouldn't there be more damage on the victim; a more frenzied attack? There were only two blows. Possibly calculated ones.'

'Maybe after the first couple of blows, the murderer suddenly realized what he'd done,' suggested Wallen. 'And then it was too late; he'd gone too far. Left in a panic, body in situ. After all, he didn't take the phone, which, for all he knew, may have led us to the perpetrator.'

'Talking of the phone,' said Hakim, 'it does raise one question: even though Iqbal may have been concentrating on switching it back on, would that be enough to distract him so he was unaware of someone creeping up behind him with a cricket bat? If not, it increases the possibility that he was with someone he knew.'

'Or there were two people – one to distract him, the other to do the deed. Lots of possibilities. Rule out none at this stage.' Anita wanted to move on. 'OK, we need to talk to the other two keyholders – Sarfraz Khan and Usman Masood – Abbas referred to them as Sarfraz and Usman. We'll let them stew over the weekend after we've taken their bats away. That'll give them plenty to think about. Hakim, we'll go and talk to Sarfraz here in Malmö on Monday; and Klara, can you and Bea take on Usman at the Lund head office? He's family, so go carefully. Liv, I want you to look into Happy Electricals. We can't dismiss Iqbal's death being business related considering that so many of the club work for the company. Female employees, too. Given that sex was involved shortly before death, it does indicate a crime of passion, perhaps jealousy. However, we can't rule out other motives. This was a successful businessman, but we don't really know that much about him. His wife and daughter were giving nothing away. Abbas talked about him being respected. Let's dig a little deeper. His staff may be willing to talk more openly about him now that he's dead. By the way, Liv, any more luck with his phone and computer?'

'Not a great deal. Endless business calls all over the place to stores and suppliers. A lot of his computer emails are to do with the running of the cricket club, including a couple berating the Swedish Cricket Federation for not picking Sarfraz Khan for the national team for some tournament. He's obviously their star player.'

'Any porn on the computer?' asked Brodd. There were some audible sighs. 'Look, it's legit to ask given what he was up to that night.'

'None that I could find.'

'Right, anything more, Liv?' Anita didn't want the meeting to get sidetracked.

'Just one thing. I've been able to trace all the numbers on the phone except one unregistered one. The odd thing is that Iqbal made half a dozen calls to that number over the last few weeks but was never rung back by the caller. The last time he contacted that particular phone was the Friday afternoon before he died. I've tried the number half a dozen times – it never appears to be switched on, so it may have no relevance to his death.'

'Worth flagging up, though. Well done, Liv. Right, any questions?' There were none. 'Let's meet here tomorrow at one.'

As they broke up, Hakim caught Anita's eye.

'I know that Iqbal attended the same mosque as my father.'

'Could Uday give us a different insight?'

'I was wondering that. I'll try and have a word – that's if he's still speaking to me.'

*

On Saturday morning, Anita enjoyed a lie-in. A lazy breakfast followed. She even put on her favourite Santana album and swayed to the rhythm as she made her way from the living room to her bedroom to get properly dressed. She was babysitting Leyla tonight, which she always delighted in. She still worried about her granddaughter's sugar levels taking a change for the worse while she was in charge, but she was getting better at coping.

She knew it was the case that had revitalized her after the last few downbeat months and the frustration caused by the death of Markus Jolis. Now she had a real challenge, and Zetterberg seemed to be taking a back seat. She felt she was in charge and that the team were up for it. Today's swoop could well identify the specific bat that was used to kill Iqbal Nawaz.

Just as she was coming back into the living room and Carlos Santana's guitar was reaching searing heights, Anita heard her phone. Her heart sank when she saw Alice Zetterberg's name come up.

'Hello.'

'Polishus. Half an hour.' The phone went dead.

'Shit!'

Zetterberg was more casually dressed than usual, but the sleeveless top and jeans only accentuated her bulk. Neither did the clothes make her any more relaxed. She demanded to be brought up to date on the Iqbal Nawaz investigation. Anita took her through all the points that had been mooted in the previous day's meeting, including their planned swoop at the match this afternoon; and her conversations with Bismah and Muneeba, and Mohammad Abbas.

'So, you think Mohammad Abbas is a possible suspect?'

'I don't know yet. He may have arranged to meet up with Iqbal down on Limhamnsfältet. There might be something between him and Muneeba, but that's pure conjecture.'

Zetterberg huffed. 'At least I'll be able to keep on top of things now.' Anita's heart sank at the thought of Zetterberg getting involved. 'But the case is not the real reason I called you in.'

'Oh?'

'Something more serious. I've been made aware that someone in this team has been trying to probe Zander Security.' Anita's heart sank even further. 'Now, we know that Markus Jolis worked for Zander twenty years ago. That case is as good as closed. So why is someone looking into Zander and using methods that have neither been sanctioned nor are technically legal? I thought you might know something about it?' This was accompanied by a gimlet stare.

There was no use denying it. Someone somewhere must have monitored Liv's searches. She couldn't allow her young colleague to get into trouble. She had only acted at Anita's bidding.

'It was me.'

Zetterberg couldn't keep the elation out of her voice.

'I *knew* it had to be you. I warned you to stop snooping. If I had my way, you'd be suspended or even out on your ear. But it's your lucky day. You're due your annual vacation.' She glanced at her watch. 'It began five minutes ago.'

CHAPTER 19

Anita sat numbly outside The Pickwick, a virtually empty pint glass in front of her. The sun was out, and people were taking advantage of the weather. Her planned swoop on the Malmö Gymkhana cricket team had been hijacked. Zetterberg had effectively taken her off the case and would now be overseeing events down at Limhamnsfältet. They'd find the murder weapon – and with a bit of luck it might lead them to the murderer – and Zetterberg would take all the credit. It was galling. Anita had rung Hakim to warn him that she wouldn't be around and that Zetterberg was going to be in charge. If the team had the chance, they should still do the planned interviews with the other two keyholders – unless Zetterberg had other ideas. He wasn't best pleased at the news. Anita hadn't told him the real reason for the enforced holiday, as she didn't want Liv to feel that she should own up to her internet searches. Before Anita left the building, she'd had a word with Liv, warning her not to bother with Zander Security any more. She brushed it off by saying the case was as good as closed. However, she did give her one last task. Again, it wasn't for public consumption – it was to satisfy Anita's curiosity.

Anita wondered who had discovered what Liv had been up to in the first place. Zander Security? If so, did they have a relationship with the police or higher authorities? Or was it some internal police department that she didn't know about? Or even Säpo, the Swedish security service? But why would it worry them? Unless they were looking into Zander Security themselves, and Liv's delving was compromising an ongoing investigation. It was a minefield best left alone. Anita had done her best to stay on the murder case – she wanted to find Iqbal Nawaz's killer – but it hadn't washed with an intransigent Zetterberg, who told her not to come back for a month, which she was in fact due. But there was always a silver lining: Alice Zetterberg would be gone by her return, and Erik Moberg would be back in place. She'd never see Zetterberg again. She drank the rest of her pint. Tempted as she was to have another, she had babysitting to think about. She smiled to herself – she would have an evening with her favourite girl and then a month to forget about work.

She was in the middle of weighing out the portions for Leyla's five o'clock meal. She'd worked out the carbohydrate content so that she could inject the right amount of insulin. Her phone sprang into life.

'Hi, Hakim! Have a nice afternoon at the cricket?'

'Thought I'd report in.'

'Not my case.'

'So you don't want to hear how it went?' he teased.

'Of course I bloody do!' Then she guiltily glanced round to see if Leyla was within hearing distance. She was too absorbed playing with her toy unicorn to notice.

'All the bats were collected. The players were not happy. Some of them can be quite volatile. A lot of shouting. Then Zetterberg read them the riot act and said she'd arrest the whole bunch of them if they didn't cooperate. All the bats were labelled with the owners' names.'

'Were all the club members there?'

'Two didn't turn up. Pontus and Bea were sent to find them. They got hold of one, and the other doesn't own a bat – he's a very occasional player who only gets chosen when they're desperate. Anyhow, Pontus has taken all the bats up to Lund, so now we'll just have to wait and see.'

'Good. Are you going to be talking to the other two keyholders?'

She could hear him titter at the other end. 'Yes. It came out as *her* idea.'

'That's why she's been offered a top job in Stockholm!'

'We were lucky to hold on to her for so long. Anyway, what are you going to do with your holiday?'

'Not sure yet. As little as possible. Meet up with Kevin at some stage. At least he'll be pleased at the outcome.'

'Do you want to be kept informed? Unofficially, of course.'

'Naturally.'

'Oh, by the way, Zetterberg has sanctioned the release of Iqbal's body on Monday. The funeral will take place the next day.'

By the time they'd finished talking, Anita had forgotten what stage she was at with Leyla's food, and she had to start all over again. However, one thing was crystallizing in her mind: she'd decided how to utilize her unsolicited vacation – by finding out how and why her father died.

'I was in a state of shock. The whole country was.' Anita was FaceTiming Kevin on Sunday morning. 'And maybe my way of coming to terms with his death was not to question the official version of the sinking. The car deck door coming off seemed to be a reasonable explanation. Of course, I was aware that people – many of the relatives of those who drowned – questioned the findings. I should have done so, too. I know Björn was sceptical, though he didn't want to make much of it in front of me for fear of upsetting me further. But I was a young cop with a young son to bring up. I had an unshakeable faith in the system. I was part of the system. I saw my role as upholding it. If the government said something, I thought it must be true. Why would they lie? Now I realize, with what's going on in the world at the moment and what I've experienced here (and so have you), that it's often in governments' interests to cover up the truth; to deliberately distort the facts. And if necessary, eliminate those who pry too much, or know too much. I was incredibly naïve back then. Or maybe I was just in denial. I couldn't have carried out my job if I'd thought that the people I believed in were deliberately lying. I may not have been a hippie, but I was a dreamer. Sweden...' Anita's voice trailed off. 'That's what I believed in...'

'I understand.' Kevin was sitting in a blue garden chair. A man of habit, he'd already mown the small patch of lawn on which it was placed that Sunday morning. 'Just be careful it doesn't become an obsession.'

'No. I've decided simply to treat it as a case. Gather the facts. I'm seeing someone from the World Maritime University tomorrow. Just to give me a steer on the actual sinking. Why it happened. Then I plan to pop over to Copenhagen.'

'What for?'

'To see Tord Jolis. Try and get a bit of background.'

'Oh, yeah.' Kevin didn't try to hide his scepticism.

'Honestly, I'm not trying to revive the Markus Jolis investigation. I've drawn a blank there.'

'You never give up.'

'You totally misunderstand me, Ash.'

'I know you well enough by now, Sundström.'

'Well, you've got this wrong. Anyway, I'm thinking of going to Tallinn.'

'Are you sure that's a good idea? It might stir up suppressed feelings.'

'I have to. I need to see where Dad spent his last days. Then I'm going to take the same ferry route from Tallinn to Stockholm.' His flicker of concern was touching. 'I want to see where he died. Pay my respects, I suppose.'

'Anita, I hope you know what you're doing.'

CHAPTER 20

Sarfraz Khan was subdued. His mood wasn't improved when Hakim walked into his Happy Electricals store in Mobilia. He recognized the young detective from the group of police who had suddenly appeared at Limhamnsfältet and confiscated all their cricket bats. Why, he had no idea. A couple of the team had speculated that a bat might have been the weapon used to murder Iqbal, but the police hadn't enlightened them. And after an argument with the visiting team, the game hadn't even got started – none of the Gymkhana players were in the mood.

Sarfraz was small and wiry with a thin, clean-shaven face. He had a sharp, ferrety look. Hakim's immediate speculation was whether he could have smashed Iqbal over the head with a cricket bat. Of course he could – this man was the team's star batsman; the man that Iqbal was trying to get into the Swedish national team.

They went out of the shop and stood in the mall, which was only slowly coming to life at that time on a Monday morning. There were a few early-bird shoppers around, though it was the coffee shops that were the busiest. On his way in, Hakim had seen some families gathering at the complex's play area outside, taking advantage of the weather to escape their apartments. It was clear that Sarfraz didn't want the police presence putting off his customers, so they had wandered along to the outside of another shop.

'When will we get our cricket bats back?' he asked straightaway in a nasal voice with a hint of a Scanian accent.

'With luck, later this week.'

'We've got a match on Saturday against Malmöhus. Big local

game. We can't postpone that as well. I don't know why you want them, anyway.'

'Just following one line of enquiry. You do want us to catch your boss's killer?'

'Of course, of course.' Hakim could sense his nervousness.

'You are one of four people who have a key to the cricket hut?'

'Yes.'

'Where do you keep it?'

'At home.'

'Now, Iqbal was killed on Monday night. When was the last time you were down at Limhamnsfältet before then? And when was the last time you used the hut key?'

Sarfraz's hand twitched across his chin as he pondered.

'I was playing in the match on the Sunday. And the last time I had the key was to unlock the hut before the game. Then afterwards, Abbas and a couple of the others took the visiting team off for a curry. I didn't want to go. I wanted to get back to my family.'

'Did you lock up?'

'No. Usman did. Or was going to when I went. That's Usman Masood.'

'And you didn't go back the next day at all?'

He shook his head vigorously as though the thought was ridiculous.

'When you left, can you remember if one of the fold-up chairs was still opened out?'

His glanced down the mall in search of distraction – his disquietude was palpable. 'I don't know. Usman locked up, so I think everything would be tidy. Just as Iqbal liked it.' There was deference in his voice as he mentioned his employer's name.

'I hear he was very hands on. That he could turn up at stores unexpectedly.'

'We never had a problem here in Mobilia. It's one of the company's flagship stores,' Sarfraz added proudly.

'I'm sure it is. What was he like with the staff?'

'He was very good. We all thought very highly of him.' He was too gushing.

'He never used his position to take advantage of anyone?' This wasn't a line of questioning that Hakim was comfortable with. 'Over-friendly?'

'Never! Never!' Was the protest too vehement?

Anita emerged from her shower. The run in Pildammsparken had cleared her head. She felt better. Zetterberg could do what she liked; at least she'd be out of her hair. This month off would do her good – recharge her batteries. And then it would be back to work under Erik Moberg. During her run, she'd thought about embarking on her father's final journey; retracing his last days. Last night, she'd booked the flight to Tallinn for Thursday, and then the Baltic Queen ferry from there to Stockholm on the Saturday evening. She saw it as a sort of pilgrimage. She hoped it would bring her closer to him – as well as gaining *closure* (a word she had learned to loathe in her job). She had a slightly uneasy feeling of morbidity that she would be sailing over the same sea her father had died in, but she brushed it away. This was what she wanted, what she needed now that both her parents were gone.

The hairdryer drowned out any other noise and it was only when that stopped that she realized that her phone was ringing. She wasn't expecting a call, as she'd FaceTimed Kevin yesterday. It wouldn't be work. The only other possibility was Lasse, and that something awful had happened to Leyla. No – she breathed a sigh of relief – it was Martin Glimhall. He was one of the few journalists she still trusted. He was a crime correspondent, and they'd been mutually useful in the past.

'Hi, Anita.'

'Is this a social call, Martin?'

'You know I'm always interested in what my favourite cop is up to.'

'That's gratifying. This is an early start for you.'

Torquil MacLeod

'We journalists never really have time off. There's always something.'

'Well, this cop is having time off. I've just started on my summer holiday.'

'Oh.' He sounded disappointed. 'So you know nothing about what went on down at Limhamnsfältet on Saturday afternoon?'

'I wasn't there.'

'By all accounts, Zetterberg and the rest of your team were. I know we have to take security seriously at major sporting events, but having a dozen police officers at an amateur game watched by one man and his dog... now that *is* strange.'

'We like to protect the public.'

'Yeah, yeah. Has it something to do with the Happy Electricals guy's murder, by any chance?'

'If it has, I'm sure Acting Chief Inspector Zetterberg will inform the press in due course.'

Glimhall laughed. 'You'll be glad when she's off.'

'You know about that?'

'Course. She let it slip out on purpose a week or so ago. Look, Anita, is there anything you can give me?'

'Sorry, Martin.'

'Fair enough. It was worth a try. Anyway, going anywhere nice on your hols?'

'I'm thinking of going to Tallinn.'

'Attractive town. It'll be a bit crowded at this time of year.'

'It's personal really. I'm following up on my dad. He was on the *Estonia*. Just wanted to retrace his steps.'

'The *Estonia*? Heavens, that brings back memories of when I was a young reporter.'

'Why?'

'I was in Stockholm at the time and doing some follow-up stories. Into how the official investigation was going... that sort of thing. Then the editor called me in one day and told me the paper wasn't giving it any more coverage. No proper explanations. He put me on other things. That's when I got into crime reporting.'

This was interesting. 'Look, can we meet up? I'd like to know more about what happened. Anything you found out.'

'Sure, I'm free tomorrow afternoon. I'll tell you what I know.' He coughed. 'And if anything you happen to know about Iqbal Nawaz accidently slips out...'

Flaming journalists!

Hakim thought he'd grasp the nettle. His parents' home was only ten minutes' walk from Mobilia. He would use this opportunity to tackle his dad about Iqbal and the mosque. He was quite prepared to be rebuffed; the *other* issue might get in the way. His father wasn't in, but his mother was pleased to see him. Was it because her husband wasn't there? He had a quick chat before heading off to Möllevångstorget, where his father was shopping at the market. He would probably be sitting with his friends, complaining about life or his children, or discussing the latest news from Iraq.

Beyond the colourful stalls, Hakim spotted Uday sitting by himself on a bench, soaking up the sun. Two full shopping bags were at his feet. He was in no hurry to return home; a home which, over the years, seemed to have got smaller and more claustrophobic. Even Sweden itself seemed to have contracted, making him feel trapped. It wasn't the country that was to blame. It was just that his life – so full and stimulating before they were forced to leave Iraq – had shrunk to little more than trips to the market, talking to equally disillusioned exiles, the mosque, and the four walls of his apartment.

Uday had his eyes closed when Hakim reached him. Was his father back in the old Iraq, the land he loved? He appeared so peaceful. Hakim felt bad that there was now this rift between them. His father was a man he had always looked up to, yet now his own priorities and loyalties had changed.

'Dad.'

Uday opened his eyes and blinked. He sat up quickly as though he'd been caught out.

'I was just...'

'It's OK. Mamma said I'd find you here.'

Uday eyed his son with suspicion. Then a half smile played on his lips.

'You've changed your mind.'

'No. Not about that.'

'Why did you come then?' he said gruffly. 'Your mother sent you? I was on my way back, anyway.' He leant down to pick up his bags of fresh produce.

'It's not that. She knows you usually end up talking to your friends.'

'Hmm.'

'I was wondering if you could help me. Professionally.'

Uday pretended that he wasn't interested. 'I'm not good at dealing with police.'

Hakim tried not to sigh. 'This is not Baghdad. Do you mind if I sit?'

'It's a free country.' Hakim thought that's exactly what his father should be reflecting on. It wouldn't help if he pointed out the fact.

'We're investigating the death of Iqbal Nawaz.' There was no reaction. Hakim pressed on. 'He owned Happy Electricals.'

'I know who he is. His funeral is tomorrow.'

'He attended your mosque.'

'It's your mosque, too, in case you've forgotten.'

'My mosque, too. It's just we're trying to build a picture of him. What sort of man was he?'

'I spoke to him after worship a couple of times. I didn't really know him.'

'I was wondering if you could ask around. Was he respected? Was he disliked? Did he have any enemies? What sort of reputation did he have?'

'I can't believe a son of mine is asking me to spy on a fellow worshipper. This is what was happening in Iraq. People informing on others.' Uday was becoming heated.

Hakim stood up angrily. 'This is not Iraq. And I'm not asking you to spy. The man's dead! Someone killed him and it's my job to make sure we catch the murderer. We don't want anybody else ending up dead just because people like you don't want to help.'

Hakim knew he was going over the top. He marched off across the square. He shouldn't even have bothered.

CHAPTER 21

The World Maritime University was situated along the canal from the Central Station. It was established in 1983 by the International Maritime Organization, a specialized agency of the United Nations, for postgraduate studies to encourage safe, secure and efficient shipping on clean oceans through education and research. Well, that's what it said on the official website that Anita had consulted before calling and arranging to have a chat with an Alasdair Roberts, a visiting associate professor from Hull University in England. He was the one the receptionist had put her on to, as, she said, there weren't many people around at this time of year. He'd agreed to meet between tutorials. They met on the other side of the canal, next to a golden sculpture of a ship's propeller, to which the sun gave warmth and animation. Roberts had emerged from a rather grand, Venetian-Renaissance-style edifice, complete with campanile, which had been built at the turn of the 20th century for the Harbour Master. The recent extension, consisting of triangular shards of glass and aluminium, melded to form a futuristic gable in sympathy with the old building; the whole sitting comfortably between the traditional and the contemporary city.

Roberts was far younger than Anita had expected. He had large glasses, tight curly hair and animated hands, which she managed to stop moving by offering him a coffee. This was an undisguised enthusiast.

'Thanks,' he said in English, with a wide-beamed smile.

'Thought you might need it.'

'Shouldn't really be drinking out of one of these.' He pulled a face. 'They're paper.'

'Outside, yes. But lined with plastic polyethylene. Plastic top. Too much plastic in the oceans already.'

'Don't worry, I'm not going to throw them into the Sound.'

'The coffee's appreciated, though. It's been a busy day. Some great students in there. They're so keen. They want to make a difference.'

Anita thought it politic to steer him onto the matter in hand before he got too carried away. 'It's about the *MS Estonia*.'

'You mentioned that on the phone. What's your interest?'

'My father was on it. He didn't survive.'

'Oh, I'm so sorry.' He retreated into his cup.

'It's taken me a long time to come round to dealing with the sinking. I just want to really understand how it happened, or why it happened. Make sense of it, I suppose.'

'What, in particular? I do know about it, obviously. Fishing's my main field, but within that, I've made a special study of accidents, collisions and sinkings involving fishing vessels. Since my connection with the uni here, I've looked into Baltic disasters, too. So along the way, I was intrigued by the *Estonia*. One theory was that it hit a submarine; there have been cases of fishing vessels, certainly round Britain, being hit by subs, or dragged down by subs caught in their nets.'

'I've read the official findings of the Joint Accident Investigation Committee. They seem to focus almost solely on the bow visor being ripped off in the rough weather and letting the water flow into the car deck. They put this down to inadequate lock design specifications. Basically, they were blaming the German company that had built it – and the German company blamed it on poor maintenance by the ferry operator.'

'Yes,' Roberts said, pursing his lips. 'Worked like a medieval knight's helmet visor: up and down. The investigation committee seemed obsessed by the whole visor thing. That was probably the fault of Carl Bildt, your prime minister at the time. Only hours after the disaster, he said he wanted the Swedish Maritime Administration to investigate bow visors on other ferries because a construction fault might have caused the accident. I think this may have influenced the

Committee's thinking. It's as though they started with a conclusion and ignored the facts that didn't fit instead of looking at the facts first and then drawing a conclusion.'

'Are you saying that it wasn't the bow visor that caused the sinking?'

'Oh, it may have contributed. Certainly, when they recovered the visor, it created a striking image which people could focus on. However, it doesn't explain the speed with which the ship went down. That defies the law of physics.'

'How so?'

He took a swig of his coffee before launching into an explanation. 'What some people can't get their heads round is the speed issue, given that the ferry wasn't in a collision or torpedoed.' Warming to his theme: 'For example, the other great Baltic maritime disaster of the last century was the *Wilhelm Gustloff.*' Anita knew of the ship: a great German cruise liner that was full of evacuees fleeing from the advancing Russians in 1945. An estimated seven thousand people, many of them children, went down with the vessel in freezing waters.

'The point is that it was hit by three Russian torpedoes which blew massive holes in its hull. It took fifty minutes to sink. The *Estonia* took thirty-five. In a vessel like the *Estonia*, water, in theory, takes time to accumulate. It should be slowed down by watertight areas: the various decks, closed cabin doors, etcetera. Basically, it takes time to fill up what was the equivalent of an eight-storey building. There was a Swedish naval architect who did stability studies based on the findings in the final report. What the report was saying was that when the visor was ripped off, the water flowed into the car deck, which was above the waterline.' To illustrate, he pointed to a point about two-thirds down his coffee cup. 'Below the car deck, you have a watertight hull – fourteen compartments on which the ship floats. That's around eighteen thousand cubic metres of trapped air. Anyway, this study showed that if the water came in as the report suggested, the ship would initially list to starboard... to the right.' He demonstrated by slowly tilting his cup. 'It would then flop onto its side and then turn turtle – basically upside down. Crucially, it wouldn't sink. All the air in the hull would still keep it buoyant... like this. Oh, shit!' He'd turned his cup upside down; the plastic top flew off and coffee sprayed over his shoes. 'I'm sorry. Hope there's nothing on you.'

Anita had seen the possibility of an accident and had stepped back out of harm's way. Roberts didn't bother to wipe his shoes but just carried on.

'According to survivors who made it from the deck below the car deck, they didn't see water flowing down the steps from above, which they should have done if that's how the sea got in. They were escaping from water below them.'

'You're saying the water might have come in elsewhere?'

'Very possibly. There were a couple of conferences later on where researchers presented the theory of a hole in the hull. I did read about some Dutch naval architect or engineer – can't remember his name offhand – who tried out various scenarios on some specialized software, which is used all over the world, that predicts the capsize behaviour of ships and damage stability. To cut a long story short, this chap tested various theories, including the official version of the event. Obviously, all the data was fed in, including the ferry's internal geometry, the size of all the compartments, the conditions that night – wave and wind forces – and propeller propulsion forces. He tried two scenarios – one with the ferry doing the reported fifteen knots and the second as a drifting ferry. In neither case did the ship sink. He did other scenarios, and the ferry still didn't go down. Only when he programmed in the car deck flooding, along with a hole below the waterline, did the computer simulation show the *Estonia* sinking. His conclusion was that it could have only gone down as it did with a hole in its hull.'

'If that's true, why didn't the report pick up on it?'

'I've no idea.'

'And what made the hole?'

'A lot of people have asked that question.'

CHAPTER 22

Usman Masood greeted Wallen and Erlandsson with a wry grin. He welcomed them into his office, from which, through cleverly positioned glazing, he could monitor the activity of two rows of head-phoned staff sitting at computer terminals, dealing with customer enquiries or checking on the transport of products. The Happy Electricals headquarters was situated in a modern business block on Scheelevägen, close to the E22 and Lund's Northern Ring Road intersection, and shared the building with half a dozen other companies.

'Welcome, ladies.' His voice was deep and resonating.

Erlandsson tried not to bridle at the greeting.

Usman was undeniably good looking. Even Erlandsson would acknowledge that. For someone in his late twenties, his career was doing well, judging by the size of his office and the cut of his grey suit. His jet hair was neatly trimmed, as was his beard. The dark eyebrows virtually met above his coal-black eyes. These were twinkling in amusement as he went back behind his desk and swung back and forth on his swivel chair. Though outwardly relaxed, his eye kept straying to his workers beyond the glass.

'Thank you for seeing us,' Wallen began.

'Naturally, you're here about Iqbal. Terrible tragedy.' He managed to look suitably troubled.

'As you know, the murder took place close to the cricket ground and cricket hut.'

'I know. Did someone try to rob him? He's a rich man, you know. The turnover of Happy Electricals is staggering. I've seen the figures.'

'We don't think the motive was robbery. We're pursuing various lines of enquiry, one being the cricket club connection.'

'Hence the cricket bats. Was he really killed by one?'

'We can't comment.'

'You caused mayhem last Saturday. Some of these young men spend the whole week looking forward to their game. It's the most important thing in their lives during the summer. Most of them have been born and brought up in Sweden, but cricket gives them a cultural identity: a connection to their roots. And then they spend the miserable winters dreaming about playing again the next year.'

Wallen was not going to be deflected.

'I believe you are one of the hut's four keyholders.'

'Correct. Can I get you ladies coffee or some refreshments?'

'No,' Wallen said firmly. 'Where do you keep your key?'

'I have it here at the office.' He leant over to a metal cabinet behind his chair. 'In here.' He produced his key. 'Sometimes, when we have practice nets in the evening, I go straight from work.'

'Is that cabinet locked?'

'No. There's nothing important in it.'

'So anybody could come in and take the key?' said Erlandsson.

'I suppose so. There are a couple of the boys in the office here that have borrowed it when I've been unable to go to practice.'

'When was the last time you used it?' Wallen asked.

'Sunday before last. After the match, I locked up at the end. Iqbal usually did, but he was away in Karlskrona.'

'And everything was in order when you left?'

'It was tidy. It was a bit of an obsession with Iqbal, so we kept it neat.'

'What about the chairs? Were they all put away?'

'I think so.'

'And where were you on Monday night between ten and twelve?'

He blew out his cheeks. 'I was at home. Here in Lund.'

'Anybody verify that?'

'No. Surely I don't need to account for where I was. Why would

I want to harm Iqbal? He's been brilliant to me. I owe everything to that man. I've got a fantastic job in a great country. I'm the company's main buyer. I get lots of travel and all the perks. Am I going to jeopardize that?'

'You might end up running the company now he's dead.'

'That's up to Bismah. Anyway, I wouldn't want all that responsibility. I'm young. I like to have fun.' He winked at Erlandsson and got a scowl in return.

'Right. An obvious question. Is there anybody who would want to harm or get rid of Iqbal? Anybody that he might have upset? Either of the other two keyholders, for example?'

'You mean Sarfraz Khan and Mohammad Abbas?' Wallen nodded. 'Not Sarfraz. Like me, he owes his position to Iqbal.'

'And was Iqbal's star player.'

'Oh, yes. He's very good. If he hadn't come here as a small kid, I'm sure he would have been good enough to become a professional cricketer in Pakistan.'

'We saw from Iqbal's emails that he was trying to get Sarfraz into the Swedish national team.'

Usman flashed that amused smirk again. 'Typical Iqbal. He was desperate for one of us to make the national side. Reflected glory for him and his team. And poor, humble Sarfraz actually seemed upset that Iqbal was trying to promote his cause! Now if he'd done the same with my bowling...'

'Bowling?'

'You Swedes really do need educating. A bowler is the person who bowls – or to the ignorant, throws the ball – at the player holding a bat. That's the batsman. *He* tries to hit the ball. The bowler tries to get the batsman out.' He saw their blank expressions. 'Forget it. Look, if I'd been good enough to play for Sweden, I'd have jumped at the chance and let everybody know about it.' He shook his head in disbelief. 'Not our Sarfraz, though.'

'What about Abbas?'

Usman stood up, slipped his hands into his pockets and glanced over their heads to the office beyond.

'Ah, that's difficult. One doesn't want to be disloyal to one's colleagues... one's teammates. Don't get me wrong, Abbas is a first-class man. But the problem is he's in love with the boss's daughter. And I have a feeling my cousin returns that affection, though I'm sure she's said nothing to her parents.' This didn't come as a surprise to Wallen. 'Of course, it's a non-starter. Iqbal would never have countenanced such a marriage. I'm sure he had plans for Muneeba: someone with connections to the family or a potentially useful business contact. He would never have allowed her to be betrothed to one of his workers – a social inferior.'

'What is Bismah's attitude?'

'I don't know, though I'm sure she'd be in agreement with her husband. That's her place.'

Now he was upsetting both women, though Wallen felt a sudden wave of relief – she knew that until recently, she'd been in a similar situation with Rolf.

'Do you know if Abbas had ever made a formal approach?'

'I doubt it. He'd have known it was impossible. Would have cost him his job.'

'So with Iqbal out of the way, could Abbas have hopes of such a match?'

Usman sat down again. 'I suppose he might.'

CHAPTER 23

Martin Glimhall didn't dress to impress. He wasn't exactly unkempt; he just didn't seem to care what he looked like. He was a similar age to Anita. He must have been a typical, tall Nordic blond in his youth. His boyish good looks were now distorted by a stomach that protruded over his still-thin legs, and the jowly features that hung hangdog over a narrow neck. And his height was now reduced by a pronounced stoop, giving the impression that he must be constantly interviewing people smaller than him. That downward squint greeted Anita as they met near the Kallbadhus. One thing that hadn't changed since she had first got to know him was the cigarette clamped between his lips.

Anita had expected that they would meet in a café or a bar, the natural homes of journalists like Glimhall, but this Tuesday afternoon, the weather was trying its best to be hot (though Glimhall still wore a thick jacket), and they wandered slowly along the fringes of the town beach; the sand and sun a siren to those who were still on holiday. It was busy.

The small talk was quickly dispensed with. Both wanted something out of this walk.

'I was the same as everybody else – I was devastated by the whole *Estonia* episode, though I wasn't personally affected by it like you. I was also a young journo who wanted to make a mark. In the months following the sinking, a number of things didn't seem to add up. But it wasn't until the Swedish Maritime Association suggested that the wreck be covered up by a concrete blanket that I really took notice. Until then, the talk was of raising it and recovering the bodies. I believe that's what most of the relatives wanted.'

'I didn't take that in. I sort of blotted out all these things; these reminders. A refusal to face up to what had happened, I suppose. Even though my mother was divorced from my father, any fuss I made over him would have upset her. Does that sound daft?'

'No,' he said, flicking away his nearly smoked cigarette. 'Everybody has their own way of dealing with things.'

'Sorry. Carry on.'

He didn't speak until he'd lit a replacement.

'It just seemed an odd decision. They'd already hoisted up the bow visor. Its mangled state was a strong media image and helped promote the theory that the visor was the culprit. The divers who went down later reckoned the ship could be salvaged. The SMA's reason for the concrete was to prevent looting, despite the diving company survey concluding that the only place that items could possibly be targeted was the bridge, as there was too much haphazard debris about in the public parts of the ship to find anything. There was only one officially sanctioned dive, which took place over four days at the beginning of December. The bridge was an area of particular interest. The divers found three bodies there. Strangely, they didn't bother identifying them, which would have been easy enough through their insignia. And it would have been useful for the investigators to know whether the captain, Arvo Andresson, had been on the bridge at the time or in his cabin. Yet the divers went to great lengths to look in certain cabins that had been specifically pinpointed by the Swedish police, who were watching the dive on monitors.'

Glimhall waved his hand, and a flurry of ash fluttered onto the path.

'Someone who might have been useful to the investigators was the ferry's relief captain – another Estonian, Avo Piht. He wasn't on duty that trip. On the night, he was seen giving out lifejackets before the ferry sank, and one survivor claimed he was in the next hospital bed to him. The press reported he'd survived. Then, puff! He mysteriously disappears. He's never been seen since.'

'Mix up?'

'Don't think so. Too many people claimed to have seen him.'

They stopped at a bench and sat down. Runners and cyclists sped past. Anita was oblivious to them all.

'I spoke to someone at the World Maritime University, and he told me about the theory that there was a hole in the hull.'

'Ah, yes,' Glimhall nodded amidst a plume of smoke. 'That's what I was looking into at the time. The dive produced nineteen videotapes, which were placed in the custody of the Swedish police and the SMA. The dive company had another set but had to destroy them as required by their contract. The Swedes, who basically seemed to have muscled in on every aspect of the investigation despite the fact that it was all meant to be a joint venture with Finland and Estonia, sent an edited version to the Estonians, who weren't very happy. The missing bits allegedly showed bodies, and the Swedes' excuse was that they were deleted to protect the dignity of the dead. Interestingly, however, a group of German experts managed to get hold of a copy of the Estonian tapes and send them to a specialist video production and analysis company in the UK. *They* found that the tapes were full of unexplained cuts, unchronological editing, cassettes incorrectly numbered – a total muddle. Not what you'd expect when dealing with such an international disaster.'

'What did they think was missing? What had been cut out?'

'For starters, there was no footage of the starboard hull, where any hole might have been.'

'Do these tapes still exist?'

'No one knows. Politicians who've requested to see them have had no luck. Anyway, they ended up not covering the wreck in concrete, as it wasn't practical. But they had allocated the same amount of money for the concreting that it would have taken to salvage the vessel. That in itself is inexplicable.'

'But if there was no concrete blanket, what about the possible looting?'

'They banned any expeditions and set up twenty-four-hour surveillance. Basically, the Swedish authorities declared the wreck a grave site and instituted a Gravesite Treaty, which they encouraged neighbouring countries to sign, including the UK for some obscure reason – what the hell it had to do with them, heaven only knows. This was supposedly to protect the wreck out of consideration for the relatives of the deceased, and involved round-the-clock observation by the Swedish navy and Finnish coastguard. It's an awful lot of bother for the wreck of a non-military boat.'

'Heavens! Murky waters. What made you stop digging? You mentioned your editor.'

He shook his head. 'I was starting to ask questions that all good journalists should ask. Was there a hole? Was something happening on the ferry that we didn't know about? I went to Tallinn and discovered there was something called the Baltic Drainpipe. I've got no real details or anything, as I got called back before I'd gone very far. My editor said that the story had run its course. The Swedish public didn't want constant reminders. It was clear he didn't want the official report to be questioned. I got the impression someone had got to him.'

He stamped out his cigarette with the heel of his shoe. 'I was easily bought off. I got promoted to crime and handed a decent pay rise. The attitude was let sleeping dogs lie.'

'What's the Baltic Drainpipe?'

'I didn't have time to get the full picture. You have to understand what was going on in Estonia at the time. The whole breaking up of the old Soviet Union. But if you're going over there, I can give you the name of someone to contact. He'll fill you in.'

'Thanks, Martin.'

'No problem.' He stood up. 'As it happens, we're not far from where you found the body of Iqbal Nawaz. Anything you'd like to tell me in return?'

Hakim decided sitting in the office wasn't being very productive. The team had interviewed Sarfraz Khan and Usman Masood yesterday and decided between them that Sarfraz wasn't killer material – though

Hakim thought he might be hiding something – and that they didn't like Usman ('too slimy', according to Erlandsson). They all agreed that Usman could have had a motive if he was to emerge at the top of the Happy Electricals greasy pole after the dust had settled. But then it had materialized that so could Abbas: their suspicions about his thwarted relationship with Muneeba having been confirmed. The late-night phone call he'd made to Iqbal and then his lack of an alibi certainly fitted their murder scenario – one that Zetterberg was keen to pursue. What they couldn't figure out was the sex aspect. Was that coincidental? Was Abbas Iqbal's partner in lust, and did he kill him because he couldn't live with the shame? But if he was in love with Muneeba, would he have had sex with her father? That really did seem off the wall. And, as a matter of interest, where was Muneeba when all this was happening? Wallen would find out. The questions had sparked much debate. What they were really waiting for was to hear back from forensics. Zetterberg had sent Brodd to chase them up. Seems they had a backlog and the earliest the team would get any information was tomorrow, Wednesday.

The need to get out and be doing something probably explained why Hakim found himself wandering into the second-hand shop on Lundavägen which was run by his old school friend, Reza. The place was packed floor to ceiling with familiar clutter, from out-dated furniture to racks of cast-off clothes; tables covered in a patchwork of crockery, glass and knick-knacks; and a stack of ageing electrical goods. It seemed as though everything was still in the same place as the last time he'd called in. The items rarely moved, yet Reza appeared to be making a decent living – the car parked on the street outside the door was flashier than the last one, and the casual clothes he wore were from the kind of upmarket stores that Hakim couldn't afford to venture into. Reza blithely sailed through life, close to the wind while never actually hitting the rocks. Hakim never delved into his contacts for fear of what he might uncover. Long ago, he'd come to the conclusion that Reza's friendship was more important – as were the nuggets of information that only he appeared to have access to.

Hakim had been in his friend's deserted emporium for nearly five minutes before anybody appeared. When someone did, it was Reza, a broad smile of greeting on his handsome, boyish face.

'Is this a police raid?' He held his hands up in mock horror.

'I think you're more likely to be raided by the tax people.'

'Tax? I've never heard that word before.'

'Bet you haven't.'

'I don't sell enough to pay tax.'

'I'm beginning to regard the items here as old friends. I recognize most of them.'

'Well, if there's anything you need for your new home, I can give you a generous discount.'

'I'm sure Liv wouldn't go for any of this...' said Hakim, glancing around. 'It makes Myrorna look like a posh department store.'

'Bring her down anyway.'

'I wouldn't be able to get her wheelchair in here. That's another violation.'

Reza slumped down into the comfortable armchair which constituted his office.

'Is this a social call?'

'Erm... sort of. Liv and I would like you to come to our wedding.' It just slipped out.

'Wedding? Great – about time you got married! Are you inviting the whole mosque?'

Hakim sat down on one of two rickety chairs that had once formed part of a dining set.

'No. No religion.'

Reza whistled.

'How have Uday and Amira taken that?'

'It wouldn't be an exaggeration to say that they've taken it badly. They don't want to come. We're holding the ceremony in our garden. You can represent the Muslim community.'

'Won't Jazmin be there?' Reza said with some concern. He'd long been an admirer of Hakim's sister and still couldn't believe that she'd ended up with a white boy.

'I don't count her as Muslim anymore.'

'Remember, if she ever gets fed up with Lenny...'

'Lasse.'

'Whatever. I'm always here.'

'I'm sure she'll appreciate the sentiment.'

Reza took his smartphone out of the breast pocket of his shirt and flicked through it idly as Hakim continued to survey the junk around him. Reza replaced his phone.

'OK, why are you really here, Hakim?'

'Told you.' He paused. 'I just wondered...'

'Yeah?'

'I just wondered if you knew anything about Happy Electricals. More precisely, the owner, Iqbal Nawaz.'

'He's the guy you cops found down near Limhamn. Read about that. Yeah, I knew of him. And Happy Electricals, obviously. Tough cookie, so I heard. Very, very successful. Some of his products have ended up in here,' he said, waving at a little, hand-scribbled notice with the words *Quality Electricals* above an assortment of lamps, kettles, toasters, a DVD player and a couple of microwaves. Hakim assumed none had ever been properly checked since their arrival in the shop and would probably be lethal if ever used.

'Do you know any rumours about him?'

'What sort of rumours?'

'Business dealings. Personal as well. Does he have a reputation for women? Or men?' Hakim could feel himself blush. Reza looked quizzical. 'Anything, really. Trying to build a picture, that's all. His staff aren't very forthcoming.'

Reza's smartphone burst into some music Hakim couldn't place. It was loud and thumping.

'Sorry, Hakim, business calls. But I'll see what I can do.' He put the phone to his ear. He mouthed 'Thanks for the invite.'

CHAPTER 24

The train was late. That wasn't unexpected. The Öresund Line trains weren't the most punctual these days. Border controls hadn't helped, but on the days they weren't operating, there was still an annoyingly flexible timetable. As Anita wasn't rushing off to catch a plane at Kastrup – her trip to Tallinn wasn't until tomorrow afternoon – she wasn't among the frustrated passengers who kept glancing up at the signage and then down at their watches as though that would magically make their transport appear. She usually took this train to get a flight to Manchester on her visits to Kevin in Penrith, but it had been a while since she'd been to Copenhagen proper. She'd had a night out in the Danish capital at the beginning of the year with Klara Wallen, when she'd felt they deserved a break. They'd let their hair down in Nyhavn, but it hadn't been a roaring success, as the more Wallen drank, the more maudlin she grew about her domestic situation. She'd even wondered drunkenly if she'd done the right thing leaving Rolf. Anita had been sober enough to give her a lecture, and then she followed it up by threatening to leave her in the bar if she didn't come to her senses. After that, the night had improved, though they had both suffered for it the next day.

The train sped across the Öresund Bridge. Rain rattled against the windows, and Malmö's Turning Torso was lost in the gloom. On the Danish side of the bridge, airport passengers with huge pieces of luggage fought their way off the train at Kastrup, only to be replaced by recently landed arrivals with equally large cases, heading for Copenhagen. Anita always marvelled at how much holidaymakers seemed to take with them on their trips. She could probably get her entire wardrobe into one such case. The train took a further fifteen minutes to reach the centre of the city. From the Central Station, it was only a short walk to the National Museum of Denmark, which was on the other side of the Tivoli Gardens. The museum was where Tord Jolis worked. Anita thought that it would be easier for him to talk about Markus away from his home and family; his father's death still raw. The good news was that Wallen had rung last night to tell her that Nina Jolis was out of danger at last. They were expecting a full recovery. Now there would be no murder case.

She flicked as much rain as she could off her small umbrella before entering the grand museum. Instead of pulling out her warrant card to get through, she paid for a day ticket. She'd have a nose around afterwards. She'd never been in here before and thought it might be a place to bring Kevin on his next Scandinavian visit. She knew there was a lot about the Vikings on display, and Kevin was into the Vikings. Actually, he was into bloody everything! And if she got bored and he wanted to spend hours wandering around, there were plenty of nice coffee shops and bars nearby for her to escape to.

She met Tord Jolis in the main entrance hall, which was large and airy. The atrium area had previously been open to the elements before being covered by an impressive pitched, glazed roof. At one end was the museum shop; open-plan staircases led up to other floors housing the exhibitions; and in the centre were low, light-wood benches placed in a large rectangle, upon one of which Anita sat, relieved to get out of the rain. Above her head was an enormous hanging with the image of a beautiful, red-headed warrior princess encouraging patrons to 'Meet the Vikings'.

Tord Jolis appeared from an upper level down one of the staircases. He explained that he worked on the museum displays. He said it was the mix of creative and practical skills which he most enjoyed; yet it was hardly the best-paid job in the world. A far cry from his father's financial situation, thought Anita. Liv had got access to Markus Jolis's accounts: he would leave his widow a very hefty sum – nearly nine million kronor. Anita and Liv had speculated how someone working for a government service for so long could have accumulated so much. Liv wondered if he'd perhaps been paid particularly well at Zander Security after leaving the customs. Again, that appeared unlikely. Admittedly, he'd probably been given a significant salary hike to work in the private sector, but he'd only spent five years with the security firm. It didn't explain the amount of money sitting in his various bank accounts. And that was the money they could immediately trace.

'I'm pleased about your mother.'

'It's such a relief. If she'd died as well, it would have been unbearable. When this is all over, she's coming to stay with us. She can't go back *there*.'

'Understandable. Look, I don't want to rake up old memories, and I stress that this has nothing to do with what happened between your mother and father. I'm not here on official business.'

'Oh,' was all Jolis said.

'It's personal, actually. My father was on the *Estonia*.'

'He didn't make it?'

Anita shook her head. 'I just wanted to know a bit more about it. You understand?'

'Of course I do. You know where Dad was on that day... the day the ferry was scheduled to come in? At the customs.'

'Yes, I know.'

'He took it hard. I was in my first job in Stockholm at the time. I could see that he was very upset. That's stupid – everybody was upset. But I suppose it was more personal for him. He knew some of the crew and some of the regular truck drivers.'

'I noticed that he moved to Malmö a week after the sinking.'

'Did he?' Jolis's thoughts were temporarily elsewhere. 'Yes.' He was back. 'I'm not quite sure why. Maybe there was some fallout from the whole incident. Or he was so affected by it, the service thought it better that he start somewhere new. It was quite an upheaval. Mamma wasn't that keen to move, but she settled eventually. In fact, he was down here for a while before they managed to sell the house in

Stockholm. I think she only came down once he'd started at Zander Security six months later.'

'Yes, he didn't remain with the Swedish Customs in Malmö very long. Do you know why he left?'

'Mamma said he got a better offer. But I think the real reason was that he found it difficult to come to terms with the sinking... the *Estonia*. Everything he did reminded him of the... well, you know.'

'He certainly seems to have taken it very personally.'

'Well, you more than anyone must know how it affected lives. It must have been appalling for you and your family.' Anita acknowledged this with a pained grimace. 'I suppose when I look back, he was never the same again.'

'Did he ever talk about the incident with you?'

'No. Not with me. It was a taboo subject. All I know about his reaction to it came through snippets from my mother. From what she said, he just tried to shut the whole thing out.'

The museum now had a steady stream of visitors. Anita noticed that there were numerous parents corralling young children, with more determination than enthusiasm. A wet day during the school holidays – the museum made a decent, dry distraction for an hour or so.

She wasn't sure if she should mention it, but she did so, anyway. 'The last time I talked to your father, the *Estonia* came up.'

It was clear that Tord Jolis was taken aback.

'I wouldn't have thought he'd remember it in his state.'

Anita wasn't going to admit that she had instigated the topic.

'Yes. Quite clearly. He said that it shouldn't have happened.'

'We can all agree on that.'

'Then he said a weird thing: "He was wrong.". As though your father was talking about an individual. Does that mean anything to you?'

'No.' Jolis shook his head. 'The captain of the ferry? I have no idea. He came out with all sorts of stuff that didn't make sense in the last year or so. I don't know how Mamma coped.'

'I just wondered, that's all.'

She could see that Jolis was itching to return to work.

'I noticed your father retired early.'

'Wanted to get the most out of life. And he did before the Alzheimer's kicked in. Trips to India, South Africa, America. Lots of cruises. All sorts of places.'

'So he could afford it?'

'He always seemed to have plenty of money. He helped me and Ina buy our place here in Copenhagen.'

'He must have been paid well by Zander Security.'

'Probably. He once mentioned that he'd done well out of investments. Certainly more shrewd than I've been,' he laughed. She wondered if Jolis had any idea how much money his father had left. He'd soon find out.

'Thank you, Tord. It's been very good of you to give up your time.'

'I'm sure I haven't been much help.'

Before Anita said goodbye, Tord Jolis gave her the name of an ex-colleague of his father's from his Stockholm days – 'He might know more.'

As she wandered into the first gallery, she realized her chat had raised more questions than had provided answers. The one that was uppermost in Anita's mind was where had Markus Jolis's money come from?

'He's our man!' Alice Zetterberg couldn't hide her delight.

Eva Thulin had just been through her latest forensic results on the cricket bats. The one that had killed Iqbal Nawaz belonged to Mohammad Abbas. Attempts had been made to wipe the back of the bat clean, though not enough to fool simple forensic tests on the piece of wood.

'I think we can wind this up quickly.'

'I have to point out that Abbas's were not the only prints we found on that bat handle. There are others, which we'll need to rule out. You have to consider that he may have let other people use the bat. I've been reading up about this eccentric sport. Another thing to think about is that when players use these bats, they are wearing thick gloves.' She produced a pair of batting gloves, which were chunkily padded, making them look like overfed crabs. 'This is to protect their fingers when the ball, which is incredibly hard, is bowled at them. Your killer may have been wearing a pair of gloves like these, so his fingerprints might not be on the handle. There were a number of pairs in the hut.'

Zetterberg was losing patience. 'The murder weapon belongs to Mohammad Abbas. He has no alibi and he's got a possible motive – Iqbal would never allow his relationship with Muneeba. We know that he phoned Iqbal shortly before ten on the night of the murder. Presumably, it was to arrange to meet down at the cricket hut. He meets up with Iqbal. I'm not sure what exactly went on there, but the upshot is that he got his bat and whacked his boss over the head. He may not have meant to kill him; we don't know yet.'

'Whatever happened in that hut, it was where the sex took place.' Thulin had their attention. 'We've been over the fold-up chair thoroughly and there are traces of semen: Iqbal's. No one else's.'

'So he was having a wank.' Brodd was pleased that his pervert theory was correct.

'Not necessarily,' Thulin countered. 'There are various prints on the plastic arms. But lots of people would have used the chair over the summer, and not necessarily the players. Family members that come to watch. Players from visiting teams or—'

'You're saying that he wasn't necessarily having sex with himself?' interrupted Zetterberg.

'Yes. Whoever he may have been with could easily have been sitting on him while he was in the chair.'

'He's an arse-bandit!' This was Brodd again. 'The gay thing.'

'Or a woman sitting on his lap. Some men like it that way. That's all I'm saying.' Wallen wondered if Thulin's observation came from personal experience.

'My money's on Iqbal being secretly gay,' ploughed on Brodd. 'And Abbas, too. Iqbal didn't have a key with him, yet had sex in the hut. Abbas carried the hut key around. He lured Iqbal with the promise of sex. It was he that let him into the hut. Killed him afterwards outside, put his bat back and then locked up.'

Zetterberg had had enough of all this speculation. 'Makes sense to me, Pontus. Whatever happened, the end result is that he tries to clean the murder weapon and hide it away in his cricket bag. And we seem to have at least two possible motives. He's gay and it all went wrong somehow, or Iqbal wasn't going to allow Abbas to marry his daughter.'

'Maybe Abbas wasn't gay but just went through with it to get Iqbal to the hut.' Brodd was on a roll. He was getting approving looks from his boss.

'Even if that's true, we're not sure that Bismah will allow the match,' observed Wallen. 'That's according to her nephew, Usman.'

'I'm sure Abbas thinks otherwise,' said Zetterberg. 'From the description of Bismah, she isn't going to say boo to a goose. Don't Muslim women just do what they're told?'

'That's not always the case,' pointed out Hakim, his sister springing to mind.

'Talking of Muslim women, do we know where Muneeba was when this was all happening?'

'She didn't get back home until about half eleven,' said Wallen. 'I've spoken to her and she said she was watching a play with a friend. One of their classmates was in the production. But I'm still checking that out.'

'The question is: did she know what Abbas was up to? Or was she part of the conspiracy?'

'We don't know for sure that she *is* in love with Abbas.' Zetterberg was finding Erlandsson's interventions aggravating. 'We only have Usman's word for it.'

'He should know. He's family.'

'What I can't figure out,' Hakim began, 'was why Abbas would use his own bat. There were half a dozen bats leaning against the wall he could have picked up. Why go into his own bag? And even if he did use his own bat, why leave it there for us to find? Why didn't he get rid of it?'

'He probably assumed that we'd never work out what the murder weapon was.' Zetterberg wasn't in the mood to countenance awkward questions when it was obvious to her who had done it. 'Maybe he just panicked after killing Iqbal. As I've said before, maybe he didn't mean to. Realized he'd done something awful. It wasn't planned. Wasn't in the right frame of mind to make rational decisions.'

While doubts were swirling round the room, Zetterberg had none. And it was time to act.

'I want Mohammad Abbas brought in for questioning. Now!'

CHAPTER 25

Anita had decided that after her visit to the National Museum, she deserved a treat. She'd ended up with a cup of strong coffee and a piece of carrot cake sitting on the table in front of her. Heavy rain had greeted her departure from the museum and hadn't given her time to weigh up the options available. Dashing out of the downpour, she found herself taking shelter in a colourful courtyard. Despite the rain, covered candles and burners flickered on an array of brightly painted tables, not surprisingly, bare of custom. Beyond, was a not-so-inviting sign: Bastard Café, but Anita was past caring about the inappropriate designation as she pushed through the doors out of the weather. What met her on the other side was totally unexpected. It was game heaven! Tiers of shelving, lining every wall and filling every alcove, groaned with boxes and boxes of every conceivable board game from Risk to Rummikub. Almost every table was occupied by excited enthusiasts shuffling cards, moving counters and throwing dice. Interestingly, there didn't seem to be a computer in sight. When she found a quiet corner spot, it occurred to her that she was probably the only person in the place over the age of twenty-five.

After the amount of time she'd spent walking round the exhibitions – she'd marvelled at how much of early man's activities had been preserved in Denmark's peat bogs – she reckoned she deserved something stronger than a coffee, but was still grateful for the shelter. And the cake was exceptional! Besides, she was on holiday. Yet her thoughts were back at the polishus: she'd just had a call from Hakim alerting her to the fact that Abbas was being brought in for questioning. Hakim had explained Zetterberg's reasoning after hearing Eva Thulin's forensics report on the cricket bats. He also voiced his concern over the fact that Abbas was unlikely to use his own bat and then leave it to be found. Furthermore, the sex angle had got them stumped. Anita advised Hakim to probe Abbas's lack of alibi – and why he'd phoned Iqbal when he did. The timing was crucial. Hakim said he wouldn't have a chance, as Zetterberg had allocated Klara Wallen and Pontus Brodd to handle the interview. Why Brodd? Because he was her man on the inside. 'She doesn't trust me,' he said. Anita replied that Zetterberg didn't trust any of them, which had been a problem for the last two years. If he wasn't going to be part of the interview, she suggested that he check out the warehouse CCTV. Abbas might be on there, leaving either before or after he said he did.

She finished off her last mouthful of cake. The skies had cleared, and the wet courtyard outside shimmered in the fresh sunlight. The forecast for the next few days, according to her weather app, was sunny with occasional cloud both in Sweden and Estonia. She chided herself for worrying about the Iqbal Nawaz case. What was the point of that? The only titbit she'd offered Martin Glimhall in return for his *Estonia* information was that he should look into the hut and the members of the cricket team. Which was pretty obvious, given that he already knew about the police turning up at the cricket match. However, he'd seemed satisfied enough. Besides, the case would be solved by the time she returned to work. Even better, Erik Moberg would be back in place – now there's a thought she'd never envisaged having – and Zetterberg would be a distant, if disconcerting, memory. Four weeks stretched ahead of her. She'd already bought a guide to Tallinn. She was looking forward to the visit with a mixture of trepidation and relish. It might bring back unsettling memories. On the other hand, it might draw her closer to her father, who had left her far too young. She hoped the trip would rekindle reminiscences of the good times they'd shared – especially the ones when they were still a happy family back in England.

She finished her coffee. She even contemplated moving onto a beer in celebration of the change in the weather. However, she decided it would be more sensible to head back to Malmö and pack – OK, bung a few things in a bag – for her flight tomorrow. She made her way through the throng towards the station. Her mind was still whirring in bewilderment at what she had so far discovered about the *Estonia*. What more would she learn in Tallinn? And how disturbing would it be? She was well aware that the Markus Jolis case would now be officially wound up, but for her, there were too many imponderables – Jolis's sudden move to Malmö; his stack of money; his abrupt death and swift cremation; the mysterious doctor and lawyer. By the time she reached the station, she wished she'd stayed put for that beer.

The recording clock clicked over to 17.00. They had been in the increasingly sticky interview room for nearly forty minutes. There were only three of them, as Mohammad Abbas had declined to have a lawyer present. Wallen thought it was a mistake; Brodd saw it as an opportunity. Neither Wallen's low-key approach nor Brodd's attempted aggressiveness (instructed by Zetterberg to get a quick confession) appeared to be working. Abbas was still sticking to his story: he was working late on two outgoing deliveries for the next morning, and he had phoned Iqbal to keep him up to date with his progress. This, he claimed, was normal practice. Iqbal liked to be kept abreast of every aspect of the company's operations. He also denied that he had feelings for Muneeba, though Wallen wasn't entirely convinced by his protestations. Brodd had called him a liar at this point, which hadn't helped.

Wallen started again.

'How do you explain that your cricket bat was used as the weapon that killed Iqbal Nawaz?' The bat in question was lying on the table between them, carefully wrapped in clear polythene.

'I can't.'

'Or won't,' accused Brodd.

'I was never down at the hut that night. I told you where I was.'

'How did you do it?' Brodd persisted. 'Was it planned or spur of the moment?'

Abbas simply folded his arms and said nothing.

'For the record, Mohammad Abbas has refused to reply to my questions.'

'I've already answered them. Nothing was planned. Nothing was spur of the moment. I was nowhere near the scene of the murder. And for the record...' he leaned towards the recorder '...I had no reason to kill a man I owed everything to.'

'That brings us back to Muneeba,' Wallen said quietly. 'We've heard from a source that you were sweet on her. And that she fancies you. My boss thinks that she might have been involved. As in the two of you together. Planned it together, carried it out together, cleared up afterwards together.'

Abbas shifted in his chair. It was plain he didn't like the direction the questioning was heading.

'Muneeba would have nothing to do with something like this. She couldn't.'

'Why couldn't she?'

'Because she was...' He stopped himself abruptly. 'Because she just wouldn't. She loved her father.'

'I'm checking out her whereabouts that night.'

'She was at a play.'

'So she says. But how do you know that?'

For the first time in the interview, he failed to meet his inquisitors' gazes.

'Someone must have told me,' he muttered.

Wallen sensed that she had breached his defence. Maybe Zetterberg was right. She would have to discover if Muneeba's alibi stood up.

CHAPTER 26

'I've tracked down the friend of Muneeba's who went to the play.'

Wallen had popped her head round Hakim's door the next day. He was halfway through the sugar-saturated coffee he'd been looking forward to all morning. He'd been out to the Happy Electricals warehouse in Bulltofta to pick up CCTV footage for the whole of Monday, the 29th of July. He wanted Mohammad Abbas's movements checked from when he went into work to the moment he left. Naturally, the time of most interest was from about nine onwards. Liv was now going through the footage.

Wallen came in and leant against the door. She seemed pleased with herself.

'I've spoken to the friend – a Kitty Harris, an American doing the same course. They went to see...' Wallen flipped open a notebook '...Deathtrap by Ira Levin put on by Guanabana Productions. They're an amateur, English-language theatre company here in Malmö. It took place at AmatörteaterForum on Norra Skolgatan. Interestingly, the play finished just after nine-thirty. They were hanging on for their course mate, Liam O'Donnell, who was in the production. He's Irish. They were going for a coffee afterwards. Anyway, as they were leaving the theatre, Muneeba got a phone call.'

'Time?'

'Kitty says just before ten.'

Hakim raised his eyebrows knowingly.

'Exactly. She tells Kitty that something has come up and she has to rush off. Her car was parked on Torpgatan on the other side of the block, so she could have been down at Limhamnsfältet by about quarter past ten, given that the traffic wouldn't be heavy that time of night. It would have taken a similar length of time for Abbas to get down there, too. Of course, he might have phoned her from his car on the way. He'd have to have been at the hut reasonably early if he let Iqbal in, as we suspect.'

'And the sex?' Hakim queried.

'I don't know. Could Iqbal possibly have had intercourse with his daughter first?'

'I don't want to believe that.'

'He was a controlling man. Could he have been abusive to his daughter? Possibly for years. Incest isn't exactly new. And in that sort of group.'

'What are you implying?' Hakim said angrily. 'Because they're Muslims?'

'I've read things,' she replied warily. 'That's all. How else do we explain Iqbal's sexual encounter if it wasn't with Abbas? Iqbal isn't likely to assault his daughter in the family home with Bismah around.' Hakim took a swig of his coffee before it went cold. 'It fits whether you like it or not.'

Hakim was loath to agree. His impression of Muneeba was that of a confident young woman. But you never know. This job was always throwing him curveballs. 'OK. Reluctantly, I'll go with that scenario for the time being because, as you say, it fits. Besides, we've nothing else to go on.' He thought for a moment and put down his cup. 'It might explain something that Anita wondered – why Iqbal hadn't heard someone come up behind him. She speculated there might have been two people there. That might be right. So, for example, Muneeba is distracting him while he's turning his phone back on, and Abbas creeps up behind.'

'Most of it is falling into place.' Wallen's hand was on the door handle. 'We need to put the two of them at Limhamnsfältet between say... a quarter past ten and eleven.'

'Liv's checking the warehouse CCTV now. If we see Abbas leaving around ten, we're really onto something.'

'Maybe *Deathtrap* was an appropriate title for the play. Was that what Abbas and Muneeba were creating that night for Iqbal Nawaz?'

Tallinn's lack of importance in the world of aeronautical travel could be gauged by the fact that the SAS flight was waiting at the very extremity of Kastrup's tarmac, and it took several minutes to reach the plane by bus. The flight was only an hour and a half, so it didn't seem long before the descent over Estonia. Unsurprisingly, as only the Gulf of Finland separated the two countries, the aerial views of expanses of pine, birch and spruce forest dominating a flat landscape reminded Anita of when she'd flown into Helsinki a couple of years before, though, unlike Helsinki, few man-made structures were visible until you were almost above Tallinn itself.

The airport was small and compact, and Anita quickly passed through it. She took a taxi and joined the crawl of traffic heading into the centre of the city. Once past the modern suburbs, the driver managed to skilfully manoeuvre the vehicle up narrow, twisting streets into the Old Town, with its massive walls and imposing towers, soaring church spires and pepper-pot domes – for all the world like an historical theme park. The taxi squeezed through impossible gaps and bumped over yawning cobbles before coming to rest outside the small hotel close to Fat Margaret's Tower that Anita had booked into for a couple of nights.

The weather was fine and sunny when she stepped out of the hotel and meandered through the medieval, Renaissance and Baroque hotchpotch of dwellings and businesses, now adapted to today's requirements and tastes. One grand, 16th-century townhouse turned out to be the Swedish embassy – Estonia had once been part of the Swedish Empire, and the embassy occupied one of the best slices of real estate on the desirable Pikk Street.

The Old Town was packed with tourists. Anita noticed a huge group which had poured off one of the gargantuan luxury cruise ships berthed in the harbour. Tallinn was merely a short stop-off on their hop around the Baltic capitals. She wondered what impressions these visitors would glean from such fleeting jaunts ashore before returning to their floating hotels and tucking into their next extravagant meal. Anita sucked in the atmosphere. Despite the crowds, the place had a calm, almost ethereal ambience, which she found comfortingly therapeutic. Wandering away from the main thoroughfares and into the back streets nestling under the old city walls, she felt an unexpected peace. She worked her way up to Toompea, the upper town, with its castle; Alexander Nevsky Cathedral; and the Riigikogu, the Estonian parliament. From this high vantage point, she could take in both the old and the new Tallinn. Immediately below where she stood was a jumble of red pantile roofs pierced by the spire of St. Olaf's Church and the graceful tower of the ancient town hall. Beyond, was the modern Tallinn; a microcosm of the wider Estonia which had, in a mere twenty years, miraculously transformed itself from a broken-down Soviet satellite state into an innovative, go-ahead European country with an eye firmly on the future. It had come a long way in a short time.

But what had it looked like to her father and his friends? In the middle distance was the harbour with a couple of colossal liners dominating the waterfront; further out, languishing in the haze, the Tallink ferries, one of which would be taking her across the Baltic to Stockholm in a couple of days. It was down there that her father must have landed. What had been his plans? How did he spend his final days? Her heart gave a little start as she realized she was staring at the last place her father had been before boarding the fateful ferry that had taken his life. The life of the man she had loved so much. Tears sprang to her eyes as she thought of all the years she had spent without him. It all seemed such a waste.

She tore herself away from the scene. The bright sun seemed to scoff at her sadness. But now she was even more resolved. However difficult it might be, she was doubly determined to find out more of what happened that night. Tomorrow at noon, she was to meet up with the academic Martin Glimhall had put her in touch with. It was the start of her quest.

*

Liv wheeled herself into Hakim's office, a tablet on her knee. Hakim glanced up expectantly.

'I think you'd better get Klara in for this.'

Hakim fetched Wallen.

'Fire away, Liv.'

Liv held up the tablet, and they could see the Happy Electricals warehouse car park. She touched the screen.

'Right, this is 7.56 on the Monday morning of the murder.'

They watched a blue Volkswagen come through the gates and park alongside three other cars. A man gets out.

'That's Mohammad Abbas coming into work. Note the car he's driving.' Liv then touched the screen a few times, and the same car park was lit up at night. 'This is 22.16.'

There was only one car left – the blue Volkswagen.

'Keep your eyes on the gateway.'

As they watched, another car appeared. This was a large Volvo. It parked next to the Volkswagen. A figure slipped out of the driver's side. Liv froze the footage and increased the size.

'Recognize her?'

Wallen's sigh confirmed that the figure in question was Muneeba.

'What the hell was she doing there?' said a mystified Hakim.

Liv cast him an unsympathetic look before a broad grin spread across her face.

'Can't you work it out?'

'She's going to see Abbas?'

'Of course she is.'

'What about Abbas's call to Iqbal?'

'You're not very romantic, are you, my love? You'll have to ask him yourself, but I suspect that it was exactly what he claimed – it was about orders going out the next day. That would be the excuse anyway; the real reason is likely to be that he wanted to find out where Iqbal was to make sure the coast was clear for Muneeba to come and see him at the warehouse. When he was sure Iqbal wouldn't suddenly turn up out of the blue, as presumably he often did, he called Muneeba outside the theatre, and she rushed to Bulltofta to see the love of her life. Given her parents' negative attitude and a control-freak father, there can't have been many places they could meet up away from prying eyes.'

Liv touched the screen again. The time is now 23.12. Muneeba appears again and drives off.

'He could have given himself an alibi all along! But, of course, he wanted to protect Muneeba, and he'd rather face the consequences than dishonour her name and reveal their secret relationship.' Liv flicked the screen, and five minutes after Muneeba's departure, Mohammad Abbas gets into his car and leaves, closing the gates before disappearing out of shot.

Wallen groaned. 'Are *you* going to tell Zetterberg, or am I?'

CHAPTER 27

Maksim Kask was in his forties. Not what Anita expected. She had conjured up an image of the professor from the University of Tartu as being a grey-haired academic with wise features and a tortured frown. Professor Kask couldn't have looked younger or more energetic. With his short hair and smart suit, he would have been more at home in a stock exchange than emerging from a lecture in an historic palace. She was greeted with a firm handshake and brisk smile.

With time on her hands, Anita had taken a leisurely walk out of the Old Town, past the port and along streets of fine but faded 18th-century mansions to reach Kadriorg Park. Kask was waiting outside the park's magnificent raison d'être – Peter the Great's Baroque Summer Palace. The pristine building had been lovingly maintained and each column, arch and relief looked spanking new. He led Anita round to the back of the building. The sun was high and reflected brightly off the cinnamon red, buttermilk and white of the stucco and decoration, combining happily with the sage-green roof tiles. The colours were cleverly mirrored by the beautiful formal gardens.

After brief introductions and a quick explanation as to why he was there in the first place – a talk to foreign students on Russian Tsarist influence on Estonia (nowhere was more appropriate than the Summer Palace for his homily on the subject) – he didn't need much persuading to launch into his pet subject: Estonian history. After starting off in faltering Swedish, Kask was grateful to switch to English, in which he was fluent.

'The curse of Estonia is that it's a new country with a long history – a long history of suppression. First, it was the Teutonic

Knights – and the German influence has never really gone: all our great manor houses were built and lived in by German aristocrats until the end of the Second World War. After the Germans, it was you Swedes. We were used as a battleground between the Swedish Empire and the Russians, until Peter the Great defeated your Charles XII in 1721. Then we were swallowed up by Tsarist rule for the next two hundred years. You know, Peter the Great and his wife loved it here so much that they built this wonderful palace. Ironically, neither lived long enough to see it completed. But what's interesting is that if Peter had beaten the Swedes earlier at the Battle of Narva, he would have built his capital here and not St. Petersburg. I'm glad he didn't.'

Anita wished he'd get to the point; she wanted to know about late 20th-century Estonia. Kask must have noticed her impatience.

'My dear Anita, to understand what happened – or may have happened – to that ferry in 1994, you need to see the bigger picture.'

'I'm sorry. Please carry on.'

'We had the Russians here until the end of the 1917 Revolution. Their empire collapsed, and we gained our independence in February, 1918. I can only imagine the joy. But it was short lived. The Russians were back in 1940: Soviet-style this time. The Germans returned and threw the Soviets out and got rid of most of our Jews. Then the Soviets were back again in 1944 and got rid of huge numbers of leading Estonians. Yes, they drove the Germans out but forgot to leave themselves! They eventually did in 1991 in the midst of the Soviet Union's disintegration, and we declared our independence. Except, they didn't all go – over three hundred thousand stateless Russians were left behind. That's a lot in a small country like ours.'

'I can imagine that was disruptive.'

He shook his head wistfully.

They stopped walking and, for a few seconds, Anita focused on the splendour of her surroundings. The sun felt good on her skin.

Kask continued, 'After the Second World War, Russians were encouraged to settle in Estonia: the Russian language was introduced at pre-school stage, and they took all the elite jobs – bankers, bureaucrats, the police. The country was full of Soviet troops, and we provided ports for their Baltic Fleet. Then with independence, they lost all that at a stroke. Overnight, they turned from repressive rulers into a mistrusted minority. Their jobs were gone, and the KGB and security officials were sacked. They were all legally obliged to learn a new language. Their ruble salaries plummeted because we'd pegged our new kroon currency to the deutschmark. And that was just the civilians. The big problem was thousands of disaffected Russian military were still stationed on our soil. That's when Estonia, and Tallinn in particular, became like the Wild West of America. Tallinn is peaceful today as the tourists wend their way through our quaint streets, but back in the early 1990s, it was one of the most violent cities in the world. Murder and contract killings were commonplace – it was awash with weapons.'

'The Russian Mafia?'

'Partly. There were so many criminal groups then. As I say, we had all these resentful troops with nothing to do, no money to spend, nowhere to go. To make ends meet, they started selling off their weapons, their equipment, their technology. There was a roaring trade in armoured personnel carriers, anti-tank rockets and Makarov pistols. To a Russian officer earning the equivalent of about thirty dollars a month in a currency that was useless, selling your weapons or your killing skills to one of the many so-called private security firms must have looked an attractive option. The street price for a contract killing was around eight hundred dollars.'

'I see what you mean.'

'The country was swamped by illegal activities, much of them to do with items flowing out of the old Soviet Union towards the West. Everything was on the move – armaments, drugs, illegal immigrants, religious icons, Tsarist antiques and dangerous materials. Poorly paid border guards and customs officials were easily bribed to look the other way – or even help. For the criminals, fortunes were made, and the newly formed private banks were only too happy to take in the proceeds for start-up capital. Corruption was everywhere and murderous, competing gangs took full advantage.'

'Is this where the Baltic Drainpipe fits in?'

'Exactly. The gangs wanted to make money from the crumbling Soviet Union. Buyers in the West, including Western governments, wanted cheap contraband. Tallinn was smuggling central. And not just to the West. It was also the gateway to rogue states such as North Korea, Libya, Iran and Pakistan. They were all particularly interested in submarines.'

'Submarines?'

'There were plenty of them. It was a great way for the Kremlin to generate much-needed revenue. They had a lot of submarines down at the Paldiski naval base, not far from here. Good deepwater harbour. At one time, there were sixteen thousand Soviet personnel down there. Anyway, one of the main routes for the Baltic Drainpipe was the recently established ferry to Stockholm. What better way of moving illegal merchandise than on an innocent passenger ferry?'

'I can understand drugs and artefacts. That's easy. But you reckon they were also shipping weapons?'

'And more besides. It's said that radioactive materials were smuggled, too.'

'Surely not!'

'There was no control over the old Soviet sites. For example, the Saku Repository outside Tallinn was a radioactive waste facility. It had one security guard covering seventy-two hectares. Needless to say, it was thoroughly looted. Western governments were worried that materials from Saku would fall into the hands of terrorists and extremists. They were being sold on somewhere. Radium, uranium and cesium-137 were all radioactive materials that were confiscated at that time. And the Paldiski naval base had two nuclear reactors. These had 460 nuclear fuel rods, each containing twenty-percent-enriched uranium. The Russians claimed that they decommissioned the reactors, but they also trashed the base before handing it over to the Estonian authorities. The rods were supposedly transported back to Russia. Or were they? Each one was three metres long, so could fit into a truck.'

'Are you suggesting one of these rods could have been on the ferry?'

'You never know.' Kask shrugged expansively. 'That or some other material, such as plutonium. It might explain why the Swedish government was so keen to cover the wreck in concrete. That's what happened to the Russian nuclear submarine *Komsomolets* that sank off Norway. That had a concrete blanket to make it safe.'

'That's a frightening thought!'

They started to walk again. Anita found it difficult to speak as she let all this new information settle in her brain. It was almost too much – too horrifying to take in. They reached the boundary wall, which was crested by a parapet, and began to climb the steps to one of the exits. Anita turned back to absorb the view. The geometrically designed garden with its box hedges, parterres, gravelled spaces, and fountains twinkling in the sun exuded a tranquillity that was at sharp variance with the turmoil inside her head. 'What do you think happened to the *Estonia*? I've spoken to someone at the World Maritime University in Malmö, and he believes there must have been a hole in the hull.'

'I would agree with him. What made it is another matter. Some say it might have been in a collision with one of these ex-Soviet submarines heading out of the Baltic. The year before, an Iranian crew in their newly acquired sub was detected off the Swedish coast. It could have been another of these. Or maybe it hit a submersible. Again, it might have been a bomb. A criminal gang trying to stop whatever a rival organization was smuggling on the ferry that night from reaching Stockholm. Or conceivably, it was on orders from a Kremlin that was fed up with so much of their arms and technology being spirited out of the country. In those days, you only had to turn up at a factory or military base or installation with bundles of hundred-dollar bills, and you could buy anything.'

'What's your personal view? Gut instinct?'

'To be honest, Anita, I have no idea.' He caught Anita's frustrated expression. 'Nothing really makes sense, though an underwater collision of some sort might explain the speed with which the *Estonia* went down.' Kask shrugged apologetically. 'I'm afraid we'll probably never find out the truth.'

CHAPTER 28

Hakim stopped the electric lawnmower. The grass was neatly cut. Most of their modest garden was laid to grass. There was one deliberately raised border which Liv enjoyed tending, though it involved a lot of stretching. Hakim's offers of help always lacked enthusiasm; he wasn't one of nature's gardeners. He'd never thought he'd end up anywhere with its own bit of green. The beauty of apartment living was that any grounds were looked after by a landlord or a residents' committee. After some effort, he was just about getting the hang of the mowing.

Liv sat on the patio in the sun in her special lounger, a pad of paper on her lap. The wheelchair stood next to her. She appeared to be drawing. Hakim knew it was a plan of how she wanted the garden laid out for the wedding. He assumed the tent-shaped thing was an open gazebo. Ever practical, Liv was planning for all eventualities, especially in this unpredictable summer.

He cleaned the mower, wound the cord, and put it away in the small shed in the corner of the garden.

'Want some juice? I'm getting one for myself.'

Liv was preoccupied. 'What sort of booze should we get in?'

'Booze?'

'Alcoholic beverages. I know you don't drink, but all the others will. My brother, certainly.'

'I suppose. Wine. Beer. I don't know what people like, except Anita. I know she drinks red wine, and beer at the pub.'

'Don't worry. You won't have to go to the *Systembolag*. I know you wouldn't have a clue what to buy. I'll make up a list for my brother, and we'll pay him back. And Malin is doing the food. She'll put on a great buffet spread.' Hakim knew that his sister-in-law-to-be would serve up something special which would include dishes that would satisfy an Arab palate. Sadly, his parents wouldn't be there to savour them. He'd secretly hoped that they would come round to the idea, and that his mother would do the catering.

'With us, there'll be ten. That's not including the kids. Twelve if your parents change their mind.'

'Little chance of that.' He paused at the patio doors. 'What about the lady from City Hall who's actually going to marry us?'

'She's not staying afterwards. She's on a tight schedule, which is why the wedding has to take place exactly at eleven.'

'Have you included Reza?' He slipped in the question as though it was totally natural to ask.

Liv's head jerked up. 'No. Your mysterious school friend? Didn't realize he was that close. Have you asked him?' Her surprise was transparent.

Hakim hadn't really intended to ask Reza. He'd just blurted it out. Subconsciously, he must have thought it would be easier to get information out of him if he softened him up first.

'Yes. He's very keen.'

'How come I've never met him?'

'Don't know really.' He knew exactly. Reza's skirting round the law might not sit well with Liv. On the other hand, he was good company – as long as you left nothing of value lying around, or at least made sure it was nailed down. Seriously though, Hakim was confident that Reza would behave himself at the wedding, especially in the company of four cops in a compact garden. Klara Wallen was the fourth member of the force attending. The advantage of Wallen was that she didn't come with a partner. Liv had also wanted to ask Bea Erlandsson, but Hakim had had to veto that one. If she was asked, they would have to invite Pontus Brodd as the only other member of the team. Coping with Brodd at work was one thing; having him at his private wedding gathering quite another. Hakim had remained firm on the subject. It wasn't often that he won the day with Liv.

He went into the kitchen, took down two glasses and filled them with passion fruit cordial and water. While he was extracting some ice cubes from the freezer compartment of the fridge, his phone went off. Talk of the devil, it was Reza.

'Hi, Reza.'

'How are the wedding plans going?'

'OK.'

'And Liv's happy for me to be there?'

'Just been talking about you. She can't wait to meet you.'

There was a pause at the other end as though Reza couldn't quite believe it.

'Same here. Look, I'm calling about what you mentioned in the shop. Been asking around. Have to be a bit careful, as Iqbal Nawaz was not a man to cross. Has powerful friends. Had. That's the word, anyway.'

'What sort of friends?'

'By and large, legit ones. Certainly these days. You'd expect that of a man running a big retail organization. Where it's a bit hazy is his sudden rise from small-time trader to national chain. Took off in the early nineties. Someone I've spoken to suggested that he had a backer.'

'Doesn't that happen a lot? Someone who sees a company's potential?'

'Maybe. But it's quite a risk putting money into an immigrant's business. All I'm saying is that if he had a silent partner, no one is shouting about it.'

There didn't seem to be much there.

'Anything else?' Hakim asked hopefully.

'Oh, yes. A rumour anyway. The old goat was knocking off a younger woman. Beautiful apparently. Get this – the wife of an employee.'

'Does this employee play in the cricket team?'

'No idea. What's cricket all about anyway?' Hakim's own mystified reaction had been the same.

'Do you know where? I mean where the employee lives?'
'Down here, I think. Malmö.'

'Do you sail this way often?'

Anita glanced up abruptly. The man spoke in English with a heavy accent. Russian, she presumed; she'd heard a lot of Russian voices since boarding the *Baltic Queen*.

They had left the harbour behind a couple of hours before. Anita had watched the fairytale battlements and spires of Tallinn slip out of view as the ferry went ever further out into the Gulf of Finland. Unlike the last voyage of the *Estonia*, the passage was smooth. She'd retreated to her cabin and showered and changed. She'd even put a short summer skirt on. It was one that Kevin was particularly fond of.

Before sailing, she'd spent the day doing the tourist route and had visited the City Museum, the Great Guild Hall, and one religious building to satisfy Kevin's curiosity – St. Olaf's Church, whose spire once made it the tallest structure in the world until a lightning strike cut it down to size in 1625. Drawn to the art and craft workshops in St. Catherine's Passageway, she'd picked up a colourful salt and pepper set as a token gift for Lasse and Jazmin (it would brighten up their kitchen if nothing else), and she'd found a small wooden horse for Leyla, which she hoped would be sturdy enough to resist the high jinks of a three year old.

What had brought her up short was stumbling across the memorial to those lost on the *Estonia*. On a grassy knoll just down from Fat Margaret's Tower and the city gates were two curved steel beams, about a hundred metres apart. One end of each beam was embedded in the ground, the other hung in mid-air. They reached towards each other, one from the top of the bank, the other from further down, but were never destined to meet. Anita wasn't sure what the sculpture was trying to symbolize; maybe it was the breaking apart of the ship, or the splitting of so many families. All she could discover was that it was called *The Broken Line* monument. Then suddenly, she saw something else which had her gasping for breath: etched on a plaque by the monument were the names of the dead. There it was – *Jens Ullman*. She sank to her haunches and gently ran her fingers over the raised lettering, dark against the grey granite, of her father's name. She was touching him again after all these years. Then she realized she was crying. The tears came out in an uncontrollable rush, and her body shook. All her suppressed feelings came welling up in those tears: the sense of loss, of unfairness, of loneliness. A yawning chasm within her that had always been there but she had never allowed herself to acknowledge. Why had it happened? Why to him? She was wallowing in self-pity, but she didn't care. So many others had suffered, too, but at this moment in time, it was only her loss. Then she realized that her public display of grief was attracting attention and she fled the scene, a handkerchief covering her embarrassment.

An hour later, she had returned, now composed. She noticed that someone had sprayed some graffiti in English on the monument: *Still Don't Care*. But she cared. Staring at the memorial, she realized how deeply she cared. She was going to find out the truth – it was the least she owed her father.

The man standing at the bar had a shock of silver hair. Despite the colour, Anita judged that he wasn't much older than herself. He was casually dressed in slacks and a light-green polo shirt. Normally, she wouldn't have noticed the watch, but after Iqbal Nawaz's murder, she was more aware. It looked pricey. She also had to admit that he was what she would describe as 'dishy' – someone younger, like Jazmin, would probably say 'fit'. He had a glint in his eye. He smiled in amusement as he waited for Anita's reply.

'No. My first time on board.'

'I find it a pleasant trip. Even more so if the company is good.' It was so long since she'd been chatted up that she didn't immediately pick up the signals. 'Can I freshen up your drink?' he asked, nodding at her nearly empty wine glass.

'Thank you.' Why not? This was rather nice.

He caught the attention of the barman. He was the type that instinctively did. 'Same again for the lady. And I'll have a vodka.'

The barman hurried off to carry out the order.

'I usually find out the name of a person who wants to buy me a drink before I allow them to do so.'

'Alexander. Though my friends call me Alex.'

The barman slid a fresh glass of red wine onto the bar in front of Anita.

'Thank you, Alex. My name's Anita.'

'I am so pleased to meet you, Anita.' He raised his neat vodka. '*Nostrovia!*'

'*Skål!*'

'Here's to an evening of possibilities.'

The most liberating thing about reaching fifty was that it had taken half a century to dawn on Anita that she didn't give a damn what people thought of her appearance. When she was younger, she hadn't really been aware of her beauty and her body until she'd fallen for Björn. He'd taught her so much in and out of the bedroom. He'd made her conscious of her physical presence and how other men viewed her. She realized that many found her sexy. At first, it was a flattering novelty. It could also be something of a curse; especially in her working life, when it became clear that some people – mainly men but not exclusively – were judging her on her looks and not on her ability. When Björn began chasing after his students and Anita had thrown him out, her self-confidence had taken a battering. Wasn't she sexy enough? Is that why Björn's eye had wandered? To cope with this vulnerability, she'd launched into a series of unsuitable relationships and one-night stands. If nothing else, she knew men wanted her. And thanks to Björn's guidance, she knew how to give them what they wanted. It turned out to be an unsatisfying way – with the odd exciting and pleasurable exception – to get back at her ex-husband. Once he'd moved to Uppsala, he wasn't even around to be jealous. Now, as far as she was concerned, she could look like a bag lady and she didn't give a fig. No, that wasn't quite true. She still wanted Kevin to fancy her. And she'd almost been disarmed by Alexander's attentions in the bar. They'd had a meal together afterwards, and she'd enjoyed his company. He was amusing and attentive, and he'd made it crystal clear how he hoped the evening would end. And for a few moments, she'd been tempted. What was the harm? One night. They'd never see each other again. But she'd resisted. Not because of guilt about being disloyal to Kevin (though she didn't kid herself that he wouldn't be upset if she told him), for there were no strings attached; he'd accepted that. In the end, she'd only allowed Alexander a parting kiss because the reason she was on this particular ship, taking this particular route, was in memory of her father. Nothing, including her own gratification, must get in the way of that.

The alarm on Anita's phone went off at ten to one. She hadn't really been asleep: more like dozing fitfully. She got up, dressed and, picking up the three red roses she'd bought in Tallinn, opened the cabin door. All was quiet except for the thrum of the ferry as it ploughed its way across the Baltic. She stepped outside. The sea breeze caught her hair, and she had to push it back into place. The sky was clear, and thousands of stars winked at her as though they knew what she was up to. Had the weather been as benign as this in September 1994, would her father have survived? Or were there other factors at work? She was beginning to believe that the tragedy *had* been engineered. The more she found out, the more she couldn't come to terms with the official explanation. Did the ferry hit a rogue submarine? Was there a bomb on board? Anita shivered.

She glanced at her watch in the light coming through the corridor window. It was a minute to one. Twenty-five years ago, this is when the first explosion or unnatural banging noises were heard. What had her father done? Was he asleep in his cabin with his friends? Had he had time to get out before it filled up with water? Or were they trapped in there, helpless, trying to force the door open above their heads? Not knowing was killing her. She prayed that his end had been quick. She leant against the barrier and watched the broiling bow wave created by the ferry. One by one, she threw the roses into the sea. Each one disappeared from sight before it reached the water.

'I love you, Daddy.'

Whether it was through the wind or the emotion, Anita had to wipe the moisture out of her eyes. She suddenly felt really down. Had she expected that this would be the cathartic moment which would allow her to move on and let her father go? If so, the gesture had failed.

CHAPTER 29

'I've an idea. Someone who might know a thing or two.'

Anita was sitting on the quayside in Slussen, looking over the water at Gamla Stan, the old centre of Stockholm. Opposite her was the imperious dark-red-brick City Hall with its iconic monumental tower. The ferry had docked mid-morning. Having given up any idea of sleep after returning to her cabin, she'd got up early and watched the sunrise, and then taken an early breakfast as the ship glided through the Stockholm Archipelago. The morning was still, the vista so serene. She'd forgotten how beautiful the islands were – hundreds of them randomly scattered along the coast; blobs of colour on the expanse of sea. The only signs of movement were the little ferries ploughing between them. What she had remembered were the houses – many painted in Falu red – perched on every available chunk of land and rock. They were predominantly holiday homes of well-to-do Stockholm folk, and Anita had always been envious of the cadets at the Police Academy who had family or friends with access to these pieces of paradise and who were able to join the weekend exodus.

Now that she'd booked into her room in a small hotel in Gamla Stan, she was ringing Kevin. She needed someone to confide in; someone to share the information she was unearthing. She outlined her conversations with both Martin Glimhall and Professor Kask in Tallinn. She told him about Glimhall's doubts raised by the official secrecy surrounding the site, and it was when she mentioned Kask's theories surrounding the Baltic Drainpipe and the possibility of the West buying arms and technology, that Kevin intervened. If that was the case, he reckoned you could bet your bottom dollar that the

CIA would be involved – and if they were, MI6 wouldn't be too far behind. At that time, they were working very closely together. Anita was quite willing to believe that Kevin had a better understanding of these things than she did.

'Peter Tallis. Used to work for MI6. Certainly around in the mid-nineties. I know he left the Service, but he must be traceable.'

'How do you know him?'

As a young cop in 1988, Kevin had been drafted in to babysit someone who had to be spirited out of London to Essex, where he was on the local force. Kevin and his handpicked colleagues had assumed it was witness protection, but it turned out to be a Russian defector whose life was in danger from a KGB hit. ('It was pre-Novichok, but they still had some pretty lethal stuff around then.') Tallis was in charge of the operation. Kevin got to know him and found him amusingly indiscreet. They stayed vaguely in touch for a while through a few heavy drinking sessions in London.

'Quite a womanizer, I remember, so I wouldn't let him anywhere near you. I'm not sure that he was ever stationed in Sweden, but I'm sure he might be able to put me onto someone who was.'

'Don't they take some sort of oath? Official secrets type thing?'

'I'm sure he broke the Official Secrets Act every time I met him. Terrible gossip. Look, I'm due some days off. Why don't I try and locate him? We've nothing to lose.'

'You don't have to.' Her protest was feeble.

'No problem. I'm here to help.' One of these days, she would have to stop taking advantage of Kevin.

'Thanks. I'm seeing an old colleague of Markus Jolis's tomorrow. Got his name from his son, Tord. He might be able to shed light on why Markus left Stockholm so quickly after the disaster.'

'You still think he was murdered, don't you?'

'Oh yes.'

There was the first real break in the case on Monday morning. Erlandsson had taken a call from a man called Doug Mitchell. He was an Australian living in Malmö. He'd been away in Italy on business and had only just returned. He played rugby at weekends at Limhamnsfältet, and he'd been down on the pitch, which was adjacent to the cricket field, on the evening of the murder. He'd been doing some kicking practice by himself and was about to head off, as the light would soon be fading. He noticed a man wearing a tracksuit entering the hut. Time? He wasn't exactly sure, though it wasn't long after ten. Did he see anybody else? Not that he was aware of. Did he see whether the man was unlocking the door or just opening it? He couldn't say. He was too far away.

The witness statement, taken at the polishus later, confirmed what the forensic evidence pointed to – that Iqbal Nawaz had been in the cricket hut that night. What they couldn't establish was whether he opened up the hut himself or someone had already done so and was waiting for him inside. Whoever it was, it wasn't Mohammad Abbas. When confronted by Hakim and Wallen with the CCTV footage, he'd admitted that he'd met Muneeba at the warehouse. The phone call had been, as Liv had surmised, to check the whereabouts of Muneeba's father. He had wanted to protect her honour. He assured them that nothing untoward had happened at the warehouse that night – not that either Hakim or Wallen cared one way or the other, as it wasn't relevant to the enquiry. However, it mattered greatly to Abbas. He outlined the opposition they'd faced from Muneeba's parents and the difficulty they had in continuing their relationship in a claustrophobic environment. He was also worried that he might lose his job if they had done anything rash. Being of immigrant stock, it would be hard to find another one if Iqbal kicked him out. He pleaded with them not to mention his relationship in front of Bismah. She could just as easily have him sacked.

Naturally, Alice Zetterberg hadn't been too pleased at the loss of her number one suspect. However, she would be in court Monday and Tuesday with the cold case that she was tying up, so she was prepared to give them a free hand while she was away. Wallen and Hakim found themselves virtually in charge of the case, and the first avenue they decided to pursue was Reza's titbit about Iqbal's dalliance with an employee's wife. It might solve the conundrum as to whom he might have been having sex with.

They wouldn't get anything out of Bismah, even if she suspected. She knew her place, and it would also involve saving face. The same applied to Muneeba. Abbas hadn't been helpful either – he thought it was unlikely that his boss would be capable of committing any impropriety. Even if he had, he was sure it wouldn't have been with the wife of anyone who worked at the warehouse. That left the shop in Mobilia and the head office in Lund. Mobilia was nearest.

Just like the first time Hakim had met Sarfraz Khan, the cricket team's star player appeared distinctly uncomfortable. In fact, he was positively nervous when he saw the two police officials walk into his shop.

Wallen came straight to the point.

'We've heard a rumour that your boss, Iqbal Nawaz, was having an affair with the wife of one of his employees.'

'That cannot possibly be true. He was a good man. He was a religious man.' As he spoke, he avoided eye contact. Hakim put it down to embarrassment talking about such a subject.

'So you don't believe such a rumour can be true?'

He shook his head almost violently.

There was little point in causing him further discomfort. They left, with Wallen observing that they might all be closing ranks to preserve the reputation of the man who had controlled their lives. Lund could wait until the next day.

They were strolling down the mall on the way back to the car park when Wallen's phone chimed into life. She took it out.

'It's headquarters,' she said with some perplexity. 'Klara Wallen here.'

They continued to walk as Wallen listened to the voice at the other end. Her expression changed from puzzlement to shock.

'Thanks for letting me know,' she said finally.

'What is it?' Hakim asked in some alarm.

CHAPTER 30

The pleasure boats that sailed to the Royal Palace at Drottningholm and the old Viking settlement at Birka sped away from their moorings, carrying their cargoes of eager tourists. Behind them, hordes of visitors milled around the piazza awaiting their turns to enter the Radhus, Stockholm's famous National Romanticist City Hall. To her shame, Anita had only ever been inside the Radhus once, but she did remember the grandeur of the interior and the wonderful mosaics in the Golden Hall; it was also the venue for the Nobel Prize banquet. She knew Kevin would love it – another one for the list. Over to the left, beyond the church towers of Gamla Stan, there was a large Viking Line ferry that ran daily from Stockholm to Helsinki.

Ulf Garde kept glancing around him as though he was expecting someone to suddenly appear. He'd turned down the chance to meet at Anita's hotel, or in a bar or café. Instead, he'd chosen one of the busiest spots in Stockholm, yet, evidently, he was still uncomfortable, his right leg constantly jerking up and down. His edgy demeanour was immediately apparent from the moment they'd sat down on a bench close to the water's edge.

'I'm not sure I should be speaking to you.'

'This is nothing official,' Anita said, trying to sound casual. 'As I said on the phone, I got your name from Tord Jolis. My interest is purely personal. My dad was on the *Estonia*. He didn't make it out.'

'And Markus's death?' It was as though he hadn't registered what Anita was saying.

'I was attached to the enquiry. It's closed now. I'm on holiday.'

He seemed relieved. 'I heard he attacked Nina.' Anita nodded. 'She was a nice lady.'

'Still is. She's making a recovery.'

'I'm pleased.'

Garde took a tin of snus out of his pocket and pushed a sachet under his lip.

'Were you on duty the day the *Estonia* was meant to come in?'

'Yes. We were all there. We were on full alert.'

'Full alert?'

'We'd had a tip-off from Tallinn that there was going to be a number of illegal immigrants being smuggled in in one of the trucks.'

'Was that typical?'

'A tip-off, no – that was unusual. Illegal immigrants, yes. It was nothing like the last few years, of course. Since the Arab Spring, numbers on the move have gone through the roof. You'll have noticed that down in Malmö at the Öresund Bridge. Back then, a number of the ones coming through Tallinn were the result of the First Gulf War. A lot of them were Iraqi Kurds. Then there were the Iranians, as well as a flood from the former Yugoslavia. Earlier that year, sixty-four Iraqi Kurds had been found in a container on board the *Estonia*. They were only discovered when one of the crew heard banging. They were lucky to be alive. We knew there was a general problem, as the ferry wasn't the only way into Sweden. There were other routes, other boats. It was certainly worth the smugglers' while. Some said the going rate at the time was at least ten thousand kronor per head. Could have been a lot more.'

'Why were they coming through Estonia?'

'The collapse of the Soviet Union. Well-armed gangs could transport them from the Middle East, mainly through the old territories where there was very little law and order, and chaos reigned. Drugs came that way, too. The Baltic States, and Estonia in particular, were ideal routes to the West and a better life for the poor buggers.'

'And do you know who was behind the tip-off?'

'We assumed it was a rival gang. We were never given details at our level.'

'If that tip-off was correct, there are even more bodies at the bottom of the Baltic.' Anita found it hard to fathom the agony that these people – if indeed they existed – must have gone through as they died trapped in a container or truck. 'Did the tip-off come through before the ferry left Tallinn?'

'I think so, though I'm not a hundred percent sure.'

Anita mused over the timings. They might be important.

'How do you think the ferry sank?'

For the first time, Garde seemed to relax.

'Well, it was the bow visor, wasn't it? Got torn off in the storm. Water gushes in, vessel tips over and down she goes.' She could tell by his eyes that he didn't believe a word of it.

'What about Markus Jolis?'

Garde sat up as though a volt had shot through his body.

'What about him?' he said defensively.

'Hey, don't worry. I'm just interested. I met him before he died. He had Alzheimer's so he wasn't making much sense.'

'Are you sure this isn't official?' he asked suspiciously.

'Honestly, I assure you the case is closed. Anyway, it was only open because of the attack on Nina.'

'Nothing else?'

'No. Why should there be?'

'No reason. No reason at all.' Something was bothering him. 'Obviously, we had to go into Jolis's background. We saw that he was transferred from Stockholm the week after the sinking. Do you know why that was?'

Again, Ulf Garde's eyes scanned his surroundings as though he was worried they might be overheard. He lowered his voice.

'It came out of the blue. One day he was with us, the next he was gone. Then we heard he'd been moved to Malmö. It was a bit strange, as his job here was a better one.'

'He didn't stay in the Swedish Customs that long. Six months.

Joined an outfit called Zander Security.'

'Doesn't surprise me. Better money, I'm sure. He was always keen on the cash was Markus. Never short of a krona or two.'

'Weren't you that well paid?'

He gave a mirthless laugh. 'You're a cop. You should know. Public servants. Course we weren't.'

'Where do you think he got his money?'

He patted his mouth as though checking that the snus was still in place.

'There were rumours.'

'What sort of rumours?'

'That he was on the take.'

'In what way?'

'Markus was often in charge. He could wave things through.'

'What things?'

'I don't know... drugs maybe. Other illegal items that found their way onto the ferry.'

'Weapons? Radioactive materials?'

He flapped his hand as though dismissing the subject.

'I've said enough.' He stood up, again glancing around at the crowds. 'We never had this conversation.'

Ulf Garde quickly disappeared amongst the selfie-snapping sightseers.

Anita remained seated. She ruminated upon what Garde had just told her. She had got to know Markus Jolis that little bit better. And maybe she was getting closer to why he had had to be silenced.

Further thoughts were put on hold when her mobile phone began to buzz. It was Klara Wallen. She wasn't expecting a call from her.

'Anita, hi.'

'Is everything OK?' Wallen's voice had sounded edgy.

'No. It's Moberg. Erik Moberg.'

'What about him?'

'He dropped dead this morning.'

CHAPTER 31

When Klara Wallen bumped into Zetterberg after her day in court and told her that Chief Inspector Erik Moberg had collapsed and died of a heart attack, it was no surprise that Zetterberg didn't show much sympathy for a team who'd lost their long-term boss. At least she'd refrained from making any derogatory observations about a man she clearly had little time for. Hakim and Brodd were hit the hardest. Hakim hadn't always been treated well by Moberg, but he'd learned to respect the chief inspector, and he'd almost been looking forward to the prospect of working under him again. It was more personal for Brodd. Moberg had been his only real social outlet. Both had needed each other in that regard – the bond of the after-work beer. Wallen and Erlandsson were more ambivalent. Neither had really been comfortable with Moberg, but they positively disliked Zetterberg. But now they knew that Zetterberg was moving on and someone fresh would be taking over. Nevertheless, despite the multifarious feelings among the team, the news had come as a real jolt, and Moberg was still very much on their minds the next morning when Wallen and Hakim drove out to Lund to speak to Usman Masood.

'I hear that you pulled Abbas in for questioning. Do you think he's responsible?'

Hakim and Wallen were sitting in Usman's office, the blinds pulled down because the sun was beating on the window. The air conditioning kept them cool.

'He's no longer a person of interest.'

'Really?' Usman's brow creased in astonishment.

'You seem surprised.'

'Well, thinking about it after you were last here, he appears to be the only person that I know who might have had a motive.'

'You're referring to his relationship with Muneeba? I can see where you're coming from,' agreed Wallen cordially. 'However, he has an alibi which checks out.'

Was that disappointment that flitted across Usman's face? Wallen had got the impression on her last visit that Usman didn't really like Abbas, despite referring to him as 'a first-class man'.

'Where are you looking next? I pray that it's someone un-connected with the company – or the cricket team.'

'Worried about the company's reputation?' Hakim asked.

'Naturally. Iqbal built up Happy Electricals from humble be-ginnings. He personally appointed everyone who works here, from head office staff and store managers down to drivers and stackers in the warehouses. He saw us as an extended family. And with a family comes loyalty. See what I'm saying? Of course I want to protect the company's reputation.'

'I appreciate that it would be a shock if someone from the company – or the cricket team – was found to be responsible for his murder.' Wallen chose her words carefully. 'Despite that, we have to look at those closest to him. And we have heard a rumour that Iqbal was having an affair with the wife of an employee.'

She was expecting the usual denial.

'Ah.' Usman began to swivel back and forth in his chair. 'I'm afraid there may be some truth in that.' Wallen and Hakim exchanged glances. 'Where did it come from, by the way? The rumour, that is.'

'I can't reveal the source,' said Hakim. 'What I can say is that it didn't come from within the company, so word has gone further afield.'

'Oh dear! I would hate Iqbal's name to be sullied, especially as he's not here to defend himself. I hope that this won't become general knowledge. Not just for Bismah and Muneeba's sakes but for all of us who loved him.'

'We can't promise anything if it turns out to be relevant to the case.'

'I don't see how it can be.'

'That's for us to judge. So can you tell us what you know about Iqbal's activities?'

Usman stopped swaying about and leant over his desk. He lowered his voice, though there was no chance that anybody outside the office could hear what he said.

'Sadly, it is true. I have no exact proof, though I suspect it has been going on for some time. In fact, I overheard him on the Friday before he died, here in the office, arranging to meet this person.'

'Where and when?' Hakim asked. He remembered that the last time Iqbal had called the unregistered number was the Friday before his death.

'Oh, I don't know that. I just walked into the middle of a conversation. When I realized it was of a personal nature, I left. Well, he waved me away irritably. I took the hint.'

'And who was he talking to?'

'Arrgh,' Usman said through gritted teeth. 'Do I really have to say?'

'Yes. It may have nothing to do with the murder, of course.' Wallen knew she was stretching the truth. Neither Usman nor anyone else outside the investigating team knew about the sex that had taken place in the hut that night.

'I'm sure it hasn't. I'm afraid to say it's Sidra. I don't blame Iqbal. She is a stunningly beautiful girl.' This was accompanied by a nervous laugh.

'And who's Sidra?' Wallen was on the edge of her seat, awaiting the answer.

'Sidra? Of course, you won't know, will you? She's our star batsman's wife.'

'Sarfraz Khan's?'

'Yes.'

In the car park outside the Happy Electricals headquarters, Wallen and Hakim stood next to the pool car. Wallen took off her jacket and

Hakim slipped on a pair of sunglasses. They were unaccustomed to the heat.

'That was very enlightening,' Hakim observed.

'Not half! If it *was* this Sidra that Iqbal met up with that night, that would explain what went on in the hut.'

'Get her prints and see if they appear on the chair.'

'And she would have access to a key.'

'Yeah, that's right. Sarfraz told me he kept his hut key at home.'

They opened the car doors to let some air in.

'It all fits in with the unaccounted-for phone calls, too. The last one was made on the Friday before he was killed so was probably the one Usman barged in on.' Wallen was now fanning herself with her notebook.

'We have Sidra meeting up with Iqbal for sex. That would explain him turning off his phone. Didn't want to be interrupted. What we have to piece together is what happened afterwards. A disagreement? Could she no longer be unfaithful to her husband?'

'Or was Iqbal dumping her and she couldn't take it?' Wallen said with some feeling.

'Whatever. She takes a cricket bat – though why she would go into Abbas's bag for one, I don't know – and creeps up behind Iqbal while he's turning his phone back on. He sounds like the type of man who wouldn't expect a mere woman to attack him.'

'Then she goes back to the hut, returns the bat and locks up. It all makes sense to me.'

'What should our next move be?'

Wallen patted the roof of the car. 'Ask her.'

The train sped through the flat Swedish countryside. Anita was one hour into her five-hour journey to Malmö. Next to her empty plastic coffee cup was her notebook. In it, she'd been trying to make sense of all she'd found out about the *Estonia* and the death of Markus Jolis. She was sure that they were somehow connected. But in what way? This she couldn't piece together. It was just too much of a coincidence that Jolis had been moved so quickly after the disaster. She knew from Ulf Garde that he had probably been on the take. It explained his money and lifestyle, which was way beyond the salary of a customs officer, however senior. If he was turning a blind eye to contraband coming through on the *Estonia*, who was paying him to do so? A Russian or Estonian gang? Or had it been her own government? Were *they* complicit, as Professor Kask had hinted, in allowing the flow of weapons and technology and God knows what else through to the West? And what about the fated ferry: the tip-off about the illegal immigrants? If it were true, who made it and who received it? Had it put the kibosh on whatever Jolis was going to let through that day?

As for the sinking itself... too many unanswered questions. It was hurting her brain, which was still addled after last night. She'd drunk too much. And her throat was rough and sore. On hearing the news about Erik Moberg, the first thing she'd done had been to buy a packet of twenty cigarettes and a lighter. She'd smoked the lot. She was paying for it now. The cigarettes had been her way of coping with the stress. The silly bastard! She knew deep down that he'd still been smoking, and he'd probably been drinking more than he'd admitted to. He was so close to coming back, and he'd ruined it. But who for? Initially, she'd convinced herself that he had done himself a disservice. He'd still had years ahead of him in the police. It was the thing he loved – it kept him going; it justified his existence. He'd thrown that away through lack of will power and self control.

It took a few drinks for her to confess that she was also upset about his death because of the effect it would have on her. She admitted that she resented the fact that his damn heart had been the cause of Zetterberg coming back and blighting her life – that was Moberg's fault. But latterly, she'd grown fond of him. Of course, it had helped that he wasn't around to drive her mad. But they were reaching an understanding. She'd missed him at work, and she'd looked forward to her occasional visits to his apartment. Now she couldn't imagine life without him.

Anita leant forward and flipped shut her notebook. That was another thing, she thought ruefully. Moberg would have let her dig further into the Markus Jolis business – he'd begun to trust her instincts; he'd encouraged her to go her own way. Now she really was alone.

CHAPTER 32

The home of Sarfraz and Sidra Khan was in a modest, flat-roofed, white terraced block in Kulladal. It was perfectly situated for Sarfraz, as it was a five-minute walk to the Mobilia shopping centre and his place of work. An ageing Ford was sandwiched between the property's outside shed and the one belonging to next door. Two large plastic bins stood on a gravelled area next to the postage-stamp-sized garden. Sprawled on its side in front of the door was a small bike; on the grass a deflated football and a faceless doll stuffed into an upturned beach bucket. Evidence of children.

The woman who answered the door, clutching a young girl in the crook of her arm, was instantly wary. She was caught off guard and was immediately conscious that her head wasn't covered. Confusion enveloped her undoubtedly beautiful face. Usman had been right about that. The deep dark eyes, the fresh smooth skin and the voluptuous mouth wouldn't have looked out of place on a Bollywood film set. It was those wonderful eyes that betrayed Sidra's panic.

'Police,' said Hakim, holding up his warrant card. Wallen had been quite happy for Hakim to take the lead. She reasoned that Sidra might respond better to a fellow Muslim. 'Do you speak Swedish?'

Sidra nodded.

'I'm Inspector Hakim Mirza and this is Inspector Klara Wallen. Can we come in?'

She spoke for the first time. 'My husband is at work.' Her free hand reached out for the handle to close the door.

Before she could shut them out, Hakim said 'Are you Sidra?'

Again, she nodded.

169

'It's you we've come to see.'

Sidra almost dropped the child she was holding. The little girl, sensing her mother's alarm, burst into tears. Using this as an excuse to ignore her callers, the agitated woman retreated from the doorway. Hakim and Wallen stepped into the house, but Sidra appeared determined that they wouldn't get any further than the hallway. They were greeted by the strong aroma of curry; it made Hakim hungry. They stood patiently while she calmed the child with some soothing words in Punjabi. It worked, and the little girl ceased crying and stared wide-eyed at the visitors. Sidra made no attempt to set her daughter down.

'How well did you know Iqbal Nawaz?' Hakim was scrutinizing the young woman, wondering how she would react to his questions.

'Not well. My husband works for him.' Her voice was soft and strangely hypnotic.

'Did he ever phone you?'

She shook her head.

'Are you sure?'

'I'm sure.' The child was losing interest in their visitors and was keen to escape; her mother turned away and stroked her head.

'Have you got a mobile phone?'

'I have.'

'Do you mind if we see?'

'Why?'

'Please.'

Sidra left them standing in the hall and returned a minute later, still holding her child; a mobile phone in her left hand. She handed it to Wallen. Wallen got out her own phone and punched in a number from a piece of paper she had in her pocket – the unidentified number that Iqbal had called. She and Hakim braced themselves, ready for Sidra's phone to go off. Nothing happened.

'It says the number is unobtainable.'

That's a pity, thought Hakim. Perhaps Sidra got rid of it after she'd killed Iqbal? A boy of about five suddenly popped his head round the living room door. Almost immediately, he disappeared again.

'I need to ask you where you were on the night of Monday, the 29th of July. It was the night that Iqbal Nawaz was murdered.'

She flinched. 'I was here.'

'Are you sure?'

'I was here,' she said with more determination.

'Can anybody vouch for you?'

'My husband was with me. Ask him.'

Hakim realized it would be difficult to prove she was down at Limhamnsfältet if her husband was going to alibi her. Maybe he needed to be more direct.

'Were you and Iqbal Nawaz having an affair?'

Her eyes widened in fury. 'Get out of my house!'

Hakim glanced at Wallen, and she nodded towards the door. They left without another word.

Alice Zetterberg was surprisingly upbeat at their Wednesday-morning meeting. Her time in court had been well spent, and she was on the verge of getting a conviction in her last cold case. It would increase her credibility. Though she'd lost Mohammad Abbas as a chief suspect, she was pleased with the work that the team had done in coming up with another very plausible candidate. As she said to them, it was just a case of breaking Sidra's story and they were a hop, skip and jump away from a successful conclusion. She was all for letting Wallen and Hakim continue to the next stage by talking to Sarfraz and putting pressure on him to break his wife's alibi. What she suggested was to put the frighteners on Sidra by bringing her in to the polishus for fingerprinting.

It turned out to be the most cordial meeting with Zetterberg that any of the team could remember. Bea Erlandsson put it down to her being demob happy. They'd also noted that Zetterberg didn't make one reference to Erik Moberg's death. Nor had she indicated if she knew who would be succeeding her. The reason was that she probably didn't care about either circumstance.

While Wallen and Hakim headed off to Mobilia to speak again to Sarfraz, Erlandsson and Brodd were dispatched to Kulladal to get Sidra's prints. Wallen had thought that as children were involved, it was best not to drag her into headquarters. If they found that the prints matched those on the seat from the hut, Wallen was confident that she would have to come clean. It was up to Hakim and herself to shatter her story.

This time, they interviewed Sarfraz in the little office at the back of the store. He'd been on a landline in there when they arrived and he was unable to escape its confines. It was clear that he was fearful, and the narrowness of the room only exacerbated the sense of being trapped. This is how they wanted him. They knew he would have had time to talk to his wife last night. Had she mentioned their visit? If she had, had she been honest with him about her relationship with Iqbal? Or did he already know? As they drove down to Mobilia, Hakim had voiced a further thought that had struck him – if Sarfraz had discovered the affair, was it possible that he'd followed Sidra to her rendezvous and then, in a fit of jealousy, attacked his boss?

'We talked to your wife yesterday,' Wallen began.

Sarfraz couldn't stop fidgeting in his seat. 'I know. You shouldn't be talking to her. It's not right.'

'Where were you on the night that Iqbal Nawaz was killed?'

'I was at home.'

'And was your wife there?'

'That's her place. It is our home.'

'Yes or no?'

'Yes, she was.'

'Are you sure?'

'I am sure!' The first hint of anger.

'You know, we've been told that Sidra was having an affair with Iqbal, and we think they were together the night he was murdered.'

'No, no!' Sarfraz was on the verge of tears. 'Don't say such a thing.'

'And what about you?' said Hakim, taking his turn. 'Did you go down to the cricket hut that night? Follow your wife?'

'I don't know what you're talking about. I was in my house all night. It's the truth.'

'At this moment, we have two detectives visiting Sidra to take her fingerprints.' This really hit home, and Sarfraz's anxiety was fast turning to terror. 'We might be able to prove she was in the hut that night.'

'She wasn't there! Please, please leave us alone. We're good people.'

Wallen and Hakim took advantage of Mobilia and treated themselves to a coffee at one of the mall's cafés. Wallen paid.

'We haven't broken Sidra's alibi, but Sarfraz is seriously rattled,' Wallen contended while wiping away flecks of *caffè latte* from the side of her mouth.

'That's an understatement. I'm sure he's lying. Or covering up.'

'Covering up for his wife?'

Hakim blew out his cheeks. 'Could be. The results of the prints will be interesting. But I'm not sure if the affair is what this is all about.'

'Come on! You're the one who suggested that Sarfraz might be our killer. And we've got good reason to think so if Sidra was carrying on with Iqbal. Boss or no, a cuckolded husband might not be responsible for his actions. And Sarfraz is the best player in the cricket team so would certainly have the skill and the strength to land the fatal blows. More so than Sidra, however angry she may have been. I really think you're onto something there.'

'Hmm... but you know... the guy we just talked to is a nervous wreck. Nor was he comfortable the first time I talked to him. There's something nagging...'

'Of course he's a wreck. His wife was having an affair with the victim. Either *she* killed Iqbal, or *he* did. Either way, he knows the truth, and it's getting to him. Can't handle the guilt.'

'Probably. Oh, I don't know! It's just that thing he said: "We're good people.". Don't you think it's an odd thing to say?'

Wallen picked up her cup. 'Don't overthink things, Hakim. We're on the verge of solving this.'

Liv wheeled herself onto the grass and got into a position where she could look across the park. Hakim sat on the ground next to her and pulled out two Tupperware boxes. They contained their homemade lunch – humus and a selection of salads, with some olives on the side. He produced two plastic forks and handed one to Liv along with her box. They sat in silence as they concentrated on their food and took in the sights and sounds around them. It was just good to be out of the polishus, even if it *was* just across the road.

Liv finished first. Hakim was always surprised at how quickly she ate. The only thing that ever slowed her down was nattering.

'Klara seems pretty sure that either Sidra or Sarfraz Khan is our killer.'

'Well, that depends on what forensics come up with.' He popped an olive into his mouth. 'They're checking Sidra's prints against what they found on the chair in the hut. Should hear tomorrow.'

'Do either of the Khans seem the type?' Liv unscrewed a new bottle of water.

'You never know with murderers. On the face of it, no. Given the circumstances though, anybody can be pushed into something that's against their nature. There's certainly something going on. When we go back, can you do some checking on them, particularly Sarfraz? His background: where he was born, parents, time in Sweden, when he started at Happy Electricals, financial info. The usual stuff. Anything you can find out. He's frightened of something.'

'I should imagine being done for murder or worried for his wife in case she is would frighten anybody. Oh, I had Anita on the phone today.'

'Did you?' Hakim's fork was spearing the last of his lunch. 'She'll be upset about Moberg.'

'Yeah, she is. That's not why she was calling, though. Wanted me to send her a link to the passenger lists for the *Estonia* the week it went down. Not for when it actually sank but for the days before. Wanted to trace her father's last trip, I suppose.'

'Did she say how she was getting on?'

'Not really. She's thinking of going off to the UK soon.'

'That'll be to see Kevin. Uh oh, I've just thought of something. Should we have invited him to the wedding?'

'Found him!' Kevin sounded exuberant.

Anita wanted a bit of good news. After hearing about Moberg, she felt she was just floundering. Even an evening with Lasse, Jazmin and Leyla hadn't raised her spirits. She even got to the stage of thinking that all her digging had just been a waste of time and was simply fuelling her sense of loss. It was a ridiculous thing to be doing. She should be concentrating more on the here and now. She was lucky to have a family to love and support. It was the living that were important. However, such arguments did little to assuage her angst, and she'd still put in a call to Liv that morning for some help.

'Where?'

'London. Chelsea, to be exact. You won't believe what he is now!'

'Probably not.'

'Have a guess.'

Anita wasn't really up for this game. 'Banker?'

'No.'

'Oh, I don't know... florist?'

'No. A vicar!' Incongruous to say the least. Was it to atone for sins committed when he was in MI6? 'Look, I'm getting an early train down tomorrow, and I'll have a chat. Nothing to lose.'

'If you're sure.'

'Anything specific you want me to ask?'

Anita thought for a moment. 'I'd like to know if various governments were unofficially involved in the illicit trade coming through Tallinn. It might give me an idea who Markus Jolis was working for and who might have wanted him dead. I think he'd suddenly become a loose cannon. A man with dementia attempts to kill his wife. The police get involved. They – whoever *they* are – send in a supposed lawyer when I'm interviewing him. Jolis suddenly comes out with "It shouldn't have happened!" and then "He was wrong.". The more I think about it, the more I believe those words sealed his fate. Next thing we know, he's dead after a visit by a mysterious doctor. Quick cremation – bam! Case closed down. Everything cleared up. All too neat.'

CHAPTER 33

'It's a match!'

Wallen came into Hakim's office, brandishing a piece of paper.

'Sidra's prints?'

'Yep. Well, her palm prints are on the plastic arms of the chair in the hut. She must have sat on him as Eva Thulin described.'

'Right. We'd better have another word with her. She'll have a job denying this one.' Then he thought for a moment. 'Unless she'd been down to watch a match and happened to move or sit in that chair. It's possible.'

'We can easily check whether she's been at the ground recently.'

'What about Sarfraz? His potential involvement?'

'Let's deal with her first. One may lead to the other.' Wallen checked her watch. 'Head off in fifteen?'

'OK.'

Wallen was about to exit the room when her way was blocked by Liv.

'Sorry, Liv, we're just about to go out.'

'I think you'd better hear this first, Klara.'

Wallen stepped back and let Liv wheel her way into the office. Hakim shot her a quizzical look. Liv addressed Wallen.

'Hakim asked me to do some digging into Sarfraz Khan's past.'

'And?'

'He hasn't got one.' Liv waited while she let this little nugget sink in. 'But he must have,' protested Hakim.

'Nope. Absolutely nothing. Officially doesn't exist. He's not registered anywhere. Tax office has no record. There's no record of parents, or when he came to this country. Zilch.'

'That's impossible,' said Wallen, shaking her head in bewilderment. 'Presumably, Happy Electricals pays him. He's got a house. He must pay something for that even if it's rent.'

'The house in Kulladal is in Sidra's name. And he hasn't got a bank account. But Sidra has. I haven't got access to the Happy Electricals payroll, but monthly payments from the company go into *her* account. I assume that's *his* salary, unless they're paying him cash, though I can't believe *that* in our virtually cashless society.'

Wallen sat down. 'That's extraordinary!'

Hakim leant over his desk. 'Were there any other regular payments to Sidra's account?'

'No,' Liv confirmed.

'Right. I just thought that she might get something for services rendered to Iqbal.'

'That might have come in the form of the house. It was bought as a *bostadsrätt*: half rent, half mortgage. She suddenly settled the mortgage they owed seven months ago.'

'Interesting,' Hakim mused. 'I wonder when Iqbal's calls to the unidentified phone started.'

'I'm ahead of you there. The first call was within a week of the repayment.'

Wallen was impressed. 'Good work, Liv. Right, Hakim, I think we'd better go and talk to the Khans. We'll start with Sidra. Maybe she can tell us why her husband doesn't officially exist.'

Kevin got off the tube at Gloucester Road and began his walk through the leafy streets of Chelsea. Passing brick and white-stuccoed mews cottages snuggling in characterful side streets, and rows of grand Georgian houses, many now converted into offices or flats, he cogitated on the eye-watering prices such homes would fetch on the property market. Only the super rich lived round here.

St. Thomas's church was typically Victorian: stone-built, strong and substantial with a high pitched roof and an impressive bell tower. It was set back from the road and was surrounded by a small graveyard.

Most of the gravestones had been moved for easy maintenance and were now resting against the boundary wall. Despite its position in the heart of London, sandwiched between two rows of five-storey town houses, there was a sense of tranquility about it – there was little traffic on the road, and in the gated gardens opposite, which obviously belonged to the houses, trees rustled in the wind and birds twittered in their branches.

As soon as Kevin entered the church, there was an immediate hush. The constant background noise of a normal London working day was severed. The stress of the streets melted away into a world of cloistered calm. He wandered down the nave, taking in his surroundings. The vaulted ceiling was so high that the altar and pulpit were Lilliputian in comparison. Also impressive was the massive stained-glass east window. The sun was streaming through it, giving animation to its colourful biblical characters.

Close to the altar, a man in a black clerical shirt and white dog collar was putting out books in the choir stalls. Kevin knew him straight away. The garb may have been distinctly different, but the chiselled face hadn't changed – square jaw, firm mouth, and blue, deep-set eyes. All were instantly recognizable – except for the florid complexion, no doubt testament to his previous bacchanalian lifestyle. The light-brown hair was thinner and the colour was fading into tufts of grey, though the smile – which he liked to call rakish – was just as bright. He obviously didn't recognize Kevin at first – he thought him another punter to add to his diminishing flock.

'Peter,' said Kevin as he approached Tallis.

'I'm afraid you have the advantage of me.'

'You don't remember. Take yourself back to 1988. An ex-KGB agent – defector – whom you were babysitting. You thought the Russians were onto him. Might be trying to kill him. Pre-Novichok but after the Markov poisoned umbrella killing. You whisked him out of London to a safe house in Chelmsford. You figured no one in their right mind, especially the Ruskies, would think of looking there. I was a young...'

Tallis clicked his fingers.

'Young Ash. Kevin Ash.'

'That's me.'

Tallis grabbed his hand and shook it warmly.

'How are you, old chap? Lovely to see you. Slightly different surroundings, of course. And the local pubs are smarter than the ones I remember us frequenting down in Essex. When was the last time we had a few snorters?'

'Think it was probably around the mid-nineties.' Kevin looked around him. 'Nice church.'

'Early Victorian. Grand without being over the top. Took a bit of a battering during the Blitz. The east window is fifties; the original blown out in '41. Not as much damage as old Angus's church over at Pont Street, though. That had to be completely rebuilt. Sorry, Kevin, please, take a pew.'

Kevin remembered that Tallis talked a lot; always going off at tangents. He thought it might be a ruse to put people off their guard. He sat down on the wooden bench. Victorians didn't believe in comfort – the mind should be concentrated on higher things.

'You're the last person I'd have thought of finding God. If I remember rightly, you were rather fond of the good things in life.'

'Past sins, old boy. Dark deeds. Did a lot of them in the Service. Penance, I suppose you'd call this. Time to settle down and make amends. Instead of trying to read people's minds for the evil therein, I look into their souls to find the good instead.'

'Not that your conscience has sent you to a deprived inner-city parish,' Kevin observed wryly.

'Chelsea's inner-city. Just a tad posher than say... Brixton. People still have to grapple with the same emotional and spiritual problems, however well-heeled they may be. And they do give awfully good drinks parties. All for good causes, naturally.'

'Naturally.'

'But you've been up to your old tricks, I hear. Rather ruffled a few feathers at the Met.'

'Got me suspended from the Cumbria Constabulary for my trouble. All sorted now. Anyway, how did you know?'

'I may not be in the Service any more, but I still keep my ear to the ground. I still have contacts in Legoland.' Tallis was referring to the modern MI6 headquarters on the South Bank of the Thames. This was what Kevin wanted to hear.

'That might be useful.'

'Useful? What are you up to, young Ash?'

'What do you know about the sinking of the *Estonia*? The Baltic ferry. 1994.' Kevin caught a hint of recognition in Peter's eye.

'Why do you ask? Can it really be the official business of the Cumbria Constabulary?' His eyes twinkled in amusement.

'Not exactly. I've got a friend... her father died in the disaster.'

'Estonian?'

'No, Swedish.'

'Is she a beautiful blonde? I always had a soft spot for Scandinavian girls.'

Kevin laughed. 'The collar's changed, but you haven't. Better not let your bishop find out. She *is* actually blonde – and beautiful.'

'I wasn't in Scandinavia at the time, but I knew about it. I don't think it's wise to meddle. Murky waters, my friend.'

'Is that a warning?'

'Might be. Besides, there is such a thing as the Official Secrets Act.'

'Come on, Peter. Even when I knew you, you weren't exactly discreet.'

'So, what are you after?'

'Not sure really. Anita... that's my friend... has been trying to find out what happened to her father. Obviously, he drowned. She wants to know why. She's been on a journey – both literally and emotionally – to find out more. She's gone into the background and the various theories as to why the boat sank. Collisions, bombs, smuggling of every variety: the lot. However, what has intrigued her most was how the whole aftermath got very political. But she's drawn a blank in Sweden. She believes that maybe other sources outside Sweden might be more likely to enlighten her. Secret sources. Let's say MI6 for example. Of course, being a simple copper, I didn't think I knew anyone in those elevated upper echelons—'

'Tautology, my dear old thing.'

'You see. Proves my point. I didn't go to the right school. And then I remembered this charming operative I'd come across many moons ago who was great company...'

'And indiscreet?'

'Accommodating.'

'And she's turned to you because you're a policeman?'

'That's not the reason. She's a detective herself over in Malmö. What kick-started her on all this was a case she was involved with. Someone died who had a connection to the *Estonia*.'

It was an indulgent smile that Tallis directed at Kevin: a teacher humouring a favourite pupil.

'I'd probably come up against a brick wall.'

Kevin took out his wallet and produced the photograph of Anita he always carried around. It was well-thumbed.

'You would be doing it for her.'

Tallis's eyes flickered appreciatively.

'I can see why you're so willing to do this lady's bidding. I will make a call. But don't hold your breath. MI6 aren't answerable to me – or to God, more's the pity.'

Sidra wasn't in when they called. Wallen and Hakim had taken a female officer with them in case the children needed to be looked after while they interviewed their mother. They waited in the narrow street for about half an hour before Sidra appeared round the corner, pushing a buggy with one hand and holding her son's hand with the other. She was startled when Wallen and Hakim stepped out of the car.

'I'm afraid we need to talk,' Wallen announced. There was a look of resignation on Sidra's face as though she'd been expecting them back.

Sidra, accompanied by the female officer, took the children into the house. Wallen waited for her to come back out and they both got into the front of the car, Hakim hovering over them in the back.

'When was the last time you went to watch your husband play cricket?'

She half turned to Hakim. 'Erm... I don't know.'

'Two weeks ago? Three weeks? A month?'

'I think it may have been June. Near the beginning of the season. Sarfraz is not happy for us to go. It makes him nervous when he's batting. He thinks if he doesn't score many runs in front of us, he is letting his family down.'

'Isn't that strange?'

'Not to him. He is a man of honour.'

'What about you?' came in Wallen. 'Are you a woman of honour?'

Sidra's gaze was now firmly fixed on the windscreen and the street beyond. She didn't answer.

'We found your palm prints on a chair in the cricket hut. The same chair that was used for sex the night of the murder. Can you explain how they got there?'

'No, I can't.'

'You can't explain or you won't explain?'

'I can't tell you.' Was this the nearest they were going to get to an admission? wondered Hakim.

Wallen tried another tack.

'Your husband. We can't find him.' Sidra instantly looked alarmed. 'Don't worry, he's not physically missing; he's officially missing. We have no record of him.' This didn't seem to come as a surprise to Sidra.

'How long have you been married?'

'Six years.'

'Do you know where he was born?'

'Pakistan.'

'And when did he come to Sweden?'

'When he was young. About three or four, I think.'

'Are his parents still alive?'

'No. They were both dead by the time I met him.'

'Was your marriage arranged?'

'Of course it was.' Judging by her tone, any other way would have been unthinkable.

'So, who agreed the match?' Hakim asked as one who was about to buck the Muslim marriage system.

'My parents... and Iqbal Nawaz.'

'Iqbal Nawaz? Why him?'

'Because Sarfraz had no family and he was working for Happy Electricals. The company was like his family; Iqbal, his father. He was always good to Sarfraz.'

'The star player in his team.'

'He was very supportive of Sarfraz's cricket.'

It was starting to get stuffy in the car, and Wallen cracked open a window.

'Does your husband's pay go into your bank account?' Sidra, still looking straight ahead, nodded. 'Why hasn't *he* got an account?'

'Sarfraz doesn't trust banks.' It sounded like the first thing that came into her head.

'But his salary goes into your bank account.'

'Happy Electricals wanted it that way. It was something to do with tax. That is what they said.'

'The house here. It's in your name. Are you saying that's also because Sarfraz doesn't trust banks?'

'It was just easier.'

'And you paid off the mortgage seven months ago. How did you do that?'

She didn't answer immediately. Then she said 'My father died. I have no brothers, so he left me some money. I used that.' If that were true, then Hakim's mortgage-paid-off-for-sex theory was well wrong.

'OK, Sidra. You can go and see to your kids now.'

Sidra's relief was palpable. They watched her hurry into the house.

'Believe her?' Wallen asked.

'Difficult to say. Not trusting banks was rubbish. No one trusts banks, but they're a necessary evil. As for the salary payments, I think we'd better tip off the tax people. Sounds like Happy Electricals are doing something iffy there. Of course, she might be right about her father leaving her money. I'll get Liv to check that out.'

'We're not going to get her to confess she had sex with Iqbal in the hut that night. Her prints alone aren't enough. Prosecutor Blom won't let us arrest her until we have further proof. We need more conclusive evidence that places her at the scene.'

The female officer came out of the house. Hakim got out of the back of the car and slipped into the passenger seat.

'What about Sarfraz? Shall we go and talk to him?'

'No,' said Wallen, turning on the ignition. 'Let them sweat. She's going to tell him that we know about his background, or lack of. And that we've matched her prints to the hut. They'll have a lot to think about. Soften them up. They'll crack soon enough, and then we'll be able to give Zetterberg the leaving present she so desperately wants.'

Anita sat at the kitchen table with her laptop open in front of her, a glass of red wine and a bowl of peanuts at hand. Since returning from her Tallinn/Stockholm trip, she had been in a contemplative mood. She'd learned a great deal, yet that knowledge didn't seem to be getting her any nearer the truth. Submarines, bombs, criminal gangs, disappearing radioactive waste, illegal immigrants, venal banks, a disintegrating Soviet Union, a newly independent country struggling to establish itself, and a flawed maritime inquiry into a ferry sinking – it was difficult to know what was relevant and what wasn't. She'd also had a call earlier from Kevin to say that he'd located his old MI6 contact. Peter Tallis had had no information, though he had been persuaded to talk to some of his ex-colleagues still working for the Service. Would that just further complicate matters?

Furthermore, Anita still wasn't sure how this plethora of data would help her solve the mystery of Markus Jolis. She was still convinced he was killed unlawfully. If he was waving contraband through customs, he was clearly corrupt. That would explain the money but not who was paying him. Then there was his sudden move after the sinking. Who was responsible for that? Was it the result of the *Estonia* going down, or something connected to the smuggling racket? She took a sip of her wine. It was all doing her head in.

OK, she would forget about Jolis for the time being. On screen, she had the passenger lists for the *Estonia*, which Liv had sent her. There was no real reason for looking through them other than that she wanted to establish when her father had actually sailed *to* Tallinn. That detail had got lost in the horror of the sinking and the realization that she had lost her beloved dad. Back then, she hadn't been sure of the timing of his trip because it had been a last-minute decision. Now, she just wanted to know. It was as though things didn't quite fit together without that information. The *Estonia* had left Stockholm on September 22nd – the Thursday before, but she couldn't find her father's name on that list. The next sailing was two days later: the Saturday. That would have given him nearly three days in Tallinn. She scrolled through the names and, with sudden goosebumps, there he was: Jens Ullman. It was there in black and white. It brought a lump to her throat. She exhaled heavily – why was she putting herself through this? Alongside her father were the names of David Josefsson and Sven Kallenberg, his friends on the trip. She had known Sven and had attended his memorial service. It had been a kind of substitute ceremony for the one her father didn't have. As Jens had been a life-long atheist, her mother wouldn't countenance a service of remembrance, and Anita went along with that. She could see that even though they were divorced, it would have been an acknowledgement that he was never coming back. Anita's mother had spent the rest of her life struggling with a bizarre dichotomy: bitterness at the break up of her marriage to Jens and a denial that he was actually dead.

Anita couldn't bring herself to open up the passenger list for the night of the tragedy. That would be too much. She was about to exit the page when she suddenly stopped herself. She had to look twice to make sure she hadn't misread what was in front of her. But there it was, further down the list, a name she knew. She was stunned.

What was Iqbal Nawaz doing on the ferry bound for Tallinn?

CHAPTER 34

Sofie Sorensen liked this time of the morning. It was nearly half past five and it was ideal for walking her dog. Jolly was a young, boisterous German shepherd, who had free rein to bound around before most of Malmö stirred. Sofie and Jolly had the canal walk to themselves. This had become Sofie's daily routine since her husband had badgered her into getting a dog. When she'd reluctantly given in, it was Sofie who'd ended up looking after the animal. It was Sofie who fed her and kept her clean, and it was Sofie who got out of bed to give her the exercise she didn't get in their apartment. Winter could be hard, but summer mornings like this one were perfect. The early hour was dictated by her job; every weekday she still commuted back to her native Copenhagen. Of course, her husband was still in bed. Once, she would have resented the situation but now she didn't. She'd become inordinately fond of Jolly and couldn't imagine life without her.

Sofie's route was a pleasant one since they'd tidied up and landscaped this section of the canalside. It was a narrow stretch squeezed between the water and the railway tracks that spewed out from the Central Station. Surrounding her was Malmö – old and new. To her left, elegant early 19th-century apartment buildings with the church spire of Sankt Petri peeping up behind them; ahead, the modern blocks of the Malmö Live complex.

She was lost in her own thoughts when she was abruptly torn away from them by Jolly's rough barking. Her immediate reaction was to shout at her to shut up. She was conscious that the sounds would reverberate across the canal to those still asleep in the apartments on the other side. Jolly must have smelt something interesting that had got her going. Except that she wasn't sniffing the ground but was standing rigidly at the water's edge. Sofie rushed over to quieten the hound, who was totally ignoring her commands. Then she saw what the dog had spotted. Something was floating in the canal. Sofie gasped and took an involuntary step backwards. Her brain reeled as she realized she was looking at a body.

'How was Tallinn?' Hakim asked.

'It was good,' said Anita distractedly. She'd had the whole night to mull over finding Iqbal Nawaz's name on the *Estonia* passenger list. Was it simply an extraordinary coincidence or did it actually indicate that she was missing something? What it did do was perhaps provide a link between Iqbal and Markus Jolis. She had wrestled with possible reasons as to why Iqbal had gone to Tallinn. He was unlikely to have been on a jaunt like her father and his friends. Business made more obvious sense. Given that she now knew the sort of things that were coming out of Estonia at that time, maybe he was buying up cheap Russian electrical goods and flogging them back in Sweden. Had that been the secret of his successful growth? The timing certainly coincided with his transformation from itinerant market-stall holder to multiple-shop owner. But did Iqbal's nefarious dealings tie him in with Markus Jolis, who appeared to have been swimming with bigger fish at the time? Whatever, she thought she would at least pass on the information to Hakim.

'Any clearer as to why the ferry went down?'

'Not really. The more I find out, the less I seem to know what really happened. The whole world has a theory, and they're all different. However, that's not why I'm calling you. It may have no significance with regard to your ongoing case, but I discovered that Iqbal Nawaz took the same ferry over to Tallinn as my father.'

'What was *he* doing in Tallinn?'

'No idea, though he could have been buying up ex-Soviet stock for his shops. There was a lot of that sort of thing going on then. Just thought I'd flag it up. All I'm saying is that Iqbal's murder might not be connected to the cricket club. There might be a business angle to it.'

'I think that's a red herring. We're pretty sure who's involved.'

Anita was naturally inquisitive. 'So, are you going to tell me?'

'Well, we believe that the woman Iqbal was having sex with that night was Sidra, Sarfraz Khan's wife. The Mobilia shop manager. We found her palm prints on the chair. And if she *was* at the hut, his alibi for her is out of the window because he says they were at home together. And interestingly, Liv discovered that Sidra's husband doesn't have an official past. No records. He doesn't exist. Anyway, we think that either she killed Iqbal after sex or her jealous husband was waiting outside and smashed him with the bat. He's the best in the team, so his aim would have been good. Jealousy is a very strong motive. But we'll find out. Wallen is just waiting for one of them to crack.'

Kevin was sitting at a wooden table in a pub garden when the call came through. He put down his cool pint and picked up his phone.

'Hello, Kevin, old chap.'

'Good of you to ring, Peter.'

'As I thought, I'm afraid. Nothing doing. I don't think they were very pleased that I was even asking. The *Estonia* must still be off limits. I have no idea why. It was a long time ago. However, places such as Legoland like to hang on to their secrets, even if it is just for the pleasure of infuriating the rest of us. Sorry.'

Well, it had been a long shot, Kevin reflected. It wouldn't help Anita though.

'Don't worry, Peter. It was good of you to try. Hope it didn't compromise any of your old contacts.'

'Talking of old contacts. I did have a thought. There *is* someone who might be worth talking to. There's a rather smashing lady called Annie Hagen. A Yank. She's ex-CIA. Now I'm pretty sure she was in Stockholm around the time of your sinking ferry. We came across each other in Delhi in the late eighties. Just after I met you, actually. That was my next posting. The lucky girl became a member of Peter's Pushovers.'

'Bloody hell, Peter, you even have a collective noun for them all!'

'It was a youthful peccadillo.' Kevin doubted that – the membership was probably still rising.

'So we'll have to cross the pond to see this woman.' A trip to America suddenly appealed.

'Oh, no. She's over here. In Oxford. She's an academic these days. She'll be teaching some rot to do with the US.'

'That's convenient. I can easily get Anita over here.'

'Look, I'll find out what her number is and text you. But go carefully. If I were you, I would use a pretext to visit her. If she thinks it's old CIA business, she might not be very forthcoming. Never spook a spook.'

'That's brilliant, Peter. I owe you one.'

'You could go to church occasionally. Do your soul good, young Ash.'

'We must meet up for a drink when I'm around your neck of the woods again.'

'What a good idea! And you might think about bringing along that scrumptious Swedish detective.'

Kevin blinked into the sunshine and finished his beer. His phone pinged. It was Annie Hagen's number from Peter. If this was an actual case, he would regard this as a lead. He rang Anita.

As they couldn't find Zetterberg, Klara Wallen chaired the meeting. She and Hakim took Brodd and Erlandsson through what had transpired yesterday. Their attention was firmly focused on the Khans, and Hakim didn't bother to mention his call from Anita. There was evidence – albeit flimsy at the moment – that Sidra was the person with whom Iqbal had had sex in the cricket hut on the night of the murder. That led to two possible scenarios. Either Sidra had killed Iqbal after their encounter – and cleared up afterwards and locked the hut – or her cuckolded husband was waiting for them to emerge and did the deed himself. In both scenarios, Sidra must have been present.

'Why don't we just go and bring them in and sweat a confession out of them?' suggested Brodd.

'We can hardly do that,' explained Wallen. 'Prosecutor Blom wouldn't let us, for starters. We haven't got enough on them. And Zetterberg would have to have her say, too.'

'Which one is the weakest link?' Erlandsson asked.

Wallen and Hakim exchanged glances.

'I'd say Sarfraz is the more nervous of the two,' conceded Hakim.

'Concentrate on him, then,' Erlandsson suggested.

'He's got a lot of questions to answer as it is,' Wallen agreed. 'Like who the hell is he?'

Brodd accompanied Hakim to Sarfraz's shop in Mobilia. Wallen reckoned that the sight of two tall police detectives might help intimidate the smaller man. It might work as long as Brodd kept his mouth shut and Hakim did the talking.

Friday was a busy day in the shopping centre, and Hakim and Brodd had to wend their way through the crowds. It was still 'SALE' time, and there was plenty of enthusiasm about for a bargain. When they entered the Happy Electricals outlet, they were greeted by a beaming assistant.

'How can I help you today? We have some very good offers at the moment that will be gone after the weekend, so now is the time to buy. May I suggest—'

Brodd flashing his warrant card put an immediate stop to the sales spiel.

'We're here to see Sarfraz Khan,' said Hakim.

The young man gave an apologetic grin. 'I'm afraid Sarfraz isn't here today.'

'Do you know where he is?'

'When I say he's not here today, I mean that he was supposed to be here. He comes in early and opens up. It's just that he didn't come in this morning.'

'Does that happen often?'

'Oh, no! I've never known him to miss a day's work. Well, not since I started here, and that's a couple of years ago.'

'Do you think he's ill?'

'Probably, but he hasn't rung in sick. That's the usual procedure. Mind you, he's the store boss.'

Outside in the mall, Brodd turned to Hakim. 'Sounds as though he's done a runner.'

'Are you sure?'

This was a call from Stockholm that he hadn't wanted to take. If the man was calling again, it was bound to be bad news.

'MI6 alerted us. Some retired spook has been on to them. Asking questions about you know what. He was stonewalled.'

'Why was he asking?'

'It must have been for someone else because he wasn't stationed in Stockholm at the time. We suspect it's something to do with our original problem in Malmö.'

'I thought you'd got someone to sort that out.'

'We had. Just that she appears to have gone rogue. Turning it into a bloody crusade. We've done some quick checking, and she took a flight to Tallinn last week. Then a ferry to Stockholm at the weekend. Don't know if she saw anyone significant in either city, as she wasn't under surveillance.'

'Christ! This has got to be stopped!'

'I'll see if I can put pressure on at this end. Rein her in. If that doesn't work, the best way is to cut off the sources of information. She'll soon end up in an impasse. Then it'll all blow over.'

'I agree. Are you going to deal with it?'

'I think it would be better if it was handled, shall we say, privately.' It had only been a matter of time before he passed the buck. Stockholm keeping their hands clean.

'OK, I've got people in London. Leave it to me.'

CHAPTER 35

Hakim phoned into headquarters to speak to Wallen.

'Sarfraz Khan didn't come into work this morning. Didn't ring in sick. Apparently, that's unusual behaviour. Do you want us to go over and see his wife?'

'No. I'd rather be there when that happens.'

'We'll just come back then.'

'No, wait... are you still at Mobilia?'

'Yeah.' Hakim glanced over at Brodd, who was leaning against a shop window with a coffee in one hand and a bun in the other.

'Pop along to the hospital, will you? There's a body that was hauled out of the canal this morning, along from the station. It hasn't been moved to Lund for a post mortem yet. But Eva Thulin's come down to have a quick look in case there's the suspicion of foul play.'

'Why us?'

'They think he might be Middle Eastern or Asian.'

Hakim still wasn't comfortable looking at corpses. A dead body was so diminished. He found it particularly hard if the person was young. Maybe it was something to do with all the life that had been theirs by right but they now wouldn't have. It wasn't the fact that he himself had been close to death on a couple of occasions that made him so melancholic – it was what had happened to Liv. He still had nightmares in which she hadn't made it. She, too, could have been lying on a metal trolley just like Sarfraz Khan. Hakim had recognized him immediately despite the time the body had spent in the water. It explained his failure to turn up for work.

'Was this murder?'

'I'll give him a thorough examination when I get the body back to Lund,' said Eva Thulin in between taking chunks out of a chocolate bar. 'There's no indication at this stage that it was anything more than an unfortunate drowning. Why he fell in, I haven't a clue. No sign of drugs or alcohol.'

'He was a Muslim.'

'That figures then. Maybe he slipped in the dark. He'd certainly been in the water for about five or six hours. Might not have been able to swim.'

'I wonder if he called for help.'

'There are some apartments on the other side of the canal, but they might not have heard him. Though it's pretty quiet round there in the early hours.'

'Unless he didn't call out.'

'Suicide, you mean? Possible. I'll leave it to you experts.'

Hakim phoned Wallen after leaving Thulin to finish her chocolate bar.

'Guilty conscience?' Wallen suggested. This echoed his own thoughts. 'Couldn't live with what he'd done?'

'I assume Sidra must have told him about our last conversation with her, so he'd know that we knew about his non-existent background. He must have been living for years with the knowledge that he was an illegal immigrant and would be deported if discovered.'

'That's a thought. What if Iqbal had discovered his secret? That would be another reason for Sarfraz to kill him.'

'That doesn't fly. Iqbal must have known all along. That would explain why Sarfraz wasn't paid directly by Happy Electricals. And here's another thought: Iqbal had such tight control over the business, he may have had similar arrangements for other employees.'

'I'll get Bea onto that. Meanwhile, we'd better go and let Sidra know. She'll have to make a formal identification. You head down there and send Brodd back here. I'll meet you at the Khans' place.'

'Are you going to run all this past Zetterberg?'

'Can't. Turns out she's pissed off to Stockholm for the weekend. Apartment hunting.'

Anita sat in Pildammsparken looking over the lake. The wind was rippling the water. Was she doing the same in her own pond? She'd spoken to Kevin about the possible contact in Oxford. Anita could tell over the phone that he was torn between wanting to discourage her about following the lead – Peter Tallis had warned him that the *Estonia* was still officially off limits and that prying into sensitive and potentially dangerous areas was decidedly risky – and wanting to see her. She'd encouraged him to ring this ex-CIA operative, Annie Hagen, to see if they could fix up a meeting. Kevin called back within the hour and said the woman was willing to see her. He'd explained that he'd been given her name by Peter Tallis, a mutual acquaintance, who'd said it was worth speaking to her, as she'd worked for the CIA in Stockholm in the 1990s. Kevin warned Anita that Hagen was now under the impression that Anita was a journalist who was doing research for a new book on American influences on Swedish foreign policy. 'It was the best I could think of off the top of my head,' Kevin had explained. 'Anyway, it must have appealed to her academic side, as she seems quite happy to talk. At some stage, we'll have to disabuse her but, hopefully, she'll be hooked by then.'

Anita had immediately booked her flight to Gatwick for tomorrow, and they'd decided that they would head to Oxford on the Monday morning after a weekend in London. 'Making up for lost time,' was how Kevin put it. She would be happy to oblige.

That sorted, as if she didn't have enough on her plate, what was of more immediate concern to Anita was the curt email she'd just received from Alice Zetterberg informing her that she was expected to give the eulogy at Erik Moberg's funeral. The Skåne County Police were organizing it and she had been designated spokesperson for the force. The gall of the woman! As acting chief inspector, it was Zetterberg who should have been giving the tribute, but, as usual, she'd managed to worm her way out of a sensitive situation. And Anita was irked by Zetterberg's use of the word 'spokesperson'. Moberg had been flesh and blood – albeit a lot of both. It wasn't a damned press conference with someone spouting a few facts and figures. Moberg wasn't just a serving officer who had been on the force for thirty years, had risen to the rank of chief inspector and had solved x number of cases. He was so much more! Yet ironically, when her initial annoyance had waned, Anita realized that she knew very little about the private Erik Moberg. She'd only ever been to his home after his first heart attack. She'd never met any of his wives or the last live-in girlfriend. She knew nothing about his family background and upbringing. Did he have any hobbies or interests outside work? Somehow, she doubted it. The police seemed to be his life. What did he do during his holidays? She had no idea. They had been at loggerheads for so many years, she'd never shown enough interest in him to find out. Neither had known how to deal with the other. For so long, she'd only seen the abrasive side of his nature, yet there must have been a gentler Moberg – she'd glimpsed a more vulnerable man on her recent visits. And presumably, you don't attract three wives by being nothing more than an overweight grouch. That in itself sounded cruel and disrespectful. Too late, she'd begun to appreciate that Moberg had been a far more complex person than she had ever given him credit for. She fiddled with her smartphone and erased Zetterberg's email. There was no escaping the fact that she didn't know enough about Erik Moberg the man to pay him appropriate homage. What on earth was she going to say?

Crumpled beauty. That's how Hakim saw Sidra Khan as she sat slumped and quietly crying in the living room of her home. The children had been taken for a walk by a family liaison officer while Hakim and Wallen broke the news of her husband's death. Though there would have to be a formal identification, Hakim's confirmation had brought the tears, though it was clear that she wasn't totally surprised.

Hakim made her a cup of sweet tea before they broached the events surrounding Sarfraz's death. They waited patiently for her to open up. Hakim could tell that she wanted to unburden herself. Eventually, she did.

'I knew something was wrong last night. Sarfraz spent a long time in the children's rooms after they'd gone to sleep, just watching them. Then he said he'd stay up for a while when I went to bed. He wasn't one for showing his feelings, but he hugged me tight and told me how much he...' She couldn't get the words out and her hands went to her eyes as she tried to stem more tears. 'In the morning, he was gone. He hadn't come to bed.'

'Did you mention our visit yesterday?' asked Wallen. 'The things we talked about?'

Sidra nodded dolefully. 'I had to. To warn him. He was greatly upset. Frightened. He talked wildly about being sent away. The family would be broken up. But after he'd been upstairs with the children, he was calm. As though he'd made up his mind. I thought everything would be all right then.'

'We don't suspect foul play,' Hakim said gently. 'An accident possibly.'

Her wide, tear-rimmed eyes gazed back at him.

'No. It was no accident. It was deliberate.'

'Was it because he thought the Swedish government would deport him back to Pakistan?'

Sidra shook her head slowly. 'He was trying to protect me.'

CHAPTER 36

Sidra had gone upstairs. Hakim and Wallen looked at each other.

'The confession?' Wallen queried.

Hakim shrugged. It would make their lives a lot easier if she did confess.

Sidra came back into the room and gave Wallen a piece of paper. She couldn't decipher it and passed it to Hakim. He, too, appeared nonplussed.

'I can read the Arabic script, but the words are in Urdu.'

'What does it say?' Wallen asked.

'He wants Allah to forgive him for abandoning his family but he has no alternative.' Sidra was finding it difficult. 'He says how much he loves us.' She no longer consulted the note and let it rest on her lap. Then she whispered 'He goes on to confess to the murder of Iqbal Nawaz.'

This was a result. Hakim felt elated. A case solved. He could see Klara Wallen was experiencing the same rush. He quickly doused his excitement. The situation wasn't appropriate: this woman's grief was so raw. And then another thought occurred.

'Wait a minute,' said Hakim. 'How was that protecting you?'

Sidra didn't answer straightaway. It was as though she was seeking help from the note. Then she spoke slowly and deliberately.

'He thought *I'd* done it.'

'He thought you'd done it? You mean, killed Iqbal?'

'Yes.'

Hakim's throat went dry and he found it difficult to speak. He sensed how tense Wallen had become. It was Sidra who broke the silence.

'But I hadn't. Of course, I hadn't. I couldn't do anything like that, however much I hated the man.'

Now Hakim was confused. It had all seemed so simple a moment ago. It was Wallen who took charge again.

'So, you're saying that neither you nor Sarfraz killed Iqbal?'

Sidra nodded confirmation.

'OK. Let's go back to the night of the murder. Were you down at Limhamnsfältet in the cricket hut with Iqbal?'

Sidra could no longer hide her sense of dishonour. The consequences had been too awful. It had cost her beloved husband's life. And for what? She wiped away the last moisture from her eyes.

'I *was* with that man in the hut.'

'And you had sex?'

'Yes.'

'So, when you'd finished, what happened?'

'I left.'

'You left? As simple as that?'

'I didn't want to stay there a moment longer than I had to.'

'So he was still there?'

'Yes.'

'Did you see anyone near the hut when you were leaving? Or when you arrived?'

'I saw no one. When I left, I took the path towards the Kallbadhus. I got a taxi from the car park there. Iqbal gave me the money for one.'

Wallen turned to Hakim. 'We'll need to check that out.' Her attention returned to Sidra.

'What time did you leave?'

'I'm not exactly sure. I got home before eleven. I wasn't in the hut for long. The act,' she virtually spat the word out, 'never took much time. He would always feel so guilty afterwards and ask for my forgiveness. Each time I hoped was the last. And then a few weeks later, another call would come. I dreaded that phone ringing – the phone he gave me.'

Wallen nodded almost imperceptibly for Hakim to take over.

'You say that Sarfraz wanted to protect you. That he thought you'd killed Iqbal. That implies that he knew what was going on.'

Sidra put the suicide note on the table.

'Yes. Not at first. But I couldn't hide the truth from him. I loved him.'

'So why were you unfaithful to him?'

'To protect him.'

Hakim tried to keep the perplexed expression off his face.

'Protect him? I don't understand. Protect him from whom?'

'Iqbal Nawaz.'

'I'm sorry. This doesn't make any sense. We were under the impression that Sarfraz was Iqbal's golden boy. The star of his cricket team.'

Sidra's smile was sad. 'He was. Loved him as his own. I think Sarfraz replaced the infant son he lost. And the fact he turned out to be a wonderful cricket player only made him shine brighter in Iqbal's eyes.'

'If that was the case, why not make Sarfraz more important in the business?'

'My husband was many things. He was humble and loving and honest. But he was not a clever man: a man of business. He ran the shop at Mobilia diligently. That gave him a position. A place of some authority. As Iqbal said to me, he'd reached his limit. To Iqbal, it was the cricket that mattered. He has a gift from Allah. That's what Iqbal said.'

'We heard from Usman Masood that Iqbal tried to get your husband into the Swedish cricket team. Yet Sarfraz was reluctant.'

'It worried Sarfraz. He thought if he was in the spotlight, his background would come out. That he would be sent away.'

'It would emerge that he was not here legally?'

'Exactly.'

'What was his background? You said that he came from Pakistan when he was three or four.'

Sidra closed her eyes for a few seconds. It was as though she were composing her thoughts. Or was she elsewhere? With Sarfraz? She opened them again.

'He came to Sweden then. What I didn't know when I married him – and neither did he – was that he wasn't even Pakistani.'

Hakim spluttered. 'If he wasn't from Pakistan, where was he from?'

'Iraq.'

Hakim found this bewildering. Sarfraz's roots were the same as his. 'How come he was supposedly Pakistani?'

'He came in with other illegal immigrants. His real father had died in Iraq in a police cell. His mother escaped the régime with him and a sister. On the overland journey, they both died. Young Sarfraz was with a group smuggled into Sweden. Of course, I have no idea what his real name was. Iqbal called him Sarfraz after his favourite Pakistani cricketer, Sarfraz Nawaz. He liked to claim they were related. And the Khan was because it stands for something like ruler. He expected great things of the little boy. Iqbal found him a Swedish Pakistani couple who had no children of their own, and they brought him up.'

'How did Iqbal know about Sarfraz in the first place?' Wallen asked.

'He brought him in.'

'Iqbal Nawaz was human smuggling?'

'I think so. Or was close to those who were.'

Wallen puffed out her cheeks and let out a massive sigh. This was a startling revelation. It hit Hakim, too. Had he dismissed Anita's information about Iqbal's Tallinn connection too readily?

'Was he still involved in bringing illegal immigrants in?' Hakim asked.

'I don't think so. He once said that he was proud that he was a legitimate businessman, respected by his peers. He didn't want anything to endanger that. It helped that he'd set up the drugs charity.'

'If you met up for sex, isn't it odd that he was discussing these things?'

'He liked to talk. The time I met him before the last one, we didn't do anything. He just wanted to talk.'

'What about the last occasion?'

'That was pure... you know. Quick and over. It suited me. I could escape.' Sidra was finding it hard to discuss these details in front of two strangers, yet there was a feeling of release. 'He was never violent with me, but I could sense his anger that night. He was upset about something. Something was preying on his mind.'

'Do you know what?' Sidra shook her head.

'Right, let's go back,' continued Wallen. 'You told us that Iqbal had set up your marriage.'

'By then, the couple that had taken Sarfraz in were dead. He was working for Happy Electricals and was a member of the cricket team. Iqbal wanted a wife for his "son" and chose me. My parents knew him from the mosque. And, as he told me later, he had always had his eye on me. It brought me closer to him.'

'And you were conscious of this?'

'Not at first. Gradually, I became aware that he looked at me in a way a man shouldn't look at someone else's wife. Sarfraz didn't notice. He was too in awe of Iqbal. Iqbal ruled his life.'

'Did you encourage Iqbal?'

Hakim thought that Sidra was going to weep again. Wallen's question had stung her.

'No. Never. I wouldn't do that.'

'But you slept with him. You had sex.' Hakim thought Wallen sounded brutal.

'I had no choice,' she wailed. 'That man...' She stopped. The words failed her.

'Tell us. Why did you have no choice?'

Sidra composed herself again. 'It's what I have been telling you. Iqbal approached me. He made it plain what he wanted from me. I refused. Of course, I refused. Then he told me all about Sarfraz's background. That he was in Sweden illegally. That it only took a word from him, and the authorities would deport him. And not to Pakistan. To Iraq.'

'Surely,' said Hakim, 'if Iqbal did that, wouldn't questions be asked about who was behind bringing illegal immigrants like Sarfraz into Sweden in the first place?'

'I challenged him on that. He just laughed. "I'm untouchable," he said. "I've got powerful friends. Sarfraz has got nobody to help him except me." He said I was the only one who could protect him. And you know the price I had to pay.' She shivered at the thought.

'Was that all?'

'No. I lied to you about where the money came from to pay off this house. Iqbal paid it. It was to soften his guilt after the first time.'

'A nice softener,' said Wallen.

Sidra ignored the comment. 'Then he gave me the phone. He called it his hot line to his hot woman. It was horrible.'

'And when did Sarfraz find out?'

'After the second time. I felt such shame.'

'What was his reaction?'

'At first, he didn't believe me, and when he did, he cried. He cried like a child. His whole world had changed. The faith he had in Iqbal. What Iqbal had done to me. He'd known from being a teenager that he was in Sweden illegally. Iqbal had told him when he first gave him a job. But he said no one would ever find out. He would ensure that. He was safe. But it had haunted Sarfraz ever since. That worry. Now he knew that Iqbal was using that secret to have his way with me. Yet we could do nothing – this man had total control over our lives.'

'You could have killed him,' Wallen baldly suggested.

'No. We may have had those thoughts in our hearts...' Sidra's voice trailed off.

'And you're sure it wasn't Sarfraz?'

'He was here when I left and here when I got back. He would never have left the children on their own. And he didn't know where I was meeting Iqbal. I spared him that detail. But when he heard about the murder, he must have thought it was me. It didn't occur to me that he would think that. If only I had talked to him about it, he wouldn't be dead now.'

CHAPTER 37

Alice Zetterberg was fuming. She was on the early Monday-morning flight from Stockholm Arlanda to Malmö. What should have been a pleasant weekend searching for a swish apartment that would reflect the status of her new job had turned into a nightmare. Firstly, she'd got a call from Wallen. Instead of good news on the Iqbal Nawaz case, the latest two suspects appeared to be in the clear – one even managed to kill himself. Wallen had filled her in on the details. They'd checked out Sidra Khan's taxi home on the night Iqbal was killed. The timings would have been very tight for her to have done the murder and tidied up afterwards, so she wasn't totally ruled out – at least that was something. Sidra had also officially identified the body in the canal as her husband, Sarfraz Khan. He appeared to have drowned and no foul play was suspected. They'd had the suicide note translated – it confirmed what Sidra had told them – and the handwriting was definitely Sarfraz's, as it had been compared to samples found at the Mobilia store. Basically, Wallen and Hakim didn't believe Sidra to be guilty – or her husband. Again the timings would have been too tight. Or had the woman pulled the wool over their eyes and she was lying through her teeth? Perhaps she, Zetterberg, shouldn't have left them to their own devices. The last thing she needed was for the case to drag on. She was due to leave Malmö in a fortnight.

And that brought her to a far more serious problem. A fortnight before, she'd had a call in the office from a very senior member of the secret service. The Säpo voice at the Stockholm end said that it was imperative that the Markus Jolis case was closed down permanently. She wasn't given a reason other than that it had national security implications. This she was in the process of doing anyhow. The second half of the instruction was to ensure that Anita Sundström stopped her 'meddling'. Again, she was more than happy to comply. It would get Sundström out of her hair while being able to denigrate her at the same time. Win-win. She had thought about suspending her. That was the more humiliating option, though it might have consequences if the suspension was looked into officially and information emerged that compromised the national security the Stockholm voice had referred to. So, Zetterberg had reflected ruefully, the only sensible course would be to send Anita off on her annual leave. Get her away from day-to-day policing and stop her snooping. Stockholm had been pleased with her actions and had indicated that she would have a warm welcome when she took up her new role in the capital.

But then, while enjoying a glass of wine in the Gamla Stan sunshine yesterday, she'd received a second call. This time, the tone was far from friendly. What the hell did she think Anita Sundström was up to? Zetterberg was at a loss, as she hadn't been in communication with her nemesis, except to dump Erik Moberg's eulogy on her lap. Liberally sprinkled with expletives, the man had described Sundström's movements over the last week (visits to Tallinn and Stockholm) and said that it was clear that she was following up on Markus Jolis. She was now flying to England, for God's sake! Why the fuck hadn't Zetterberg killed this as per instructions? A flabbergasted Alice had no idea why this was particularly problematic, as the man hadn't filled her in as to why the Jolis case needed to be closed. She had just been pleased to carry out orders. And she'd learned from past experience that when Säpo were involved, it was best not to ask questions. She tried to point out that she had no control over what Sundström did on her vacation, but this didn't wash. The man was clearly agitated. He finished off with an unreasonable and very worrying warning – if Zetterberg didn't put a lid on both the Jolis case and Sundström's activities once and for all, she could forget about her Stockholm job. After the call, she'd hit the bottle with a vengeance as she mentally fulminated against that unspeakable woman who was now jeopardizing her whole future career. When she'd woken up with a hangover the following morning, the hatred was still buoyant, but her heart sank at the thought that she had no idea how to rectify matters.

Anita and Kevin took a mid-morning train from Paddington to Oxford – the journey took an hour. Kevin had arranged for them to meet Annie Hagen that afternoon. He was still pleased with his ruse about Anita doing research into American influences on Swedish foreign policy. The only worry was how Hagen would react when she twigged there was more to it. Hagen had suggested that they meet her on her allotment because she wasn't teaching that day. It was an odd location, but it was a sunny day and after London, it would be good to breathe in some fresh Oxfordshire air.

From the rather dull 1970s station, a short walk into the town brought them to the hotel on George Street where Kevin had managed to get a good two-night deal. After dumping their bags, they wandered out and along to the Tourist Information office on Broad Street. As neither of them had ever set foot in Oxford before, Kevin thought it would be a good idea to get a map (he liked maps). He grudgingly bought one – complaining that it should have been free – and a small guide book. They retreated to the café of the University Church of St. Mary the Virgin. They sat outside for their coffee and sandwiches, admiring the adjacent neo-classical domed rotunda of the Radcliffe Camera. It was one of the city's many iconic buildings. Itself a former library, it was now a reading room for the nearby Bodleian.

'Sums up Oxford,' remarked Kevin, his gaze torn away from the map he was busy studying. 'A stunning creation that's now simply somewhere to read. I bet Malmö University library doesn't look like that!'

'Don't think so.'

'Apparently the Bodleian – that's just the other side – has twelve million books and documents dating back to the pharaohs.'

'I don't think they'll allow you in there with your Kindle, then.'

'Very funny.' His attention returned to the map. 'More to the point, I've found Annie Hagen's allotment. She said we can't miss her, as she keeps bees.' He pointed to the spot. 'It's across the canal and railway line in the Walton Manor area of the city. I reckon it's about half an hour's brisk walk. Unless you want to take a taxi?'

'It's a nice day – we'll walk. Besides, it'll give me time to get my story straight.'

'Honestly, don't worry. We're going to have to come clean at some stage. And if she tells us to bugger off...' He shrugged.

'It's a long way to come for nothing.'

'What do you mean? You've got two romantic nights in the "city of dreaming spires" with the man of your dreams.'

'As I say, it's a long way to come for nothing.'

Kevin managed to look hurt for a couple of seconds before a grin burst through.

Zetterberg sat sullenly through the meeting she'd called to review where they were with the Iqbal Nawaz case. The team went through all that they'd done while she was away in Stockholm. She'd muttered that she'd been there because of her new job, which they appeared to accept. Actually, she realized that they didn't care. They just wanted to see her go as quickly as she did. But now she had this threat hanging over her head. She was still undecided as to what she should or could do.

'Where does this leave us?' she asked.

'Sidra Khan is still a possible suspect.' Wallen had taken on the role of summing up. 'As we've said, she could be lying, though our feeling is that she isn't. She's a broken woman who believes that she's responsible for her husband's suicide. All we know is what she's admitted – she had sex with Iqbal Nawaz in the cricket hut on the night he was killed. Having sex with someone else's husband isn't illegal.'

'Just as well, as we'd be arresting people all over the place.' Brodd's jocular intervention wasn't appreciated.

'Have we any other suspects?' Zetterberg's irritation was growing. 'What about the fourth key holder?'

'Usman Masood doesn't have an alibi as such,' Hakim admitted. 'Nor does he have an obvious motive. He's got a fancy job at Happy Electricals. Would he want to jeopardize that?'

'Unless he ends up running the company,' suggested Erlandsson. 'It's in Bismah's gift, and they're related. He did indicate that it would hinder his lifestyle – but he might have been lying.'

'Look into that. Any other angles?' Zetterberg really wanted the meeting to end so she could formulate a plan as to how to handle Anita Sundström.

Hakim wasn't sure whether to mention it, as it was probably going to raise Zetterberg's hackles. Then he thought it was worth airing for the sake of the case, which seemed to be floundering.

'We've assumed all along that the killing of Iqbal Nawaz was tied in with people who were close to him, either personally or professionally. Or that it's somehow tied up with the cricket club. The business with the hut keys, etcetera... But what if the murder has broader implications? Iqbal was a powerful man with all sorts of contacts. Many may have been dubious. As Klara has just told you, Sidra indicated that he may well have had connections with human smuggling back in the 1990s. That's how Sarfraz arrived in Sweden. And I know he may well have had business dealings with Estonia, which was a funnel for human smuggling back then.'

Zetterberg's head shot up. 'How do you know this?'

Hakim coughed. 'I just know he sailed on the *Estonia* ferry to Tallinn just before its sinking. He's on a passenger list.'

'How do you know this?' This time it was a demand.

'Anita told me,' he replied sheepishly.

'And why in God's name was she looking at passenger lists for the *Estonia*?'

'It's to do with her father.'

'Her father?'

'Yeah. He went down with the ferry. I think she's just finding out about the disaster to satisfy her own curiosity.' He was trying to downplay it as much as possible.

Zetterberg hadn't known that. On the surface, it was innocent enough. Maybe Stockholm had got the wrong end of the stick. Sundström wasn't following up on Markus Jolis. Then again, she had mentioned Jolis's connection to the *Estonia*. Bloody hell! Was that what all this was about? It wasn't Jolis that Säpo were getting their knickers in a twist about – it was the *Estonia*. Like many Swedes, she'd accepted the official version, though she'd been aware of some rumblings. Was there something more to it? Is that why Sundström visiting Tallinn had caused such consternation in secret service circles? One thing was for sure: she couldn't afford to upset Stockholm any more. Whatever the situation was that was panicking them, she'd better put the lid on it right now.

'It's ridiculous to think that Iqbal's movements in 1994 have any bearing on his murder. If they had – human smuggling or something else – surely any retribution would have happened by now. They're not going to wait over twenty years. We shouldn't be distracted by events that happened so long ago. This is about the here and now. The facts point to a much more personal motive. The person who did this was close to the victim.'

CHAPTER 38

Anita and Kevin crossed the canal. Anita stopped to admire the scene, delighted by the colourful narrow boats with their beautifully painted roses and castles, and adorned with a profusion of decorated tubs and pots and buckets, out of which tumbled a riot of floral displays. Over the railway line, with the wide, green expanse of Port Meadow on their right, they cut down to the allotment gates, which were open. The allotment area covered a considerable acreage and was bordered by the River Thames on one side and several unimaginative, modern apartment blocks on the other, the latter providing yet more accommodation for the ever-growing student population. The allotments themselves were at their most productive at this time of year. Each one reflected the character of the holder: some organized, some organized chaos and some just chaotic; but all fruitful and bursting with produce. Dotted throughout was an assortment of huts and shacks housing gardening paraphernalia. There weren't many people around today, just the odd few busy at work gathering their harvest. A couple of retirees were sitting on rickety old chairs enjoying the sunshine and a bottle of beer. A pair of red kites soared overhead on the lookout for a late lunch.

Anita and Kevin had to walk the full length of the site to reach Annie Hagen's plot. She was easy to spot: a figure in full beekeeper's gear – boots, baggy white suit, blue gloves, and a wide-brimmed hat and veil which obscured her face. Except for the headwear, she might be Eva Thulin at a murder scene. Hagen was standing next to one of two hives, which had head-high netting on three sides. She had a smoker in her hand. The hive top was open and she was peering inside, keeping the inmates calm with the odd puff of smoke. Bees were zipping around her head and above the netting. Their proximity made Kevin nervous. He didn't venture too close and called over.

'Hi! Annie Hagen? I'm Kevin Ash. I called you two days ago.'

'Yeah, sure.' The unmistakably harsh drawl of a New Yorker rasped from behind the anonymity of the veil. 'Look, give me five minutes to finish up. Best stand over there by the hut. Might be safer.'

Kevin and Anita gladly retreated to the wooden hut at the end of the plot and watched in fascination as Hagen fussed over her thousands of charges. Hagen walked over to them and took off her hat and veil. She rubbed her sweaty forehead with the back of her hand. 'Sure is hot in this get-up.'

'Looks it.' Kevin couldn't think of a suitable reply. 'Anyway, I'm Kevin by the way.' He offered a hand to shake.

Hagen slipped off her gloves. 'I know. You've already said.' She didn't shake his hand.

Anita estimated that the woman must be in her early sixties. If Peter Tallis was the skirt chaser that Kevin claimed, she could see why he'd gone after Annie Hagen. Her short auburn hair (subtly dyed), her remarkably un-lined face (no signs of Botox), and her generous mouth and wide, blue-grey eyes combined to create a striking presence. Yet she wasn't so pretty that she would turn every male head when she entered a room. That was useful in a spy. And there was something else that immediately struck Anita: she wouldn't take any bullshit – the sort of bullshit she was about to serve up.

'And this is the journalist I told you about. Anita Sundström.'

Hagen gave her a cursory nod but said nothing. She pushed past them and went into the hut. She emerged with a bottle of water, which she guzzled thirstily.

Kevin could see it hadn't got off to a good start. He decided to jump in with some small talk.

'I saw Peter Tallis the other day. He sends his love.'

This brought a faint smile. 'How is the old rascal? I hear he's a clergyman now. Who would have thought?'

'Busy ministering to the poor of Chelsea. Even the super-rich have their spiritual problems, allegedly.'

'When I knew the old lech, he was ministering to me and a string of others.'

'Peter's Pushovers,' quoted Kevin.

'Jeez! Is that what he called us? I don't think God was much on his mind in those days. I suspect he's brilliant with the ladies of the parish. Could add a new meaning to "tea with the vicar".'

'I don't know when he had his Damascene moment. Maybe it was all the awful things he had to do while working with MI6. I believe you came across him in India?'

'Sure did. I was working at Delhi Station. Early nineties. Pete and I took Anglo-American cooperation to a whole different level. Then I got posted to Stockholm. I think I was meant to be a cultural liaison officer.'

'You were there at the time of the sinking of the *Estonia*. September 1994.'

Hagen fiddled with the plastic bottle and stared hard at Anita.

'Is that why you've come? You're not writing a book, are you? I looked you up last night and couldn't find a journalist or any writer called Anita Sundström in Sweden or any place else.'

'Sorry about the deception,' Kevin said apologetically. 'We weren't sure if you'd speak to us if you knew the real reason.'

'My father died in the tragedy,' put in Anita firmly. She wasn't here to waste her time. 'I'm trying to find out the truth behind his death. As you've discovered, I'm not a journalist. I'm a detective.' Hagen arched an eyebrow. 'But I'm not here in an official capacity. Purely personal.'

'And what do you think you've found out so far?' It was clear that Hagen wasn't going to play ball easily.

'I've talked to various people. I've been to Tallinn, too. From what I can gather, the ferry may not have sunk as per the official findings. Seems the route was used for smuggling all sorts of illegal contraband from a dysfunctional Estonia still coming to terms with its independence. I've heard about criminal gangs and their goings-on, and I've found out from the Stockholm end of things that the Swedish Customs had been tipped off about the possibility of people being smuggled on that particular sailing.'

'So why come to me? You seem to know enough already.'

'Come on, the CIA must have known what was going on. It wasn't just desperate illegal immigrants that were passing through Tallinn. Drugs were big and, maybe of more interest to the Americans, weapons and, shall we say, interesting materials? I'm sure there must have been concern in certain circles that these might end up in the wrong hands.' Hagen watched her dispassionately. 'And the sub-marines. Submarines heading out of the Baltic and being used by states that the US might disapprove of. Am I getting warm?'

'You might be, honey.' Hagen pointed with her bottle. 'You see those little beauties over there? It's not exactly the proverbial hornet's nest, but it works in the same way. They can be stirred up just as easily. They can get upset; difficult to control once they're out. The real problem is that they can turn very nasty. And it's often the innocent bystanders who get stung.'

'I know what you're saying. I've no intention of stirring anything up.' Anita wasn't going to mention the suspicious death of Markus Jolis.

'Look... Anita. You're a cop. I spent much of my professional life dealing with cops. The good ones don't let go. Dog with a bone and all that. Now, I don't know if you're a good cop or not. But you've come all the way here. You've been to Tallinn. That doesn't sound like a gentle meander down memory lane. You want something more than simply discovering what happened to your daddy.'

Anita shuffled self-consciously. She wasn't used to being dis-mantled so adroitly.

'Possibly.'

'I don't think you know what you're getting into.'

'I'm starting to.' Anita decided to come clean. 'It began with the unexplained death of a customs officer in Malmö. There were things that didn't add up. Non-existent people appeared and disappeared. It left unanswered questions. And it started me on a quest to find out what happened to my father. So, it got personal.'

Annie Hagen didn't speak for a while, and the three of them stood in a tense silence. Anita and Kevin exchanged nervous glances.

'You two have strayed onto dangerous ground. My advice is that you go home and enjoy the rest of your lives.' She could see that Anita was about to object. 'On the other hand, if you really can't let this thing rest, I might be willing to give you a little information. If you still want to go ahead, you can come to my place tomorrow night. Around nine-thirty. There's a back gate. I'll leave it open. But I'm warning you that your investigations should stop here, right now. Think about it. I hope for your sakes I never see you again.'

Hakim sat at his desk, staring at his computer. So much had been going through his mind since the morning meeting. Was Zetterberg right? Should they be concentrating on the cricket circle – those who knew the victim? It would explain why he was off his guard. Or had Anita got a point? It could have been a professional hit job carried out on behalf of a rival from the past to look like the work of an amateur. The cricket bat had signposted the cricket hut and the team, but was that just to throw them off the real reason for the killing? Yet he had to concede that Zetterberg's argument about no one waiting for twenty-five years for revenge was convincing. With these conflicting theories vying for pole position in Hakim's mind, he decided to email Anita. She might be interested to know that Iqbal Nawaz had something to do with human smuggling and that it was linked to Tallinn. Would that tie in with Markus Jolis? That wasn't his problem now, of course, though he was sure that Anita was still pursuing it.

His office phone rang. He could see it was reception.

'There's someone here for you.'

'Send them up.'

'He doesn't want to come to your office. He says he'll meet you outside the front gate.'

This was very odd. 'Who is it?'

'Says he's called Uday Mirza.' That was a shock. His father had never visited the polishus before. Hakim knew he had a dread of such places after his experiences in Iraq.

Five minutes later, Hakim was approaching his father, who was hovering in the street. He was visibly uncomfortable in this vicinity. Had he come about the wedding? Had he changed his mind?

'I hope I'm not disturbing you from your work.'

'Not at all. It's good to see you.'

'Your mother was asking about you.'

Hakim didn't answer, and Uday shuffled awkwardly from foot to foot. Hakim thought he'd better end his father's discomfort.

'Do you want to go somewhere to talk?'

'No, no. What I have to say can be said here.'

Hakim waited for him to speak.

'You asked me about the mosque.' Hakim could see the internal struggle.

'About Iqbal Nawaz. I shouldn't have asked.'

Uday waved away the suggestion.

'I spoke to the imam about him. In a general way, you understand. I didn't want the imam to think I was interfering. Or helping the police. Iqbal did a lot of good in our community. Helping our young people off drugs. Many have no hope you know. No jobs. No prospects. That's why they turn to such things.' He was starting to get agitated.

'Dad, I know. I was at school with many of them.'

'Of course you were. You were strong. You were different. That's why I'm proud of you.' It came out in a rush, and Hakim could tell he was immediately embarrassed. Hakim felt a burst of affection. His father had never really complimented him before.

Uday coughed. 'Anyhow... anyhow,' he went on hurriedly, 'the imam did tell me that Iqbal was a worried man before his death. Something was deeply troubling him. He didn't enlighten the imam as to the reason and the imam wouldn't have passed it on to me if he had,' he said, almost accusingly. Such a thing would be reprehensible. 'That's all,' he added brusquely.

'Thank you. That could be very useful.'

'I must go.' Uday half turned to go. 'Oh, and your mother says you must come round and see us. With Liv.' And then he was gone.

Hakim watched his father stride down the street. He knew how difficult the whole business had been for him. He smiled to himself. Was the healing process beginning?

He wandered back into the polishus. So, Sidra had been right. Iqbal had been struggling with something. But what?

It was on wet days like this that Peter Tallis wished he was back in Delhi, or Johannesburg, or Athens. Not exactly the good old days, but warmer ones. Back then, the things on his mind were the machinations of the enemy, the Cold War, the untrustworthy régimes that were your friends one year and foes the next depending on Britain's constantly shifting foreign policy. And then there were all the delightful female distractions that made even the grimmest of postings more acceptable.

Now his concerns were more mundane: the parish newsletter and website (so important in this world of modern communication); the weekly visit to the local primary school; seeing a young couple about a christening (neither had been members of the congregation until they suddenly realized church attendance might help their little angel get into said primary school); and the maintenance of this wonderful church he loved so much. He and his flock were busily raising money for a new roof. The old one was starting to leak, especially in the tower. His painfully persistent parish clerk, William, was forever nagging him to monitor it. With this in mind, and with the unexpected heavy burst of rain that he'd just scampered through, he thought he'd better check there wasn't any more damage. The roof fund was still well short of its target.

He opened the creaking door to the tower. The hundred and six spiralling stone steps to the top seemed to be getting harder to climb. He always joked with himself that it meant he was getting closer to God. As he panted his way up, he realized that if he had a heart attack here and now, he would reach heaven more quickly than he'd planned. He was nearing the opening into the belfry when he thought he heard a noise below. Was someone else on the stairway? He must be hearing things. He continued upwards and opened the door onto the tower roof. The rain had relented, though the surface he was standing on was very wet, and there were a couple of ominous pools of water. He sighed heavily. On Saturday, there was to be yet another fundraising fête at which the usual suspects would appear. What they needed was a rich sponsor. It shouldn't be that difficult – Chelsea was full of rich people.

The charcoal skies above threatened yet another downpour. He looked over the crenellated parapet at all the fine dwellings below. Surely somebody could be sweet-talked into helping? He walked gingerly towards the largest puddle, making sure he didn't slip on the chipped tiles.

It was an old instinct that made him turn when he did. The Service's tough training methods had instilled in him a natural wariness that had saved him in the past. But now age and a sedentary life had dulled his physical reflexes. Before he could move, his arms were pinned to his side in a vice-like grip. He struggled in vain. He was no match for his assailant, who walked him back towards the parapet. His feet couldn't get any purchase as they slid over the tiles. God moved in mysterious ways – this wasn't the ending he'd envisaged. He felt himself being hoisted over the barrier, and the ground came hurtling towards him.

CHAPTER 39

The kettle bubbled to a halt and Kevin filled up the two cups with hot water – tea for him and coffee for Anita. The television droned on in the background. He handed a cup to Anita, who was sitting up in bed, scrolling through her smartphone. He went back to his tea and, with difficulty, tore open the sachet of milk without spilling it. He glanced at the TV screen. 'Bloody Brexit!'

He wandered over to the bed and slipped in next to Anita.

'By sleeping with a Swedish government employee, will that qualify me for an EU passport?'

'Depends on how good you are in bed.'

'That sounds like a demanding criterion. Maybe I'll have better luck trying to find an Irish ancestor.'

Anita sipped the instant coffee and pulled a face.

'I'm sure there'll be real coffee down at breakfast.'

She wasn't confident. She rarely had what she'd call a 'proper coffee' on her UK visits. Then she squinted at an SMS message that had just come in.

'Problem?' Kevin asked.

'Sort of. It's from Jazmin. Leyla's got a stomach bug.'

'Sounds horrid.'

'Trouble is, illness raises her blood sugar levels – it can throw her whole system off balance.'

'That lot over there,' Kevin said, nodding in the direction of the television. 'I got so fed up with the BBC lumping type 1 and type 2 diabetes together, I wrote a snotty email complaining and explaining the bloody difference. When I mention to people that Leyla has type 1, they just think she must be fat. It winds me up something rotten.'

'Good for you.' Anita leant over and kissed him on the side of his head.

They lapsed into silence while Anita wrote a message back to Jazmin. Kevin stared at the TV screen, not really taking in what was being discussed, as the sound was too low. He was waiting for the sports bulletin to come on.

Anita finished her message and put down her phone.

'Well, are you going to see Annie Hagen tonight?' Kevin asked with some concern.

'Of course.'

'Look, I totally understand you wanting to find things out about your dad. It's only natural. But I don't want you putting yourself in harm's way. Annie warned you off. And I have to say that Peter Tallis effectively did the same. The *Estonia* is officially a closed book.'

'Exactly. That's why I've got to open it up. What are they hiding? If Annie Hagen can shed a bit more light on what happened, I'll get closer to the truth.'

'But at what cost? You've got so much going for you. Think of Lasse... Jazmin... little Leyla. Your family is what really counts in your life. Maybe it's time to just forget all this. Move on.'

'Sorry. I can't.'

Kevin knew she couldn't. At least he'd tried to dissuade her. He couldn't shake the fear that this was all going to end badly.

After dropping Liv off at headquarters, Hakim drove up to Lund. Liv had suggested it the night before when they were discussing Uday's appearance at headquarters. Coupled with what Sidra had told him about Iqbal's state of mind during their last tryst, it made sense to get confirmation from a source closer to the murdered man. They decided it was more likely to do with business rather than anything personal. Other than his periodic bouts of guilt about Sidra, his home life appeared settled. They'd thought about asking Bismah but then decided to steer clear, as she would still be in mourning. Besides, if it *was* connected to the business, their understanding was that Iqbal had kept his family and commercial lives separate. Lund was the natural place to start – it was where Iqbal spent most of his time when he wasn't surprising his store staff around the country with unscheduled visits. And Usman Masood would know as much as anybody.

As Hakim drove into the office block car park, he saw Usman standing there, smoking with a colleague. Hakim parked and approached him. There was something about Usman that put his back up. Too smooth? Too confident? Or was he, deep down, a bit jealous? When Usman spotted him, he nodded to his colleague, who quickly put out his cigarette and hurried back into the building.

'Good morning,' Usman called cheerily before taking one last drag and stubbing out his cigarette with his foot. 'I wouldn't have been able to do this if Iqbal had been around. Didn't like his workers smoking in office hours,' he added with a smile. 'Anyway, have you come to see me or someone else?'

'You, actually.'

'How can I help?'

'You've obviously heard about Sarfraz Khan?'

'Of course. Dreadful. We were all shocked. Killing himself. And so close after the death of our founder. In an awful way, I'm glad that Iqbal wasn't alive to see this. He loved Sarfraz like a son.'

'It didn't stop him lusting after his wife,' Hakim pointed out.

'I know. It wasn't a good thing to do, though she's a real... Sorry, that's inappropriate. Let's say Sidra was his one weakness.'

'It was Sidra who was in the hut with Iqbal that night.'

Usman looked stunned. 'Did she kill him?'

'We're keeping an open mind about that. That's not why I'm here. You worked closely with Iqbal.'

'I suppose. Whenever I was here, that is. As the main buyer, I'm often away. Pakistan, mainly, because we have factories there. Also Europe, America and China. We stock most of the main electrical brands as well as our own. But when I was here and he wasn't on one of his checking-up trips, I probably saw more of him than most.'

Hakim watched the sun glinting off a red Aston Martin parked near where they were standing. He would put money on it being Usman's. It stood out like a beacon of defiance and prosperity among the serried ranks of more sensible cars like Volvos and Volkswagens. Many from the Indian subcontinent would admire such an ostentatious symbol of success, while most Westerners probably wouldn't. The Swedes have their own expression: *Jantelagen* – an unwritten law which states that no one is any better than anyone else. They don't approve of showing off. Neither did Hakim, who realized how Swedish his thinking had become, despite his parentage.

'We've heard that before his death, Iqbal was worried about something. Preoccupied. Does that ring any bells with you?'

Usman shrugged. 'Not particularly. Who said this?'

'A couple of sources.'

'He had the usual worries that anybody in his position has. He'd built up a big chain. That's the easy part. Staying ahead of the competition is the difficult bit. You see, we always have competitors snapping at our heels. The internet, too. I think if Iqbal had anything on his mind, it was that he was contemplating slowing down. Let other people do the donkey work. Delegate more. He sometimes talked of retiring back to Pakistan. But it was not so easy. His problem was that he was a control freak, and he wasn't sure who to trust to handle the business if he took his eye off things.'

'Not you?'

Usman laughed. 'As I've said to your colleagues, it's not my thing at the moment. *I* wouldn't trust me to run a business this size. Maybe in a few years.'

'So who's running things now?'

'Bismah has put Abbas in temporary charge. Don't know what she'll decide in the long term. My guess is it'll be someone like Imad Wasim. He runs things in Stockholm and all points north.'

'And there couldn't have been anything personal bothering him?'

'Doubt it. He loved Bismah and Muneeba, whatever he got up to with Sidra.'

'Could they have found out?'

'I don't think Bismah would have been too fussed. As long as it was discreet. Sometimes wives are happy to pretend these things aren't happening. That's one of the side effects of arranged marriages. You should know that.'

Hakim merely responded by thanking Usman for his time. Maybe his father's information hadn't been that useful after all. As he walked away, he heard a car lock clicking. The red Aston Martin *was* Usman's. Hakim disliked him that little bit more.

Anita reached the Walton Manor area of the city. The street consisted of tall, red-brick town houses. She recognized the road end because they'd passed it on the way to the allotments. Kevin had insisted on escorting her as far as the back lane that ran along the rear of the terrace. She'd persuaded Kevin not to come in, though he'd not been happy. She was convinced that if they were to get anything out of Annie Hagen, she had to do it alone. After all, it was her personal crusade, and she reasoned that Hagen would be more accommodating on a woman-to-woman basis. What she hadn't mentioned was the fear that she might be dragging Kevin into a risky situation. As he'd pointed out, Hagen's warning at the allotment hadn't been issued frivolously. He said he would wait in a pub nearby in Jericho. He'd found it on the map, and Anita knew how to get there after her talk with the ex-agent.

The day had been interminable. Oxford is a beautiful place to wander round, but Anita's thoughts were not on its thousand-year-old history or the almost overbearing weight of academia which was round every corner. Her mind was far too engrossed with what Annie Hagen may have to tell her. Of course, Kevin had been in his element and had dragged her all over the city. The highlight for him was the Ashmolean Museum, where he'd gone into paroxysms of excitement at the sight of the Alfred Jewel – a tear-shaped, filigree-gold-encased piece of quartz and cloisonné enamel showing the image of a man. Created for King Alfred the Great, it is one of the most significant Saxon relics ever found. Anita had to admit that it was beautiful, and she was happy to see Kevin so euphoric. In between regular breaks in pleasant cafés, he'd marched her round the ancient colleges and buildings he considered were of architectural merit. Her feet were starting to hurt by the time they had their evening meal. She knew he wasn't just indulging his passion for history but was trying to keep her mind off things. It hadn't worked, though she *had* been distracted by the ducks waddling along Parks Road, a reminder that Oxford was a city of rivers and waterways. Though not the university term time, the streets were crammed with people – mainly tourists, and foreign students doing summer schools – and simply getting from A to B took a lot of concentration. Now, after this exhausting and jam-packed day, she was glad to be standing in front of a wooden gate in the wall of the back lane – everywhere was quiet, as dusk surrendered to night.

Anita opened the gate and walked along a path which ran the length of the narrow garden. It was too dark to distinguish the contents of the flower beds except for a splash of large, white daisies, picked out by the dwindling light; but she was able to see well enough to carefully negotiate the brick steps that led down to the basement of the four-storey house. Through the French window, she could see a dimly illuminated kitchen beyond. She went in as instructed. Annie Hagen had said that she was to make her way up to the living room on the next floor.

Anita wound her way up the flight of creaking stairs and saw a shard of light cutting through the gloom.

'Annie?'

'Come in, honey.'

Anita pushed open the door of a high-ceilinged room and stepped into the glare. Annie Hagen was draped along the length of a blue chaise longue, wearing a full-flowing, green and brown kaftan; a whisky glass clamped in her hand. The room, which occupied almost the entire floor, was tastefully furnished: chintz-upholstered chairs gave it a homely feel, an elaborate marble fireplace presided over one end, a Georgian grandfather clock nestled comfortably in one corner, and a couple of family portraits and some agreeable water colours adorned the walls. Hagen smiled when she saw Anita staring at the chaise longue.

'Came with the house. I rent.' Hagen waved her glass around. 'Not really my scene. But when in Oxford...' She eased herself up into a sitting position before hoisting herself onto her feet. A little unsteadily, she shuffled over to an open cupboard in a manner which reminded Anita of the ducks she'd seen earlier in the day. Hagen reached into the cupboard and came out armed with a half-empty bottle of whisky.

'Since I've been here, I've developed a taste for Scottish malts. Want one?'

'OK. Small, please.'

The cut-glass tumbler was half filled. Anita didn't like whisky, but if it made Hagen happy, she might be more forthcoming.

'So why the UK? Why Oxford?'

'It's a classy place and it's full of secrets. Makes me feel like I'm still at the Company. Academics are even more devious and back-stabbing than spooks.'

After refreshing her glass, Hagen plonked herself back down on the chaise longue, though she remained sitting. Anita hadn't noticed anything in the way of personal possessions – photos, trinkets of travel, or mementos of a long career that had taken her round the world.

'Have you been here since you left the CIA?'

'No. I sort of dropped out. Took myself off to Alaska. Out in the wilds. Except even there, there were reminders of my old life. Did you know Alaska used to be part of the Russian Empire? But it's a good part of the world to exorcise one's demons. And the average spook usually has plenty of them.' She stopped her flow to take a gulp of whisky. Anita's was still untouched. 'When I got my mind together,

I put myself through university again in the States. Ended up with a doctorate and a lectureship. But I could see the way the wind was blowing politically, and I decided to move out. Besides, I had no family left alive to keep me there. Conned my way into a post here lecturing on American history. I've got a unique perspective on the run-up to 9/11. That goes down well. I think it tickles them that I'm ex-Company.'

'And those demons you were so busy trying to erase? Did they include the sinking of the *Estonia*?'

It was clear that Hagen had already been drinking. Had their visit to the allotment set this off? Or was it a regular occurrence? She held her glass out in Anita's direction.

'You're quite perceptive for a cop. Probably because you're a woman. Swedish, of course. You're better at giving women breaks over there. Gender equality and all that. Here's to Sweden!' Hagen raised her glass in a toast, which gave her the excuse to drain it, which, in turn, gave her a pretext to refill it. Anita covered her own glass with her hand. Once Hagen was back in position, Anita began prompting her.

'How long were you working at Stockholm Station?'

Hagen pursed her lips. 'Nearly three years. Long time. '93 to '95.'

'So, the *Estonia* happened right in the middle.'

'Sure did.'

'And you must have heard of the Baltic Drainpipe?'

Hagen guffawed. 'You like to get to the point! I remember Swedes being quite abrupt. Yanks like that. None of your British prevarication. God, I'm surrounded by that here. Chrissake, why don't Brits just say what they're thinking?'

'I hear gangs were moving all sorts of illicit items across the Baltic – and a lot of them on that ferry route.'

'Not only criminal gangs, honey. We brought our fair share across. The old Soviet Union was like a goldmine just waiting to be exploited. Such riches – technology, electronics, vital intel. Military hardware too. These sensitive transports came in by the ferry, were waved through customs, and driven straight to some Swedish airfield and loaded onto US military aircraft. Whizzed away to the States,' she said with a flourish of her hand, nearly spilling her drink, 'or via our airfields here in the UK. The Brits were fine with that. Of course, if there was particularly useful intelligence or information coming across the Baltic, we'd let Säpo and MI6 have a peek at it too. Keep our allies in the loop. Keep them onside.'

'So the Swedish authorities knew?'

'Couldn't be done without them. Of course, they wanted to keep their hands clean. We used a third party, so if it was discovered, they could pretend it had nothing to do with them. Put it down to private enterprise.'

'What sort of third party?'

'Some influential person. I wasn't at the pay grade to know who it was. Used various companies as cover to move stuff through. It all had to look above board. There were enough problems with the Russian and Estonian gangs getting hold of dangerous materials. It was better that we got our hands on them first and they didn't end up with the wrong people. The wrong countries. There were some rotten apples around. Well, we thought they were rotten. Al-Qaeda might not have been a serious player then, but terrorists were still a constant danger. Look at Britain at the time with the IRA.'

'And you paid for these services?'

'Oh, yeah. Big bucks. But still cheap because everything coming out of the Soviet Union came at knockdown prices.'

'How did you cover up all that money coming into Sweden? Surely that could be traced?'

'Because it never came into Sweden. We paid it into a bank in Tallinn.'

'Do you know what bank? A Swedish one? Swedbank are big over there now.'

'No. It wasn't a Swedish bank, though it wouldn't surprise me if it was owned by a Swede. It was something to do with independence...

erm... oh, yeah, the Independent Bank of Estonia... that was it.'

Anita remembered Kask telling her about the new banks that had started up after independence and where much of their capital came from.

'And the Swedish Customs just let all this material sail through?'

'Yeah. That was part of the deal. About ten years after the sinking, there was a guy who blew the whistle on a couple of shipments of military equipment passing unhindered through Stockholm earlier that September when the *Estonia* went down. The Swedish government were obliged to look into it and had to admit that the shipments had happened, though they refused to reveal what was being transported on the ferry. But that was just the tip of the iceberg. It wasn't called the Baltic Drainpipe for nothing.'

Anita was finding this mind-numbing. The scale was far greater than she could ever have dreamed of in her worst nightmares.

'Does the name Markus Jolis mean anything to you?'

Hagen pursed her lips thoughtfully. 'No. Should it?'

'He was the customs official I mentioned. I think he may have been one of the officials waving through the Soviet goodies. Would he have been told to do so by you or the government?'

Hagen gave a caustic laugh. 'He'd nothing to do with us. We just picked up the merchandise and moved it on. And the Swedish government wouldn't have given him official orders to turn a blind eye. He probably wasn't even aware of the government's position. Most likely, he would have been paid handsomely by whoever was behind the movement of the "Soviet goodies".'

That could explain where Jolis's money came from. Anita took a swig of her whisky to try and fortify herself. She coughed as the alcohol bit the back of her throat. When she'd recovered her composure, she knew she had to get to the nitty-gritty.

'Was there anything on the ferry the night it sank? I've talked to an ex-customs official who said there'd been a tip-off about some illegal immigrants on board.'

'Didn't know about that. Not our concern.'

228

'Was there anything that was your concern on board that night that you Americans were smuggling back to the US?'

Hagen stared thoughtfully into her glass. She didn't react for so long that Anita wondered if she hadn't heard her question.

'There was. And I'm sure it led to all those lives being lost. I still think about it. I'd been due to go to the harbour the next morning to make sure that everything went smoothly.'

'What the hell was it?' Anita demanded.

Another pause. 'Electronic chips. Contained crucial information on the accuracy and range of Russian missiles. The Soviet Union might have been falling apart, but it didn't make their missiles any less dangerous to the West. More dangerous, in fact. More so with the loss of central control.'

'And you think these chips were the reason the *Estonia* was sunk?' Hagen nodded. 'How and why?'

'We weren't a hundred percent sure, but we believed that it was probably the Russians who blew a hole in the ferry. Survivors talked about hearing an explosion.'

'Wasn't it a bit drastic to kill all those people just for some bloody electronic chips?' Anita was angry.

'I don't think they were meant to be killed. I think the Russians were pissed off – there was so much important military material disappearing off to the West, they wanted to stop the trade. We thought that the bomb on board was a warning.'

'A warning?' Anita almost screamed in her exasperation.

'We believe they wanted to cripple the ship so that it would turn back to Tallinn. Then they could retrieve the chips and whatever else might have been on the vessel that night. I wasn't privy to everything that was going on. But the stormy weather didn't help. It just all went wrong.'

'You can say that again,' said Anita bitterly. Her thoughts were in turmoil. 'And the aftermath? The inquiry?'

'Sweden was very cooperative. Took a firm hand and made sure that the inquiry came to the "right" conclusion.'

'Protecting the wreck?'

'Of course. No one could afford to have unauthorized people poking around down there. God knows what they might have found. Can you imagine the international scandal that would have ensued if all this came out? Governments closed ranks. You won't find any of the states involved giving up their secrets anytime soon. Even in the US, the National Security Agency has fobbed off nosy journalists' freedom of information requests with the old "could cause serious damage to national security" excuse. They won't even release heavily redacted documents from the archives. Basically, nothing will come out until long after all the participants are dead, including me.'

Anita put down her tumbler. She'd got information that she hadn't been expecting, even if some of it she'd rather not have heard.

'Does the name Happy Electricals mean anything to you?' Iqbal Nawaz had been on the same ferry over to Tallinn as her father three days before the sinking. And she'd had an email from Hakim informing her that he may well have been involved in smuggling illegal immigrants at the time.

Hagen squinted at Anita.

'Rings a bell. Didn't one of their vehicles go down with the ferry?'

'Did it? That's not public knowledge.'

'I must have seen something at the time,' she said airily.

'And did you come across Zander Security?'

'Swedish company?'

'Yes.'

'They had something to do with Tallinn. Can't remember what.' Hagen finished her whisky. 'Look, Anita, I need to go to bed. Got an early tutorial tomorrow. The graduate students might be on vacation, but there are still a few of my post-grads beavering away.' She stood up unsteadily. 'I've probably said too much. Not that you can do anything about it. The past is dead and buried. I suggest you keep it that way.'

CHAPTER 40

Anita made her way along the canal towpath. The light of the three-quarter moon, reflected in the glassy water, guided her along. Further ahead, she could make out the shapes of a line of narrow boats. She crossed over a small bridge which led her down into Canal Street. Ahead of her, she could see the illuminated sign of the Old Bookbinders ale house. It was still warm enough for the benches outside to be occupied with drinkers and smokers. She was gasping for a beer to take away the taste of the whisky that Annie Hagen had given her. She entered a low-ceilinged, half-timbered bar. An eclectic and eccentric mix of paraphernalia, from pans and copper jugs to ice skates and boxing gloves, was suspended from the beams and plasterwork. None of it seemed to have much to do with books, though Kevin had chosen this particular tavern because that area of Jericho had been built mainly for the workers at the nearby Oxford University Press on Walton Street, hence the name of the pub. It wasn't as full as some of the city-centre inns, as it was off the tourist trail. Most of the patrons seemed to be locals, which created a cosy and friendly atmosphere.

She spotted Kevin nursing a pint and reading a newspaper in the corner by the window. As soon as he saw her, he got to his feet.

'I expect you need a drink.'

'Yes, please.'

Kevin shuffled off to the long wooden bar and came back with two fresh pints.

'You'll like this. Nice ale,' he said, plonking a glass down on the table in front of her. 'We should have come to eat here. The grub looks great.'

'Thanks. And here's a pot of honey in return.' She took out of her bag a reused glass jar with the label *Hagen's Honey* handwritten in blue biro. 'Her exact words were "honey for you, honey".'

Anita gulped her pint then put her glass down with a huge gasp.

'Well?' Kevin was impatient to hear if she had gleaned anything from their beekeeper.

'Annie was very forthcoming. I think a hefty dose of whisky helped.'

'Any closer?'

'I don't know. She confirmed that the American and Swedish governments were heavily involved in the Baltic Drainpipe. Brits were beneficiaries, too. Everything being waved through customs, which must have been Markus Jolis's role.'

She took another swig.

'Does she have any idea how the *Estonia* sank?'

'She blames it on the Russians. The trouble is that everyone I speak to has a different theory. No one is actually certain. Annie was only guessing. I'm starting to think that I really am wasting my time and yours.'

Kevin drained the remains of his old pint and pushed a newspaper towards her.

'Someone left this.' Anita could see it was an *Evening Standard*. 'A London commuter, I suppose. While I've been waiting, I've read it from cover to cover, or back cover to front cover, as I always start with the sport. But I found this,' he said, tapping a small article.

Anita squinted through her glasses and read: VICAR'S FATAL FALL.

'And?'

'Read it.'

It was only three paragraphs at the bottom of page nine, but it described how the Reverend Peter Tallis of St. Thomas's in Chelsea, had been up on the roof of his church tower and had slipped in wet conditions, falling to his death. It was a tragic accident, and his parishioners were deeply shocked and saddened by the loss of their popular priest.

Anita pushed the paper away. 'That's really sad.'

'Can't believe I was talking to him just a few days ago. I liked Peter a lot.'

'I'm sorry,' said Anita, putting a comforting hand on Kevin's arm.

'St. Peter will have his hands full when Tallis turns up at the Pearly Gates.'

Alice Zetterberg stared out of the window of her apartment, vodka in hand. All she could see were other blocks. In recent months, the more she resented her time in Malmö, the more the apartment became like a prison. As a result, she'd spent as much time as she could away from it. That usually resulted in sitting alone in restaurants or bars; unless she managed to find someone for a quick one-nighter, preferably at their place. And that was getting harder at her age. She'd been dissatisfied with her temporary role running the Criminal Investigation Squad, always aware that Moberg would be back. And she'd lost interest in the Cold Case Group when the commissioner had cut the funding and Erlandsson had been moved. It was only a matter of time before it was allowed to quietly fade away – there were more pressing priorities than digging up old cases that might embarrass the force.

Then the offer of the Stockholm job had come along, and life was good again. But now, due to Anita Sundström's inability to do as she was told, that new life was under threat. She raged against the injustice. She'd helped the secret services out twice now. And look where it had landed her! It was so unfair! Somehow, she had to stop Sundström doing whatever she was doing. If only she knew what Stockholm were trying to protect; to keep under wraps. Whatever it was, it was incredibly sensitive. And she guessed that it probably had something to do with the sinking of the *Estonia*.

She swigged what was left of the spirit in her glass and returned to the bottle: it was nearly empty. She normally resorted to it out of despair, and it hardly ever helped, yet this time, it gave her a moment of inspiration. She'd sent Sundström on holiday. She could just as easily bring her back. That would make sure she cut short her trip to England. God knows what she was hoping to dig up there, but Stockholm had been alarmed by her visit. It was the only way she could monitor what Sundström was up to. Keep her busy and be in a position to thwart any surreptitious enquiries. And she had a good excuse to get Sundström back to work. The Iqbal Nawaz case wasn't going well. An extra hand would be useful. She was desperate to tie it up. With Moberg dead, she was worried that the commissioner might ask her to stay on until the case was solved.

Zetterberg sat down to ping off a sharply worded SMS to Sundström. Basically, it was an order to get her arse back as soon as possible. Needed on Iqbal Nawaz case urgently. Then she poured out the last of the vodka and downed it in one gulp.

Kevin woke. He glanced at the digital clock. It was just past three. He was about to turn over when he realized that he needed to get up to have a pee. The beer he'd had at the Old Bookbinders was catching up with his bladder. He slipped quietly out of bed in the dark and tiptoed to the en suite bathroom. On his return, he could make out that Anita wasn't in bed. Then he noticed her sitting in a chair, staring out of the window.

'Can't you sleep?'

'Sorry. Did I disturb you?'

'No. Call of nature.'

He joined her at the window, the curtain slightly parted so she could look out at the street below.

'What's on your mind?'

'Oh, things,' she murmured distractedly.

'Zetterberg's text ordering you back?'

'Not really. I know from Hakim that they're struggling on the case. I didn't want to leave it in the first place.'

'What things then?'

'Annie Hagen. Peter Tallis.'

'Peter? What about Peter?'

Anita shifted in her seat and glanced up at him, her face half in shadow. In some ways she was even more beautiful without her glasses on.

'His death. Was it an accident?'

'Says so in the paper.'

'What if it wasn't? Don't you think it's a coincidence that within a few days of him contacting MI6, he's dead?'

'The poor guy just slipped on a wet roof.'

'Or was he pushed?'

'Are you saying that MI6 might have done this?'

'No. But don't you think that when Tallis contacted them, they would have passed the information on? It's obviously all still classified on both sides of the Atlantic. What if they got onto the CIA? Or Säpo? What if the whole *Estonia* thing is a big cover up? Maybe Peter Tallis getting in touch with his former employers had, in Annie Hagen's words, upset the bees.'

'But why him?'

She shook her head. 'I don't know. Is it just my over-active imagination?'

'If you're right, then I put him in danger. Christ! And what about Annie Hagen? She's spilled a few beans to you tonight. Have we put her in the spotlight, too?'

'What about us?'

'What do you mean?'

'Well, we're the ones upsetting the hive. Will they come after us next?'

Kevin marched over to the kettle. He switched it on.

'Let's have a cup of tea. Everything seems worse in the middle of the night. Time to stop our imaginations running riot and view things rationally.'

'Do the British really think a cup of tea is the answer to every problem?'

'Of course. It's a well-known fact. And I bet after a nice cuppa, Peter Tallis's death will be back to the accident the world thinks it is. It'll all look different in the morning.'

CHAPTER 41

It hadn't looked different in the morning. Not to Anita. That's why she was standing on the steps leading up to Annie Hagen's front door. Kevin stood on the pavement while Anita rang the bell for the third time. Over an early breakfast, she'd returned to her theme of last night and was concerned that they should warn Hagen, or at the very least, tell her the news about Peter Tallis and let her draw her own conclusions. After half a dozen phone calls that Hagen had failed to pick up, Anita had marched from the hotel and right up the street – this time not skulking through the back lane and garden as she'd done last night at Hagen's insistence.

'She's obviously gone out,' said Kevin. 'You said she had a tutorial.'

From the top step, Anita leant over the basement cavity as far as she could and tried to peer through the bay window of the living room where she'd sat drinking whisky the night before.

'You're probably right. Do we know where her tutorial will be?'

'According to the academic website I found her on, she works at the Rothermere American Institute.' He got out his now well-creased map. 'Yeah. It's on South Parks Road. Fifteen minutes' walk.'

The Rothermere American Institute was tucked away in among some modern buildings, opposite the more established ones of the university science site. They walked round the concrete, rectangular block until they found a more adventurous tubular glass appendage, complete with revolving door.

'I'll go and ask.'

Kevin let her. He turned his attention to the contrasting building over the wall – the Victorian Gothic splendour of Mansfield College.

The creamy Cotswold stone bathed in sunlight was easy on the eye, and Kevin allowed his thoughts to wander. As usual, his inquisitive nature got the better of him, and he took out his phone to find out more. He smirked at the irony – during the Second World War, Mansfield College was home to forty members of staff from the government's Code & Cypher School decoding enemy secrets. At least *they* knew who they were up against. But in Anita's case, who were the enemy? Did they really exist?

Anita reappeared with an expression that Kevin could only describe as pensive.

'Is she in there?'

She shook her head.

'Has she been in?'

'No. But she phoned in first thing this morning cancelling her nine-thirty tutorial and her other appointments for the next couple of weeks.'

'So, she's just gone away?'

'Her brother's been taken seriously ill.'

'There you are.'

'Except for one thing. She told me one of the reasons she came to Britain was because she had no family left in America. And I'm not the first person to ask for her this morning. Someone rang in earlier asking if she was here.'

Anita and Kevin headed through the gates into the University Parks: a large expanse of sports fields and recreational greenery that wended its way to the banks of the River Cherwell. Neither had spoken since leaving the Rothermere American Institute. Anita had been glued to her phone. Kevin knew that she was checking up on the flight she'd booked out of Gatwick that evening. He didn't want her to go. He had to admit he'd rather enjoyed their bits of sleuthing together. She might not agree, but he felt they made a good team. Simply being with her always gave him a buzz. Life was never boring when she was around, which only made his Penrith existence seem rather prosaic by comparison.

As they wandered along the path, he noticed a cricket pavilion.

'Oh, this must be The Parks!' he said with the excitement of someone who'd just discovered El Dorado. 'The Oxford University cricket ground!'

Anita glanced up from her phone. 'Very nice.' Then she returned to her screen.

Kevin could see some players in cricket whites gathering at the foot of the pavilion steps.

'Look, I think there's going to be a game.' He ushered Anita over to a bench on the boundary. 'Some great cricketers started their careers here. C. B. Fry, Douglas Jardine, Colin Cowdrey, Nawab of Pataudi...'

'That last one doesn't sound very English.'

'He wasn't. He was Indian.'

'Any Pakistanis?'

'Yeah. Their first ever captain. A. H. Kardar. He was here just after the war.'

Anita watched the players stretching and warming up. Was this the routine Iqbal Nawaz's team went through each weekend? Except they didn't do it in front of an elegant late-Victorian pavilion, but outside a wooden hut. One thing Anita was now certain of: Iqbal's murder had nothing to do with the cricket club or its members.

The gentle sun beat down on the bench. 'I wish you weren't going back today. Bugger Alice Zetterberg!'

'It's not just her. I want to go back. I need to help solve the case. I'm now convinced that Markus Jolis's death is connected to Iqbal Nawaz. And I think that I may have inadvertently set both deaths in motion.'

'What do you mean?'

'If I hadn't asked Markus Jolis about the *Estonia*, he wouldn't have said what he did in front of the so-called lawyer. I reckon the lawyer was something to do with the secret service, who sent him in to make sure that a poor man with dementia didn't blurt out anything he shouldn't. And the unidentified doctor at the hospital probably came as part of that package, too; as did the hastily arranged cremation paid for by the same so-called lawyer. After all, we know that Jolis was working in customs and was on duty the day the *Estonia* was meant to dock. He was on the take, which explains his wealth. It's extremely likely that he was one of the officials waving through illicit items for the Americans. Then when things go wrong, he's swiftly moved down to Malmö.'

Kevin had his eyes on the cricketers taking up their positions for the start of the game, though his mind was firmly on Anita's thought processes.

'I get all that. And I can see there being a clandestine operation to shut Jolis up. Not sure where your Pakistani businessman fits in, though.'

'We know Iqbal was on the same voyage to Tallinn as my dad.'

'Business. Annie Hagen told you that a Happy Electricals vehicle was on board. He was probably in Tallinn buying up old Soviet electrical goods. They'd be cheap. Maybe that's why his enterprise took off at around that time.'

'Yes. That makes sense. But I think it's the human smuggling that's the link. Hakim said that Sarfraz Khan was smuggled in as a child and that his wife Sidra believes that Iqbal was involved. And low and behold! Jolis's ex-colleague says they were tipped off about illegal immigrants being on board when the boat sank. If that were true, then those poor people must have experienced a harrowing death trapped in a truck or container. It doesn't bear thinking about. What if Iqbal was over in Tallinn, not for electricals but a people smuggling operation?'

'Again, you might be right. But why would anybody want to get rid of him now?'

'Maybe he knew what was going on with the various governments and that all sorts of things were passing deliberately undetected through customs. It was common knowledge in Tallinn at the time. He just used the system.'

'Still doesn't answer my question.' This was followed by Kevin clapping. One of the players on the field had just played a good shot.

Anita sat silently as she rummaged around in her mind for an answer.

'What if Markus Jolis was waving the illegal immigrants through, too?'

'For your theory to work, Iqbal would still have to be in cahoots with the authorities. Snuffing him out now means he had knowledge that was still potentially dangerous. And Jolis was the catalyst.'

'The timing fits.' She was still racking her brains. 'What if...'

Kevin turned to Anita and grinned. 'You're a "what if" sort of person.'

'No, I'm serious. What if Iqbal was more involved in the illicit trade than we think. Not the smuggling, though that might have been a sideline. Actually, that's a thought!' She felt a mounting excitement. 'The Happy Electricals truck or van or whatever. This is a really big "what if". What if the authorities were using Iqbal's firm to transport some of the contraband? Certainly the electrical-related material. Annie Hagen said that the cargo that night included electronic chips containing crucial information on Russian missiles. What better cover than using a company making regular trips dealing with everyday electricals? That could be it!'

'Plausible.'

'If that was the case, then Iqbal would know all about the illegal, government-sponsored operations. The secret service guys seem intent on stopping any information leaking out. After they killed Jolis, Iqbal would be an obvious candidate for elimination. He knew too much.'

'Followed by Peter Tallis. *You* might feel bad. His death might have been *my* fault!'

'You contacted him because of me.'

'Doesn't absolve me from guilt.' Now Kevin had lost interest in the cricket. 'What about Annie's disappearing act?'

'She heard about Peter Tallis. Thought she might be in danger.'

'Brilliant! That means that if Peter *was* killed, they, whoever they are, are operating over here. And if they've tried to track Annie down, then it's probably us who led them to Oxford. Which means someone

is following our movements. They might be observing us right now.'
He glanced around the park. Not many people about: a couple of
joggers, a dog walker with five animals straining at their leashes, a
mother pushing a buggy and a young couple walking hand in hand –
and then there were the cricketers. 'Not a comforting thought.'

Anita took Kevin's hand and squeezed it. 'I shouldn't have put
you in this position.'

'Don't worry about that. You're the one in more danger if this *is*
a government cover up.'

They lapsed into an uneasy silence.

'What if—' Kevin started.

'Not you now. It's catching.'

'What if this isn't a government cover up?'

'Must be. Peter Tallis's death indicates that. Whoever is behind
all this must have found out about him making enquiries about the
Estonia when he got in touch with MI6.'

'Christ, you don't think MI6 killed him?'

'I don't know. I definitely think MI6 passed on the information
to their opposite numbers in Sweden. Maybe *they* were acting on
behalf of the Swedish government. After all, presumably the British
don't want anything to come out either.'

'Or the CIA. They seem to have been involved. Annie Hagen's
proof of that.'

'We know these people are completely ruthless. Look what they
did to Albin Rylander and poor Klas Lennartsson. That's never seen
the light of day. When they want something hushed up, whatever the
cost, they do it.'

'I hear what you're saying, but if you'll just let me finish my
"what if"...' Anita tipped her hand in a gesture of *be my guest*. '...I
still think there might be another player in all this. You told me that
Annie Hagen spoke about the Swedish government being very hands
off. She mentioned there being someone who fronted, or facilitated
anyway, for the government and various other countries.' Anita
nodded agreement. 'He or his organization was probably Markus

Jolis's paymaster. Jolis would have to be on their books when you think about it. Isn't it significant that after he was moved to Malmö, he joined this Zander Security outfit? And Hagen had heard about Zander in connection with Tallinn. Then there's the banks. One of them was used by the Americans to pay off the Russians. What was the one Hagen mentioned?'

'The Independent Bank of Estonia.'

'Well, we need to check if it still exists and who was behind setting it up.'

'When I go back, I could get Liv to do some digging. Mind you, she'll have to be careful. Someone cottoned on to the fact that she was looking into Zander.'

'There you are. There might be a link between Zander and the Independent Bank of Estonia. And another thought: you said that Markus Jolis's funeral was paid for by a well-wisher – singular. That sounds like one person.' Kevin was warming to his theme. He clicked his fingers excitedly. 'And didn't Jolis say to you "*He* was wrong."?'

'This all happened twenty-five years ago. The original person masterminding the government-sponsored parts of the Baltic Drain-pipe back then might not even be alive now.'

'You have three deaths so far. If my "what if" is correct, then he's very much alive.'

CHAPTER 42

The Bulltofta car park was full, and Hakim found it difficult to find a space. He wasn't entirely sure why he'd come here to see Mohammad Abbas. Though he'd pretty much drawn a blank in Lund with Usman Masood, he'd discovered that Abbas was now running the company, albeit on a temporary basis. For a moment, it had crossed his mind that Abbas was behind the murder to gain control of Happy Electricals. He even flirted with the idea that he'd deliberately involved Muneeba to give himself an alibi. But his reasoning didn't really stack up. Abbas would have to have had another accomplice to carry out the murder for him. Somehow, he couldn't see the man ordering a hit. And, disappointingly, Usman hadn't been able to shed any light on what was supposedly worrying Iqbal. He was beginning to think that the imam and Sidra had read too much into his moods. Maybe someone in the Bulltofta warehouse would enlighten him. It was more out of hope than expectation that he'd persuaded Zetterberg to let him come and ask around. The team was stumbling around in the dark, and Zetterberg was itching to get a conviction. Knowing Zetterberg as he did, it was definitely an act of desperation on her part to recall Anita – he couldn't think of any other reason. Hakim, of course, was delighted that she would be rejoining the investigation, though he suspected she wouldn't be happy being dragged away from her holiday in Britain.

There was a lot of activity inside the massive building, though he detected a sombre atmosphere. Abbas was in a meeting, so Hakim wandered through the maze of aisles and spoke to a few of the employees. The story was always the same – Iqbal Nawaz was a marvellous boss and had regarded them all as family. No one seemed to think that he had anything on his mind: when he appeared he was always his usual self. He visited the warehouse once a week for a catch-up meeting with Abbas, and sometimes came round and checked the stock. The only time he lost his temper was if the products weren't in pristine condition or had been badly stacked, which might result in them getting damaged. One brave soul actually ventured that the boss might have had OCD, an opinion he'd never have uttered if Iqbal had still been alive. Hakim was on the point of leaving, when he saw that Abbas's meeting was breaking up. Abbas waved through the glass partition for him to come into the office.

'Sorry, I'm a bit busy at the moment. I'm trying to keep the operation running as smoothly as I can.'

'It's a lot of extra responsibility.'

'Yes. I may have to give the cricket a miss this weekend.' He sat down at his desk. 'Coffee?'

'No thanks. Look, maybe you can help.' Hakim remained standing. 'I've heard from a couple of sources that Iqbal was worried about something in the days or weeks before he was killed. I can't get any confirmation. So it might have been personal, or it might have been to do with the company. Any ideas?'

Hakim was expecting the party line – businessmen have business worries.

'Yes...' Abbas said, extending the three letters into a longer word. 'A possible business problem. It was me that started it off.'

'OK. How exactly?' Hakim took a seat and whipped out his notebook.

Abbas sighed deeply. 'I was checking the deliveries about three weeks before... you know. Each month, we get two shipments from our factories in Pakistan coming through Trelleborg. The containers are driven straight here from the port, so we know exactly the distance the trucks should rack up on each trip. It should be around forty kilometres. I happened to notice that for the previous six months, one of the shipments was clocking up around seventy kilometres.'

'That's quite a difference.'

'I pointed this out to Iqbal.'

'What did he think?'

'Well, like I did. The driver – and it was the same one each time – was going somewhere else first.'

'Things falling off the back of a truck type of thing?'

'That was what was so odd. Every item was accounted for. Nothing had been stolen.'

'Did you or Iqbal speak to the driver?'

'I didn't. Iqbal said he would look into it. Stefan wasn't a full-time employee. He was only used to do those runs and similar routes when needed.'

'And did he track him down?'

'I don't know.'

'Can you give me this driver's name and contact details?'

'Sure.' Abbas worked on his computer keyboard for a few seconds. 'We get our drivers through the same agency. It's not worth employing full-time drivers for those runs: not enough work.' He copied down the details for Stefan Sundewall on a piece of paper, which he handed to Hakim.

'It's certainly odd,' said Hakim as he gazed at the information. The employment agency was based in Trelleborg.

'I know. If there'd been any missing merchandise, it would be understandable. But there wasn't.'

No immediate explanation came to Hakim.

'And this troubled Iqbal?'

'Yes.'

'Enough to really upset him?'

'You wouldn't have thought so. But he was the type of person who didn't like anything that couldn't be explained.'

'And?'

'Strangely, the last call I made to him that night... the night he died... as you know, I was doing it to make sure that he wouldn't suddenly turn up here as I was going to meet Muneeba. Anyway, my mind was on other things, and it only came back to me afterwards. I don't know if he talked to the driver, but he said he'd found out why the shipments had gone on their round trips.'

'And?' Hakim said again in anticipation of some great revelation.

'That was it. He said he'd tell me the next day.'

'She appears to be in league with a man called Kevin Ash. British citizen. And a police detective. Cumbria Constabulary, wherever that is.'

'So we have two cops sniffing around?' The voice at the Stockholm end sounded perturbed.

'Looks like it.'

'Where are they now?'

'Heading back to London. But they've been to Oxford.'

'Why Oxford?'

'They went to see an Annie Hagen. It just so happens that she worked for the CIA in Stockholm at the time of the event.'

'Oh, God! Did your people manage to get hold of her?'

'No. She'd disappeared.'

'Did someone warn her?'

'Don't know. Maybe she saw something about the vicar. And, yes, that went smoothly. A tragic accident.'

'We have to stop this getting out of hand.'

'Absolutely. Do you want me to see to the two detectives?'

Stockholm couldn't keep the anxiety out of his voice. 'No way! Far too dangerous. It would be difficult enough covering up the death of one police officer. Two in two countries could really open up Pandora's box. The police don't like to lose their own. It might draw too much unwanted attention. As I mentioned before, we need to cut off the sources of information that they can access.' There was a pause at the other end of the line. 'Look, let us take over now. We'll use our resources.'

'All right,' he said warily. 'If you're sure.'

'Yes. I'm sure.'

'She'd better not turn up on my doorstep. Remember, if anything comes out, I'm not going to go quietly. I'll bring the whole damn house of cards crashing down – and you with it!'

CHAPTER 43

The flight back from London Gatwick to Copenhagen was not a relaxing one for Anita. As the booking was made at the last minute, she found herself squeezed in between an overweight businessman who should have been able to afford a better, wider seat on an international carrier and not a budget airline, and a young woman who spent most of her time playing something on her phone. That wouldn't have mattered if she hadn't been expressively using her elbows, which kept intruding into Anita's diminishing space.

She was also worrying about her conversation with Kevin in the Parks in Oxford. Was she really being followed? With a detective's forensic eye, she'd scrutinized her fellow passengers while they gathered and queued at the gate, in the hope that she might spot someone taking an inordinate interest in her. The only person who looked remotely suspicious was a young man who was giving her funny looks, until she realized he probably had a lazy eye. No one fitted her idea of an undercover operative. Presumably that was the point – a good one would be undetectable.

She quietly fretted about the situation. It wasn't helped by the awful coffee she'd stupidly ordered with the bacon roll and packet of crisps as part of her meal deal. The tray in front of her was crammed with all the inflight food. She should have just gone for a couple of the miniature bottles of red instead. She wasn't sure what she should do next. Clearly, she would be joining the team tomorrow to work on the Iqbal Nawaz investigation. That had now taken a twist and, in her opinion, might well be connected to the death of Markus Jolis. How was that going to play out if Alice Zetterberg was still keen to kill the

Jolis case? Of course, Zetterberg's actions suddenly made sense. What if she was getting orders from elsewhere? That would explain how she knew someone had been delving into Zander Security. If there was a conspiracy going on, they would have got to Zetterberg. If her past actions were anything to go by, she would be happily compliant. She had discouraged Anita virtually from the word go – certainly after her meeting with Markus Jolis in the hospital. And when she couldn't get Anita to stop, she'd sent her away on holiday. It all added up. With intervention from shadowy figures above, how could they possibly solve the murder of Iqbal Nawaz? Would Zetterberg try and put a stop to that investigation, too? Yet now she was yanking her back off holiday to help the team. That didn't make sense. Unless Zetterberg hadn't been informed of the connection.

And was she, Anita, going to pursue the connections to the *Estonia*? She realized that she was swimming in dangerous waters. Her instinct was to continue to look into how and why her father had died – she would never rest easy until she knew. But at what cost? Was her meddling responsible for three murders? Would she be putting more lives in jeopardy if she carried on? Could her family be targeted? That was an unbearable thought. And what of Kevin, whom she'd dragged in without thinking of the consequences? OK, he'd volunteered, but he wouldn't have done so if she hadn't told him all about her *Estonia* findings. Their farewell at the airport had been hurried. He'd tried to be upbeat, coming out with his terrible jokes until their final hug. But there was no hiding the fact that he was far more worried about her than he was about himself. Is that what love is all about? He'd embraced her with an extra urgency, and she'd found it difficult to break free. Would *he* now be watched? Regarded as a risk by the British intelligence service? He'd nearly lost his job once before because of her.

Then her mind strayed to Kevin's 'what if'. A single person – a mastermind. A middleman backed by acquiescing authorities. A man with a lot of power and, given his role, a great deal of leverage with several governments. A man, if he existed and was still alive, with the protection of various national states and their most secret organizations. With the scale of forces mounted against her, the most sensible thing to do would be to walk away. But she knew she couldn't. She hated to admit it but she had her mother's obstinacy, which is why she would continue to make her surreptitious enquiries. At least Kevin had given her a couple of places to start looking – the mysterious Zander Security and the Independent Bank of Estonia.

The other matter on her mind was the link between Iqbal Nawaz and the human smuggling carried out at the time of the ferry sinking. The evidence wasn't clear cut, though it wasn't difficult to draw conclusions. Iqbal had been heading for Tallinn only days before (albeit allegedly) a group of illegal immigrants had set off on that fateful voyage. Then there was the paradox of Sarfraz Khan. Iqbal had virtually adopted an Iraqi child and must have gone to great lengths to keep his identity from being discovered over the years. As she tried to open her crisp packet without spraying the contents all over her tiny tray and the bulbous businessman's lap, she had an idea. She knew a man who might be able to join the dots. And she knew exactly where to find him – in prison.

Anita was greeted in the next morning's meeting by Zetterberg's sarcastic 'I'm glad you could make it.' She made it sound as though Anita had been skiving off for a few days: she didn't rise to the bait. She was determined to keep Zetterberg in the dark as much as possible. The main thrust of the discussions was Hakim's discovery of the circuitous route taken monthly by the delivery truck from Trelleborg. He'd checked up on Stefan Sundewall, the driver on each occasion. He was forty-two, divorced and was on their database. He had two convictions for handling stolen goods. His last offence was seven years ago. He was no longer around. He'd got work in Germany, according to the agency he worked through. The timing had been odd – he'd gone the weekend before Iqbal was murdered. Liv had gone into the possible places Sundewall could have got to, taking into account the extra thirty kilometres. The favourites were around Lomma, Lund or Svedala. Lund appeared the most obvious because the company head office was there, though Wallen pointed out that if the truck went via the Lund HQ, Iqbal should have been aware of it.

The logistics of the container truck's movements led to speculation as to why it would deviate in the first place. The driver flitting off to Germany had been very suspicious. What extra freight could the container hold that could be unloaded en route to the warehouse? Much to Zetterberg's annoyance, Hakim raised the subject of human smuggling. Iqbal might have been involved before. Was he doing it again? This was countered by Bea Erlandsson, who postulated that if he *was* involved in such an operation, why was he so concerned about the truck's extra mileage? Hakim responded that his concern might have been because Abbas had discovered the discrepancy. As to the load, drugs was another theory, as was ancient artefacts smuggled in from the Indian subcontinent, for which there would be a ready market in the West.

'It might be simpler than that,' mused Brodd, who hadn't so far contributed much to the debate. 'The driver might have been doing something more personal. Seeing a married woman, for example. What better time than during the day? Or maybe he was doing a favour for a mate. Hakim, you said he'd a record of handling stolen goods. Maybe he still was – and using his truck to do so. A legit delivery would be good cover.'

'Maybe that's what Iqbal found out,' suggested Zetterberg.

'I don't think so,' said Wallen, looking over at Hakim. 'Remember, Sidra said that he was angry that night. She actually said he was upset about something. Would such a simple explanation have upset him so much?'

The argument petered out as the team became lost in their own thoughts, and the meeting broke up shortly afterwards. Nothing concrete was decided other than that they would keep pursuing the leads they had. Specifically, Wallen was to have a word with the drugs squad, and Erlandsson was to enquire about the trade into smuggled artefacts. As they left the room, Anita collared Hakim.

'Can I have a word at lunchtime? I'll treat you to a sandwich.'

They ended up with falafels after Anita realized how hungry she was. She hadn't eaten since her snack on the plane, discovering there was nothing in the fridge when she got home. Breakfast had consisted of two extra-strong coffees, which had gone down very smoothly after suffering from the English offerings. Anita's falafel was covered in a creamy garlic sauce. Kevin would be jealous.

'How did you get on in England?' Hakim asked between bites. They were sitting in Drottningtorget, the square that had featured heavily in Anita's professional life. The day was warm and languid, and no one around them seemed in a hurry.

'I learned a lot. Not all of it I wanted to hear.' As she spoke, she scanned the square. It was the paranoia again. 'One thing I'm certain of is that the deaths of Markus Jolis and Iqbal Nawaz are connected.'

'I'm not sure.'

'Well, I'm convinced it's all to do with the *Estonia*, or rather the smuggling the ship was being used for. I also think there's a big cover-up going on, and if there is, I suspect our chances of clearing up Iqbal's murder aren't great.'

Hakim wolfed down another chunk of falafel, salad and pitta bread. He knew that when Anita got on one of her hobby horses, there was very little chance of unseating her. He let her go on.

'We're pretty sure Iqbal was into smuggling. You found out about Sarfraz Khan's origins; I discovered Iqbal was over in Tallinn at the time of the *Estonia* sinking. I think that, somehow, some source tipped off the Swedish Customs that there were going to be illegal immigrants on board. They were waiting for them at the point of arrival. Among the officials was a dishonest Markus Jolis, whose job it was to let all sorts of illicit merchandise pass through unchallenged and unchecked. He was probably doing this for the Americans, the British and the Swedes.'

Hakim nearly choked on his food. 'Come on, that's a bit steep!'

'Trust me. It's what was happening. That's one of the things I found out in England.' She briefly described the Baltic Drainpipe and what the various governments were up to. 'You can see why they need to cover the whole thing up.'

'You're not saying they were behind the sinking of the *Estonia*?'

'No. Of all the theories out there, either an accident or the Russian bomb makes the most sense. But whatever the cause of the sinking, it induced panic in government circles. They made sure that nothing on the wreck could be touched. If those Russian computer chips were found, all sorts of embarrassing questions would be asked, which might expose the whole trade. Which brings me back to Markus Jolis. *He* knew all about it, as he was an integral part of its smooth running. The secret service probably sent in that phoney lawyer to make sure this old man with dementia didn't say anything he shouldn't. But of course he did, and he had to be silenced. Hence the phoney doctor. Jolis's death was definitely murder, but we couldn't prove it because the body was cremated in double-quick time.'

'And Iqbal?'

'He was involved, too, somehow. I believe he was using the ship for human smuggling. We know it was happening, as illegal immigrants had been found on board earlier that year. He had the perfect front – he was running his legitimate business through that route. My ex-CIA contact mentioned one of his vehicles was on the ferry.'

'Carrying the immigrants you think were lost on board?'

'Possibly. Depends on the size of the truck being used. There's also the strong possibility that whoever was behind the smuggling of those chips was using Happy Electricals as cover. Perfect way to do it.'

Hakim finished the last of his falafel and managed to suppress a burp.

'It's all speculation. You can't prove any of it.'

'I know. I've just got this feeling that Iqbal was killed because he knew too much.'

'A professional hit?'

'Yes. But made to look like it was connected to the cricket club. We conveniently obliged. When I think about it, this whole business might explain why Iqbal was so worried – he thought his involvement might be dredged up.'

'If you're right – and I have to say I'm not totally convinced – where do we go from here? The Markus Jolis case is history. That'll not be reopened. How would we even begin to link Iqbal to the *Estonia*? You heard Zetterberg's reaction.'

'She's part of the problem.' Anita didn't go into any detail. There was no point in burdening Hakim with all the behind-the-scenes machinations. 'Look, you and Klara are really leading the case now. All I'm saying is that the motive behind Iqbal's murder might neither be connected to the cricket club nor to his company as it is today.'

Hakim had learned to trust Anita's instincts over the years – not that her record in that regard was unblemished. Still, her theory was worth considering, though how he was going to explain it to Wallen, he wasn't quite sure.

'So, what are you going to do?'

'I'm going to keep digging.'

'Well, make sure you keep me in the loop.' He was fairly sure she wouldn't unless it suited her. 'I'd better be getting back to head-quarters. Coming?'

'No. I've got a prison visit to make.'

Anita hadn't been in the prison since the last time she'd visited Ewan Strachan nearly six years before. It wasn't the same room, though the atmosphere was just as oppressive, the furniture just as minimal. When she'd talked to Ewan, she'd insisted on speaking to him alone without a prison guard. With Dragan Mitrović, she insisted on exactly the opposite – a guard was present throughout the interview. Mitrović didn't exactly scare her – he just did a good line in intimidation despite being behind bars. After all, he had once broken into her apartment and threatened her, albeit in a charming, well-mannered way. She'd heard that most of the inmates gave him a wide berth unless he needed something from them – woe betide anyone who couldn't deliver.

Anita had dealt with Mitrović over the murder of the investigative journalist known as The Oligarch. One of the main suspects, an ex-boxer named Absame, had worked as an enforcer for the Serbian. Both he and Absame had had an alibi for the murder – they'd been picking up a shipment of narcotics from Trelleborg on the night in question. Mitrović was channelling narcotics through his state-of-the-art gyms. The alibi had been provided by a member of the drugs squad who had been working under cover. So, it wasn't that particular shipment that had resulted in the gaol sentence Mitrović was now serving – it was a bigger one later that year. Prosecutor Blom had thrown in prostitution and extortion for good measure. Mitrović had pleaded guilty on all counts. As he greeted Anita, she noticed he didn't seem to be suffering any obvious hardship from his imprisonment. His manner was relaxed and his smile beatific. He wasn't wearing his trademark sharp suit, yet he still managed to appear stylish in a white T-shirt and grey tracksuit trousers. The black, slicked-back hair was still dyed to within an inch of its life. The granite features, cloven by a scar down the left-hand side of his face, were still as rugged as she remembered them; only now he was starting to look his age. Anita reckoned he must be nearing seventy. He'd be a very old man by the time he got out – unless he bribed, intimidated or blackmailed his way to an early release.

'You know, Inspector Sundström, my visitors are usually met by sniffer dogs. I suspect that didn't apply to you. I hope you haven't brought in any drugs. They're prohibited in here.' His heavy-handed humour was delivered with an alluring menace.

'I'm sure that hasn't stopped your supply.'

The dark eyes flashed in amusement. 'I always liked you.'

'That's only because I didn't put you in here. I'm sure there are some inmates who are not my biggest fans.'

'I've met a few. For some reason, they find it more humiliating being put away by an attractive cop.'

'They've no worries on that score these days.'

'I don't know...' It was the first time she'd been flattered by a gangland boss.

Mitrović took a seat at the table. His movements were deliberate, as though he was still wearing his more sophisticated clothing.

'So, how is life on the inside? As palatial as we out there all think? We had a laugh down at the station when there were complaints about the quality of prison toilet rolls.'

There was a wry smile. 'Not as comfortable as I've been used to, of course. But if my dear, departed mother could see my present accommodation, she would think it the height of luxury – my cell is far better than the shithole she was forced to bring us up in.' He crossed his legs. 'But I'm sure you're not here to discuss prison conditions, Inspector. Do I need a lawyer present?'

'No. I'm here because I want you to give me a history lesson.'

'In exchange for?'

'I've got nothing to trade. I thought you'd do it out of the goodness of your heart.' She wasn't sure whether he was about to stand up and walk out. The thought must have crossed his mind, but curiosity got the better of him. He gestured for her to continue.

'I want to know about human smuggling.' She held up a warning finger when he was about to interrupt. 'I don't mean the trafficking that's going on now. You've clearly been bringing in your prostitutes from somewhere. I'm not interested in that. I want to take you back to 1994.' He pulled a puzzled pout. 'You'd have been operating at that time.'

'Yes. I was working for Bilić back then. In Stockholm and here.' Anita remembered when Bilić had mysteriously disappeared off the gangland scene. The police assumed that Dragan Mitrović had had something to do with it, as he had emerged as top man after a series of shooting incidents. Clearly, it was a case of intra-gang restructuring.

'There was a growing number of Iraqis coming in then after the First Gulf War. Some of them were being shipped across from Tallinn on the *Estonia*. Does this ring any bells?'

He nodded.

'Was Bilić involved in the same trade?'

'Not too much. He was more interested in bringing in girls from Eastern Europe. It was easier to convey them through Trelleborg or along the east coast. Plenty of remote islands that the coastguard couldn't cover.'

'Weren't illegal immigrants lucrative enough?'

'Oh, you could make good money. Very good. But the Tallinn link was all sewn up. Everyone wanted a piece of that action, and Bilić attempted to muscle in. He tried it once, but his cargo was discovered.'

'Was that before the ferry sinking?'

'Could have been. About that time.' That fitted in with what Ulf Garde had told her. 'Bilić thought he'd been grassed up because he knew other immigrants were getting through undetected. We thought it was a warning not to trample on someone else's territory.'

'Does the name Iqbal Nawaz mean anything to you?'

'Of course. He was murdered the other day. King of the cheap electricals. I met him a couple of times.' Anita registered her surprise. 'Malmö is smaller than you think.'

'He had connections with Tallinn. I think he was buying cheap Soviet electricals.'

'Makes sense.'

'I also think he might have been doing some human smuggling on the side.'

'Possibly. Bilić suspected that he was.' Mitrović ran a finger down the crevice of his scar. 'If he was, he'd have to have had someone in authority turning a blind eye.'

'You mean someone in the government?'

'Your guess is as good as mine. Put it this way... no one official was kicking up a fuss.'

It still wasn't cast iron proof that Iqbal *was* people smuggling, but it was another pointer in his direction. And if his trade was being protected, then he was inextricably tied up with Markus Jolis. If Iqbal was also involved as a go-between for the CIA and associates, he was definitely a danger to someone.

'Thank you.' Her eyes strayed to his scar. 'Don't mind my asking, but how did you get that?'

Mitrović gave her a lopsided grin.

'Bilić. We had a disagreement. He'd had my most loyal courier killed. He didn't do anything like that again.' The meaning was clear.

Anita stood up, as did Mitrović. Her mind flashed back to the meeting when the team were discussing what the container truck might have dropped off on the way to the Happy Electricals Bulltofta warehouse.

'How's the narcotics business now that you're in here?'

Mitrović cocked his head. 'You mean are my rivals trying to move in on my territory?'

'I suppose so, yes.'

'Someone's trying. I hear heroin from Afghanistan is coming in on different routes. Not so easy now to come overland through the Middle East. Too unstable.'

Anita quickly formed a mental globe.

'By sea?' His eyes flickered agreement. 'The most obvious place would be through Pakistan.'

'I'm not saying anything more.'

'Could Iqbal Nawaz have moved into drugs with you out of the way?'

He gave her an indulgent smile as though humouring a child who didn't quite understand the conversation.

'Iqbal was more than capable of working outside the law. But not drugs. He was a big anti-drugs campaigner.'

'What better front?'

'You don't understand. He hated them with a passion. He even berated me once about causing unnecessary distress and death. The silly bastard had a thing about them. I told him I'm just a business man like him supplying public demand. It was just heroin and cocaine instead of hair dryers or food mixers. He was very cross.'

257

Anita could imagine the scene. It would be water off a duck's back to Mitrović.

'Thank you for visiting,' Mitrović said, holding out his hand for her to shake. She was so taken aback that she took it. 'I've enjoyed our trip down memory lane. And it will give you something to ponder when you're back at that nice apartment of yours.'

'At least while you're banged up in here, I'm safe in the knowledge you won't break in again!'

CHAPTER 44

Kevin cleared away his supermarket lasagne and put his plate and cutlery in the sink. He stared out of the window. In the distance, he could see the lights of the M6 motorway as the cars and trucks whizzed past Penrith and the village that he lived in two miles south of the Cumbrian town. The house was rented, as he still couldn't afford his own place – the divorce had seen to that, together with helping his daughters out financially. If grandchildren came along, he'd have no spare money at all.

He leaned over to the fridge and took out a bottle of beer. He flipped the top off. He thought about pouring it into a glass then decided he couldn't be bothered. He'd got back that morning on the train from London. He was missing Anita, and he was still concerned over what she might be getting herself into. Was she already in too deep? He had tried to persuade her that he should fly to Sweden, too. She was adamant that he didn't. He'd learned not to argue with her. As he still had a few days off, he might go over to Newcastle and visit the girls. If nothing else, they'd let him treat them to a slap-up meal at one of Tyneside's trendy restaurants. Every visit cost him.

He sauntered into the living room and collapsed into a comfy green armchair. It was one of the few items that he'd managed to salvage from the divorce settlement. Anita had suggested that he get it reupholstered: the material was now threadbare, and it sagged every time he sat in it. He knew she was right, but he also knew he'd probably never get round to it. It fitted his bum perfectly. He flicked the television on with the remote and took a sip of his beer. The BBC 10 o'clock news had just begun. He hadn't paid much attention to current events over the last few days so it would be interesting to catch up.

He was halfway through his beer and the news when the front door bell rang. It was unusual to get a visitor at this time of night. He didn't have much of a social circle beyond work, and if it was police related, he would have had a phone call.

With much huffing, he went to the door and opened it. At first, all he could make out was a figure in the blackness. One thing he could tell: it was a woman.

'Sorry, no hawkers or traders.'

'Kevin Ash?' The voice was pleasantly crisp. She wasn't from round these parts.

'Yes,' Kevin answered guardedly.

'I need to have a word.'

'Can't you come back tomorrow?'

'I'm afraid it can't wait.'

Kevin could hear the newsreader in the background. It sounded like more doom and gloom. As his eyes grew accustomed to the dark, he could make out the woman standing in front of him. She was taller than him – a lot of people were – and she had her red hair swept back in a ponytail.

'And what is so important that you've come here at this time of night?'

'It's about Peter Tallis.'

Kevin showed the woman into the sitting room. He grabbed the remote and turned off the television.

'Take a seat.' The woman slipped off her black mackintosh and draped it over the back of the sofa. Now he could get a better look at her. She couldn't have been more than mid-thirties. The freckled face was chubby. The brown eyes surveyed her surroundings like an estate agent weighing up how best to tart up the house to make it sellable.

'MI6 or MI5?'

'Six.'

'Want a drink?'

'No, thank you.'

'Don't mind me,' said Kevin as he reached for his half-drunk bottle of beer. He settled down in his familiar armchair.

'Peter Tallis...' the woman started. Kevin noticed that she hadn't offered a name. Nor had he asked for ID. Sloppy.

'I hear he died in a tragic accident. Fell off his church roof.'

'You were in contact with him before his death.'

'Was I?'

'Don't be coy, Kevin.' He bristled at her calling him by his first name when she hadn't divulged hers. 'We have your mobile phone calls to him – and his to you.'

'OK, I did contact him and I did see him at his church. But I was in Oxford when he died.'

'We know. We don't suppose you had anything directly to do with his death.'

'Well, that's a relief,' he said, though he didn't like the word 'directly'.

'Was it on your behalf that Tallis contacted Albert Embankment?'

'You mean Legoland? Yes, it was, as a matter of fact. It was his idea, being ex-Service.'

'I'm well aware of who he was.'

'And his reputation?' he smiled, in an effort to lighten the conversation.

'And his reputation. Fortunately, the Service has moved on from those more sexist days. Even we've heard of *MeToo*. Tallis enquired about Sweden. At the time of the *Estonia* ferry disaster in 1994.'

'Correct. And it's also correct to say that he didn't find out anything. The Service kept shtum.'

'Why was he enquiring about the *Estonia* disaster on your behalf?'

'I was trying to help out a Swedish journalist I know. She was doing some research,' he added vaguely.

'And this journalist is called Anita Sundström, the woman that you stayed with at hotels in London and Oxford last week?'

'You have been checking up. Is it a crime to date EU citizens now?'

'Except she's not a journalist. She's a member of the Malmö police force. A detective.'

'Bloody hell, is she? She had me fooled!'

'Don't piss about, Kevin. What was she up to?'

'Don't you know?' He reasoned that after what they'd been through, she *must* know. MI6 *must* know.

'I wouldn't be asking if I did.'

'Right, I'll level with you. Anita's father died on the *Estonia*. You can check that out. She just wants to know some of the background. I was trying to help. That's why I approached Peter, because I'd met him when he was working for your lot years ago. Anyway, he got nowhere.'

'And Oxford? Why were you in Oxford?' Didn't she know about Annie Hagen?

'A break. Anita had never been there before. Neither had I, as a matter of fact. We loved it. But she had to go back to Sweden to work on a murder case, and she flew out last night. I presume you already know that. There was nothing official in what she did. She was on holiday, for goodness sake!'

'And how many times did you see Tallis before his death?'

'The once.'

'Are you sure?'

'Look, I saw him at his church a week ago. I hadn't seen him in over twenty years. He phoned me the next day to tell me that he hadn't found out anything.' If this woman didn't know about Annie Hagen, he wasn't going to enlighten her. They'd find out soon enough when they dug further.

'What did you think Peter Tallis might discover for you?'

That was a nasty question. He had to be at his most evasive.

'Anita found that no one in Sweden was being particularly helpful. The disaster scarred their national psyche. Until the Indian Ocean tsunami, it was the most people they'd lost in one event for two hundred years. I figured there might be more information from another source, another country. I mistakenly thought that Peter had been stationed in Stockholm at the time. Turns out he wasn't, but he was just trying to be accommodating. He was that sort of guy. That's probably why he ended up as a vicar.'

The woman abruptly stood up and swept her macintosh off the back of the sofa.

'That's it?' Kevin was incredulous. 'You've come all the way up from London for that?'

'Yes. That's all.'

'Wait a minute. The only reason you're here is because you don't think Peter Tallis's death was accidental.'

'I can't comment on that.'

'Anita was right. She thought it might not be an accident. Thought your lot might be behind it.'

'We're not in the business of dispatching our own, past or present.'

'Then who do you think did it?' Kevin was growing angry. Part of that anger was generated from the culpability he now felt more acutely. The woman might not admit it, but her presence confirmed that Tallis's death was murder. 'The Swedish secret service?'

She shrugged on her coat. 'I suggest that you and your Swedish detective steer clear of anything to do with the *Estonia*. You particularly. You're not highly regarded in certain circles in the capital after all the brouhaha you caused at the Met. Important heads rolled because of you.'

'They only got what they deserved.'

'That sort of thing doesn't go down well. Make any more waves and you could find yourself in a great deal of trouble.'

'You mean I might fall off a roof.'

'That's not our style. It's just a gentle warning. And you can pass that on to your girlfriend.'

Kevin followed her to the front door. She pulled up her collar. It was starting to drizzle.

'Peter Tallis didn't deserve what happened to him.'

'I know.' She retreated into the dark.

'I hope you bloody find who did it,' he shouted after her. But he knew that even if they did, no one would ever hear.

Though it would be late in Sweden – and she might be in bed – Anita had to be brought up to date. The MI6 visit had unsettled Kevin. He and Anita had stumbled into a highly secretive and disturbingly sensitive area. This was crossing international boundaries, and no one was safe. He even wondered if he should be calling her. What if his phone – or hers – was bugged? It was a risk he'd have to take. Anita was awake when he rang. She'd been wrestling with her eulogy for Erik Moberg's funeral, which was on the following Monday. She'd managed two sentences. Neither was usable. Kevin didn't bother with a preamble.

'I've just had a visit from MI6.'

'What? Really? In Penrith?'

'Right to my front door. Very nice young lady. All the way from London. Probably needed a dose of oxygen coming this far north.'

Anita found it one of Kevin's many irritating habits that he made light of crucial moments that demanded a more serious perspective.

'What did she want?'

'To know about my meeting with Peter Tallis.'

'They don't think—'

'No, no. Nothing like that. They know I was in Oxford. And with you. They also know that you're not a journalist. I tried to spin her that one. They'd checked out the hotels we stayed in: London as well as Oxford.'

'It fits. The big cover-up. All these conniving secret services. Working together.'

'I don't think so. The reason she was talking to me – other than warning me off... you too, by the way – the reason is that they're obviously investigating Peter's death. It does confirm what you suspected – he was pushed. It clearly wasn't MI6. And it's unlikely to have been the CIA or Säpo. They're hardly likely to kill an ex-operative on another's turf unless it's been sanctioned by the home team. Shit would hit the diplomatic fan otherwise.'

'But to kill Tallis, someone must have known that he was asking questions about the *Estonia*. And that had to be MI6.'

'Granted. It depends who they passed that intel on to.'

'Säpo would be the obvious people.'

'OK. And who would *they* alert? Our mastermind? It worried someone enough to take Peter Tallis out of the picture. The dreadful thing is that he wasn't even a threat.'

'They didn't know that.'

'Whatever. It was a bloody pointless killing!'

CHAPTER 45

On Friday morning, Anita asked Liv if she could come to her office. Her conversation the night before with Kevin had made her think more seriously about a mastermind who could be mixed up in the whole *Estonia* cover-up; someone with a network of connections or companies that took advantage of the Baltic Drainpipe and facilitated the movement of goods out of the crumbling Soviet Union via Tallinn. This network could have included Happy Electricals, among others. As the ultimate middleman, whoever it was would have made huge profits at both ends of the Drainpipe. If Iqbal Nawaz was also doing some human smuggling as a lucrative sideline, the chances were that the middleman was allowing him to do so. Another money-spinning slice of the action. Dragan Mitrović had joined some dots. If he was right, the smuggling through Tallinn and then onwards via the *Estonia* was a monopoly. It would take some clout to achieve that. She hadn't told Kevin about her visit to Kirseberg prison. He was apprehensive enough about her without her making it worse by telling him of her continued pursuit of her quest.

Liv was her usual sunny self. 'Just over a week to go,' she said excitedly. Anita remembered her own exhilaration just before her wedding; her girlish glee at the prospect of a lifetime of happiness. A false dawn, though she wasn't to know that at the time.

'I know. I can't wait.'

'You know Uday came and saw Hakim? He actually came *here*.'

'You're kidding!'

'I couldn't believe it! Neither could Hakim. We know what Uday's attitude to the police is, as well as everything else at the moment.'

'Is he coming to the wedding now?'

Liv shook her head. 'Still don't know. It was about the case. Something Hakim asked him to do. He wasn't at all keen at first. But he did it. Gave Hakim some useful information about Iqbal Nawaz at the mosque. So, I'm hopeful. Hakim pretends it doesn't matter if they're not there, but I know he'd be really hurt if they fail to show.'

'I know. His parents' approval means so much to him.'

'Anyhow, how can I help?'

Anita suddenly felt uneasy about asking Liv for yet another favour. This was a young woman with an upcoming wedding to plan as well as her busy job to do. It would be too much.

'I shouldn't ask. You've got so much on your plate. Another time, maybe.'

'Look, Anita, what do you want? You know I'll do anything for you. Without you, I wouldn't be here. And I suspect your reticence is that it's about what I looked into before. Am I right?'

Anita couldn't help but smile. 'Yeah. That caused some trouble.'

'If it helps nail the bad guys, then let's do it.'

'I'm afraid it can't be official again. And we definitely can't use the computers here. Your Zander Security search was monitored. You'll have to do it at home. I'm not sure if Hakim would be too happy.'

'I've got plenty of jobs for him to do this weekend. That'll keep him out of the way.'

Anita went to a drawer in her desk and produced a small black laptop. 'Use this. It's mine. If anybody's tracking what we're up to, then I'll be in the firing line.' She scribbled the password on a scrap of paper.

Liv hid the computer down the side of her wheelchair. 'What am I looking for?'

'Well, Zander again. I want to know if there's a common link between them and the Independent Bank of Estonia based in Tallinn – I'd like to know who set up the bank. I know Zander were working in some capacity in Estonia in the mid-1990s. What I'd really like is a name that connects the two. And if anything crops up to do with Happy Electricals, that would be a bonus.'

'No sweat.' Liv's grin was broad.

'I tried to find things out last night – got nowhere. I'm crap at internet searches. Please don't take any unnecessary risks. If you stray into areas that worry you, just stop. Promise?'

'Promise.'

Hakim came in just as Liv was leaving. He looked suspiciously at Anita. He hoped she wasn't dragging Liv into her Markus Jolis campaign.

Anita read his mind. 'Wedding talk.'

'Ah.' Hakim was relieved. He shoved his hands into his pockets, which made him look even more like a beanpole. 'Any thoughts where we can go on the case?'

'Not really. I saw an old friend of mine yesterday.'

'Oh, anybody I know?'

'Dragan Mitrović.'

'Wow! I thought he was inside.'

'He is.'

'And why him?'

Anita took off her spectacles and rubbed the bridge of her nose. It might be time for another eye test.

'After what was mentioned at the meeting, I asked him about the drugs scene. He did admit someone's been trying to move onto his turf while he's in the cosy custody of the Swedish Government. He says that Afghan heroin tends to come through Pakistan these days. That got me excited until he categorically stated that Iqbal wouldn't touch drugs – he'd even once ticked Mitrović off for pushing. So, whoever is behind this new team is maybe getting their merchandise through Pakistan but not through Happy Electricals.' Anita replaced her spectacles. 'How about you?'

'Nothing really. I'm going to have a closer look at Usman.'

'Because he was the fourth person to have a key to the cricket hut?'

'Partly. And partly because I don't like him. Too flashy by half. Too cocky. Too friendly.'

Anita smirked. 'That's not a crime, even in Sweden.'

'Trouble is, he hasn't got an obvious motive. It sounds like he's not going to end up running the company. But he hasn't got an alibi, either.'

'From Klara's description of him, it strikes me that if he *did* kill Iqbal, he's the type of person who would line up an alibi.'

'You're not being much use!'

'I'm just a minion on this case.'

'Very funny.' Hakim made to leave the room. 'If you're not going to be more helpful, you're not invited to the wedding!'

Anita playfully threw an empty paper cup at the closing door.

Reza was sound asleep when Hakim entered his shop. Again it was deserted – it always was whenever he visited. His old school friend was lying out on a sofa that had seen better days. He gave a guilty start when Hakim gave his shoulder a gentle shove.

'Anybody could have pinched stuff while you were asleep.'

Reza rubbed his eyes. 'Who in their right mind is going to pinch any of this?'

'That's not a great advertisement for your merchandise,' said Hakim, laughing. It also confirmed – if confirmation were needed – that the place was merely a front for Reza's other activities.

'Want a coffee?'

'OK. Looks as though you need one.'

'Long night.' Hakim thought it best not to enquire further.

Reza disappeared into the back, and Hakim heard a kettle click on. He sat down on the sofa and reflected on the different routes he and his friend had taken in life. Different sides of the law, though Reza *had* avoided picking up a police record. Hakim wasn't sure if that was because he was particularly smart or the police were particularly dim. But he'd always liked Reza, despite his only passing acquaintance with the truth sometimes. His constant positivity was in sharp contrast to his own guarded view of life and his innate cautiousness. Maybe it was the attraction of opposites.

'Here you go,' said Reza, re-entering the shop with two chipped coffee mugs. Hakim took his and noticed that it hadn't been cleaned out first – the stained rim was a giveaway.

Reza sat down beside Hakim and surveyed his emporium.

'All set for the wedding?'

'I think so.'

'It's my social event of the year.'

'Don't get out much, do you?'

'Too busy working, my friend. Commerce never stands still.' He took a sip of his coffee and pulled a face. 'Forgot the sugar.' He didn't bother to go back and add some. 'What can I do you for? I assume it's not to do with the wedding... unless you want me to be your best man.' His voice suddenly perked up.

'I'm not having one.' Reza's face fell. 'You're all witnesses.' That seemed to satisfy him. 'The reason I'm here is that you might know something about Usman Masood. He's the nephew of Iqbal Nawaz's wife.'

'Did you find out if the old bugger was screwing one of his worker's wives?'

'We looked into it.'

'And?'

'That's all.'

'So, he was. You see,' Reza tapped the side of his nose knowingly, 'you get quality information from me.'

'And now I'd like some quality information on Usman Masood.'

'Flash fuck. Always has money to spend. Drives round in an expensive red Aston Martin Vanquish.'

'I've seen it.'

'Hangs around the smart clubs. Not meant to drink, like a good Muslim boy, but does.'

'He's part of a very successful business.'

'Yeah, course.' Reza took another sip of his sugarless coffee and grimaced again.

'Are there any rumours about him? I mean, sailing close to the wind?'

'What are you getting at?'

Hakim wasn't sure if he should tell Reza about the Happy Electricals deliveries. That information wasn't in the public domain. He tried another tack.

'Anita, whom you'll meet at the wedding, has heard that there's a new player in the drugs market.'

'While Dragan Mitrović is banged up?'

'You *have* got your finger on the pulse.'

'Not my scene, but it pays to keep the old ear to the ground.'

'Heard anything about heroin coming in from Afghanistan via Pakistan?' Klara Wallen had reported back from the Drugs Squad, and they'd confirmed that they were aware of a new outfit trying to make inroads into Mitrović's patch. They hadn't been able to firm up on details beyond the initial rumours, but the Russian mafia were the prime suspects, though there was no hard evidence to that effect.

'Might have.' Reza stood up. 'I can't drink this anymore.' He walked out of the shop into the back room.

'So, what *have* you heard?' Hakim called after him.

Reza re-emerged without his mug. 'No bloody sugar left. If I had an assistant, I'd sack him.'

'Come on, Reza. This could really help.'

'I hear there's a new lot in town. Undercutting the existing suppliers. Bit like Happy Electricals with their... well, electricals. Don't know who this player is and I'm not about to ask around. I treasure my balls too highly. But the route sounds familiar.'

'And how best to bring the stuff in?'

'You're the cop.' Reza rested his hands on the back of the sofa. 'But I'd use... I don't know...' he scanned the shop '...everyday objects that are unlikely to be too thoroughly searched.' His eyes came to rest on a microwave. 'That, for example. You understand what I'm saying?'

'Thank you, Reza.' Hakim finished his coffee. Then he eased his long legs up from the sagging sofa. 'And we'll see you a week tomorrow.'

'Of course. Can't wait. By the way, your wedding present. Is there anything here that takes your fancy?'

CHAPTER 46

Over the weekend, Anita struggled with her eulogy. She wanted to do Erik Moberg justice and go beyond what she knew most of her colleagues thought about him – an oversized bully with poor social skills. He had been a daunting figure around the polishus and hadn't endeared himself to many of his underlings, or the powers that be. After a while, she gave up and decided to go to Kristianstad and sort out a few of her mother's things. And she felt she'd better find out if her aunt was coping. Not too well, as it turned out. A spinster who had had no known male friends as far as the family could remember (Björn had always made unkind jokes about that), Elsa was bereft without her sister. The two had happily moaned together about the state of the world and what pathetic scraps life had thrown their way. Though Anita had never warmed to her aunt, she had made a promise to herself that she would try and visit her more often – more often than she'd ever visited her mother.

She had brought back a box of things that she'd found in her mother's bedside table drawers. There were two surprising items. One was a childish drawing Anita must have done when she was about five or six. It depicted a wobbly house with a bright sun above it, and three stick figures: two large and one small. The Ullman family. Why had her mother kept that? A reminder of happier times? More unexpected were the letters – written by Jens to his sweetheart Margita before they were married. He had come down from Stockholm to Nybrostrand on the outskirts of Ystad and had met Margita there. A holiday romance. Neither had been tactile with each other, let alone anyone else, yet the letters were full of tender love and yearning. Had her letters to him reciprocated the sentiments? She'd never found any when clearing out her father's belongings all those years ago. Anita had always thought of her mother as aloof. Maybe life had changed her. Maybe by the time Anita was more aware, the flame that had burned brightly in the early years of Margita's romance with Jens had been extinguished. Maybe everything changed when she came along. Her relationship with her mother had always been a battle of wills – neither of them prepared to back down; the more indulgent Jens defending his daughter on occasions. As their marriage disintegrated, Anita's parents had used her as a stick with which to beat each other – an outlet for their own unhappiness. But the fact remained that despite the divorce and the years of bitterness, Margita had kept her father's letters. Why? Now she would never have the chance to ask – not that her mother would have told her: all intimacy between them had long since dissipated. Maybe she had judged her mother too harshly. Looking back, Anita choosing Jens over Margita can't have helped.

Alice Zetterberg sat in the front pew of the dour crematorium chapel alongside Commissioner Dahlbeck and Prosecutor Blom. Further back were members of the force in their official uniforms, including Moberg's old team. Anita Sundström was sitting in the row immediately behind her. She could feel her malevolent eyes boring into the back of her head. She didn't care. She was interested to know if Sundström had been able to come up with anything nice to say about the unpleasantly boorish chief inspector. The gathering on the other side of the aisle was very sparse. There was some obscure cousin they'd managed to unearth, a sprinkling of old acquaintances, and one gaunt woman whom speculation outside the chapel had labelled as one of Moberg's three ex-wives. Zetterberg shifted in her seat as the pastor read out some tedious address. She had better things to do on a Monday morning.

She hadn't really had a choice about attending once she'd realized that Commissioner Dahlbeck was going to be there. She wondered whether he was privy to her conversations with the secret service in Stockholm. If he was, he wasn't giving anything away. She rather liked the thought that even someone in his elevated position might not know what she knew. Now things had settled down. Bringing Sundström back off holiday had been the right move. She'd informed Stockholm, though they seemed fully aware of Anita's movements. 'Just keep her busy,' was the instruction. After the call, she'd sighed with relief. Her Stockholm job was safe again. She only had to keep Anita out of trouble for the rest of the week, and she'd be away. Even solving the Iqbal Nawaz case before she left no longer seemed important in the great scheme of things. They would just have to get on with it without her. It would be a pity not to go out on a high, but after the fright she'd had over the Markus Jolis business and the ensuing threats, she was just grateful to get out with her career unscathed.

Zetterberg had been so deep in her thoughts that she hadn't even been aware that Anita Sundström was standing at the little wooden lectern. The light through the window caught the side of Sundström's face. Zetterberg had to admit that she still had elements of her youthful years. And her figure still wasn't bulging out of the uniform that Zetterberg herself had found so difficult to tuck herself into that morning. This was the woman she had so desperately wanted to befriend at the Police Academy. During their short intimacy, she had basked in the glow of her more glamorous fellow student. She'd attracted interest by association until people had tired of her. That was the start of the niggling jealousy which had blossomed into dislike. And then the betrayal with Arne had opened the floodgates of outright hatred that had continued to fester through the intervening years. She was suddenly aware of gentle laughter around her. Sundström had managed to dredge up some vaguely entertaining anecdote.

'Erik wasn't the easiest colleague to get on with.' Cue for a further ripple of amusement. 'For a long time, I felt some trepidation whenever I dealt with this bear of a man. But over time, I realized that his bark was worse than his bite. Underneath it all, I knew that he was a good policeman trying to do a difficult job; a job that he devoted his life to; a job that he was still desperate to return to even though his heart had had enough. And that heart was a big one, though he often didn't show it.'

Did Sundström really believe all the drivel she was coming out with? Zetterberg's attention started to drift again. She was so looking forward to leaving this rabble behind. She had no idea what Anita Sundström saw in them. She, too, seemed quite content to plod along: the woman had no ambition. She hadn't even used her fancy arse and flirty eyes to progress beyond inspector while she, Alice Zetterberg, had worked her butt off to get her advancement without all the natural advantages that Sundström possessed. In an uneven contest, she was going to come out on top despite the odds. So why wasn't it giving her the satisfaction she craved?

Then she was aware that Sundström was looking in her direction. She was no longer reading from her notes.

'Above all, Erik Moberg respected his team, despite our many faults. He expected high standards, which sometimes we failed to match. When we didn't come up to muster, he would let us know in no uncertain terms, but it never stopped him being there to fight our corner when things got tough, because he believed loyalty was a two-way street. It's a street that fewer believe in walking down these days.' Zetterberg felt uncomfortable in the defiant glare of those grey-green eyes. 'He was a man who had integrity; another diminishing quality.'

Anita slowly folded up her notes. For the first time, emotion crept into her voice.

'I'll miss Erik Moberg... more than I can say.'

Anita felt drained after the funeral. She'd found it difficult to choke back the tears when Moberg's coffin had slipped out of sight to be consumed by the flames. That in itself had caught her by surprise. It felt like another chapter of her life was at an end. What would the new one bring? In fact, the first thing it brought was Liv, who'd stayed at the polishus to man the fort. She hadn't worked with Moberg, so hadn't attended the ceremony. She wheeled herself into Anita's office.

'Hakim said you spoke very well.'

Anita didn't know what to say. Considering all the battles that she'd had with the chief inspector over the years, the whole business had left her feeling rather raw. Better to talk business.

'Did you get a chance over the weekend?'

'Yes.' She produced Anita's laptop and handed it back. 'Not a huge amount of luck. I couldn't find who had founded the original Independent Bank of Estonia. Seems to be clouded in mystery. The only Swedish connection nowadays is Henning Kaufer.'

'The oil magnet?'

'The same. He's on the board with three others. Checked them out, and they're all Estonian. That's not unusual in itself, as Kaufer does have various interests in all the Baltic States, and his company's been involved in shale oil in that region. And he owns a hunting lodge in Estonia. Big hobby of his. Wild boar, moose, lynx and deer. Shoots on his Scanian Lugnadal estate as well. The red deer shooting season has just started, in case you want to know. Unfortunately, I can't find a personal connection between the bank and Zander Security, though I have found some references to the company in Estonia around the time of the ferry disaster. Zander might have worked for the bank offering security. Dangerous and unstable times. As I found out before, Zander have been heavily involved in Kaufer's Surt Oil installations in Africa, so there is a tentative link.'

'Right, that doesn't get me any further really.'

'Sorry. Still came up with nothing new about Zander or who took the company over from the founder.'

'Long shot. Thanks for trying, though.'

'There was one thing of interest I dug up, though. Nothing to do with the Markus Jolis case and Zander. And I can't see that it has any relevance to the Iqbal killing. But it's this: the Independent Bank of Estonia was making lavish loans to a Swedish business in 1993. Happy Electricals.'

CHAPTER 47

Three birds were on the feeder at the end of the garden. Hakim couldn't identify them, though Liv was trying her best to educate him. Despite being on an urban estate, to Hakim this was like living in the country – so much open space around. He put down the breakfast tray on the garden table in front of Liv. The sun was already warming the day even though it was only a few minutes past seven. On the lawn was the gazebo party tent that he and his future brother-in-law had erected over the weekend in readiness for this Saturday's wedding. Only five days to go.

He placed Liv's tea and bowl of muesli, covered in a copious amount of *filmjölk*, in front of her. His breakfast was a strong black coffee accompanied by a bun with slices of *Västerbotten* cheese and hard-boiled egg. He sat down opposite Liv and took a bite out of his bun.

'What was that other computer I saw you with over the weekend?'

Liv hadn't realized that Hakim had noticed. 'It was Anita's. Some glitch. Managed to sort it.'

He eyed her suspiciously. 'She hasn't been trying to get you to do some checking up on the side?'

'No,' she said evasively.

'She still thinks that our case is linked to the death of Markus Jolis, and we don't even know if that was murder.'

'We'll never know.'

Hakim breathed out heavily. 'That won't stop Anita. Can you imagine what she'll be like when Zetterberg goes on Friday?'

'Any word on a replacement?'

'Nothing.'

'That means you and Klara will be running the investigation.'

'Exactly. How are we going to control Anita?!'

'Maybe she'll go back on holiday. Anyway, why did Zetterberg bring her back?'

'Haven't the faintest. It's not as though she's letting her get involved much. Today, she's sending her and Brodd out to try and find a possible location for the truck driver's mysterious drop off en route to Bulltofta. So they'll be looking at every warehouse, container park, outhouse, lock up and shed around Lund, Lomma and Svedala. It could take them weeks.'

'Maybe that's the point. Zetterberg drags her back and then gives her a hopeless task. A final humiliation.'

'Wouldn't put it past her. I saw the look on her face as we left the chapel after what Anita had said in her speech. The final bit was directed at Zetterberg, no doubt about it.'

Liv tucked into her bowl, and a silence descended between them.

Hakim broke it. 'I was thinking about Usman Masood last night.'

'I thought I heard you thrashing around.'

'Sorry, did I wake you?'

'I was just aware of it. I was out straight after. You know what I'm like with sleep. Nothing really disturbs me.'

'Yeah, I was awake for a time. Around three. Found it difficult to drop off again. There have been things that have been bugging me about Usman. Then it struck me. He's been too helpful.'

Liv's spoon was midway to her mouth. 'What do you mean?'

'I kept going over what he's said. First to Klara and Bea, then when I went to Lund with Klara. He was the one who pointed us in the direction of Abbas and his love for Muneeba.'

'That's true.'

'Gave subtle hints. When you think about it, Usman was the one who locked up the hut after the match on the weekend before the murder. He'd see that Abbas's cricket bag was still there. Then when it comes to the killing, he deliberately uses Abbas's bat, which we'd eventually work out was the murder weapon. You notice how specific the bat was – the killer could have used any of the half dozen bats that were propped up against the wall. One that was in sight; not one hidden away.' Hakim was warming to his theme. 'He probably knew that Abbas would be working late that night with big orders going out the next day. He even supplied a motive – Abbas not being allowed to marry Muneeba.'

'Of course, what he didn't factor in was Muneeba turning up and giving Abbas an alibi. I get that.'

'Exactly! I remember how disappointed he was when we told him. And when that failed, he nudged us towards Sidra and Sarfraz Khan. A big nudge, actually. He admitted he'd heard Iqbal arranging to meet someone. He implied he left before the rendezvous was mentioned. What if he overheard that bit as well? And, of course, it was true – Iqbal *did* meet Sidra for sex. And the motive was implied all along – Sarfraz was the cuckolded husband getting revenge. Or if not that, Sidra killing Iqbal herself – couldn't take any more of the degradation, or out of guilt for betraying her husband. Take your choice.'

'That didn't work either.'

'No. Then when I saw him last week, he played down the fact that Iqbal was worried about something. That was totally contradicted by Abbas. And my father, too, after speaking with the imam. If Iqbal knew about the truck driver's little detours, wouldn't he have mentioned it to someone as senior as Usman?'

Liv finished her food. 'That all makes sense.' She pushed her bowl away and picked up her mug of tea. 'But where's the motive?'

'My initial thought was his position in the company, but he's unlikely to take that over. Then I thought about what Dragan Mitrović told Anita, and my chat with Reza. I think it's drugs. Heroin in particular. Usman is the Happy Electricals buyer. Goes all over, including regular trips to the factories in Pakistan. Reza as good as hinted that it's Usman behind the latest influx of heroin into town. He could organize its transport, packed in various electrical products, and have it delivered somewhere on the way to the warehouse. Then Iqbal is tipped off by Abbas about the detours. That's why I think Usman set Abbas up. Without realizing it, Abbas had stumbled upon Usman's racket. Best way to shut him up was pinning a murder charge on him. Anyway, Iqbal digs around and finds out that Usman's up to no good – after all, Iqbal had an abhorrence of drugs. He's onto Usman's game, so Usman has to get rid of him. Blame it on Abbas, and he's killed two birds.'

'You've no proof, my love.'

'I know. It's all conjecture.' He drained his coffee. 'Better be getting into work.' He gathered up their breakfast things.

'He hasn't got an alibi, has he, Usman?'

'Probably thought he wouldn't need one after framing Abbas.'

'So let's take a different approach.'

Hakim lifted up the tray. 'What?'

'We'll start with his car.'

Anita was tired and fed up. She and Brodd had been driving round the Lund area and stopping off at every conceivable place where the container lorry might have gone on its monthly detour. They had drawn a total blank. CCTV footage hadn't come to their rescue either. And time spent in close proximity with Pontus Brodd was never time well spent as far as Anita was concerned. It was late afternoon when they got back into her car and drove out of the small timber yard they'd just visited.

As Anita turned onto the side road that had taken them to the yard, she said, 'Let's call it a day.'

'Should we? Won't Zetterberg mind?' Brodd asked cautiously.

'Not if we don't tell her.' He was still anxious. 'We'll not go back to headquarters. If she asks tomorrow, we'll just say we were out until six.'

'If you think it's OK,' he said, cheering up.

'Look, Pontus, do you mind if I drop you off near the hospital? I've got to visit someone.'

'Who is it?'

'Just an old friend,' she said noncommittally.

'Excellent. I need to do a bit of shopping.'

'And you can treat yourself to an early beer.'

'Hadn't thought of that.' It was clear he had.

Twenty minutes later, Anita dropped Brodd off opposite Pildammsparken. With a guilty grin, he nipped out of the car like a schoolboy who was sneaking out of classes early. Anita drove round to the hospital car park. It took her some time to locate Nina Jolis's ward, as she'd been moved since the last time Anita was in.

Nina, sitting in a chair next to her bed, was reading a magazine. She glanced up as Anita approached, and peered over her spectacles. The last time Anita had seen her, she'd been at death's door. Now the sallow cheeks were less gaunt beneath the wispy, grey hair. She was still bandaged underneath her pink dressing gown, though physically, she was recovering well. Whether the mental scars would ever heal was debatable.

'Hello. I'm Anita Sundström. We haven't met but I was working on your husband's case. Thought I'd just call in.'

'That's kind of you.' There was a smile of recognition. 'My son Tord has spoken of you.'

'Yes. He was very helpful. And you look so much better.'

'I'm coming out on Thursday.'

'That's good news. Are you going home?'

Nina Jolis shook her head slowly. 'No. I'm not sure if I could. Not yet, anyway.'

'I understand.'

'I'm going to stay with Tord and his family in Copenhagen while we decide what's best.' She put down her magazine. 'Please sit.'

'I'll not stay long.' Anita parked herself on the bed. 'I just wanted to see how you are. I've been away recently.'

'Anywhere nice?'

'England. London. I was visiting a friend,' she added as an afterthought.

Nina's eyes lit up. 'Ah, London. Markus took me there. We did all the sights. We saw a show. A musical. I can't remember which...' she chewed the tip of a finger thoughtfully '...it's gone. We stayed in a lovely hotel near the river. It was very exciting.'

'I heard that you both went travelling a lot.'

'We did. We were so lucky.' Luck had nothing to do with it, Anita reflected. 'We saw some amazing places. But that was before Markus took ill. Dementia is such a cruel disease, taking away an active mind. It was difficult towards the end. He didn't mean to... he didn't know what he was doing.'

Anita showed agreement with a frown of concern, though she refrained from commenting.

'You had plenty of good years before though, didn't you? Good memories. I mean it was fortunate that Markus was able to retire when he did. He was working for...' Anita feigned forgetfulness.

'Zander Security,' Nina supplied helpfully.

'Of course. I believe they are a very reputable company. It must have been a good job. Well paid.' Anita quickly cursed herself for her lack of subtlety.

Nina appeared to agree. 'They were so good to Markus. Really appreciated the work he'd done for them.'

'I'm sure they did.'

'He got a very handsome bonus when he retired.' Odd. How many people get huge pay-offs when they retire, other than failing bureaucrats and incompetent CEOs? The police certainly don't – here's your pension, now piss off! Nina's eyes lit up again. 'And we got an invitation.'

'An invitation?'

'To Lugnadal.'

'Lugnadal?'

'The home of Henning Kaufer. What a wonderful house! More like a castle, really. It has its own lake. We had afternoon tea on the lawn with herr Kaufer. Can you believe it? He was so welcoming, so polite. Such a gentleman! He spoke so highly of Markus. I was very proud of my husband that day.'

Anita tried to keep her tone conversational. 'I knew Henning Kaufer was an oil magnate. I hadn't realized that he had anything to do with Zander Security.'

'Oh, yes. He owned it.'

CHAPTER 48

'You could be right, Hakim.'

Klara Wallen had stopped fiddling with the paperwork that she'd been trying to wade through most of the day. Hakim was expounding his theory about Usman Masood's 'too helpful' approach and the more he did so, the more she nodded in agreement.

'It really looks like he set Abbas up, doesn't it? He was being so accommodating handing us that lead on a plate. It would have worked, too, if Abbas hadn't arranged his tryst with Muneeba. Usman couldn't have known that was going to happen. As you say, he probably knew when and where Iqbal was going to be when he met Sidra Khan.'

'Exactly. He could have gone into the hut before his boss arrived, taken out Abbas's cricket bat, lain in wait until after Iqbal and Sidra had had their little sex session and then smashed him over the head when he emerged from the hut. It all fits.'

'And you think it's all to do with heroin?'

'Yeah. We'll have to try and prove that, of course. But it does explain why Iqbal was upset and preoccupied. If he'd found out about the unscheduled deliveries, he would have had quite a shock, given his attitude to drugs in general. Slightly ironic for a possible people smuggler. Takes all sorts.'

'That's not the only thing we have to prove. We can't place Usman anywhere near the scene of the crime.'

Just then, Liv pushed her way into the room.

'I'm hoping you've got something positive for us?'

Liv wheeled herself in front of Wallen's desk. With a flourish, she

285

brandished a piece of paper. It had a CCTV image on it.

'It's taken me all day... this is Usman Masood's red Aston Martin Vanquish. And there's the registration. It's definitely his. Monday, the 29th of July.'

'Where is it?' Wallen asked as she and Hakim peered at the image.

'It's John Ericssons väg near the old Malmö Stadium. It's heading in the Limhamn direction. And look at the time: 20.51.'

'Interesting.' Hakim gave Liv a warm smile.

'That would give Usman plenty of time to park, get to the hut and take Abbas's bat before Iqbal and Sidra turned up.'

Liv laid a second image on the desk. 'The return journey. 22.41.'

'Don't know how he's going to explain that away. The only problem, Klara, is that Sidra told us she didn't see anybody.'

'He'd be hiding in the trees when she and Iqbal turned up.'

'What about the witness who saw Iqbal go into the hut? The Australian kicking his rugby ball?'

'Maybe we didn't ask him the right question. We were asking about anyone who was at the hut around ten – not an hour earlier.'

'I couldn't find any sign of the Aston Martin parked on the main road running along Limhamnsfältet,' said Liv. 'But, of course, there are plenty of side roads without cameras.'

'It's all residential round there. A car like his would stick out like a sore thumb; it'd be noticed just parked on the street. And it would be a bit close to Iqbal's apartment, too. Where would *you* park?' Hakim challenged Wallen.

She went over to a map of Malmö pinned to the wall. She let her index finger hover over the green expanse of Limhamnsfältet.

'If we're discounting the adjoining streets, then he'd either park down at Limhamn or up near the Kallbadhus.'

'At that time of night, there wouldn't be many people about, especially on a Monday. No cameras there, either.'

'We'll have to check both areas,' said Wallen, still engaged by the map. 'Come to think of it, Sidra told us she took a taxi from the

Kallbadhus car park. She may have seen Usman's car – we need to ask her.'

'OK. Klara, do you want to talk to Sidra tomorrow? I'll speak to the Australian.' Hakim tapped the location of the cricket hut with his finger. 'Place the car near the scene, and we've got him!'

Anita's laptop was open on the kitchen table. Her second coffee was still warm. On an ordinary night, she might have treated herself to a glass of red wine. But not tonight: she wanted her wits about her. She was searching the internet for as much information about Henning Kaufer as she could possibly find. She rubbed her eyes. She didn't like staring at a computer screen for too long and was becoming weary.

Henning Kaufer was seventy-three years old. Born in Sweden of German origin, as a young man he'd dropped the *von* in his name. His father's family had been successful Malmö merchants up until the Second World War before falling on hard times during the conflict. When Henning was born the year after the war ended, his parents were living in more straitened circumstances near Halmstad. They'd had to sell the Lugnadal ancestral estate north of Skurup to pay off debts. Henning had made it his life's aim to buy back Lugnadal and restore his family's social standing, which he did in 1993. By all accounts, he was clever and driven: a combination that landed him a position with Surt Oil, who were speculating and developing fields in Nigeria and Angola. Using his ability to mix charm with tough negotiating skills, he acquired vital concessions for the company. His achievements in Africa resulted in swift promotion up the corporate ladder, and he was brought back to the head office in Stockholm in a senior management position. By 1986, he was running the whole show. He then began to expand his portfolio both at home and abroad. Nowhere, however, could Anita find any reference to his association with Zander Security or Happy Electricals, yet she knew they must be connected. Both were operating in Tallinn at the time of the ferry sinking – and Kaufer was indisputably linked to the Independent Bank of Estonia, although she couldn't find any dates pinpointing when his involvement began. Yet the Bank (the same bank that Annie Hagen had said was used by the CIA to fund the movement of illicit materials) had made significant payments to Happy Electricals for, Anita believed, the smuggling of the smaller technological items. Presumably, there were other companies in the Kaufer web which could move larger equipment. It all fitted together. Kaufer was powerful and influential enough to be the ultimate middleman. Trusted by the various governments, his network could facilitate the illegal trade across the Baltic. The Independent Bank of Estonia's funding had enabled Iqbal Nawaz to build up his national chain of retail stores. The evidence also pointed to Iqbal using the route to transport fleeing refugees: a monopoly that Kaufer could control using the expertise of another of his companies, Zander Security. If Iqbal *was* human smuggling, Anita was sure that Kaufer would know about it. No doubt he would be taking a cut of the profits.

Then there was the association with Markus Jolis. Jolis must have been on Kaufer's payroll when employed by the Swedish Customs. He waved through cargoes on Kaufer's orders while the authorities happily looked the other way. When everything went dramatically wrong and the *Estonia* sank, Jolis was swiftly taken out of any possible firing line and sent post haste to Malmö. Six months after that, he was working for Kaufer's Zander Security and left five years later with a substantial bonus for services rendered – an inducement to keep his mouth shut.

A thought that had taken seed in Anita's mind and was growing steadily was the importance of the timing of the tip-off to the Swedish Customs that the *Estonia* was carrying illegal immigrants. Did they know about the immigrants *before* the ferry set sail from Tallinn? Ulf Garde, the customs official Anita had spoken to in Stockholm, had thought they may have done. And if the Swedes had known about the human cargo that fateful day, why didn't they alert their counterparts in Tallinn? Of course! – the light dawned: the Swedes would want to be the ones exposing the racket; and with all the corruption prevalent in Estonia at the time, could the authorities there have been trusted to do the job? The fact remained that whoever tipped the customs off – and for whatever reason – it was imperative for the Drainpipe smugglers that the ferry didn't reach Stockholm. As the Swedish officials searched for the Iraqis when the boat docked, they might well blunder across a much more important and internationally damaging cargo – the Russian electronic chips in the Happy Electricals vehicle. And if the tip-off *had* come through before the ferry sailed, Markus Jolis was in a position to warn Kaufer. Kaufer, in turn, would have had time to order Zander Security in Tallinn to disable the ship. So, someone had planted a bomb. It probably wasn't meant to sink the ferry; merely to cripple it so it would have to return to Tallinn. That's why Jolis had said 'It shouldn't have happened!'. The bomb might not have sunk the *Estonia* if the weather hadn't intervened and scuppered that last-minute plan. That made Kaufer the *he* in the 'He was wrong.' that Markus Jolis had blurted out. In his befuddled brain, he still carried the guilt for his part in the tragedy.

Anita pushed her seat back. Now she would have a drink. After a search, she found she was out of wine. There were a couple of bottles of Carlsberg in the fridge. She normally kept them in for Lasse. She opened one and sat down again. It was hopeless. The scenario made total sense. And she didn't have one shred of proof.

Then there was all the business after Markus Jolis's attack on his wife. Someone was alert enough to send in the bogus lawyer, Filip Assarsson. Jolis sealed his own fate that day. And, of course, the phantom doctor at the hospital, followed by the quick cremation paid for and organized by the well-wisher – that had to be Kaufer, too. He was sending in a team to make sure they hadn't left any loose ends. Was Iqbal Nawaz also a loose end? If he was being bank-rolled by the Independent Bank of Estonia for acting as a courier for the Americans as well as running a human smuggling operation on the side, Kaufer would have had good reason to silence him once Anita had started to investigate the circumstances of Jolis's death. For all Kaufer knew, her enquiries might lead to Iqbal, who knew far too much.

Peter Tallis's death was harder to explain. They could only have found out about his enquiry through MI6. And MI6 surely wouldn't have passed that information directly to Kaufer. Säpo or some other secret organization must have been involved. After all, certain people in the Swedish government would still be nervous about any facts emerging about the *Estonia* that weren't covered in, or contradicted, the official report. Annie Hagen's sudden disappearance only confirmed that there was some kind of cover-up going on. The whole thing stank.

She idly flicked through the few photographs she'd found of the camera-shy billionaire. There were a couple taken in Africa when he was a young man. He was tall and muscular with an unsmiling, weather-beaten face. The fair hair was cropped. It had grown by the time he was in a boardroom photograph at Surt Oil – managing director at the age of only forty. He wore a sharp suit, mid-eighties style with big lapels. The most recent shot was from a year ago in an American blood sports magazine. Taken in South Africa, Kaufer, holding a rifle, was in the centre of a hunting group standing over three dead black springboks. The caption included all the names of the group, but it was clear who was the most important. In that photo, Kaufer was smiling. The image enraged Anita and she slammed the laptop shut. Suddenly, she felt totally dejected. She knew she was utterly powerless to do anything about the man whom she now held responsible for her father's death.

CHAPTER 49

'Bring him in for questioning.'

Both Hakim and Klara Wallen appeared delighted that Zetterberg had made the decision. They had caught her after she'd returned from a long lunch. Her breath smelled of alcohol. Hakim had taken her through how, he believed, Usman Masood had on separate occasions steered them in the direction of different suspects to divert them from the real culprit. Hakim outlined the possible drugs scenario as being the reason Usman himself had killed Iqbal Nawaz and tried to frame Mohammad Abbas. He had no alibi, and now they were able to place him in the vicinity of the murder. Wallen had shown Zetterberg the shots from the CCTV footage on John Ericssons väg: clear evidence that Usman was heading towards the area and out again before and after the murder. Then there were the two statements they had taken over the course of the morning. The first one was interesting, if not totally conclusive. Hakim had tracked down the Australian, Doug Mitchell, who said he'd seen someone loafing around the cricket hut about an hour before he'd spotted Iqbal, though he couldn't confirm if the man had entered the hut or not, as he'd been concentrating on his kicking skills. But it was the second statement that had really clinched it: Sidra Khan *had* seen Usman's car in the car park while she was waiting for the taxi to take her home. She was hanging around for about ten minutes and had recognized the Aston Martin. She'd seen it at the cricket matches she'd attended and knew it belonged to Usman. Her husband had commented on it a couple of times. She'd assumed that Usman was taking a sauna at the Kallbadhus. She hadn't known, of course, that the Kallbadhus closed at nine o'clock.

'Good work.' This had surprised both Hakim and Wallen.

'Should I let Anita and Pontus know what we're doing and get them back from Lomma? They're still out searching.'

'No. Let them carry on. We still need to know where that truck went on the way to the warehouse.'

Hakim raised an eyebrow in Wallen's direction as he closed Zetterberg's office door. They knew perfectly well that Zetterberg just wanted to keep Anita out of the way.

Pontus Brodd had clearly had a curry the night before. Anita was suffering from the aftermath in the hot car as they carried on with their search for the elusive dropping-off point, if it actually existed. She was beginning to think that the truck driver had simply had a bit on the side and had been slipping into some girlfriend's bed while her husband was out at work. She managed to escape Brodd at lunchtime, when they went their separate ways.

As she drank her coffee in a small café down by Lomma harbour, Anita's mind was far from concentrating on the task in hand. She thought that the truck's vagaries were irrelevant. The reason for Iqbal's death had nothing to do with the cricket club or the present-day Happy Electricals. Why couldn't anybody else see that? Of course, they didn't have the background knowledge that she had accumulated over the last few weeks. Information that she could do nothing with. She felt impotent. She had no reason to approach Henning Kaufer, no excuse to expose him. There was nothing now that she could act upon. Everything was buried in the past. He was protected, untouchable. So what was nagging her? What was it that didn't quite fit? Or was it something that did fit and she couldn't see it? Was it something she'd read or something she'd seen? She gripped her coffee cup in annoyance. She was stuck out here when all she wanted was to get back home and go over everything again.

It was only at about half past four, after another fruitless day, that she called the polishus. She'd expected to speak to Hakim. She got Liv instead.

'Sorry, Hakim's not in the office. He's gone with Klara to bring Usman Masood in for questioning.'

'What?'

'Yes,' Liv said with some excitement. 'We've been able to place Usman near the murder scene at the right time. It was Hakim who really put it all together.' Her pride came bubbling over the line. 'He's done so well on this.'

'He has,' replied Anita in some mystification. Could this be possible? Had she got it all wrong? 'Why weren't Brodd and I kept informed?'

'Don't know.'

Anita had an idea why.

'OK, we'll wrap things up here.' She put her phone away.

'What was that all about?' asked Brodd with his mouth half-full of chocolate.

'They're bringing Usman Masood in.'

He wiped his mouth. 'Great. We can go back.'

On her return to the polishus, Anita hung around the office. She was waiting to see the outcome of the interview that Hakim and Wallen were carrying out with Usman Masood downstairs. She still wasn't sure that he was their man. Kaufer was involved somehow.

It wasn't until after six that they emerged from the interview room to consult with Zetterberg. Anita caught up with Hakim afterwards.

'We're keeping him in overnight. He wants a lawyer. He didn't want one initially. Very self-assured. Insisted he was at his apartment that evening, until we produced the CCTV images of his car. That took him aback. Then he said he'd lent it to a girlfriend. When he couldn't produce the name of the girlfriend, he demanded a lawyer and clammed up. Wouldn't answer any questions.'

'You're sure it's him?'

'Oh yes. What else would he be doing there? Besides, someone was spotted around the cricket hut earlier, which would roughly tally with the time Usman would have arrived at the Kallbadhus car park.'

'Motive?'

'We think it's heroin being brought in from Pakistan with electrical products. Got the tip-off from my friend Reza. Iqbal starts sniffing around and Usman has to get rid of him. It makes sense that he's behind the new outfit trying to take over Dragan Mitrović's territory. We know that thanks to you. Anyway, we still need to find out where the truck made its drop-offs so we can tie Usman and the drugs together because I'm sure he's not simply going to confess – he's not the type. Zetterberg won't sanction a raid on the Happy Electricals head office or the warehouse until we've found the link. I'm afraid that means you and Brodd will be on the road again tomorrow.' Before she could protest, 'Zetterberg's orders. She's still in charge until the weekend.'

By the time Anita left the office, the *Systembolag* was closed and she couldn't buy the bottle of wine she'd promised herself all day. She'd have to make do with the other bottle of Carlsberg left in the fridge. She took her laptop into the living room and set it down on the coffee table. Between sips, she went through all the material she'd unearthed last night. Still nothing of any use. She was self-aware enough to know that this was becoming an obsession. She wanted someone to be responsible for her father's death, and she'd chosen Henning Kaufer. Having put it down to unfortunate circumstances over the last twenty-five years, she now knew that there was a web of complexity behind the tragedy and that a plethora of shady characters had gone to great lengths to ensure the truth never came out. She couldn't hold a government to account. Or an organization like the CIA. Or a more obscure entity like the Russian mafia. But she could single out an individual. Her only chance of letting the world know what really happened was to flush out Kaufer. Only she didn't know how to do it. She had nothing to go on.

She went into the kitchen to prepare some food. She wasn't really hungry; she was on automatic pilot. She'd open a tin and bung something in the microwave. The cupboard didn't offer an enticing choice, and she never got round to making a decision. Because it suddenly hit her – what had been niggling her all day! She dashed back into the living room and almost knocked over her half-drunk bottle of beer as she wrenched the laptop round so she could see the screen. She fiddled around until she found the photo of Kaufer's hunting party in South Africa. There were seven men brandishing guns. But it wasn't Kaufer that riveted her. It was the one wearing glasses on the right-hand side of the group. She enlarged the picture. And there he was! He might have been wearing a bush hat, but there was no mistaking the features. She'd met this man before. She glanced down at the names – Henrik Mellin. Except she didn't know him by that name – she knew him as the fake lawyer from Ekvall & Ekvall, Filip Assarsson.

CHAPTER 50

Anita had the modern-day link she was so desperately seeking. Henrik Mellin, AKA Filip Assarsson, was directly connected to Henning Kaufer. He was probably employed by him – Kaufer's fixer. He had been at the interview with Markus Jolis and had paid for the funeral on behalf of the well-wisher, which now could only be Kaufer.

Anita had had an early call from Kevin that morning – the 29th of August – to wish her a happy fifty-first birthday. She hoped she hadn't sounded off with him, as her mind was elsewhere – she now knew what she was going to do. She was going to contact Henning Kaufer and ask him about Henrik Mellin – well, that would be the excuse. She hoped it would stir things up. She hadn't mentioned it to Kevin and she wasn't going to tell Hakim, either. They were the two professionals she most trusted in the world. But they would try to do their best to stop her and persuade her that what she was doing was sheer madness. It *was* sheer madness. It was dangerous, too. She knew it would probably kill her career. Possibly kill her. She no longer cared. All she could think about was nailing the man who had played a part in depriving her of her father, and Lasse of his grandfather.

She deliberately got into work before Brodd rolled in and they would be sent off to search the area in and around Svedala. Luckily, Liv was already in the office, as a nervous and motivated Hakim had rushed them out of the house first thing so he could prepare for another crack at Usman Masood.

'Happy birthday!' beamed Liv as soon as she saw Anita.

'Thanks.'

'Doing anything nice today? I mean after work.'

'Calling round to see Lasse and family. I've been promised a Chinese takeaway.'

'He's really pulling out all the stops.'

'Low key. We can celebrate properly on your big day.'

'Good idea.'

'Look, I've got to shoot off soon with Pontus. Can you do me another little favour on the quiet?'

'No problem.'

'Can you find out anything you can about this man?' Anita handed Liv a piece of paper with the name Henrik Mellin scribbled on it, along with another name and an instruction.

Liv stared at the paper. 'And you want me to find a direct line to Henning Kaufer, too? *The* Henning Kaufer?'

'Yes. I tried and couldn't find it. You know how to bypass the system.'

'Is this in connection with Markus Jolis?'

'Don't ask. If anyone catches you, say you were obeying my orders.'

'Don't worry, I will,' Liv said, laughing.

'As soon as you find anything, call me straight away.'

'No comment.'

To use a cricket analogy, Usman Masood was batting away every question with a negative response. He sat impassively next to his lawyer, who appeared quite happy for his client to be uncooperative.

Hakim turned to Klara Wallen and nodded. It was her turn.

'Right, let's go through this again.'

'Excuse me,' intervened the lawyer languidly. 'You've already been through this twice already. It hasn't achieved anything. If you aren't going to charge my client, then I suggest that we leave.'

'Your client isn't going anywhere,' said Wallen firmly. 'We're staying here until he decides to expand his vocabulary beyond "no comment".'

*

Anita leant back on the bonnet of the car and watched as Brodd talked to the owner of the junkyard a couple of kilometres outside Svedala. They had got into the habit of taking it in turns to ask questions while the other rested or snoozed. It was warm again and she felt drowsy. The heat off the car reminded her that she mustn't take the weather for granted. Autumn had a habit of slipping into Skåne too early. Her phone on the dashboard disturbed her, and she reached into the car to answer it. It was Liv.

'How did you get on?'

'Not a huge amount on Henrik Mellin, though there is one connection I've found. He was born in Stockholm in 1984. He did start studying at Uppsala University – a law degree – but gave up after a year. He worked in South Africa for a while for a mining group. Don't know what he did – he's just described as an executive. Various other jobs around Africa. Part of that time while he was out there, in Nigeria, he was employed by Zander Security.' Anita's heart gave a little blip. 'Now based back in Stockholm. According to his tax returns, he's a security advisor. Self-employed.'

'That's enough for me to act on.'

'Right,' said Liv uncertainly. 'And the number you wanted. Direct line. Don't ask how I got hold of it. I'll send it through to your phone.'

'Thanks, Liv. That's brilliant!'

'You're not actually going to ring him, are you?' Anita noted Liv's concern.

'Sorry, must go. Pontus is coming.' She ended the call.

Brodd was still deep in conversation with a thick-set, bearded man with two colourfully tattooed arms. Anita walked further away from both them and the car. Liv's SMS came through. There was the number. She stared at it as though paralysed. Her fingers lost all feeling. Her mind whirled. Voices in her head, which she recognized as Kevin's and Hakim's, were telling her to put the phone away. Go back to Malmö and have a pleasant birthday with the family. Don't jeopardize it all. The next thing she knew, the number was ringing in the distance and then a voice answered 'Henning Kaufer speaking.'

'Now, on the night of Monday, the 29th of July,' said Wallen, deliberately teasing out the facts, 'you drove your car from Lund to Malmö in the direction of the Kallbadhus. We know you were on John Ericssons väg at 20.51. Your car was then seen in the Kallbadhus car park by a witness at around 22.25 as the witness waited for a taxi that arrived at 22.33. That pick-up time has been confirmed by the taxi company. Your car is then seen again returning along John Ericssons väg at 22.41.'

'My client has explained in an earlier interview that he wasn't driving; that he'd lent the car to a girlfriend.'

'A girlfriend whom your client has failed to produce.'

'Protecting her,' he said weakly.

'From what, exactly?' The lawyer lapsed back into brooding silence.

'We believe that your client, after parking his car in the Kallbadhus car park, walked down to the cricket hut on Limhamnsfältet and let himself in, he being one of the four key holders.' She turned to Usman. 'You were seen by a man who was kicking a rugby ball on the next pitch.'

'A man who hasn't specifically identified my client,' interjected the lawyer.

Wallen ignored the interruption. 'Inside, you took the cricket bat out of Mohammad Abbas's cricket bag, which you knew had been left there from the weekend's game. You locked up again then waited. Iqbal Nawaz turned up for his assignation with Sidra Khan just after ten. He opened up the hut and had intercourse with Sidra, who then left. Iqbal came out of the hut some time after, and you came up behind him from your hiding place in the trees and hit him over the head twice with Abbas's bat. You then left the body and, after a feeble attempt to clean it, you returned the bat to the bag, therefore setting

299

up Mohammad Abbas as the murderer. Then you locked up after yourself and headed back to the Kallbadhus car park and your car. Is that how it happened, Usman?'

Usman was about to reiterate 'no comment' for the umpteenth time when Hakim suddenly broke in.

'Interview terminated 14.04.'

'What?' Wallen said in stunned exasperation.

'I need to speak to you outside.'

Once out in the corridor, Wallen demanded to know what he was playing at. 'You can't just stop an interview like that!'

'Sorry. I had to do it.' He cupped his head in his long figures for a few seconds before he spoke. 'I've been so stupid. It's been staring me – us – in the face all along.'

'What the hell are you talking about?'

'It's the timings that got me thinking. You've just laid them out in there.'

'And?'

'Sidra said she waited about ten minutes at the car park for the taxi to arrive, which we know to be ten thirty-three. Give or take a minute, she must have reached the car park about ten twenty-three or four. Five minutes from the hut. So she left at say... twenty past.'

'She said it was a very quick session and she got out as quickly as possible.'

'Right. So, let's say that Iqbal takes a few minutes to sort himself out afterwards. Locks the hut. Heads along the track through the trees and, bang!, he's attacked. Say that's five to ten minutes after Sidra's gone. Then Usman has to go back to the hut to leave the evidence.'

'So?'

'So, how does Usman get back into his car to be caught on camera at 22.41? I don't think he's got the time.'

Wallen leant back against the corridor wall and groaned. 'Are you saying Usman didn't kill Iqbal?'

'No. He did it all right.'

Wallen appeared flummoxed. 'So, what's the key to it all?'

'Exactly. The key *is* the key!'

'You've lost me.'

'Anita wondered right at the beginning whether there might have been two people involved. One to distract Iqbal, the other to kill him.'

'Another person? Who?'

'Let me ask you this. When you first went down to the cricket hut with Anita, how did you get in?'

'Muneeba gave us Iqbal's key.'

'What was it doing in the apartment?'

'Well, that's where it was kep— Oh my God, you're right! It shouldn't have been there! Iqbal opened up the hut with his key. He closed it afterwards with his key. It should have been on him when we found his body!'

'There's no way that Usman would have had time to return the key to the apartment. Anyway, it would have been very suspicious if he'd tried. But he didn't have to. Someone else cleared up afterwards – put the bat back – while Usman dashed off to his car and got away from the crime scene.'

'You're not seriously suggesting Muneeba was the other person?'

'She couldn't have been. She was with Abbas at Bulltofta.'

Wallen clamped a hand over her mouth as she shook her head in disbelief. 'You mean...?'

'Yes. Bismah.'

CHAPTER 51

'That fucking policewoman rang me up. Here! How did she get my private number?'

Henning Kaufer was fuming.

'I don't know,' said his Secret Service contact at the other end of the line. This was a call that he hadn't anticipated.

'She knows about Henrik Mellin. I used him to sort out the Jolis business. She's linked him to me!'

'He must have been careless.'

'Of course he wasn't being fucking careless! Without him, we wouldn't have known that this Sundström woman was nosing around. You should have ensured she couldn't have got anywhere near us.'

'I've been let down in Malmö. There will be consequences.'

'That's no fucking good now! Sundström insists on coming to see me. Here... at Lugnadal! I could hardly refuse, as she said it was part of an official inquiry.'

'It's not an official inquiry. It's closed.'

'I know that, but I could hardly say I knew. How would that look? Refusing to see her wouldn't stop her. She's come this far.'

'OK, it was the right thing to do. Don't panic.'

'Don't panic! Everything's on the fucking line here! If any of this gets out, we're all in the shit. A lot of important people will go down for this, including you. I'll lose everything. Everything I've created. And I'm not prepared to do that. She's got to be taken out! I'll arrange it.'

'No, no,' he said hastily. His mind was speedily computing all the possibilities – how the scenarios would play out, the likely outcomes. What mattered most was that he retained ultimate control; keep it in-house.

Kaufer's Zander personnel had caused enough problems. They'd already notched up two deaths. 'We'll deal with it. When is she coming to see you?'

'Tomorrow afternoon. Three o'clock.'

'Right. That gives me time. I'll get an operative there. What's the terrain like round the house?'

'The house is next to a lake. On the other side, there are woods. Beyond, a mixture of forest, open land, fields... my hunting area, basically.'

'That's good. You say there's cover close to the lake?'

'Plenty.'

'All you have to do is make sure you don't take Sundström into the house. Keep her talking; find out what she knows. There might be other avenues we have to block off afterwards. Take her to the lake. Make sure she's well in sight. By the way, is there any of your family around?'

'No. They're summering on the yacht. I'm flying to Monaco on Tuesday to meet up with them.'

'And can you make sure there are no staff, either? We don't want witnesses.'

'What about afterwards?'

'Leave that to us.'

Hakim parked the car in the street next to Bismah's apartment block. He and Wallen got out. They'd run Hakim's ideas past Zetterberg, who'd given them the green light to go and pick Bismah up. Bringing her in might loosen Usman's tongue. The thought had even got Zetterberg animated. She could have the case tied up just as she was leaving. Go out on a high.

It was Muneeba who answered the door.

'We've come to see your mother,' said Wallen.

'Oh, she's not in.'

'When will she be back?'

'I don't know. Not for a few weeks, anyhow.'

Wallen and Hakim looked at each other in alarm.

'Where's she gone?' Hakim demanded irritably.

'Lahore.'

'Pakistan?'

'Look, what's the matter?' Muneeba was bewildered by Hakim's tone.

'Did she know that we've arrested Usman Masood?'

'Yes. I passed on the message from Abbas yesterday.'

'And had she planned her trip for a while?'

'No. All very sudden. Said my uncle was ill.'

'When did she leave?' Hakim's face was firmly planted inches from Muneeba's, making her flinch.

'She took a taxi to Kastrup a couple of hours ago.'

Hakim turned to Wallen. 'She won't have taken off yet.'

Without another word, they rushed to the lift and left a flabbergasted Muneeba standing on the doorstep.

The car, siren blaring, raced through the streets and across numerous roundabouts to the E20, which would take them across the Öresund Bridge to Kastrup airport on the other side, where Bismah Nawaz would be getting ready to board a plane to Pakistan. Wallen was at the wheel, having wrenched the car keys off Hakim with 'I'm a better driver than you.'

Hakim had been trying to get on to Zetterberg so she could ring ahead and get them official clearance on the Danish side. To his frustration, he couldn't get through. She was on the line to someone else.

'You've let me down.' Zetterberg was still in a state of shock. 'Inspector Sundström is about to cause untold damage, which we're having to take drastic measures to avoid. National security is at stake, God damn it!'

'I was doing my best,' she tried to protest, but it didn't carry much conviction in the face of the fury coming through the phone.

'It's not good enough. All I asked was for you to stop her. Now, thanks to your incompetence, we'll have a huge, unnecessary mess to clear up.'

'That's unfair. I—'

'Fairness has nothing to do with it. You failed. And you can kiss goodbye to your Stockholm posting.'

The conversation was ended abruptly. Tears welled up in Zetterberg's eyes as she stared blankly at the mobile phone shaking in her hand.

Hakim gave up calling the polishus and flipped through his phone to find the flight that Bismah might be on. He found a Turkish Airways one to Lahore that was going via Istanbul. It was due to leave in twenty-nine minutes.

Wallen had to slow down when they reached the bridge tolls. She swerved the car to an empty booth and flashed her warrant card at the toll collector. 'Police! Emergency!' she shouted. She gunned the engine and the car hurtled into the outside lane of the bridge.

Hakim got through to Zetterberg and yelled over his instructions. Get them clearance as soon as they arrived, get someone to meet them and try and stop the flight taking off. It was a long list of demands that he hadn't got time to expand on.

'Is she going to do it?' Wallen asked when Hakim had finished. She pressed her foot on the accelerator as hard as she could and flashed the vehicle in front to get out of her way.

'I think so. Sounded a bit odd.'

They careered past a truck that had overlapped the outside lane, and Hakim hung onto his seat. The Sound below was whizzing by. He glanced nervously at his watch. The flight would be going in twenty minutes. It would be another five before they got to the terminal.

Bismah shuffled along in the queue at the gate. She was starting to relax. Soon she would be on her way to Lahore, her proper home. Away from any tricky questions. There, she could lie low in luxury for years – they'd never find her. Her present mood was in sharp contrast to a few hours ago when Muneeba had given her the disturbing news that Usman had been taken in for questioning. How had they got onto him? He'd been so confident that he could handle the police. More importantly, how long would he hold out before he implicated her in Iqbal's murder? They had been so sure that Abbas would get the blame. That would have achieved two aims: it would stop his ludicrous romance with her daughter but, more importantly, it would stop his prying – permanently. He was the one who'd alerted Iqbal to the shipments being dropped off at Usman's lock-up near Svedala. Usman had managed to get the driver out of the way when Iqbal had started asking awkward questions, but once her husband had stumbled on their heroin scheme, he had to go. She had spent two years setting up the route, with Usman liaising with the Pakistani and Afghan ends of the operation. The import of products from their own factories had been the ideal cover. And Iqbal would never have known. The timing couldn't have been better – conditions were perfect, with a major supplier like Mitrović out of the picture. By the time he re-established himself, they would have flooded the market with cheaper stuff. Then Abbas spotted an anomaly. They really had no choice. Carefully planned, the murder went smoothly; she'd been quite proud of that. Following his usual route through the trees that she knew he would take after being with his whore, he'd been caught off guard. He was so surprised to see her. Then Usman smashed him over the head from behind. Wearing batting gloves to avoid fingerprints was a nice touch. While Usman had got away, she'd used them afterwards when she'd replaced the bat in Abbas's bag. Before locking up, she'd even left in place the chair that she knew Iqbal must have used for his sordid sex. That would add to police confusion. And it might always come in useful to implicate Sidra Khan if their initial plan to frame Abbas didn't stick. Pleased with the night's work, she'd made her way home and prepared herself to play the part of the grieving widow.

The queue started to move. She had her passport and boarding card ready for inspection. Soon she would be on the plane.

The car screamed to a halt outside the glass-fronted terminal. It blocked the traffic that was trying to negotiate its way through the massive construction work that was going on around Terminal 2. Hakim and Wallen ran into the building, waving their warrant cards. There was an airport security guard waiting for them. Zetterberg must have acted incredibly quickly.

'Turkish Airlines?'

'Yes!' Hakim said breathlessly.

'Follow me. Gate D9.'

Immediately in front of them was an escalator. They ran up it, two steps at a time. The guard swiftly turned to his left and sped along the corridor above the check-in desks below. Hakim could see they were heading towards Security. They dashed to the head of the line of people waiting to go through the boarding-pass scanners, and pushed their way forward. One official tried to stop them, but swayed out of the way as her colleague yelled at her. Hakim vaulted the barrier and was at the security guard's shoulder as they hit the throng. They struggled past the unsuspecting passengers to reach the front of the queue. Their guide held up a hand and bawled 'Police emergency!' as he went straight through the screening booth, almost knocking aside an elderly man who was in the process of vacating it. Hakim and Wallen followed. Whatever metal they had on them set off the alarms. They took no notice and began their tortuous negotiation of the crowds in the shopping and restaurant areas. Hakim was breathing heavily now and Wallen was starting to fall behind. As he ran past the displays of gaudy gifts and overpriced food, Hakim looked at his watch. They still had time – just! At last, they were on the home run to the gate. Ignoring the travelators, too clogged with people and luggage to be of any use, they rushed past D7, and on to D8. Here, passengers were milling around ready for boarding. They heaved their way through – and there was D9! No one was there except two female officials tidying up their paperwork.

'Where are the passengers?' Hakim shouted, startling the women.

'They're... they're on board,' one of them stuttered.

'Can we stop them?'

'No. The plane's moving.'

'It's too late!' A shattered Wallen was bent over, hands on knees, staring out of the floor-to-ceiling, plate-glass window. Hakim, still fighting for breath, joined her. He rested his forehead on the cool, smooth surface. His heart sank. He could see the Turkish Airways plane manoeuvring away from the terminal, taxiing towards the runway.

Hakim beat the glass with his fist. 'Shit!'

Bismah stretched her legs. A wave of relief overcame her. Now she was free. Free in more ways than one. Free of snooping detectives. Free of Sweden, which she had never really liked. And free of Iqbal. She'd never loved him. He'd provided her with a good life, but she'd earned it. She had been the driving force. He'd only ever have been a modest success if he hadn't been approached by Henning Kaufer with a commercial offer they couldn't refuse: just add a few special deliveries to his own orders from the ex-Soviet Bloc; no questions asked. All that injection of capital into the company. Kaufer was her kind of businessman. Someone open to ideas – her ideas. It was she who'd seen the potential of using the Estonian route to bring in Middle Eastern immigrants. Iqbal hadn't been keen. Stupid, weak man. Kaufer had been quite happy to take his cut as long as nothing could be traced back to him. His part of the bargain was to ensure that there was no competition. And then the ferry sank and with it their money-spinner. Propitiously, the disaster didn't impede the growth of Happy Electricals, and that sated her avarice to a certain extent. But she didn't have a role anymore, and she wanted an outlet for her business acumen. Then, on a trip home to Pakistan two years ago, she met a man who knew a man who could supply heroin. They were looking for new outlets. She began to plan, and the plan involved her nephew. She could count on Usman's greed. The set-up was ideal as long as Iqbal never got wind of it. And when he did, she'd had no compunction in getting rid of him. Usman she could manipulate with the lure of huge wealth to come. She'd promised him control of Happy Electricals to run alongside their drugs enterprise.

The plane continued to trundle towards the runway. She liked planes and she liked going home. The one person she would miss, of course, was Muneeba. Somehow, she still needed to stop her marrying Abbas. She'd already started to plot that. She'd get Muneeba to come out to visit her in Pakistan, and once there, she would stop her returning. Marry her off to someone more suitable; of the right social standing.

Bismah was suddenly overcome by tiredness. All the strain of the last few weeks was catching up with her. She closed her eyes. After a few minutes, she became aware that the plane had stopped. It must have taxied into position and be preparing to rev up. She opened her eyes and peered through the window. She could see another aircraft passing them. They weren't in the take-off queue any more. What was the delay? She had a horrid queasy feeling in her stomach. Then a voice came over the intercom: 'This is your captain speaking. If I can have your attention. Due to circumstances beyond our contol, we are having to return to the terminal.'

CHAPTER 52

It had been easy to slip away from headquarters, which was buzzing after Bismah Nawaz had been brought in from Kastrup airport by Hakim and Wallen. Hakim was quite the hero. Deservedly so – Anita had let herself be sucked in by her *Estonia* conspiracy theories while Hakim had kept his eye firmly on the facts before him. And the team even had to give Zetterberg grudging credit for managing to pull the strings which had the plane turned round on the tarmac, though it had been a very close call. Oddly, Zetterberg didn't seem to be basking in her own or the team's success, and she'd cut Anita dead in the corridor that morning. No gloating farewell remarks on her last day in Malmö. No sarcastic comments. Anita was just delighted she'd never have to see her again after today.

Usman, on hearing of Bismah's arrest, had started to spill the beans in a desperate attempt to shift the blame onto her. It was all her idea. He'd even revealed the location of a lock-up near Svedala where the truck driver had made his unscheduled deliveries. Basically, he was trying to do a deal. Anita knew it wouldn't wash with Prosecutor Blom, though she suspected that Blom would string him along until she got what she wanted. Bismah was remaining tight-lipped.

None of this concerned Anita as she pulled her car into the side of a country lane near Lugnadal, Henning Kaufer's family estate. She couldn't remember being this nervous before. She'd stopped the car because she thought she was going to be physically sick. The doubts came barging back in. During her birthday meal with Lasse, Jazmin and Leyla last night, she'd questioned her actions. Was she risking all this? The family she loved so much. Was she putting her life on the line? She knew these were ruthless people. Yet she also knew she was driven. She could no longer suppress the righteous anger that had been slowly welling up inside her over the last few weeks as she'd unearthed more and more about the run-up to the sinking of the *Estonia* and the shameful aftermath. She knew nothing would deflect her from trying to arrest Henning Kaufer in connection with the murder of Markus Jolis. It was the only way she could see to try and highlight his other crimes. She had no authority to detain him, but the furore it would create would put her and Kaufer in the full glare of the media. She needed to expose the lies, the rottenness and the deceptions perpetrated by a corrupt system. It was the only way to the truth; the only form of redemption. She took a deep breath, checked her pistol and got back into the car.

He sat in the mucky, green van near the estate boundary. He was relaxed as he rhythmically chewed his gum, playing with the wrapper in his fingers. He knew the order would come through soon. He'd already seen Sundström's car arrive and head up the drive. He was ready. He knew that this was a case of protecting his country's national security. That's how he could live with himself.

His earpiece sparked into life.

'Get in position. Understood?'

'Understood.'

'I'll be listening in.'

He languidly stepped out of the van, went round to the back and opened the double doors. From under a blanket, he took out the Blaser R8, a discontinued German hunting rifle. It already had the telescopic sight attached. He shut the doors, hopped over the small wall and headed into the trees.

Anita parked in front of Lugnadal. It was a huge, solid, red-brick residence; more castle than stately home. The red pantile roof and stepped gables gave a roughened elegance to the building's rather uninspiring cuboid shape. But there was no denying that the setting and location were magnificent. Her heart jumped when she saw Henning Kaufer was waiting for her. She'd expected to be shown in by some lackey. She got out of the car and automatically felt her jacket pocket for the handcuffs she'd stored ready for use if Kaufer didn't come quietly. As she approached her quarry, she was conscious of how eerily quiet it was, just the occasional caw of crows in the surroundings trees. Lugnadal was living up to its name – calm valley.

Kaufer didn't bother with any preambles. 'You want to talk about Henrik Mellin?'

'Yes.'

He began to walk in front of the house and across the lawn that reached down to the lake. She followed him. He clearly didn't want to talk to her within ear shot of anyone else. She could understand that.

The man cut through the tangle of bracken and ivy that covered the roots of the trees. Through the compacted trunks, he glimpsed the lake, which curled around two sides of the house. This was easy terrain compared with many he'd operated in. He stepped lightly through the undergrowth so as not to create any sound that might be picked up across the water. When he was near to the verge, he sank to his haunches. On the opposite side to where he was crouching was a small wooden jetty with a rowing boat tied to its frame. His gaze mechanically moved up to the two distant figures walking across the grass. He laid the hunting rifle carefully down beside him and waited.

Kaufer stood still for a moment, staring across the lake as though looking for something. A bird? Something to shoot? Anita wasn't used to hunting types. He swivelled round and faced her.

'Look, I'm not going to bother beating about the bush. I know exactly why you're here.'

'To arrest you.'

'Don't be so pathetic. What for?'

'You were responsible for the murder of Markus Jolis. He was one of your ex-employees. You used him to wave through customs sensitive contraband coming in from Estonia after its independence, mainly on the *Estonia* ferry. The only trouble was that Jolis had dementia and he'd tried to kill his wife. That's why you sent Filip Assarsson – or Henrik Mellin to be precise – to make sure he didn't say something he shouldn't. But he *did*, implicating *you*, though I didn't know that at the time. That's why you sent in a bogus doctor to finish him off.'

'You've no idea how much trouble you've stirred up.'

'I think I have. I know that you were working for various governments on the Baltic Drainpipe and that you used Happy Electricals as part of your cover. I also know that you were allowing human smuggling. You were in league with Iqbal Nawaz over that.'

This was greeted by a hoarse laugh. 'For God's sake! Iqbal was useful, but he wasn't that clever. Bismah was the brains behind that. She was the one I dealt with, though Iqbal was quite happy for me to funnel money into his crappy electrical empire. But it was the immigrants who brought in the serious cash. Yet Iqbal – the fool! – was never totally comfortable with that side of our business relationship, though he was the one we used to line them up on the other side for transporting. You know, he even half-adopted one of the kids to assuage his guilt. Bismah, of course, wouldn't let him bring the child up as his own, so he palmed him off on another couple.' He shook his head in disbelief. 'Ironically, it was the fucking immigrants that kiboshed the whole business.'

'What do you mean?'

'The *Estonia*. The ferry. That night. We had a hundred Iraqis on board. Then Jolis was briefed that the Swedish Customs had got a tip-off, probably from some local Estonian gang no doubt trying to muscle in. He got word to me that the customs were preparing to search the boat the next day when it docked. I couldn't let that happen with another important cargo on board.'

'Electronic chips containing Russian missile placements.'

'Well well, you have been digging. Can you imagine the international uproar if *they* were discovered? It was too late to stop the trucks, so I ordered my Zander agents to disable the ship.'

'So, it was *you* who gave the order! It was a death sentence for those poor immigrants, as well as all the other people.'

'Collateral damage.'

Anita nearly pulled out her pistol to shoot him right there and then.

Across the lake, the man, well camouflaged, raised his rifle and squinted through the sights. He lined it up, and Kaufer's head appeared in the centre of his vision. Then he moved ever so slightly, and the blonde detective's forehead was in middle of the crosshairs.

'In position,' he whispered. 'Clear shot of target.' His finger hovered over the trigger.

'Not collateral damage, mass murder!'

'I didn't mean for it to go down. That just happened. The bomb made the hole and the weather did the rest.' Anita couldn't understand why he was so unflappable. He was confessing everything as though it didn't matter; as though she didn't matter. 'But tell me, why have *you* been pursuing this? You've been like a dog with a bone.'

'My father was on board,' she said through gritted teeth.

Kaufer bit his lower lip. 'I see,' he drawled. 'This is some personal crusade.'

'You killed hundreds of people that night. You're responsible for killing more now. Markus Jolis and Peter Tallis.'

'Who?'

'The vicar you had thrown off his church roof.'

'Oh him,' he said off-handedly. 'Shouldn't have been asking questions. Got Stockholm in all of a tizzy. Though they weren't too happy about our solution to the problem.' He was so matter-of-fact.

'That's it?' Anita shouted. The words echoed around the lake. Then in a calmer voice: 'I'm going to make you answer for it all.'

'By arresting me?'

'Yes.'

'Do you think the government or the security services are going to let this come to light? You can't prove anything. You can't prove what was on the ferry that night. Why do think the powers that be have gone to such lengths to suppress the facts? They've got too much to lose. You've got nothing that will stand up in a court of law in any country. They're not going to let me near a courtroom because I know too much, and they know that. All that will happen is that you'll look like the deranged harpy that you are. The ravings of a daughter who lost her beloved father and is trying to find a scapegoat.'

'No... I've got you now... you'll tell the world the real story.'

'You ludicrous woman!' The contempt almost dripped from his lips. This tiresome trouble-maker would be out of his life any minute now.

Anita whipped out her pistol and pointed it at Kaufer's head.

'I think you will,' she said with steely determination.

Kaufer didn't even blink. 'You're wasting your time.'

With her other hand Anita felt for the handcuffs. She knew he wouldn't come of his own accord. If nothing else, she was going to humiliate him by bringing him into the polishus. And she'd make sure the press were waiting there. Martin Glimhall was on speed dial. She would phone him from the car.

'Turn around.' Kaufer slowly twisted round without a murmur and gazed over the lake. There was even the hint of a laugh. 'Hands behind your back,' Anita ordered. This felt good. It was the right thing to do, whatever the consequences. She was about to lay the ghost that had haunted her for twenty-five years.

He squeezed the trigger.

CHAPTER 53

The sudden thwacking sound startled her; as did the wetness that engulfed her face and glasses. She could hardly see as her hand instinctively started to rub the lenses to wipe away the red smears that were blurring her vision.

She was still standing there, unable to move; a stationary target for a second bullet. Kaufer was slumped motionless at her feet, his head a raw, red crater. She was covered in his blood and splattered brain.

Anita had enough instinct left to throw herself down behind the body, still desperately trying to wipe away the detritus from Kaufer's head from her glasses. The only noise was the birds, startled by the sound, flapping and squawking above the trees on the other side of the lake. All was deathly calm; not even a ripple on the water. She waved her pistol in the direction of the gunshot, scanning for any sign of movement or a rustling of leaves. Would he pick her off next?

The initial shock was wearing off. Rage took over. It was fury that brought her to her feet. She strode down to the water's edge, not caring whether she was killed or not. Without bothering to take aim, she fired in the direction of the trees – again and again.

'You bastards!' she yelled. Her voice reverberated, mocking her frustration.

There was no movement on the other side. The anonymous assassin was gone. There was no need to kill her. She was powerless – without Kaufer she was no longer a threat.

Anita sank to her knees, tears rolling down her cheeks as one searing thought broke through. The truth about the *Estonia* would remain forever at the bottom of the Baltic. She had failed her father.

The man reached the van and slipped the rifle out of sight in the back. He got into the driver's seat.

'Target taken out. Final source of information nullified. Sundström has left the scene. Ready for the team to clear up.'

CHAPTER 54

On Saturday, the next day, Anita attended the wedding of Hakim Mirza and Liv Fogelström. It was a happy occasion. Uday and Amira were there, much to Hakim's joy. It was a new beginning for them all.

On Sunday, Anita received a call from Klara Wallen with the news that Alice Zetterberg had decided that she wasn't going to take up her posting in Stockholm. Commissioner Dahlbeck's office had sent round an internal email saying that he was delighted that such a talented officer was staying in Malmö and that soon he'd be able to confirm her permanent position as chief inspector in the Skåne Criminal Investigation Squad.

On Monday, a report appeared in the national newspapers announcing the death of business tycoon Henning Kaufer, tragically killed in a shooting accident while hunting on his estate in Skåne. His family would appreciate it if they could be left in peace to grieve in private.

On Tuesday, Inspector Anita Sundström handed in her resignation from the Skåne County Police.

ANITA SUNDSTRÖM WILL RETURN IN
MAMMON IN MALMÖ

NOTES

MS Estonia disaster

In a modern world where we can't escape conspiracy theories, the *Estonia* tragedy fits right in. The facts as we know them have been laid out in the story, and what has caused so much speculation over the years is that the official inquiry probably wasn't as transparent as it could have been and was unnecessarily cagey about its processes. Many of the theories – though not all – were put to Anita as she progressed on her quest to find the answer to her father's death. For example, there actually was a rumour that there were a hundred illegal Iraqi immigrants on board that night. Personally, I have no fixed idea as to how the ferry sank, and I would like to believe that the weather was the main contributing factor. That said, I do think that a hole in the hull would explain the incredible speed with which the ferry went down.

As I write this (July 2019), there has been an announcement that a French court has refused a claim for compensation by the survivors and the victims' families. The court in Nanterre said that the 1,116 plaintiffs hadn't been able to prove that the French certification agency (Bureau Veritas) and the *MS Estonia*'s German shipbuilder (Meyer Werft) were at fault. A lawyer for the plaintiffs alleged that 'this ship wasn't fit to sail'. Meyer Werft asserted that the ferry construction was in line with regulations but that it had not been properly maintained. Throughout, the Swedish and Estonian authorities have rejected calls for the case to be reopened.

If you'd like to read further on the subject, I would recommend a book called *The Hole* by Drew Wilson, who methodically goes through the evidence and theories and lets you draw your own conclusions. Wilson is particularly good on the background to the disaster and the fallout from the crumbling Soviet Union. If you want to know more about the wilder conspiracy theories, the internet should be your first point of reference.

Cricket in Sweden

Cricket might seem an odd sport to put in a Swedish setting. I became aware of the quintessential English game's presence in Sweden when my son started playing for the Malmöhus team. In those days, cricket wasn't widely played – though the Swedish national team had had its first match back in 1993 against Switzerland – and Malmö only had two clubs, most of the games being played against Danish teams from Copenhagen. However, in the last few years, the sport has grown rapidly and I believe there are as many as 65 teams and 3,000 players now active in Sweden. Most of the teams are made up of expats from various British Commonwealth countries who adopted the game. Many are made up from the Indian subcontinent diaspora. In 2017, there were 13,970 Pakistanis living in Sweden and nearly 30,000 Indians. Augmented by Sri Lankans and Afghans, there is a large pool of keen participants. However, cricket is still very much a minority sport within the country, and there is a lack of native Swedish players, though Swedish Cricket is doing great work attracting more boys and girls to this booming sport.

Type 1 Diabetes

I've given little Leyla type 1 diabetes, as it is close to my heart – our Swedish grandson was diagnosed with the condition just before his third birthday. Many of those who have type 1 are young, which is why it is sometimes referred to as juvenile diabetes – 90% of people under the age of twenty-five who have *diabetes have type 1*. It is a lifelong, life-affecting and, if not constantly treated, life-threatening condition that sees the sufferer having to adhere to strict diets and numerous daily insulin injections. It should not be confused with type 2 diabetes, which it often is by the public and the media, hence Kevin's complaint. It has nothing to do with being overweight, and it's not self-inflicted. Even in the time that our grandson has had type 1, there have been great strides in research, and new devices are becoming available to help deal with the condition. However, the ultimate hope is that scientists can come up with an immunotherapy drug that will stop or prevent it. There has also been huge progress made in the development of artificial pancreases, designed to release insulin in response to changing blood glucose levels.

Much of this research work is carried out by the Juvenile Diabetes Research Foundation (JDRF), which is funded through charitable gifts. That's why I'm donating 5% of any profits from this book to JDRF.

If you would like to learn more about type 1 diabetes, visit www.jdrf.org.uk (UK) or www.jdrf.com (USA).

Among the many high-profile people who have type 1 diabetes are Jean Smart (actress), James Norton (actor), Theresa May (politician), Ann Rice (author), Ed Gamble (comedian), Jay Cutler (American footballer), Gary Hall Jr. (Olympic swimmer), Wasim Akram (Pakistani cricketer), and the late Mary Tyler Moore (actress).

ABOUT THE AUTHOR

Torquil MacLeod was born in Edinburgh. After working in advertising agencies in Birmingham, Glasgow and Newcastle, he now lives in Cumbria with his wife, Susan, and her hens. The idea for a Scandinavian crime series came from his frequent trips to Malmö and southern Sweden to visit his elder son. He now has four grandchildren, two of whom are Swedish.

Also by Torquil MacLeod:

The Malmö Mysteries
(in order)
Meet me in Malmö
Murder in Malmö
Missing in Malmö
Midnight in Malmö
A Malmö Midwinter (novella)
Menace in Malmö
Malice in Malmö

Jack Flyford Misadventures (Historical crime)
Sweet Smell of Murder

ACKNOWLEDGEMENTS

This book would never have been written and completed without the encouragement of family, friends and loyal readers.

More specifically, I have to thank my medical brains trust – Bill and Justin Foster, doctors of Gloucester, for useful information and advice, which I hope I haven't distorted too much. Again, thanks to Nick Pugh of The Roundhouse for his patience over the design of the book's cover, though I regret our inability to meet up for cricket matches.

I'm most grateful for the help of Sarah and David Edwards: Sarah for showing me round Oxford, and David for demonstrating his beekeeping skills at their allotment. Also thanks to the Reverend Angus MacLeod, Liz Brutus and Olivia for their hospitality and inside knowledge of Chelsea churches, though St. Thomas's is purely fictional.

Of course, I can't forget my inspiration, Karin Geistrand and all her help with Swedish policing matters. Whether she recognizes my interpretation of procedure is another thing, as she's too polite to mention it. As well as Karin, I'd like to mention Fraser and Paula, who continue to give me useful insights into Swedish life. Fraser's knowledge and experience of Swedish cricket was also invaluable.

Thanks to Linda MacFadyen for her support and her promotion of *The Malmö Mysteries*, despite disappearing off to the Isle of Bute.

Finally, I want to thank Susan for her tireless efforts keeping my books on track and ensuring that they make sense.